THE KING'S
SCARLET

THE KING'S SCARLET

BY

JOHN M. DANIELSKI

WWW.PENMOREPRESS.COM

ISBN-13: 978-1-942756-72-9(Paperback)
ISBN :-978-1-942756-73-6 (e-book)

BISAC Subject Headings:
FIC014000FICTION / Historical
FIC032000FICTION / War & Military

Editing: Chris Wozney

Cover Illustration by Christine Horner

Address all correspondence to:

Penmore Press LLC
920 N Javelina Pl
Tucson AZ 85748

DEDICATION

This book is dedicated to Jim T. and Tom G.,
who always believed.

CHAPTER ONE

SPAIN: JULY, 1812

"Help me! Help me! Help me!" the young girl shouted in frantic, nearly incoherent Castilian. Her attackers laughed because they knew no one could hear. Her terror excited them.

Their blue uniforms proclaimed them French soldiers, but their actions proclaimed them brigands. They were drunk, angry, aroused, and in no mood for refusals. The Spanish peasant girl clawed, slapped, and kicked at them, but two of them held her while the other two gleefully tore off her blouse. She spat, cursed, even tried to bite, but they joked with each other as they pawed her and reveled in her nakedness. They liked a spitfire. It was as much about violence as it was sexual release. The sweat on their dirty skin glistened and their bloated red faces showed no humanity. They threw her roughly to the ground, pushed up her skirt, and wrenched off her under garments. She called to the Virgin Mary. She sobbed and pleaded. Their tongues flicked their lips like reptiles.

"Rot in hell, you frog-eating bastards!" The girl's whole body convulsed in rage and the powerful spasm broke the grip of one Frenchman. It only gave her a few second's respite.

1

One soldier pinned her arms, two forced her legs apart, and the last began to unbutton the front flap of his trousers. She was nothing to them, just an animal to satisfy their own base lusts. When they were done with her, they would kill her. Spanish guerrillas had caused a lot of grief to the French; the loss of one stinking peasant from a cesspool of a country would be a service to their cause. No officers were around to restrain them; indeed, some of the truly bitter ones of long service in Spain might even have encouraged them. A ridge hid them from the village of Valdencia, half mile away. There were plenty of places to dump the body afterwards.

But they were not alone. Three Englishmen watched them from the thick woods, ten yards away. Two were Royal Marines, one a servant. The exceptionally tall one, a captain, looked on in disgust and revulsion. To interfere might compromise his mission. To not do so would surely compromise his duty as a gentleman. He had to choose immediately. Her cries tore at his heartstrings, even though the military part of him did not want to hear. "Damn!" he muttered in frustration.

"Jesus, save me!"

He looked at his sergeant, whose grim expression mirrored his own. He nodded decisively and made several hand gestures. The noncommissioned officer bobbed his head and drew his hanger. The captain drew his cutlass, then motioned to the servant to stay down. The man looked disappointed, but complied.

The officer had to time it well. The ground ahead was open. The ugly soldier with the bulbous nose had dropped his trousers and got onto his knees. His ardor was obvious, and his fellow soldiers focused on what was about to happen, oblivious to anything else.

The Englishmen rose swiftly and dashed the ten yards in wraith-like silence. Their quarry saw and heard nothing of their approach. The bulbous-nosed Frenchman was about to enter the girl. The captain stopped abruptly behind the man's head and focused all his one hundred eighty pounds into a decisive stroke. The blade tore through the air, the man's head jumped violently off. Blood shot in great gouts and the body slumped forward, the manhood still engorged. The girl screamed.

The sergeant drove his hanger downwards, two-handed to increase force. It ripped through the shoulder of the man holding the girl's right ankle and pierced his heart. The Frenchman cried out and released his hold of the girl, but he lost strength as he lost blood, and his hands dropped weakly to clutch at his chest. The soldier holding the left ankle started to rise but was too slow to avoid the quick thrust of the officer's blade, which passed between his ribs and skewered the heart.

The last Frenchman, a sergeant, jumped up and drew his own sword. But his English opposite number was too quick. He savagely buried his blade in the man's groin. The Frenchman emitted a horrid, high-pitched squeal, more animal then human; abruptly silenced when another stroke severed his throat.

The blood-spattered girl yelled in hysterics, but stopped as she saw the expression on the officer's face when he bent down to her. It was pure kindness, in stark contrast to his violent actions of a few seconds ago. He spoke soothing words to her. She did not understand them, but his calm voice steadied her. He gave back her clothing. The blouse was badly torn, so he unwound and handed her his crimson officer's sash that she might bind the remnants into some more modest covering. The gesture seemed to astonish her. He very deliberately turned his back while she composed herself.

He knew she could not stay here. Blood was everywhere, the road was well-traveled, and it would take time he didn't have to bury the bodies. Furthermore, her disheveled appearance would provoke gossip in the village, and someone always had a careless tongue. The French possessed networks of collaborators who listened for just such talk. The French would piece things together, wrongly. They would think the worst, that she had lured the soldiers into an ambush. Females sometimes fought with Spanish partisans and had deserved reputations for ferocity. She would likely be shot out of hand. The last thing he needed was female baggage, but he had no choice. He had to take her someplace safe until things quieted down.

He spoke slowly, in halting, rudimentary Spanish, but it got through. He explained things as quickly as an unfamiliar language permitted. "If you wish to remain safe, you must come with us."

She was frightened, but kept her wits about her. She regarded him for a few seconds, and then nodded agreement. She made a decision to trust him utterly. "¿Cómo se llama?" she asked, with a mixture of gratitude and awe.

"Pennywhistle, Thomas Pennywhistle, your servant ma'am," he replied quickly, then, "Me llamo Capitan Pennywhistle," he said much more slowly, emphasizing the syllables of his last name, realizing it would be difficult for the Spanish tongue. He included his rank, because Spaniards set great store by such things. He took her hand, and the three of them walked towards the woods. He had to get to Wellington's headquarters as fast as possible. He had vital dispatches from Vice-Admiral Martin to deliver. A duplicitous guide had already led him far off his planned route. He'd had no business making this bloody detour.

His ears detected a troubling noise in the humid afternoon breeze: a dull, concussive thudding, with a decided rhythm; faint, but growing steadily louder. It was some distance off, coming up the main road. The carefully cadenced tramp, tramp, tramp meant soldiers. No drums, no fifes, no ceremony; probably just a patrol on routine business. He put his ear to the ground and listened closely. The strength of the vibrations suggested it was company strength, roughly sixty men.

Spanish guerrillas struck fast and viciously at isolated French detachments, then vanished into the hinterlands. The French scoured the countryside to discover and destroy their hides and arms caches. It was nasty work; no quarter given and none expected on either side. When the French found these four bodies, they would lash out violently at anyone in the vicinity. If they found no obvious culprits, the common practice was to burn the nearest village.

The three of them took shelter in a copse of oak trees at the top of large hill. Manton, the servant, joined them with canteens full of cool water he had drawn from a nearby stream. The position gave a clear view of the road, but anyone looking in their direction would see only trees and brush. Soldiers approaching them would have to negotiate the hill slowly and would be fully exposed. The captain unfurled his pocket Ramsden spyglass, balanced it on a large boulder, and surveyed the road. He needed to think.

He should leave now; simple prudence. But he could not forget his moral obligation. He had saved the girl, but set another, even more disastrous train of events in motion. He hated to think of the fate of the village when the bodies were discovered.

The French would need to blame someone. If they blamed the British, the village would be spared. The British were regular soldiers like themselves, and the state of military courtesy between the two armies was often quite chivalric. The four bodies would be seen as casualties of war, not murder victims. There would be no retribution visited upon the Spanish.

He and his NCO wore the King's scarlet, the hallmark color of British sergeants and officers. The brilliant and distinctive uniforms would stand out clearly in the hot afternoon sun. They would never be mistaken for anything civilian. It was risky, foolhardy even, but they were paid to hazard their lives. Civilians had suffered greatly under the hated rule of the usurper Joseph Bonaparte, Napoleon's brother. A King's officer had a duty to oppose acts of terror and vengeance. He had seen enough dead peasants for a lifetime.

The girl said her name was Juanita. She looked about nineteen, five-foot nine, unusually tall for a girl, slim and athletic. She had porcelain skin, raven black hair and a delicately sculpted face with expressive, vivacious features. Her terror faded quickly, suggesting a resilient core. Her rapid-fire Spanish, replete with Castilian lisp and trilled r's, caused him to miss much of her talk, but she clearly despised the French and was eager to volunteer everything she knew about their local dispositions when he asked.

"The closest garrison is at Valdez, two leagues distant. That's where those devils came from." She knew the area well and told him there was an old foot path to the rear of the hill that wound through steep terrain to Cordona. That village was fifteen miles closer to Wellington's Army. She doubted the French knew of it. The French seldom traveled alone or strayed far from the main roads because of all of the recent ambushes. She would guide them. Her uncle in Cordona would help as well.

He replied in slow, labored Spanish. *"Gracias, señorita Juanita. Estoy muy agradecido por su ayuda."* He had arrived in the Peninsula less than a month before. He had read a short grammar book on the language before departing Plymouth, but had actually spoken it on only ten occasions since crossing the Spanish frontier from Portugal. He guessed he sounded hopelessly formal, feared he made mistakes, and knew his accent was atrocious.

He had two mules and a horse. She told him the hardy mules could negotiate the trail, but it was more problematic for the horse. He looked over his shoulder at the old brown nag tied to the tree a hundred yards to the rear. He knew he had been overcharged in Lisbon for the temperamental slowpoke, inappropriately named Lightning, but it had been all he could find on short notice. He was no great rider himself and regarded horses with deep suspicion. But the beast was large and could surely handle the weight of the girl, in addition to his own, at least part of the way, and it would not do to leave it behind for the French to claim. Mules had a well-deserved reputation for stubbornness, but Manton had so far persuaded them to move on command; something he had been unable to do.

He saw the front of the French column come up over the rise three hundred yards away. He panned his glass slowly up and down the formation. The blue-coated soldiers marched in open order, their steps easy and disciplined. Their uniforms showed the wear of usage and their faces looked hard. They mostly seemed to be in their late twenties. No bandbox company fresh from training depots this, but one of veterans.

He saw two officers leading the company, one a captain, one a lieutenant. They looked fit, alert, and confident. Their expressions were harsh and unforgiving. They were out for blood. They, he decided, would not see another dawn. Kill the brain, and the body would be no threat. He would take the captain, his sergeant, the lieutenant: one shot for each. The officers' departure from life would be quick; after firing, their own departure from the hill had to be just as swift.

He explained his plan to his sergeant, Dale, who replied, "Not a problem, sir, easy enough shot." He then sent his servant Manton to the rear with Juanita and told him to get the animals ready to move. He and Dale fetched their rifles and found a suitable spot. Normally they would fire from concealment, but today it was imperative they be conspicuous.

Pennywhistle's Ferguson rifle was a rarity, a breech-loading weapon years ahead of its time, capable of six shots a minute in experienced hands. Dale's Baker rifle was a traditional muzzle-loader capable of two shots a minute. Unlike smoothbore muskets, the rifling made both pieces accurate to three hundred yards, although two hundred was a much more sensible range. Today he would sacrifice the advantage of distance. An individual was far easier to see at seventy-five yards than three hundred, and he intended to be seen.

He watched closely as the column moved closer. He noted there was no talking in the ranks, the sign of a well-ordered unit. They carried no flags or banners, and skirmishers hovered on the front and flanks of the column. Clearly, this was a patrol bent on hunting down irregulars, not out to fight a set-piece battle with a proper enemy.

"*Merde! Putain!*" The two officers swore and gesticulated when they came upon the carnage. The lieutenant halted the column, while the captain slowly walked around the bodies. His stopped and stared when he came to the headless corpse. The empty neck seemed to writhe under its cloak of flies.

Skirmishers cast about, looking for footprints and trying to identify the path by which the Spanish murderers had fled. It wasn't long before one scout waved and shouted, pointing at the tracks Pennywhistle and the others had left. The captain strode over to examine the telltale marks in the sand, then called over his lieutenants. Pennywhistle could practically read the officers' minds from the expressions on their faces: Those damned dagoes! More of our soldiers murdered! The Spaniards are monsters! They shall pay dearly!

In short order, the column was marching up the hill in pursuit of the killers. Pennywhistle tracked the captain as the range dropped: eighty-five yards, eighty, seventy-five. Perfect. "Now!" he shouted to Dale. They stood to their full heights, the red of their uniforms brilliant against the backdrop of trees, sighted their pieces, and squeezed the triggers.

The flintlocks crashed back against their shoulders and puffs of smoke temporarily obscured their vision. When it cleared, they saw that both officers had collapsed; the captain had a hole in his forehead, and the lieutenant's blue uniform was purpled with the spreading stain of his life's blood. The column faltered as soldiers saw, not the backs of fleeing peasants they'd expected, but two British soldiers armed with rifles, in command of the high ground.

The column's sergeant recovered quickly. He was an older man in his forties, whose weather-beaten face looked as if it had seen plenty of action. He saw the two red-coated soldiers on the hill and swore vividly. Then he yelled a command, and a single drummer pounded it out on his kettle drum. The men adroitly formed into a line and quickly fixed bayonets. Sixty angry men leveled cold steel toward the hilltop.

No time to be subtle. Pennywhistle waved his arms and bellowed in French, "Come and get us, you Gallic bastards!"

"Charge!" yelled the sergeant.

"Run!" shouted Pennywhistle.

CHAPTER TWO

Pennywhistle and Dale abandoned any pretense of dignity and hurtled down the steep hill just as fast as their legs could manage. They had to zigzag to avoid the many boulders that cluttered their path, which slowed their progress, but they would do the same to their pursuers and break the integrity of their line. Small, jumbled groups were much easier to defend against than an ordered company. A deep, fast-running stream lay at the base of the hill. High, wooded bluffs rose steeply on the opposite bank.

Directly below the bluffs, Juanita swayed unsteadily in Lightning's saddle. Manton stood alongside, clutching the bridles of the two mules in sheer frustration. As a good servant, he had to stand still and wait while the captain and Dale risked their necks and drew enemy fire. He looked suspiciously at the stony path in front of him. It was barely discernible as a trail, but Juanita had assured him it linked up with a disused Roman track that led to Cordona. He glared into the dull eyes of the sometimes willful Carmen and Rosita and mentally commanded their obedience. If the temperamental beasts threw tantrums, it could cause a fatal delay.

Pennywhistle heard shouts, yells, and bawled commands as the enemy crested the hill, but he did not look back. He estimated from the noise he had at least a hundred-yard lead. He and Dale pulled up hard at the edge of the stream and sucked in a few quick breaths. The current was swifter than he'd thought. The jagged rocks were covered in green slime, slick and slippery.

Zzzzip, zzzip, zzzip. A sound like angry hornets assailed his ears. They were under fire. He looked up and saw puffs of smoke from the top of the hill. Evidently, the old sergeant had decided to see if a few lucky shots might relieve his men of having to negotiate a boulder-strewn hill. The chances of them scoring hits at this range, more than a hundred yards, were small; but there was also the possibility the enemy commander sought to unnerve, distract, and delay his quarry. Clever, but that only worked with novices, not professionals.

He and Dale waded into the icy cold stream, weapons and cartridge boxes held above their heads. The water came to just below his waist, somewhat higher on Dale's shorter frame. He gingerly placed one foot after the other on the slime-covered rocks, lest he lose his footing. It ended up more of a shuffle than a walk. He could see small groups of French soldiers moving steadily down towards the stream, gaining ground—and range.

The sound of low, staccato barking caused him to halt abruptly in midstream. He snapped his head back and saw two huge, white dogs racing down the hill. Dogs moved much faster than men. The French NCO was crafty, Pennywhistle realized; he had sent the dogs to maul them, fix them in place, before sending his men down the hill to finish the business.

Pennywhistle recognized them as Great Pyrenees, famous as fierce battle companions since the time of Louis XIV. They must have belonged to one of the dead officers. Each was a hundred and fifty pounds of angry muscle, and the effect of their powerful jaws on human flesh was exceedingly unpleasant to imagine. With their precarious footing in the stream, there was no way to reach the far shore before the dogs savaged them.

He felt the blood rush to the surface of the skin and knew his face had turned a brilliant crimson. He saw Dale flash the hint of a smile; the sergeant recognized the "battle face" that manifested in moments of great peril. Pennywhistle's mind shifted into hyperactive mode and he saw the situation with sudden calmness and perfect clarity. The dogs were fifty yards out, in full gallop, closing rapidly. He had time for two shots, one for each animal; no margin for error whatsoever. Torso shots would have been easier on their large frames, but they were beasts famous for their powers of endurance and they might keep on coming. No, it would have to be head shots, right between the eyes.

He thanked God for the Ferguson. With a muzzle-loader, he would not have had the time. In one quick motion, he brought the rifle to his chest, jerked the trigger guard down and to the right, and opened the breech. He inserted a paper cartridge and .62 caliber ball in a greased leather wad that gripped the rifling. As the barks grew louder and closer, he twisted the guard up and to the left to close the breechblock, then shot fine priming powder from a metal flask into the pan and closed it. The rocks might as well have been covered in grease; he had reached a shallower place in the river, so he dropped to one knee for better balance. He winced as the cold water hit his chest, but the pain increased his concentration.

He lined up the v-shaped sights on the lead dog, barely twenty yards from the water. The world shifted to a soft blur as everything but the dog's snout faded from his vision; that was in bold relief and exquisite detail. He held his breath for a fraction of a second, let it out gently and fired. The ball penetrated the skull diagonally and fragments of brain flew out the canine's left ear. The impact lifted the body a foot off the ground and pitched it violently sideways.

The second animal, enraged by the death of his companion, snarled and put on a burst of speed. He was almost at the edge of the water, which would at least slow the brute. Pennywhistle guessed he had ten seconds. He shot to his feet, reloaded in a lightning blur of motion, crouched low, and brought the piece to the point. He fired as the dog leaped at him from three feet away. The point-blank shot exploded the dog's head into a shower of gore. The headless body's forward motion nearly grazed Pennywhistle's shoulder before it plunged into the stream and changed the flow to red.

The French had not been idle. They had progressed more than three quarters of the way down the hill. Bullets started to whine about his ears, and this time the sounds were loud and the fire well directed. Pennywhistle turned his back, trusted to luck and fate, and slogged as fast as he could toward the far shore. He actually moved quite quickly, but with bullets flying, the passage seemed interminable.

Twelve of the French soldiers charged the last few yards to the water's edge, just as Pennywhistle and Dale gained the far bank. The rest formed into a line a few yards back and prepared to deliver a volley.

"C'mon on, Captain!" Manton yelled. "Just a few more yards!" Pennywhistle and Dale sprinted up the bank. Soldiers entered the stream. Two slipped and ignominiously plunged into the swift current, soaking cartridge boxes and rendering their contents useless. The rest waded slowly and carefully forward, as if walking through a sea of molasses.

Pop, pop, pop! The French on the far bank volleyed and bullets flew over the running men's heads. One shot grazed the edge of the marine officer's blue cuff, fraying fabric but missing flesh. Damn! It was a new uniform. He and Dale positively raced the last ten yards.

Pennywhistle hastily jammed the Ferguson and the rest of his kit in the saddle bags, then executed a fast and decidedly ungraceful jump into Lightning's saddle. Juanita gripped his waist for dear life. Dale mounted the mule bringing up the rear.

The breeze carried the sound of angry bees, much louder now that the French had gained the far bank, and Pennywhistle felt puffs of air near his face. He had no spurs, but he dug the heels of his heavy hessian boots into Lightning's flanks, reached behind with a large birch rod and slapped the animal's rump, yelling "Haah!" The beast jumped and moved smartly forward. Manton's mule followed immediately, but Dale's beast was sulky. Three vicious slaps of a boatswain's starter on her backside did the trick.

They were moving. Up, up, up, ever so deliberately. The path twisted and fluctuated in width, so no great speed was possible. Juanita was familiar with the way and told Pennywhistle what lay ahead as they went around each turn. Below him, he heard the sounds of French troops, blaspheming and shouting as they puffed, panted, and stumbled upward on the unknown, sinuous path. He had hoped they would give up the pursuit, but the sergeant in command was evidently a persistent chap. He needed some violent discouragement.

The trail narrowed and rose steeply just below the crest. It was barely wide enough for Lightning's shoulders to pass without scraping two large boulders that framed the exit. Soldiers coming through would have to go single file; that made it the perfect spot for an ambush.

The little caravan moved on to the grassy plain that marked the summit. Heavy woods lay a few yards ahead. Pennywhistle dismounted and took the Ferguson out of the saddle. "Get everyone into the woods and out of sight. If I am not back in thirty minutes, get moving anyway," he told Dale. "I will find a way to catch up."

Dale opened his mouth to object. As a non-commissioned officer, he was theoretically less valuable and should be the one staying behind, but the fierce look in Pennywhistle's eye silenced him. He huffed a sigh and saluted.

"Don't worry, Sarn't. It's just like shooting deer in Scotland. It's just that these deer have guns to shoot back. I don't even have to stalk them! They will walk right into my den. What could be easier? I haven't practiced since we left Lisbon, and I don't want my marksmanship to get rusty."

Dale smiled crookedly at this brittle attempt at humor. Pennywhistle appreciated Dale's willingness to fight, but he had something Dale did not: acute eyesight. What other people saw clearly at twenty feet, he saw at sixty.

He never deluded himself about his true nature. He possessed several qualities that suited him perfectly for military service, not civilian life, at least as proper gentlemen reckoned things. He was clever, resourceful, and ruthless: far closer to crafty Odysseus than vainglorious Achilles. He liked to push his physical limits and challenge the raw edges of endurance. He possessed an almost monkish self control. Both were legacies of a vigorous, Spartan childhood spent mostly outdoors on his grandfather's estate in Scotland. Ghillie Gunn, who first taught him to shoot, said excellence was never achieved without a price, that price being constant practice. He spent much of his off duty time practicing obsessively with his rifle and his cutlass, something many of his fellow officers regarded as distinctly odd. He found their obsession with cards and games of chance equally peculiar.

When he first met Dale, the sergeant was unhappily serving under Lieutenant Carson, a corpulent, heavy drinker who gloried in being a gentleman amateur, someone who left the distasteful business of actual killing entirely to the men. Pennywhistle thought Carson had it all backwards. An officer's duty was to be the greatest warrior among his men, to take greater risks so his men might take lesser ones.

Pennywhistle relaxed for a fraction of a second and favored Dale with a quick smile. He appreciated the man's loyalty and genuine concern for his welfare. "Don't play my nanny, Sarn't, just see to the girl."

Dale took the reins of his horse and the procession vanished into the dense forest. Pennywhistle dashed back to the pass as the sound of French cursing grew louder. He found a spot in some dense bushes to the right of one of the boulders and stripped off the scarlet jacket that defied camouflage. The foliage gave almost perfect concealment; only a few inches of his four foot rifle would be visible. It would be very difficult for startled soldiers to target the source of their discomfiture.

He placed his soggy jacket on a flat rock to dry. He then carefully laid out his cartridges, balls, wads, and priming flask for quick access. He checked his flint, frowned, and inserted a new one. He meticulously applied a blend of beeswax and tallow to the breech screw to make the action fluid and easy. He loaded his piece with his usual care to ensure the oiled leather wad cradling the ball would tightly grip the eight lands and grooves of the rifling.

Since he was firing downward at a steep angle, he decided to use a stealth position favored by marksmen of the 95th. He made a bed of reeds for comfort and to absorb the water from his clothing. He braced his back against the larger of the two boulders, legs fully extended, right boot resting atop the left. He positioned the muzzle on the toe of his right boot and wrapped the front of Ferguson's sling around the tip as an anchor. He wrapped the rear of the sling around his right hand for better grip and balance then reached over with his left hand to add stability to the butt. It gave steadiness as good as a firing stand. Since the Ferguson needed no ramrod, he could easily reload. He had an excellent view of the trail below. The range would be short, exactly twenty five yards.

He felt the strong pull of the usual uninvited guests to battle: fear and excitement. He needed them reduced to quiet, unobtrusive bystanders and knew exactly how to do it. *The Ritual* always worked, but it called forth his darker, amoral self.

He breathed in and out slowly, deeply. Annoying random thoughts faded. The tightness in his chest disappeared and his pounding heart slowed to a steady, regular beat. His body temperature dropped, and his nose detected the scents of hidden beasts—a lurking Pine Marten and an alert Iberian lynx. His muscles grew supple, and the clarity of his vision increased exponentially. He heard birdsongs that had gone undetected five minutes earlier. He felt a slight metallic taste his mouth and a tingling in his fingertips. Excitement changed to profound concentration as a deeper, more subtle mind took control of his perceptions. He visualized every action in the minutes ahead in exquisite detail. He felt relaxed, comfortable, and steady, yet his senses were pitched to the highest intensity.

His moral compass stopped, icicles covered his heart, and his capacity for mercy shrank to insignificance. Everything suddenly became deathly quiet. The animals, birds, and insects sensed what was about to happen and cleared off. He noted the smell of honeysuckle in the pleasant breeze and calmly factored a two knot wind into his shot. It was actually quite a beautiful day; a good day to die, just not for him and his people.

He detected footsteps approaching the curve, then they abruptly stopped. He heard murmurs, whispers, and low voices. He understood French perfectly, but even if he had not, the problem was clear. The men were tired and winded after the long climb and weary of the pursuit. They sensed danger and debated who would expose himself first. They were cautious; no one was looking for induction into *La Légion d'Honneur*. These were experienced soldiers, not recruits seeking glory.

Someone said, *"Merde, merde, merde."* A tall fusilier tentatively poked his head round the bend, looked quickly in several directions, then pulled back to cover. He waited several minutes and repeated the process. Pennywhistle did nothing, wanting him to feel safe. The third time, the fusilier moved directly into the center of the trail and stood firm, his Charleville advanced with fixed bayonet. He swiveled his head carefully twice, then plodded cautiously ahead. "All hands repel boarders," shouted his old captain's voice in Pennywhistle's mind. He sighted the Ferguson on the fusilier's chest and smoothly squeezed the trigger. An explosion of red erupted from the Frenchman's left breast and he was knocked backwards. There were surprised shouts, then nothing. The swiftness of the death had stunned the French. After a minute, a chorus of angry whispers, hushed exclamations, and fearful maledictions drifted up toward his alert ears. They were clearly trying to figure out their next move.

He reloaded. Several minutes passed. His breathing remained slow and regular. There was a hint of movement a few feet away; unimportant, just a fox trying to remain hidden, His entire world was the small patch of trail, and nothing escaped his heightened attention.

A short, dark man moved hesitantly onto the trail. His face showed he wanted to be anywhere but where he was. He looked back towards his compatriots, who murmured words of encouragement. He shook his head in violent disagreement, snarled a curse, and then began to move forward, taking the smallest of steps. He held his musket steady, but Pennywhistle saw his finger quiver on its trigger. He was jumpy, ready to fire at anything, and likely to miss.

Pennywhistle calmly tickled the trigger and his shot hit the soldier square in the right pectoral. The man spun and collapsed, unable to cry out for help as he choked on the blood filling his lungs.

Pennywhistle smiled quickly in satisfaction at a well-placed shot. He cared nothing for morality at this point, only ballistics. The distressed cries from the French excited his emotions not at all. They were merely useful tools for assessing the state of their morale and pinpointing their position.

The sergeant who spearheaded the pursuit emerged decisively onto the trail. He had probably promised the first two volunteers promotion as a show of confidence, but now decided it was time to step up and lead by example.

Pennywhistle admired him: an enemy, but a good soldier. Still, it changed nothing. The only consideration was that his death would burn the heart out of his followers.

The sergeant advanced menacingly up the trail. The grizzled NCO stopped for a moment and looked methodically left to right, searching for clues to the shooter's whereabouts. Nothing presented itself. He sniffed the air briefly, as if his nose could locate what his eyes could not. He plodded more slowly now, as the incline steepened, and swept his barrel in slow, careful arcs; still nothing. He frowned deeply as his frustration grew.

Pennywhistle could see his square, battered face clearly. Hollow cheeked, scarred, and deeply furrowed with worry lines, probably from hard service, it bespoke the solid character of a career soldier. Soldiers would readily follow such a man. He pulled the trigger and the bullet tore the top off the sergeant's skull. For a moment, brain, blood and bone spewed in every direction. Then the corpse fell, rolling back down the hill. Pennywhistle calmly reloaded. A few seconds later, two men dashed from cover and pulled the body back with them.

That told him a lot. Risking their lives to retrieve a corpse bespoke great loyalty, a quality he valued. The Sergeant was dear to them and would no doubt receive a military funeral. That pleased him; an honorable opponent deserved a proper sendoff. He could easily have killed one of them, but decided it was pointless and unsporting. Retrieval of the corpse was a gesture of resignation. They would fight no more today and retire down the hill. It was time to go.

He breathed deeply for a full minute and came back to himself. His forehead ached slightly, the usual after-effect of *The Ritual*. He donned his jacket, a little drier now, gathered up his belongings, and walked briskly toward the woods, lost in thought. He had to find a safe spot for the night and figure out his next move. He was behind enemy lines with few assets, but at least the immediate danger had passed. He had, of course, brought it all on himself.

He had cocked things up badly, and it ate at him. He'd trusted the wrong contact at the Spanish frontier, paid dearly for maps that turned out to be worse than useless, and been betrayed by a supposedly reliable guide. Then he'd compounded his folly by risking his life to play Don Quixote to a perfect stranger of a girl. He knew why he'd done it. It was an act of atonement. He felt responsible for Carlotta's death, even though everyone assured him, repeatedly, that it had been an act of God.

The rescue had felt right, but it was militarily wrong. By inviting pursuit, he had jeopardized both his overt and covert missions. The dispatches he carried were important, but what he had in the hollowed out heel of his left boot was far more so.

He entered the gloomy forest and walked a quarter mile to where his party waited anxiously. He forced a breezy smile to his face when he saw their looks of concern. He was in command and had to put up a proper front. It would not do to even hint at weakness or regret. "That lot won't bother us any more today," he said cheerfully. "But just to be safe, we need to be miles away by morning."

It worked on Juanita. Her face assumed a deeply serious but calm expression, her clasped hands tightened once, then relaxed. Pennywhistle, seeing this, deduced she was a person of deep faith, a staunch Catholic who believed his timely appearance was a divine omen rather than a lucky coincidence. He knew Dale and Manton had been with him too long to be fooled by his almost jovial manner, but he felt honor-bound to stage the charade anyway. Dale had even said once, "It's your tell, sir. When you are at your heartiest and aggressively optimistic, that's when you are most worried." Dale was not wrong.

CHAPTER THREE

They rode slowly and in silence, through the late afternoon and into the evening. The stony path twisted and turned like a snake in a series of switchbacks as they moved ever upward. Lightning might not be a fast horse, but he was sure-footed; perhaps the 200 Portuguese dollars had been a reasonable investment after all. The mules were bred for this sort of climb. Pennywhistle, however, felt out of his element; he understood boats better than horses.

They were crossing a rugged spur of the Sierra Francia Range. The vegetation grew sparse as the ground rose and the trees gradually changed from deciduous to evergreen. Oak and ash gave way to pine, and the air turned noticeably cooler. He breathed more heavily than usual; he guessed the elevation was approaching a mile. The trees blocked out much of the sun and made the forest stern and unwelcoming. Juanita assured him they were on the right path, that they would reach Cordona by noon on the morrow. He hoped she was right; his only map was atrocious. Come nightfall he would use his compass, sextant, and the stars to get a closer fix on their position. Navigation learned at sea worked just as well on land.

He did not think anyone followed, but so much had gone wrong on this assignment, it was as well to plan for the worst. At least any opponents would have only one avenue of advance. Juanita said the area was too rough and remote for the French to bother with, and as a result, partisan bands used it as a refuge. He didn't like the sound of that. The Spanish irregulars were British allies, but they were also a very mixed bunch. Some were highly effective and disciplined partisan warriors, but others were little better than criminals who used the war as an excuse for extortion and banditry. One partisan had already tried to kill him, take his pouch of gold guineas, and abscond with the dispatches. And that chap had been represented to him as trustworthy.

More promisingly, she said itinerant hunters frequented the area because of an abundance of wild boar. He had forgotten, in all of the tumult, that he was hungry. He had plenty of hard tack and salt pork in his saddlebags, but fresh boar meat was a much more pleasant prospect. Besides, a woman would be present this evening, and he hated to subject her to Navy fare. Dale had been one of England's premier poachers before joining the Marines, and he himself had been expertly schooled in the hunter's craft by Ghillie Gunn, so dinner tonight would be something special. Dusk was the best time to hunt boar. Better to stop early to allow time for stalking, skinning, and dressing.

They would stand watches, he decided. He would take the first, Dale the second, and Manton the third. Although Manton was not a marine, he could be relied upon. Typically, a captain's manservant would have been a marine private, but Pennywhistle had found the boy's intelligence exceeded any of the military candidates who had sought the job. No one objected to an English gentleman being eccentric. Besides, the eighteen-year-old had learned much of the soldier's art from careful observation. In a way, he was as much Pennywhistle's apprentice as his servant. He was a good marksman, so Pennywhistle had given him his old fusil at the start of the mission. Manton treasured it and cleaned it regularly.

Pennywhistle glanced over and noticed Manton looking at Juanita with wide eyes of longing; nothing lustful, more puppy dog affection. All to the good; he would be vigilant in watching out for her.

He saw a small clearing just ahead. It looked like a hunter's campsite, with a carefully constructed stone fire pit with a cleared area all about it and a view of the valley below. Very defensible, and a fast-running mountain brook ran through it to boot. There was plenty of wood for a good fire. He debated whether a fire would make them vulnerable, but decided at this height it was worth the risk. A hearty, hot fire and freshly cooked meat were splendid for morale. Everyone was tired, and they were finally at the crest of the spur. Tomorrow, it would all be downhill. He gave the order to halt.

Juanita's tattered blouse troubled him; it could not be good for her sense of propriety. He also wanted his sash back. He instructed Manton to give her his spare white broadcloth shirt, adding, "Let her have my boat cloak as well."

"*Gracias, muchas gracias, Capitan Pennywhistle,*" she said with surprised delight. She disappeared into the woods to change. When she reemerged a minute later, she asked him how she looked.

The soft cotton shirt was several sizes too big and the heavy blue boat cloak overwhelmed her thin frame, yet the overall effect was quite charming, accentuating her long black hair, violet eyes, and heart shaped face. It made her appear pixyish; a sort of forest sprite. He did not want to encourage the look he saw in her eye, but it seemed cruel not to say something polite after all she had been through. "My clothing has never been shown to greater advantage," he said quietly.

She broke into a broad, delighted smile, and he knew he had said exactly the wrong thing.

"I have relatives in Cordona who will guide you toward Wellington's army," Juanita volunteered with deep seriousness.

"They will accept no money, because they value honor and chivalry."

"I shall be most grateful for any assistance they can render." That was true enough, but his good cheer was forced. He had found Spanish honor real and punctilious, but quirky and wholly unpredictable to the English mind. Spanish promises might be heartfelt, but they were often of questionable value.

She continued to explain how her countrymen would assist with a sadness that indicated she was loath to leave his company. It was natural enough, even predictable. He had saved her from what contemporary moralists called "a fate worse than death." Nevertheless, the wistful look on her face bothered him.

He did not want, need, or welcome her affection. She was someone to be protected, not loved. She was not so much a woman as a duty. She was attractive, and he certainly had normal male appetites, but there had been no woman in his life since Carlotta's death, and he was determined to keep it that way. Carlotta had loved him, and he her, with a grand passion that came once in a lifetime. Real love was precious and extraordinary, like gold. He wanted no chunks of fool's gold.

He had not been chaste since her death, but had indulged his lusts with women chosen specifically because they were utterly forgettable afterwards. He was discretion itself, so not a whiff of scandal touched his reputation or theirs. They were all women of station and quality and he'd treated them well enough, but at the first sign of nest-building he'd discarded them with the swiftness of a child dropping a hot coal. It was the height of arrogance that they should dare to lay claim to his heart. His loins and his heart were two separate entities, and the first did not inform the second. It puzzled him that women could not understand such an elementary idea. One had had the gall to suggest he was consumed by bitterness.

He prided himself on his rationality, but sometimes wondered if he were a bad luck talisman for women, what sailors called a Jonah. Carlotta, the great love of his life, died because he'd failed to see what was obvious, failed to protect her. Julia had succumbed to yellow fever a week after he had discarded her. She had never been sick a day in her life. Emma, who knew horses as well as he knew boats, had died in a freak riding accident a day after their parting. It was illogical to attribute all of the deaths to a single cause, but the Universe always seemed to exact a price when a virtuous heart consorted with a damaged soul. Juanita deserved something better, a good, stalwart young man like Manton. These thoughts brought a scowl to his face, and Juanita recoiled.

He realized how forbidding he appeared and forced a friendly expression back on his face. He needed to get things organized, and a grim countenance certainly would discourage everyone's best efforts. An hour and a half remained of daylight. Setting up camp and getting supper were the priorities. The prospect of a good meal energized him.

He would have preferred to stalk the boar himself, as it would be a great release for his riled emotions, but he allowed Dale was better than he and assigned him the duty. Dale smiled with pleasure and promised he would be back with the kill before nightfall. He vanished quietly into the verdure like a disembodied spirit.

Juanita watched in puzzlement as Pennywhistle removed a strange variety of accoutrements from the saddlebags, laid them out carefully on the ground, and methodically assembled them into a canvas structure the like of which she had never seen. He told her the design was his own; he had had Firmin's of Birmingham run it up. He'd based it on the improvised versions he had seen in the field made from blankets and sticks. Rankers called it a "dog tent." Because of its small size, he considered "pup tent" a more appropriate label. He bowed gracefully and said, "Of course, it is yours for the night." He thought nothing of it, but she looked at him in amazement that a gentleman would sleep on the ground so a mere peasant girl could sleep on a canvas floor.

He left her standing in surprise and moved briskly out to reconnoiter the immediate area. He had already examined the fire pit for any sign of recent use and had found none. He wanted to make sure the area was clear and establish a defensive perimeter. The forest had a story to tell for those trained to read its language. "Trees with tongues, brooks with books, sermons in stone"; the Bard would have made a good woodsman. He slowed his pace, minutely examining the trail, as would a scientist studying an insect under a microscope. He noted fresh tracks of rabbit, boar, deer, mountain goat, and the older ones of a lynx; nothing remotely resembling the impressions of boots, shoes, or feet. There were no mule or horse tracks, either. He then walked two hundred yards along the fast-running mountain stream, seeing nothing to indicate human presence. It looked like no one had been in the area for at least a week. He returned satisfied they were secure for the night.

Manton had a very pleasant, deliberately smoky fire going. The smoke served to keep away annoying insects. There was a crashing noise, and Dale emerged from the woods, proudly towing a handsome boar tied to a long pine bough. It was a fast kill, even for Dale.

"Caught it sleeping," he announced cheerfully. "Snoring powerful loud it was, child's play to track. Give me half an hour and I'll have it ready to cook."

Dale was as good as his word, and the steaks proved excellent. The meal gave everyone a welcome reprieve from tension and fatigue. It was fully dark by the time they finished, and the forest came alive with the clicking and cooing of night insects and animals. Pennywhistle talked with Juanita as they ate, his anemic Spanish improving rapidly with use, and got a good idea of French movements in the area. Peasants were disdained by the French; nevertheless they were everywhere, observant, and excellent sources of raw intelligence. Dale and Manton listened with interest, trying to make out words they could understand. She said the slope of the trail was much easier and wider on the other side, and they would be able to secure provisions in Cordona.

Pennywhistle liked the soothing lilt in her voice, and speaking with her relaxed him. The chat was quite pleasant, but suddenly her posture tensed and her melodic voice jumped an octave. Shrill, harsh words cascaded from her lips, and her face flushed red.

"The Virgin Mary was looking out for me this afternoon when she dispatched you to my rescue. I am far from the first girl to be attacked. You are a good man, but I think you are too reasonable and do not understand. The French are pigs! Pigs! You cannot reason with animals. They understand nothing of God, decency, or honor. They are truly Satan's spawn and must be swept away by fire. I curse them all! Spain will never be whole again until every last French soldier lies dead and rotting, food for crows!"

Her tone was pure fire and her voice vibrated with righteous anger. Her transformation shocked him, even though he should have been prepared for it. She had been through an awful ordeal and her reaction was natural enough, yet he suspected she might have said exactly the same thing before the morning's drama. He was unprepared for the depth of hatred here in the Peninsula. It was particularly strange that she believed he was some kind of avenging angel sent by God's command.

Her blazing eyes were two violet coals that burned the air and hypnotized Dale and Manton. Pennywhistle quickly changed the subject to the weather common to the area in midsummer. It was a lame attempt to cool the heated atmosphere, but surprisingly it worked. She had shot her bolt and seemed content now to talk about trifles.

He ordered the others to turn in as soon as they finished eating. Dawn was at four a.m. and he wanted to break camp at first light. They had all had a long, arduous day and would need plenty of rest for what lay ahead.

The temperature dropped rapidly after sunset and the night turned pleasantly cool. He moved away from the camp toward a rock outcrop where he could get a clear view of the night sky. The stars formed a magnificently luminous canopy and the view of the valley below was quite striking. He loved forests and had spent many pleasant summer nights as a boy beneath the Milky Way. But tonight was no holiday outing; it was deadly serious business.

He unfurled his map and placed it next to the lantern, using small rocks on the edges to hold it down. He studied it and checked his compass. He looked up and used Cassiopeia to locate the Pole Star, then took out his brass sextant and measured its height above the horizon to establish both local time and his latitude.

He next measured the angle of the moon's relation to the Pole Star, then to eight others. Consulting a pocket edition of *The Nautical Tables,* he noted the times at which those distances would occur at Greenwich. He opened his pocket watch and made sure it squared with the local time he had established via sextant: 11:20. His Swiss Blancpain was the most accurate watch available and had cost him a small fortune. Since the earth rotated 15 degrees each hour, he then had to compare local time to the Greenwich baseline to establish his longitude.

He carefully made his calculations.

They were probably twenty miles from Tormes del Rey, the nearest large town, and thirty-five miles from the city of Salamanca. They had a ways to go. The last reports had Wellington maneuvering against Marmont thirty miles north of Salamanca in the direction of Tordesillas. Marmont's army was living off the land and had to constantly keep moving; his men would starve if they stayed in one place too long. Pennywhistle wondered if what he carried in his boot might influence Wellington's movements, then decided it was silly to guess. The Admiralty clearly deemed the message important, and it was his duty to deliver it.

Something caused the hairs on his arm to rise and his skin to prickle; a tiny shift in the wind, a very faint scent, the barest hint of movement. A low level electrical current traversed his nerves, the varying intensity of the pulses a code for danger. He immediately doused the lantern, then jerked his head away from the bright stars and towards the dark tree line, trusting his instincts. Something out there was alive and active; but was it animal or human?

He crouched low and sprinted silently toward a line of boulders. He flattened himself on his belly, looked toward the brooding forest, and waited, listening carefully. As the minutes passed, his eyes readjusted to the Stygian darkness. He detected a badger and a Roe deer, but dismissed them: they were not the cause of his trepidation. After a quarter of an hour, he saw definite movement in the brackens. It was furtive, yet clumsy; not at all like the economical movements of a nocturnal beast. This was unmistakably human. He detected the faint smell of garlic. Quietly he drew the small dirk from inside his boot. He breathed deeply with anticipation. He was ready.

CHAPTER FOUR

The figure emerged from the bush and hesitantly moved a few steps onto the trail. Pennywhistle looked at the edges of the figure, rather than the central mass, as edges were much more distinct in darkness. The man cupped his hand to his ear as if he had heard something. He glanced cautiously to the left and the right. He raised his head up, as if he were sniffing the air. It was hard to tell much beyond that he was tall and excessively thin, almost a scarecrow. He sported a plumed bicorn worn sideways and appeared clad in some kind of military attire to judge from the cut of the clothing; with color filtered out, it was difficult to tell of what nation. He tightly gripped a musket under his left armpit in a poor imitation of the *secure arms* position. He acted as if he were uncertain whether the musket was a tool or a hindrance. He had to be a new recruit, or militia. No veteran would carry a weapon like that. For that matter, neither would an experienced hunter.

The man walked tentatively down the trail, which would bring him directly in front of Pennywhistle's position. He just had to be patient. The feet came closer. The shoes were cheap and crude, with the high heel favored by locals, not French army issue. He wore long buttoned gaiters, typical of Spanish soldiery.

31

He stopped directly in front of the marine and moved his head warily side to side.

Pennywhistle's hands shot out and grabbed the ankles. He jerked back hard and the man slammed violently to the ground. Then he leaped onto the man's back and jabbed his fist sharply into the base of the fellow's neck. Not as hard as he could have, just enough to render the man unconscious. He hated unnecessary death, and dead men furnish no information. He wanted this man talking.

He turned the body over and examined the face. It was angular and handsome, but care-worn and haggard, darkened by stubble. The lips were dry and cracked, the skin dirty and sunken; clearly he had endured privation, but the lack of creases and age lines suggested he was only in his late twenties. The tattered uniform was that of a Spanish regular regiment. The fact that he was alone in such an obscure place suggested he was either a deserter or that some disaster had befallen his unit.

Pennywhistle took a comfortable seat next to the man, opened his wooden canteen, and poured a steady trickle of water on the man's parched lips. He laid his dirk alongside for quick access, just in case. The man moaned briefly and bobbed his head slowly side to side, not quite conscious. His lips opened and took the water gratefully.

The marine saw a flicker of movement in the eyelids. He put down the canteen and took up the dirk. He held it close to the throat but did not touch the skin; a warning, not an attack. The man's right hand twitched briefly. His eyes snapped suddenly open; disorientation, surprise, and fear followed in swift order.

"Do not move. Answer my questions honestly and you will not be harmed. Deceive or attack, and I will cut your throat," he said in Spanish, his tone harsh. He stared menacingly into the man's shocked eyes to establish dominance. "Now sit up and nod your head if you understand." The man's face went from terror to docility. He sat up slowly as Pennywhistle retracted the dagger. He bobbed his head twice. He wanted to cooperate.

The Englishman decided a military approach might work best. "Name, regiment, and commanding officer, soldier!" he demanded. It was like hitting a switch. The man's posture became rigid. For a few seconds he forgot his fear, remembered training and rote responses. "Juan Morales, Sergeant of the 2nd Regiment, Colonel Juárez commanding."

"I am a British officer," Pennywhistle announced gravely. "We may be on the same side, but I have no idea if you are patriot, deserter, or *afrancesado*. Explain how you came to be here. Be quick about it, for I am a man of little patience." He was actually quite patient, but it was as well to sow a bit of fear and prod the man to get to the point.

"Please, *señor capitan*, I mean no harm. I am a good man and a good soldier. Until two days ago, I was in charge of a platoon of soldiers in a small village. It was a small outpost where nothing ever happened. We were told Marshal Marmont was sixty miles away and King Joseph's Army was still in Madrid. We had no reason to expect anything. It was dusk; we had stacked our arms and were going to the local tavern. That's when we were attacked by a company of French hussars. They must have lain in wait in the ravines. They galloped at us from two directions, caught us in the open. Their horses rode us down. Their sabers cut us to pieces. My men died before my eyes. I was lucky to still have my sword and I got one French horseman with it, but they were just too many. I was the only soldier left. I ran. They set fire to the town. I can still hear the screams of the women in my head." His expression changed to one of deep sadness. "I headed for the mountains. I was out of my mind with grief and sadness. I knew of a partisan hideout, but I am no woodsman and got lost. Please, *señor capitan*, I am not a bad man. I tried, I really tried; I did not know what to do."

He began to sob. "I should have stayed, I should have stayed," he murmured.

An owl hooted loudly. Morales' shoulders jerked in fear. He swiveled his head toward the source of the sound as if he expected to see some sort of forest demon.

He was probably telling the truth. His story seemed less a recounting than a confession. Reactions like his were hard to fake. His tale would account for his disoriented, disheveled state. Morales may have been in charge, but his training had been marginal. He was not the first garrison soldier to be overwhelmed by combat, nor was he the first to suffer survivor's guilt. Pennywhistle knew of men who had become brigands and worse with less cause than this wretch. Here was a man in need of redemption: he desperately wanted someone to reassure him he was not a coward and that he had done all he could. Pennywhistle's own guilt over Carlotta's death had taught him that men were willing to run great risks in search of atonement, and that such journeys often took the most unexpected paths.

Some things disquieted Pennywhistle. Why would 140 elite cavalrymen bother to raid an unimportant garrison five miles this side of nowhere? To practice swordplay? It made no sense. Hussars were scouts; they must have been looking for something, but what? A cold chill went down his back.

The marine looked sternly into Morale's eyes. "Did the troopers say anything, do anything out of the ordinary, shout any command that seemed strange?"

Morales cast his eyes downward and said, "I do not understand French, sir, but I caught the words, 'manteau rouge' several times. I heard one of the officers shout that repeatedly at some of the troopers."

"Red coat." But there were no British soldiers in the area. Maybe they were pursuing one of Wellington's exploring officers —men on fast thoroughbreds who roamed widely behind enemy lines, seeking intelligence information. They were daring chaps who operated singly and wore their uniforms conspicuously, lest they be shot as spies if captured. But a whole company seemed overkill to capture one man.

The thought that coalesced in his mind was almost too fantastic to credit. So many unforeseen things had gone wrong on this mission, starting with his betrayal by a supposedly reliable guide. The man had misdirected him onto a secondary route. What if he had done that, not for security, as he'd said, but for more sinister reasons? What if the man was an *afrancesado*, a Spaniard sympathetic to the French, a collaborator? He and Admiral Martin were the only ones who knew the details of the mission, and even Pennywhistle had no idea of the encrypted contents in his left boot. What if word had leaked? He was loath to consider the possibility, but forced himself to do so. He had valuable information. What if the troopers had been really searching for him? A thousand questions to ponder. For now, he had to deal with Morales.

He felt sympathy for the man and decided he might prove useful. It was time to relax a bit. He had used the stick, time for the carrot.

"I warn you, if you have lied to me, it will go hard with you," he said brusquely. There was no point in expressing sympathy too directly; frightened men were best tightly controlled. "For now, I chose to believe you, but require more information." He opened his haversack and handed the man some hard sausage and bread. "But you will think better on a full stomach." Morales eyes grew large as full moons. He almost snatched the food from the Englishman's hands and his teeth tore into it greedily. He resembled a hungry squirrel stuffing nuts into his mouth.

Pennywhistle waited a few minutes while he ate. He analyzed the key components of a worsening situation and asked the question he had been dreading. He thought he knew the answer. "What was the name of the village where you were stationed?"

It took a few seconds for Morales to clear his lips of crumbs. "Cordona," he mumbled.

It was as he feared. There would be no succor at the end of this journey. Were there alternate trails down the mountain, other routes to a different destination? Juanita would probably know. Morales avowed they were hussars; could he have gotten the identification wrong? Not likely. Hussars were known for their extravagant, colorful uniforms and similar behavior. The cut and composition of the uniforms were distinctive, although colors varied according to individual regiments. A regiment might sport bearskin shakos, blue-faced crimson shell jackets with lots of buttons and elaborate piping, royal blue pelisses worn over the shoulder, and tight fitting azure trousers. Hussars were the sort of troops to make a quick raid and withdraw, not settle in to permanent occupation. If they had not found what they were looking for, they would have moved on.

Morales admitted he had fled when they started their depredations. He really had no idea how much of the village was intact. There might still be something left. They could approach the village in stealth and size up the situation. Pennywhistle wondered if the hussars belonged to Marmont's army. If so, it was much nearer than he had been told, but it also meant Wellington could not be too far distant. The situation was fluid and undoubtedly had changed since he'd left Lisbon. He needed new, reliable information.

He looked at Morales, considerably calmer after food and drink and realizing he would not die tonight. Something could be made of the man. He was ashamed, and he would want to fight, to hit back at the French. He would add another musket to the little band, and there certainly was plenty of boar meat to feed him. He would put him in Dale's charge. There was not a better drillmaster in the Fleet, and if anyone could lick some sense into him, it was Dale. Dale's lack of Spanish would be a problem, but he guessed the general purport of commands would surmount the language barrier. Good non-commissioned officers always found a way to be understood. He knew exactly what Dale would do first; teach Morales how to thoroughly clean his musket. It was filthy.

"Sarn't, you will come with me," he said in a voice that brooked no argument. "We have three guns and could use a fourth. You will have a chance to take a bash at the French. It is preferable to starving, don't you agree?"

The sergeant looked dumbfounded. He could scarcely credit the stern officer was actually offering help! His reaction amused but did not surprise the marine. In the Spanish Army, officers were usually well connected and brave, but often minimally trained and capricious. Most treated their men as expendable ciphers and were bad at providing for their basic needs.

"*Si, Señor Capitan,*" he said sheepishly.

"See here, Sarn't, I'll have none of that beaten cur stuff. Hold your head up, stiffen your back, and say," here he switched to loud English, "Aye, aye, sir!" He reverted to Spanish, "Say it smartly too! Like it or not, you are on duty with the Royal Marines." He was not sure if the man grasped it all, but he had to start somewhere to give him back his self respect.

"Shoulder your weapon, Sarn't. Forward march." The sergeant complied with a surprised look on his face and began to plod into the darkness. "Follow me," said Pennywhistle, taking the lead.

A frightening thought hit Pennywhistle. What if the infantry company at Valdencia had not been out on a random hunt for guerrillas? What if they had been hunting specifically for him? It might account for their zealous pursuit, and he had certainly made things easier for them by directly exposing himself. Damn! He was a fool! Maybe he was actually caught in a widespread search pattern. His treacherous guide might have propelled him into a maze.

He heard the sergeant's footfalls close behind him all the way back to camp. He was certain he had captured his temporary allegiance, but then, where could the man run? This whole mission was spinning out of control. He wracked his brain for clever ideas, but none were forthcoming. The only thing he could come up with was a general determination to do the unexpected. He needed sleep; he would think better in the morning. For now, there was nothing more to do but play out his hand, trust to his resourcefulness, and hope Fortune would favor the bold—or the foolhardy. He was not a religious man, but prayed silently that the night held no more surprises.

Chapter Five

Pennywhistle slept little and fitfully, with a spate of unpleasant dreams. He was already wide awake at 4 am when the sky began to lighten to grey in the east. He sat up, acknowledged Dale with a quick nod, then rose to his full height and stretched his arms high above his head. His sojourn in the land of Morpheus had left him stiff, creaky, and un-refreshed. He discussed Morales briefly with Dale, amplifying the particulars he had furnished the night before. "Keep a sharp eye on him today, Sarn't. He wants to fight, but he needs training. If we run into any French, I do not want him to do anything precipitate."

"Aye, aye, sir," said Dale calmly. "I can knock the rough edges off short order." Directly he had met Morales the night before, his trained eye had appraised Morales' character, appearance, and arms. The first he'd viewed with satisfaction, the other two with grave distaste. He could not do anything about Morales shabby attire for the moment, but the musket was another matter. Dale had cleaned it thoroughly, replaced the flint, and applied a shiny layer of gun oil to the lock-plate and barrel.

Dale knew the Spanish Army's reputation for slackness; nevertheless, it puzzled him why they neglected to drill into their soldiers the supreme importance of always having a clean and fully functional weapon. Armies suffered far more defeats from a want of attention to the basics than from masterful enemy tactics. The importance of a well maintained musket was one of the first things taught British recruits and it was stressed with loud voices, mighty curses, and occasional swift kicks. After the first day of training, a dirty firelock bought a heavy-handed clawing from the cat-o-nine tails.

Manton and Juanita had regarded Morales with curiosity. The tall, cadaverous man looked exhausted and bedraggled, yet walked with an erect carriage that suggested a military dignity unlikely to be found in either a hunter or a partisan. Their lips had remained dutifully unmoving but their wide eyes had demanded some sort of explanation. Pennywhistle had been too worried and tired to furnish much of one. "Sarn't Morales is the only survivor of the massacre of his regiment by hussars. He is in shock, but I believe he will recover quickly and prove useful." Manservant and maiden nodded briefly, satisfied that the disheveled stranger was a man on the run, in the same position as themselves, marooned behind enemy lines. Morales had wolfed down some leftover meat, then collapsed into the sleep of the dead.

Now Pennywhistle woke Manton quietly, and Dale gently did the same with Juanita. Pennywhistle wanted to be moving as soon as objects could be easily distinguished at the quarter mile, but first, there was the matter of washing. He struck out fifty yards into the forest to where the fast flowing mountain brook widened and deepened. He stripped off his garments and waded quickly into the icy, clear water, splashing it on himself. It stung like an army of bees and he gasped for breath, but it invigorated him and temporarily banished the regiment of worries shouting in his head. He'd read somewhere that Beau Brummell, the Prince Regent's favorite, bathed three times a day and was starting a new trend for gentlemen. Pennywhistle approved. It was far better to eradicate unpleasant smells than cloak them with expensive colognes. However, many old school gentlemen firmly believed regular bathing was injurious to the human constitution. Still, bathing thrice daily seemed excessive to Pennywhistle. "All things in moderation," his wise French tutor had counseled him long ago.

Meanwhile, Manton revived the fire and heated some water for the captain's shave. He held the straight razor over the fire briefly. His master was eccentric and preferred to shave himself rather than let Manton do it. On his first day as Pennywhistle's batman, the captain had told him, "I regret to say, Manton, that too much exposure to combat has rendered me ridiculously over-cautious. I simply cannot abide anyone with a naked blade too near my throat." He laid out his master's shaving kit and his bone and horse-hair tooth brush. He checked to see the pouch of baking soda was full. Unlike many, the captain still had a full set of original teeth.

He carefully gathered up the uniform that his master had heedlessly cast aside. It had been exquisitely tailored by Gieve's of Savile Row and deserved meticulous attention. It was a matter of pride that even in the center of a foreign wilderness his officer should always appear a proper gentleman. He carefully brushed the captain's double-breasted scarlet coat with the blue collar and cuffs, then lovingly polished its gold buttons and fringed bullion epaulettes. The crescent-shaped gold gorget the captain wore suspended from his neck received a particularly vigorous shining. He took a fine camel's hair brush to the red and white plume on the side of the black round hat. He shined the heavy Hessian boots with blacking. He heated a small hand iron in the fire and carefully applied it to the captain's blue-grey trousers to ensure a proper crease. He then did the same to the captain's favorite shirt with the jabot. He would have everything meticulously laid out when Pennywhistle returned from his morning bath.

The thought of bathing in an icy stream seemed fanatical to him; he realized he lacked his master's iron constitution and obsession with cleanliness. Nevertheless, the captain had persuaded him to bathe at least every other day, where practicable. It was quite a radical notion, but he rather liked the way he felt afterwards. Most servants—and many gentlemen—seldom met a tub of hot water more than once a week.

He plopped boar meat into the three-legged iron spider and it sizzled pleasingly. The captain liked his well done. The aroma invigorated everyone. He broke out a baguette for Pennywhistle and began soaking hardtack in a pot for the rest. Hardtack kept for ages, but un-softened was tough enough to crack teeth. The captain wanted everyone to be well fed. He often told Manton a soldier could battle the enemy or his stomach, but not both.

He ground some fresh coffee beans with a small hand grinder. He made sure not to spill a single bean, since his supply was limited and his master guarded his coffee as jealously a miser his gold. The captain preferred stout Brazilian coffee to wine, and thought tea a dull, insipid drink fit only for rheumatic old men taking the waters at Bath.

Juanita seemed to sense Pennywhistle was holding something back when he asked her at breakfast if there was another village beside Cordona that might be reached from their present position. She looked alarmed, but replied that there was the tiny village of Agallas, six miles to the north of Cordona. She said a spur branched off the main trail five miles ahead. "But why would we go there? It has nothing to offer and Cordona is only eight miles."

He forced optimism and confidence into his voice. The heartening power of coffee had lightened his mood somewhat. "No reason, just like to know what my options are, always wise to have an alternative." Juanita appeared satisfied, but he could tell from Dale and Manton's expressions they knew something was up. Morales ate in silence, concerned only with having a full belly for a change.

After breakfast, Dale and Juanita went over the camp, picking up refuse and tossing it into the fire, lest any strangers know people had passed this way recently. They doused the campfire and carefully dispersed the ashes. Normally he would have been confident no one would have followed, but after his ruminations of the night before, he was much less sure.

He had already determined to strike for Cordona, but he now knew he had five miles in which to amend his decision. He would talk to Juanita as they rode together. He needed to discover the town layout and possible access points; he needed a hide, something defensible, a room with a view. A night entry into the village might be best, and he had two native speakers who were familiar with the townsmen.

It was prudent to take his time and be safe, but he knew the information he carried was needed as soon as possible. He had expected to meet with Wellington two weeks after leaving Lisbon. But with poor roads, treachery, and the present detour, ten days had already elapsed and he was nowhere near his destination.

It had all started to go wrong when he'd picked up the new guide at Ciudad Rodrigo. He had been given very little information on the man, just a physical description and a password and countersign. It would have been easy enough for someone to sweat that out of the real guide, dispose of him, and substitute a ringer. He hadn't liked the fellow from the start, and he'd felt there was something off about his furtive, smarmy personality. The Spaniard had tried to slit Pennywhistle's throat in his sleep two nights later. But the man had been an amateur with a blade, and the marine was not. Yes, security had been breached; possibly at headquarters. How much other information had the French obtained? Marmont had anticipated several of Wellington's moves recently; perhaps it was due to something other than luck and perception.

Most of the staff officers in Lisbon were very well connected gentlemen; the idea that one might be a sugar-tongued traitor rattled him. Such a man would be in a position to pass very sensitive information. He wondered if the French had been given general notice of a commissioned messenger or had actually been furnished with a name, rank, and description.

They departed as the top edge of the sun pierced the horizon. The mountain air was crisp and bracing. Morales rode with Dale on Rosita. Rosita was balky and disliked her new passenger. She let out a few noisy protests, but gave into the inevitable and plodded slowly forward.

It was all downhill now. The trail widened, the grade eased, and the switchbacks grew much more gradual. The air warmed rapidly as they descended. Deciduous trees made a gradual reappearance and roadside vegetation increased. Pennywhistle talked with Juanita and got what he needed in short order. There was an old Moorish fortress called the *Alcazaba de Trujillio* at the start of the trail. It was a bastion against the *Reconquista*, deserted for centuries and now chiefly a source of stones for the town, but it had thick walls and stood on a high, rocky bluff. It sounded ideal for his purposes: a defensible ruin, mostly unfrequented, with cleared fields of fire. It probably contained a fresh water source in case of siege. They passed the fork to Agellas and continued straight ahead. He was committed.

Everyone gradually lapsed into silence as the hours passed. It was a pleasant enough ride, uneventful and favored with striking scenery. Danger lay at its conclusion, but it was easy to forget that and revel in the beauty of the day. Pennywhistle relaxed somewhat, but was still careful to observe the forest signs along the way. He saw plenty of evidence of animal predators, but none of human.

They reached the *Alcazaba* just after midday. The noontime sun baked the life out of everything, a typical, stifling hot summer day on the plateau of Leon. The empty fortress looked austere and brooding, but it was exactly what he wanted. It was a compact structure of four high, squat, crenellated towers around a courtyard graced with a long rectangular pool. The marble pond was choked with weeds and surrounded by wild riots of long grass, but it was spring fed and the water tasted cool and fresh, and the grass provided a welcome meal for Lightning and the mules. Even in a state of decay, the pool radiated welcome and beauty. Being originally from the desert, the Moorish castle builders had regarded water not just as a necessity, but as something sacred to be celebrated.

The parapet of the northwest tower gave an excellent view of the village, four hundred feet below and half a mile distant. With his spyglass extended it was easy to follow the movements of people in town. He'd grilled Morales and Juanita for every scrap of information he could think of, but he wanted to confirm what they said with his own observations. He badly wanted to dash in and shove events forward, but if French troops and Spanish spies were on the lookout for him, he needed to scout the way. Patience was called for, not impetuosity.

He settled in for the long wait under the unforgiving sun and directed the others to take advantage of the traditional siesta in the shade of the courtyard. Eat and rest, he told them, it might be awhile before you get to do either. Once they left the town, they would not have the protection of the mountains and might have to travel by night: much slower, but safer. He would press his next guide ruthlessly about his bona fides. He had been a fool not to have done some local vetting on Manuel. But even without a guide, he would never be truly lost as long as he had a compass, a watch, and a clear night sky.

The hours dragged by slowly and sweat trickled down his high stiff collar. He absentmindedly consumed two apples to pass the time. He worried about the urgency of the information he carried, but decided a careful reconnaissance was still the wisest course. He saw burned buildings, but most of the town appeared intact. People looked to be going about their business, but he noted expressions of agitation on several faces.

After an hour, he saw them: two cavalrymen in black boots adorned with gold tassels. Their ornate crimson and blue uniforms were gilded and festooned with buttons. Each wore a royal blue pelisse on his right shoulder and sported a black bearskin busby. Their red trousers clung so tightly to their athletic thighs as to appear painted on, and they walked with a bold swagger. They laughed over some joke. Both were short, jaunty, brazen young men who acted as if they owned the town; definitely hussars. They did not look like they were expecting action.

They mounted their horses, rode out to the edge of town, and disappeared into the distance. They returned forty minutes later, dismounted, and entered a local cantina, thirsty after a hot ride. It had to be a routine daily scout, with a fixed patrol area and timetable. Pennywhistle watched for another hour, but no other troopers showed up. He guessed the two were alone, left behind to man an observation post.

Drinking at the local tavern in the afternoon after light duty told him no officers were likely to materialize. That was helpful; it would make his job less complicated. Two men fuddled with alcohol could be easily removed as threats and might be induced to volunteer useful information. Enlisted men tended to offer much less resistance to interrogation than officers because they had no code of gentlemanly honor to uphold. He knew little about horses, but their mounts looked to be good specimens and would be much faster than the mules.

From his perch, he saw they could enter the town from the southwest and not be visible to anyone until they exited from the long ravine. From there it was only a hundred yards to the cantina. He decided he would go in the late afternoon. If the hussars came out of a dark tavern into slanting sunlight, they would have a hard time seeing at first. Alcohol would also slow their responses. He wondered if they had better maps then he. He hoped so, but was certain they knew the location of Marmont's main army, of vital interest to him.

He checked his pocket watch. Three hours to wait. The girl should go in first and alone. She knew the town and would arouse no suspicion. She had relatives to care for her. He had played her guardian long enough. Morales would stay with him. The Spanish sergeant wanted vengeance a bit too eagerly, might well do something hasty and ill advised; he would have to be watched. He might be useful in a fight, but the marine hoped it would not come to that. He wondered if he should ask Juanita to rustle up peasant's smocks to conceal his and Dale's uniforms, but decided against the effort. British scarlet would reassure the natives and startle the French. He had been stealthy; soon he would be bold.

He picked out a spot in the deep ravine for a staging area. Lightning would be fine, but he worried the mules might decide to become unruly. Their loud braying would certainly give away the game. So far, Manton had been able to keep them in good order; he would not enjoy being left behind as a horse-holder, as he was desperate to prove himself a warrior, but he obeyed orders. Manton had real gifts and deserved a better future than being a gentleman's servant. If they got out of this mess, Pennywhistle decided, he would look into that.

The little party moved out of the Alcazaba. An old trail wound down from the rear of the fortress, leading to the ravine. It was what the Moors called a wadi: an old, dry, creek bed. It was choked with brambles and tumbleweed and sloped gently upward. He noted plenty of horse hoofprints. The French must have reached the same conclusion about concealment as he had and launched their attack from this place.

At this distance, he needed no spyglass to see the town's dusty main street. The hussar's horses were still tied to the hitching post in front of the cantina. Two older men, both gentlemen from their attire, strolled the street, engaged in conversation. A peasant woman herded her three unruly young children forward, probably headed toward home. A donkey reluctantly pulled a two-wheeled cart laden with wood, the driver cursing him to go faster. Three dandified young men smoked cigars and lounged on a long bench outside of the cantina. From their expressions and gestures, their talk looked to be boastful: three young blades nattering on about their prowess with women. They paid no attention to the fast, happy guitar music that poured from the building.

Other than the fine leather saddles on the horses tethered at the cantina, marking them as animals from an elite cavalry unit, everything was ordinary. Two buildings at the end of the street were burned out shells, but the rest of the town looked to be a typical white washed, red tile roofed Spanish hamlet on an uneventful Saturday evening.

Juanita did not want to leave them and pressed her tear ducts into service. Pennywhistle assured her she would be fine, that she only needed to head to her uncle's home, where she would undoubtedly receive a warm and loving reception. Spaniards were very keen on family. He had no idea what kind of man her uncle was, but if he was anything like Juanita, he was probably a good man. She protested she did not yet feel safe and wanted an escort. Pennywhistle wanted to be strict and military, but her sobbing unmanned him. It was far easier to face an enemy volley than a woman's tears. Still, a part of him noted that she seemed to summon them with ease, and he wondered if he was being manipulated.

Zppptt! A bullet whizzed by his ear. Where the hell had that come from?

CHAPTER SIX

All five of them instinctively slammed themselves against the side of the wadi.

The three young blades outside the cantina tossed away their cigars, shot to their feet, and departed at the run. Pennywhistle looked toward the swinging doors of the cantina for the source of the shot. It was the two hussars. They were lurching drunkenly, doubled over in laughter, and one held the cavalry carbine he had just fired.

Pennywhistle tried to puzzle out their target. Apparently, it was the peasant woman and her children, who just happened to be between the hussars and their own hiding place in the wadi. The little family broke into a run and madly fled the street. The hussars roared with laughter at their discomfiture. Pennywhistle had no idea if the man had aimed or merely meant to frighten. The one who had fired was a corporal, his companion a sergeant. Presumably the high ranking one would have better information. The corporal was expendable.

Wanton cruelty disgusted him and excited his contempt. He made his plans coldly and quickly explained them to the others, then he lined up the V sights of the Ferguson on the corporal's chest. He breathed in and out deeply for a few seconds and a soothing calmness flooded him.

The bullet pierced the corporal's left breast and exited out the back, carrying with it pieces of heart muscle. He wore a brief expression of surprise, as if someone had told him a fascinating fact or remarkable story, then collapsed onto the dusty street. His companion tried to focus his drunken eyes and dimmed attention on the body, but the reality had not yet penetrated his fogged brain.

Pennywhistle slung his rifle, whisked his cutlass from his scabbard, and rose up in a quick flash. Dale followed suit a second later. They dashed out of the ditch, shouting like demons, and rushed toward the hussar, waving their swords with clear and brutal intent. His anger was genuine, but an icy part of Pennywhistle's brain also informed him that anger would disorient and unman their alcohol-soaked foe.

Manton and Morales covered Pennywhistle and Dale with their guns as a precaution. Juanita smiled with satisfaction, knowing at least two of the cursed Frenchmen were to pay for their misdeeds.

The hussar stood frozen, his mouth agape. He could not credit the two scarlet-clad figures running madly toward him. It had to be the drink—a hallucination. The British were nowhere near! Then the brass clamshell guard of Pennywhistle's sword slammed into his jaw and Dale's boot thudded into his shin. Pennywhistle pulled his punch somewhat, lest the man's neck be snapped, but he folded like a cheap accordion and lay motionless in the street.

Dale and Pennywhistle's shouts and the gunfire had alerted the community. Many saw what happened from their windows. As the two marines pulled the hussar to his feet, people poured from their homes and a crowd began to gather. Townsmen were merely curious at first, but soon low talking and curses permeated the air—all directed against the hussar. Apparently he'd made himself quite unpopular, but had appeared dangerous and untouchable. The marines had destroyed the illusion of invincibility.

Pennywhistle and Dale dragged the limp sergeant inside the cantina and dropped him unceremoniously across a cheap wooden table. The few Spaniards inside fled into the street and joined the crowd. "Watch him," he said quietly to Dale, who nodded his assent.

Pennywhistle went back outside, intending to fetch the others, but stopped dead when he saw the rapidly growing crowd of over a hundred. The hot-blooded hatred radiating from it made his skin prickle. As more joined, it changed from a crowd to a mob. Crowds complained, but mobs acted. The power of mobs was a terrible thing and a direct affront to his devotion to reason. Mobs were unfettered by normal rules of civilization; people in a group would do things individuals would never even consider. The mobs of the French Revolution were bloody proof.

The townspeople had good reasons to be angry and aggrieved. The French had acted savagely and without regard for honor or decency; it was natural to want vengeance. It was easy to guess what the mob intended. The only uncertainty was how savagely it would be enacted. The hussar's end might be swift and violent, but more likely would be agonizingly slow and exquisitely painful.

He could not permit that to happen. The hussar might be a vile man, but he was a soldier and a prisoner of war. It was always tempting to descend to barbarity in warfare, so the few rules restraining bad conduct had to be scrupulously observed. He was a British officer, and much as he disliked it, it was his duty to see to the safety of the hussar. A more calculating part of his nature whispered that he needed the Frenchman alive for a thorough interrogation.

He could, of course, simply stand aside and let the crowd do its bloody business. It would be easy, popular, and win him plenty of acclaim and cooperation. They might even have most of the information the hussar did. He certainly was not supposed to call attention to himself; his orders had used the words "unobtrusive" and "swift movement." But in the end, orders or no, it came down to one thing. He was a British officer and had sworn an oath to uphold the reputation of King George. Oaths, treaties, and codes of conduct meant nothing if they were but empty words that never stood the test of fire.

It was also a deeply personal matter of honor. An officer's life and possessions belonged to his Sovereign and his soul to God; only his honor was truly his own. Expediency was seductive and always had to be resisted with firmness.

He doubted he could stop them alone. His Spanish simply was not good enough, they did not know him personally, and the appeals to reason he so prized would fall on deaf ears. His uniform and the high reputation of British arms carried some cachet, but it would only slow them. He needed someone emotional, someone who understood them, someone who felt their pain. Of course—Juanita! She had plenty of spirit and a certain way about her. He had to get her here, fast. He had not wanted her affection, but now it would come in very handy. He was a cynical dog.

He dashed into the cantina and looked at the hussar. He had hit him harder than he'd thought. The hussar needed no guarding, would not be conscious for some time. He told Dale the situation and tasked him to bring Juanita immediately. "Tell her it's an emergency." He added, "Bring the others as well." Morales might prove of some use, and Manton always wanted to play the hero and certainly had the heart of a stalwart. Dale vanished in a flash.

Pennywhistle walked back into the center of the street, his tread measured and menacing, his face determined and purposeful. He faced the crowd, planted his feet firmly, and drew his cutlass slowly and deliberately. He pushed the blade downward to *order arms*, its razor-sharp point extended two inches in front of his right toe and the same distance above the ground. His posture did not directly challenge the crowd, but made it clear the weapon was ready for immediate use. He brought the opened palm of his left hand up to chest level and extended his arm. The gesture to halt was unmistakable and better than any words he could have summoned.

The crowd eyed him briefly and stopped. A mere minute later, however, it started to move slowly, tentatively, toward him. Some favored him with smiles, grateful for his intervention, but the majority looked eager to blow past him, enter the cantina, and literally tear the French fellow limb from limb. Restraint and subtlety were not working. He needed to do something, anything, to buy time until Juanita arrived. A greater threat was needed.

He sheathed his cutlass and unslung the Ferguson. He attached the bayonet with great ceremony. He began to load the rifle very, very slowly and very, very threateningly. Every movement was studied, his stance one of resolve and defiance. He forced a grim expression on to his face, pretending he was about to berate a marine found drunk on guard duty. Once prepared, he held his weapon vertical, in the "make ready" position.

The weapon, uniform, and stance had their effect. The mob ground to a halt. They began to talk among themselves in heated, feverishly quick Spanish of which he was able to make out only an occasional word. He caught words like *gut*, *behead*, and *quartering* which filled him with dread. He also caught words like *talk*, *wait*, and *officer* which filled him with hope. The crowd was at cross purposes, undecided—poised on a knife's edge. He hoped no one did anything stupid.

Of course, that is exactly what happened. Idiots had the least to contribute, but were often the most volatile in a mob. Some fool with more anger then courage fired off a pistol. The bullet whined past him, wide of his ear. He had no idea if the fellow had been aiming or if it was intended as a warning. The crowd began to surge forward again, and the hussars' horses at the hitching post whinnied loudly in fear, sensing what was about to happen. He steeled himself and very dramatically full cocked his weapon. The click echoed loudly off the low, stone buildings. He slowly leveled it at the crowd, his intention clear.

Damn it, they were supposed to be allies! The French would have overrun them long ago if it weren't for Wellington! The crowd slowed, but still shuffled forward.

He heard a rush of pounding strides behind him. Dale and Manton charged up and took position on his left, while Morales did the same on his right. They all nodded quickly to him and leveled their pieces at the crowd. They all had fixed bayonets. For a brief second, Pennywhistle felt a surge of emotion at their unswerving loyalty; a few against hundreds, but no hesitation. Morales' presence surprised him; maybe there was more to the man than he thought. His expression was as determined as the Englishmen's. Suddenly the crowd faced four weapons, not one.

They stopped abruptly, pondering their options. It was stalemate, at least temporarily. No one in the mob wanted to die. At least four would if they pressed forward; more, if English used their bayonets. One old man called out, "But the English officer is on our side." He was quickly stared into silence.

The crowd inched forward again, taking the smallest of steps, as if that might prevent a confrontation. Suddenly, a female voice rang through the evening air.

"*¡Para!¡Para!¡Para!*" The emotion in it was powerful, dramatic and riveting. Juanita had arrived. Thank God.

CHAPTER SEVEN

"Stop! I absolutely command you to stop. You are all fools! Fools, I tell you." She almost spat the words. Her bewitchingly feminine voice dripped with contempt and vibrated with anger. It was not the voice of a mere girl, but the clarion of a divinely self-assured preacher. It had the effect of a giant physical slap on the crowd and pulled them up hard. Who was this strange creature who spoke with such fire?

Juanita strutted majestically forward, a peasant queen inspecting her court. She walked between the crowd and the men with guns, unafraid, her sheer will projecting some kind of invisible barrier. She radiated an odd, almost spiritual energy that was palpable. She walked up to Pennywhistle and placed her right hand on his shoulder. The touch was warm and kind, but what surprised him was its almost electric charge. Her hand on his arm, she faced the crowd.

"You would murder this man? Have you taken leave of your senses and your courage? Many of you know me, and I tell you this brave officer risked his own life to save mine! I would have been raped and murdered by the French but for him. He gave me food, drink, and shelter. He put his friends in jeopardy. Just now, he killed one enemy and laid low another. What more proof do you need of his goodness?

The mob's will wavered. People looked at each other uncertainly, short words were exchanged, and heads bobbed in agreement. The power of a single-minded, strong-willed orator over a mob was more persuasive than grapeshot. Certainly it was preferable to four bullets.

Juanita's voice rose to a furious crescendo. "This man is a gentleman and a hero! He is our friend. More than that, he is our ally! The English fight the same French we do! He is a righteous guest in our country, one who has traveled far and undergone much travail to come to our aid, yet you treat him as worse than a vagabond. I am ashamed! Ashamed!" Big tears formed in her eyes.

Guilt flowed through the crowd. Their eyes looked downward.

"I ask you, where is Spanish hospitality? Where is Spanish nobility? Where is Spanish honor? You speak of them often, but today you act as if they were strangers!"

Feet shuffled slowly and the people looked up. Shame was moving toward sympathy. Mob's moods change quickly. She had touched something in them.

"I am one of you." She stopped briefly. "I know you." There was pregnant pause and the crowd eyed her expectantly. "You are better than this!" Smiles flashed through the crowd. She definitely had their hearts in her talons. "We must help this man! Let him do what he needs to do."

She drew a dagger from under her skirt and flourished it menacingly in slow half circles in front of her. Her expression morphed from empathy to defiance in a fragment of a second. Pennywhistle blinked in astonishment; he wondered how she had conjured a knife. "If you cannot understand, then you must kill me before you touch him." The mob let out a collective gasp.

"I ask you to trust him," she paused for dramatic emphasis, "as I have!" She looked fiercely into Pennywhistle's eyes, then back toward the crowd.

"I have put my life in his hands and I ask you to do the same." She sounded like a Spanish Joan of Arc, such as would be a welcome addition to any band of partisans. Her fiery tone turned reverent. "You prayed to the Virgin for help and deliverance. She listened and dispatched this brave officer. He is my savior! He will be yours as well!" It was all extravagant blather, but the crowd gobbled it up like starving peasants eating beef at a lord's feast.

Juanita waited for the weight of the words to sink in. Her timing was exquisite. Pennywhistle was floored: beyond sheer, iron will, he sensed true guile in her address. She many not have had formal training in rhetoric, elocution, and oratory, but she was the equal of Robespierre in manipulating a crowd. She played on their emotions like a pianist in total command of a concert hall.

The change was dramatic and swift. The mob became a crowd again, a mass of townspeople rather than a pack of vigilantes. People nodded, smiled, and a chorus of "¡Sí! ¡Sí!" rose from the crowd.

Juanita eyes flashed with power as she finished the business. "Go to your homes. Be with your family and friends! Have faith, and believe in the Englishman! Stay only if you can do something purposeful to help this man and his friends." She waited for her message to sink in. In a soft, tearful voice overflowing with kindness, she ended with a simple *"Vaya con Dios."* Masterful! She had perfectly tapped the rich vein of sentimentality so close to surface in the Spanish character.

The crowd faded gradually away, almost like a troupe of actors dispersing after their final curtain call. Most were probably headed home for a quiet supper. A few remained behind and waited patiently to speak with the English officer, eager to lend what assistance they could.

Pennywhistle let the tension drain out of him. He breathed in and out slowly and the tightness in his chest abated. He lowered his weapon and quietly told the others to stand down. They all removed and sheathed their bayonets and slung their weapons.

It had been a damned close run thing. He saw relief in Manton's and Dale's eyes, but most markedly, in Morales'. Morales expression changed a second later to one of surprise, as it fully dawned on him what he had just done. The Spanish sergeant had actually been prepared to fire on his own people.

Pennywhistle turned to Juanita, who wore a triumphant expression. "You saved us," he said simply. "Yes, yes I did," she replied without a hint of humility. "I hate the Frenchmen even more than they do, and I know the Virgin trusts your judgment." Her expression softened. "I did it for you, and I would gladly do it again." She looked deeply into his green eyes, as if to impress her will upon him. "I believe in you. I believe you have been sent into my life and theirs"—she pointed toward the village—"for some important purpose. God has given me a sacred trust."

"Quite," His response sounded patronizing, although he did not mean it that way. Her words startled and unnerved him. He was not some divine emissary. It was more likely The Other Fellow had sent him. He was here because he had muddled things badly and was weak and sentimental. He was simply a marine with a job to do, not a rescuer of people in need, and if he served anyone's will, it was Admiral Martin's. He was not here to save the world, make it a better place, or rehabilitate lost souls. Quite frankly, his job was to kill people and do it efficiently. He was good at it, and it worried him.

Her eyes bothered him. He had noticed immediately upon meeting her that they were a very unusual violet: deep and compelling. In certain lights, they glowed with an unearthly luminosity straight out of Norse myth. Right now, they burned with the fervor of fanatical righteousness. They blazed with love for him as well, but it was something more complex than physical attraction.

It was the power of faith, he decided; faith that he was a man of destiny, power, and goodness. They were the eyes of the missionary, the evangelical, the zealot. They did not cross the threshold of madness, but who could foretell what lay in the future? He had a definite belief in God, but he prided himself on his Enlightenment rationality. Cosmic notions of faith, destiny, and Divine Will disturbed him. He accepted the axiom that faith could move mountains, but never considered it a proposition testable in real life. Perhaps he was being given that chance.

Stop it! He should send her packing, but a cunning inner voice demanded he reconsider. She had just proved herself highly useful as a go-between with the locals. She wanted to be used, so why not use her? She was a tool, a means to an end. So what if he liked her a little bit? He just had to be a sly, ruthless-hearted monster for a while longer and concentrate on the job.

He became his brusque self again. "Juanita, I need you to talk to those people. I require supplies for a week. I need food, a reliable guide, local maps, and some good horses. I can pay with British chits. We don't steal; they know that. Any scrap of information they have on French troops, no matter how small, is most welcome. I need to have a chat with our French friend, but I want to depart this village soon, midnight at the latest. Have you got all that?"

"I do. I will attend to it immediately. But there is no guide better than myself. My father was a mule drover and I traveled with him everywhere as a child. I know this country better than anyone. I have ridden every path, lane, trail, and highway for miles around. It is as familiar to me as your hands are to you. I also know something of horses. I will stay with you." She said the last words with calm finality, as if the matter were settled.

He had thought he was in command, but he felt as if she had just issued him an order. However, he had no reason to doubt she was telling the truth, and unlike the last guide, he had no suspicions as to her loyalty. Her conduct had been the perfect vetting. It made sense, and—her eyes said it was pointless to argue. "Fine," he said crisply. "Get cracking."

She flashed him a quick smile and departed. It was dark now, with a full moon and cloudless sky. The stars blazed bright and clear. He could take an exact fix on their position.

"Señor Capitan." It was Morales. "I, too, would like to stay with you. My unit is destroyed and I can be of no further service here, but I may be of some use to you. As you have said, you can always use another musket. I wish to strike back at the French, and I know if I stay with you I will be given the chance. Adventure follows you, as fleas follow hounds." He smiled warmly.

Christ, the last thing he needed was more drama! This was supposed to be a straightforward delivery job, but it appeared some unknown hand had rewritten the script. He just wanted to evade the French and get those dispatches to Wellington. Morales saw the disapproving look on his face and looked crestfallen. It pained Pennywhistle to see the man's newfound self-respect evaporate.

Oh, why the hell not! The mission had turned into a traveling carnival of errors and it probably wouldn't hurt to add one more performer to the circus. He wondered what flaw in his character was a magnet to the lost. Still, Morales could have gone over to the mob, but had chosen to stand with him. He would protect any man willing to give unswerving loyalty. A Spanish NCO would establish their bona fides with any Spanish troops they encountered. Morales would undoubtedly relate his sad story and generate sympathy and assistance.

"Very well, Sarn't Morales, you may stay. Please assist Juanita in assembling the supplies. It will help her to have the assistance of a man." He spoke in crisp, magisterial tones, but laughed heartily on the inside. That woman needed no man's help. She was definitely not Dulcinea! It struck him this was the first time he had not considered her a girl. But it was as well to flatter Morales she was a helpless maiden and keep up appearances with the townspeople. Morales snapped to attention and favored him with an unusually crisp salute. "*Sí, señor Capitan.*" The two men turned in opposite directions: Morales to follow Juanita, Pennywhistle to interrogate the prisoner.

The French hussar's cheek was black and blue and he grimaced with pain, and he was barely awake when Pennywhistle confronted him. Dale had just finished tying him to a chair, using seaman's knots that were well nigh unbreakable. The hussar snarled a few words at Dale. His accent was distinctive. He struggled briefly and lustily when Pennywhistle approached, almost as if playing a part, and then abruptly stopped, as if expectations had been satisfied. The young hussar wore an expression of sullen defiance, in complete contrast to the merry rampage of color in his uniform.

Pennywhistle looked him over carefully. The uniform was new, and fitted to his trim physique, albeit crudely—obviously tailored by a provincial. The fabric color was ever so slightly off, the product of a less expensive dye. The drape of the cloth indicated a lighter, cheaper quality fabric. A number of buttonholes were ornamental, not functional. Pennywhistle's tailor at Gieve's would have been apoplectic.

The hussar's hands looked smooth and un-calloused. The heels of his boots were unworn. He had seen no hard or extended service. Pennywhistle picked up the man's sword, which Dale had placed on a nearby table. The inexpensive leather on the grip had started to separate from the metal. Pennywhistle flexed the blade and decided it might well break in a hard fight. He flourished it about, to get a feel. The steel was, like the hussar's uniform, of an inferior grade. He'd probably chosen it because he lacked the money for a Chatterault or Kleigenthal. Likely he'd spent most of his funds on the fancy uniform—the poor judgment of the amateur.

You could tell a lot by a man's blade. One hazarded one's life on it. His own was a superbly balanced confection of Wilkinson's of London, made of the finest blued steel. The black leather grip fit his hand like a tight glove, making the sword an extension of his arm and his personality. He had but to intend, and his cutlass performed.

He mentally summed up the hussar. Young popinjay: lots of arrogance, little experience, son of a minor merchant or petty official, not born a gentleman, wants me to know how tough he is. Flamboyant enough when his peers are around, rough on civilians, not so brave when alone and unarmed. Good in an impetuous charge, poor in an extended fight. Bonaparte promoted on merit, so the man had enough talent to be an NCO, not enough to be an officer.

The hussar grimaced again and put on a face that shouted, "I hate you, Englishman!" Excellent! A calloused professional would sport a look of bland indifference. This young man was trying too hard. He was a puff pastry pretending to be a rock. Just so; he could be broken in short order. Pennywhistle shot the man a stern glance, and he flinched.

The hussar expected a beating. He would do the opposite. Sympathy and guile were far better weapons than blows of the hand and fist. He would kill him with kindness.

CHAPTER EIGHT

"You really should thank me, *monsieur*. I have just saved your life, at considerable inconvenience to myself. The Spanish were most eager to festoon the streets with your entrails. I would appreciate it if you could return the favor with a few unimportant considerations."

His French was flawless, with the accent of Versailles. That puzzled the French sergeant quite as much as the mild tone of his words. Englishmen typically had no facility with foreign languages, disdaining any tongue but their own. This one smiled pleasantly and displayed a peculiarly cheerful manner. The sergeant had expected anger, harsh words, imperious demands, even blows to the face. He was prepared to resist strenuously, but now was off balance.

The tall Englishman continued. "I would like an easy chat, to ask you a few simple questions. I need your word you will attempt nothing untoward, or I shall have to maintain the use of those very unpleasant restraints in which you now languish. We have our duty; our countries are at war, but it seems silly to make things harsher than they need be. No reason we cannot introduce some measure of civilization. I have some superb brandy, which might ease your pain. Have I your parole, Sarn't?"

The hussar bobbed his head reflexively. He had no idea what the sandy-haired officer was up to, but the prospect of a drink sounded wonderful. His head ached. The English officer was clearly a gentleman of honor, and his disarmingly jovial manner was infectious. He shuddered when he thought of what the peasants would have done to him. He had no means of escape, and the British sergeant standing nearby looked hard and unforgiving. Better to go along and take his chances.

The Englishman smiled. "Excellent! I am greatly pleased you have listened to the blandishments of reason. Sarn't Dale, please untie the prisoner." Dale did as ordered, although he gave the hussar plenty of nasty glares that indicated he disapproved. It was perfectly played. Pennywhistle poured the man a large tumbler of some perfectly dreadful brandy that Manton had scavenged. He doubted the hussar had the palette to notice; he would welcome the effect.

He handed it to the prisoner, who gulped the tumbler's contents greedily. Pennywhistle looked at his pocket watch. He could not take too much time with the interrogation, but he had to give the impression he had all the time in the world. In the hussar's nervous, exhausted state, the brandy would work its magic quickly. Get the man relaxed, talking about himself and home, befriend him. Keep things personal, light, and cheerful, and establish bonds of comradeship. Shift quickly and seamlessly to military questions. If the prisoner hesitated on the key questions, give him another shot. But he would have to be careful; he didn't want the man to pass out.

"Let us be civilized: an exchange of names. It betrays no duty, builds bridges, and makes talking so much easier. I am Thomas Pennywhistle. I see in your eyes, you have noted I am a captain of marines. I hail from the city of Berwick, just south of the border with Scotland. I already know from your accent and clothing that you are a Provençal and a sergeant, but could you favor me with a Christian name?"

The hussar began to feel very relaxed. The Englishman appeared quite interested in him, and it seemed the most natural thing in the world to give him an answer. "I am Christophe. Christophe LePage."

"Very good, Christophe; it is a pleasure to make your acquaintance. Tell me about your home in Provence. I understand people in your area are the friendliest in France. It is far sunnier than my rainy home, and the cuisine is delightful, particularly the bouillabaisse, which I find bewitching. I truly relish good food, at which, sadly, my own countrymen are at a disadvantage compared to yours. Mrs. Ford, our family cook, always said the secret of Provençal cuisine was the clever use of fennel and basil. She tries hard, but we English have never been able to duplicate your people's particular genius for cooking. What is your favorite dish?"

It was a harmless question, mixed with a bit of regional flattery, designed to get the man talking about a subject which all soldiers found interesting. Pennywhistle sat down, leaned languidly back in his chair, and put a disarmingly bright smile onto his face. He gave the impression of complete and total relaxation, as if he were prepared to listen to a long and delightful story.

LePage's palette matched the quality of his uniform, but he burbled on merrily about his favorite foods. It was easy to guide him from there, and Pennywhistle soon assembled a considerable dossier on LePage's' hometown, as well as his family and fiancée. The man needed very little prodding, only the repeated use of his first name, a few nods, compliments, and an occasional "Oui." He was a lonely man and positively garrulous when someone listened with attentiveness as he talked about himself. The drink's effect became more pronounced as the minutes ticked by.

He was on the point of slurring his words, when Pennywhistle smoothly switched topics to matters military. He poured the man another shot and began the real interrogation.

But it did not seem that way to Christophe. He was merely chatting with an unexpected new friend who truly sympathized with him for all the privations he had endured so stoically. It was all so easy, so relaxing. The bruises didn't hurt anymore. It was the most natural thing in the world to answer his questions.

An hour after the interview commenced, Christophe slept deeply and snored. Pennywhistle had gotten far more information than he had a right to expect. It was all useful, although some of it was disquieting. It changed things, but he was good at extemporization. They would have to move fast. He and Dale gathered up their accoutrements and left LePage to his fate. He had saved the man once; tomorrow morning, he would have to save himself. At least the madness of the mob had dissipated. If Le Page talked fast and persuasively, he might survive.

LePage had said his regiment had screened Foy's division of Marmont's army at Toro until five days ago. That was on the Guarena River, fifty miles to the east of Cordona. He'd explained that Marmont was trying to flank Wellington, who was falling back on Salamanca, with the French in close pursuit. That was considerably closer than Pennywhistle had expected.

Company B had been detached and sent to the Cordona sector to search for a British officer carrying extremely valuable information. He, LePage, had been told nothing else, save that the officer would not be incognito; presumably a lone scarlet coat would be easy to identify. This made sense to Pennywhistle: compartmentalize and limit information. There was no reason a sergeant would know anything of covert operations; he was but a tool and would be given the bare minimum of detail.

One thing was clear. He was that officer. What the blazes was he carrying in his left boot heel that merited the attention of an entire hussar company? He, too, had been given minimal information, he reflected wryly. At least the French did not know his name and rank, but that probably mattered little.

LePage had regarded the mission as a waste of time, an opinion shared by his entire company. They resented being pulled away from the main front against Wellington on a fool's errand. They'd encountered nothing but surly weather and surlier Spanish peasants until they came to the town of Cordona. They were bored, angry, and full of energy. They took out their frustrations on the garrison. The Spaniards were poorly trained and unprepared; this gave them a cheap success and the satisfaction that the mission was not a complete failure. They had at least killed a few actual soldiers. LePage had been less than pleased at being left behind in case the Englishman materialized; he and his companion had amused themselves chiefly by drinking, while the company headed north toward the town of Medina del Rey. He mentioned his captain had said, "I hope the infantry have better luck."

Pennywhistle nodded to himself. His hunch had been right. They had been looking for him at Valdencia. It was part of a pattern.

He and Dale headed to the livery stable where they had agreed to meet Manton, Morales, and Juanita. Five horses awaited riders, and two others were outfitted as pack animals. There were four local men who stared sheepishly at their feet. Juanita was berating them in blisteringly quick Spanish. He missed most of it, but it was obviously a dressing down. She appeared in absolute command of the situation. She stopped instantly and smiled brightly when she saw him approach.

"Amazing sir, absolutely amazing! She has been a dervish of energy!" Manton dashed up to him with an enthusiastic grin. "She got the horses organized first, while I wrote up a register of supplies. They tried to push some old nags on her, and she ripped them to pieces! I gave her a detailed list; the English was confusing to her sometimes, but we sorted it through. Morales helped a bit, but mostly just let her have her head. I told her to make sure we were charged a reasonable price for everything, not a gouging. I know, sir, you are frugal with King George's money. She dragooned those fellows into looking high and low for everything we needed. I think she just did some hard bargaining on the price." He handed Pennywhistle a list. "I don't think I missed anything, did I, sir?"

Pennywhistle glanced at the list and was yet again impressed with his manservant's passion for detail. They had everything they would need for a week. "You did a superb job, Manton. I expected no less." Manton beamed with pride.

Juanita touched his arm and he turned to face her. Her expression was determined. "They tried to cheat us, to sell us bad food and worse horses at a high price, but I would not permit it and prevailed on their honor. We have good quality at a fair price." She handed him an itemized bill. Pennywhistle scanned the numbers and blinked. She was quite a negotiator and a superb quartermaster.

He took a large checkbook from his haversack and Manton produced a quill and ink well. Using a spare saddle as an improvised desk, Pennywhistle wrote out the chit in the name of King George, tore it off, and gave it to Juanita, who presented to the four men. They beamed and erupted into a chorus of "*Gracias, gracias, muchas gracias, señor capitan.*" There might be some delay, but they knew they would eventually get paid. It gave them one more solid reason to trust their British allies. The best goodwill was usually financial. He could have done it with the gold guineas he carried in a small pouch, but had a feeling he should save the hard specie for an emergency.

He assembled his little band and they looked at the new maps Juanita had procured. They were crudely drawn, but she said they were much more accurate than anything the French had. He noted emendations on the edges, referring to recent changes in French positions; very useful. Based on LePage's information, they should head for the village of Nava del Campo, about six miles distant. It would move them away from the hussars and toward Wellington. Juanita had been there many times. He asked if there was a secondary path, something more secure than the main road, but she replied the main road was perfectly safe after dark. Because of heavy guerrilla activity, the French never moved in the darkness, even on royal roads, unless it was a very large force. They would be in Nava before daybreak if they departed immediately. The road was wide, surprisingly well maintained, and easier on horses than any alternative.

Pennywhistle continued to ride Lightning. Juanita had offered him a youthful, sleek replacement that clearly had some Arabian blood, which she assured him would be fast yet docile. He surprised himself by refusing. Lightning might be an old, swaybacked curmudgeon, but after an initial test, when he had tried to buck Pennywhistle out of the saddle, the beast had settled down and had apparently decided that Pennywhistle was a master worth keeping. Lightning had become like a pair of old bedroom slippers; worn and not much to look at, but comfortable and always giving sure footing. The part-Arabian was given to Morales instead.

The night was warm and alive with the buzz of insects as the little caravan clattered slowly down *El Camino Real*. Juanita rode in the lead, followed by Pennywhistle, Dale, Morales, and Manton. Manton brought up the rear because of his affinity for animals. He held the bridles of the two pack horses that clomped placidly on either side. Pennywhistle took a fix on the stars and worked out their position. The road wound up and down some low hills, but nothing as challenging as the mountain switchbacks of the day before. As Juanita promised, the road was deserted. It was possible some partisan eyes watched, but it was clear from the silhouette of their little band that they were not French, and that was all that mattered.

Pennywhistle munched slowly and absent-mindedly on some chorizo, a hard pork sausage infused with a lot of paprika. The spiciness was unfriendly to an English palette accustomed to bland tastes, but it stopped the growling of his stomach. He followed it with some garnicha, a fruity local red wine he drank directly from a goatskin bota. It was quite good, an improvement on the "miss sally" favored by British sailors. He would have preferred coffee, but time was short and his supply of beans was low; he had to use them sparingly. He guessed the others were probably eating as well. He had told them to eat while they moved, since he did not know when they would have time for a hot meal. He was getting more used to riding. His thighs didn't ache and he felt his posture was improving. He had become better at synchronizing his motions to the horse's rhythm. He did not have to keep a death grip on the bridle after all. Lightning really wasn't such a bad fellow.

They reached the outskirts of Nava just before dawn and stopped at the edge of town. Juanita said they could ride in directly, but Pennywhistle was too cautious for that. He asked her if there was anywhere with a view of town where they would be sheltered and could grab a few hours' sleep. Everyone showed signs of fatigue; they had been awake more than twenty-four hours. Juanita replied there was a small valley sometimes used by Gypsies half a mile ahead.

Sleep four hours while Dale stood watch, he decided, and enter the town quietly around noon. Yes, that seemed an eminently reasonable plan, just as long as unforeseen events did not interfere. There had been far too much of the "unforeseen" on this mission.

They made camp without delay. Dale borrowed the captain's spyglass and moved up to the ridge line. He unshipped the glass, surveyed the town, and loaded his Baker. He breakfasted on bread and cheese, allowing himself two sips of wine.

Manton tethered the horses near a stream where they could drink the water and eat the grass. He did not unsaddle them, in case quick movement become necessary. Pennywhistle unfurled a blanket at the base of a welcoming juniper tree and lay down comfortably, keeping his loaded Ferguson next to him. He looked up at the sun peaking above the horizon, felt a moment's content, and dropped into a deep sleep.

Five minutes later, Juanita lay down chastely next to him. She knew that God often used Unbelievers for His own purpose, the better they might come to understand Him. The Englishman might not sing with the angels, but he certainly fought on their side. Her meeting with him was no accident, but God's design. She was playing a small but important part in a much grander scheme. She did not have to understand, merely have faith. No harm would befall her as long as she stayed close. A great peace washed over her as she looked at him before sliding easily into sleep.

He had pleasant dreams of trout fishing back in Scotland as a boy. He laughed and joked with his childhood friend, the ghillie's son, and they merrily compared their amazing hauls of fish. The Tweed was bountiful today. Some part of his subconscious knew it was a dream, but nevertheless wished it could go on forever with no responsibility, no duty, and no treachery.

Pop, pop, pop. The sound resembled champagne corks being pulled and was all too familiar. What killjoy would be firing off weapons along a fine trout stream and upsetting the concentration of determined anglers? It took a few seconds for reason to penetrate the dreamscape. His awoke with a start, fully alert and on edge, not a trace of grogginess. Danger always had the effect. It was musket fire he was hearing: faint, distant, sporadic, but unmistakable.

Dale stood over him, concern on his face. Unspoken words flashed between them. "I'll come," Pennywhistle said simply. He grabbed his rifle and followed Dale two hundred yards to the crest. They lay down and Dale passed him the spyglass. "Over there," he said, pointing to the northwest.

Pennywhistle could see puffs of smoke. It was some kind of a fire fight. It was hard to make out shapes and color, but men were moving in formations. Judging by the volume of smoke, the numbers involved could not be too great.

"Damn!" He was trying to avoid a fight, not become embroiled in one, but he seemed to have stumbled onto an infantry skirmish. His first instinct was to break camp and get moving into the hills above, but a part of him wanted to assess the situation. He was coming to have an unexpected regard for the Spanish. It puzzled him that he should find their struggles even vaguely heroic; that was the kind of rank sentimentalism that he had always distrusted. Maybe Juanita's faith was having a bad influence on him. Maybe it was just his instinctive curiosity. Maybe it was a fascination with lost causes. He decided to stay a few more minutes.

CHAPTER NINE

The firing increased in intensity and the rolling banks of smoke grew into thunderheads. The pungent stink of rotten eggs assailed his nose as more and more rounds were fired. The battle moved inexorably closer with each passing minute. Heroic paintings to the contrary, it was hard to see much of anything. All he could tell was one side was steadily advancing, the other slowly retreating. The retreating side was moving uphill toward them. The almond and oak trees broke the smoke into segments and disrupted efforts to form a continuous line of battle. Men were fighting in small groups. He wondered how much control either commanding officer was exercising over the engagement.

Manton ran up and plopped down next to him. He had been with him in battles at sea, and certainly knew how to handle himself. His fusil was loaded, bayonet attached. Morales joined the group a minute later, with his musket and bayonet. Behind him, Juanita bounded up the hill, skirt flying, to join them. Her eyes blazed with ferocity, like some feral animal in the night. The prospect of battle was energizing her. Pennywhistle wondered if this was the first time she'd witnessed battle; probably not, he decided. Her speech in the village had been the voice of certitude.

It looked like no one would be getting any rest. Pennywhistle looked back down at the horses, but they were securely tethered, placidly chomping grass, and appeared uninterested in the battle. He panned his glass left and right and was finally able to discern glimpses of color, as a rising breeze blew away isolated sections of smoke. The retreating men closest to their position wore drab, dirty brown; those further away and advancing wore midnight blue. The first had to be some sort of Spanish militia, definitely not regulars. The second were voltigeurs, French light infantry: skirmishers chosen for individual initiative and well suited to fighting in broken country. The Spanish probably knew the terrain and were brave enough, but militia was never a match for well-trained regulars. It did not surprise him that the fight was going against the Spanish. Yet they were not in headlong retreat, and they appeared to be yielding ground grudgingly. But they were moving toward his position faster than they had been minutes before. He estimated they would reach the ridge line in about five minutes.

Now would be an excellent time to depart. He furled his glass and tried to think. He told himself to concentrate on his assignment and leave these impetuous peasants to their own devices. It was not his fight. Juanita looked at him with intensity, her mouth saying nothing, her eyes shouting, "Do not leave them! God will guide you." Damn her and her peasant faith! He was no emissary of God, no avenging angel, just an officer doing his job, and rather badly at that.

He looked away from her and opened his glass again. His eye was caught by something he'd noticed before; now it riveted his attention. The stoutly built, brooding stone structure was a truly remarkable specimen of Gothic Revival architecture gone wrong. The ugly chapel, too tiny to be a real church, was enclosed by a four-foot high limestone wall. The miniature monstrosity was probably a local shrine; these were found all over Spain and had usually been built by wealthy individuals to commemorate some religious event, local saint, or miracle, often a sighting of the Virgin Mary. Their eagerness to believe in miracles puzzled him, but Spanish religiosity was heavily invested in driving the French from Spain, and it was unwise to discount its impact. "Bandits led by monks," was how LePage had phrased it.

The chapel would make a fine, easily defensible strong point, even with only four men, and it would position them on the left flank of the advancing French. If they opened fire from the rear, once the French had passed, it might have a devastating effect. Troops surprised from the rear were far more prone to break than those attacked from the front. Confident advance could change to precipitate retreat in the space of 3 heartbeats. But for best results, he needed some way to coordinate with the Spanish commander, and he had no idea who that was. He had to find him, explain his plans, and hope for cooperation. His uniform would vouch for his legitimacy, but it was still asking for a lot. Spaniards were very touchy about honor and protocol, even when an engagement was spiraling out of control. They might react badly to an unknown foreigner demanding quick improvisation.

But... the Spanish supremo might well listen to an impassioned *native* missionary who was convinced the Englishman could pull off the kind of miracle the Spaniards loved to celebrate. A French peasant girl armed with a vision and a voice had driven the English from an impregnable position four hundred years before. Maybe Juanita could duplicate the feat of the Maid of Orleans. She had a definite gift. Faith did not need to move a mountain, just one man. What he proposed was madness, but it would appeal to a certain mad, heroic strain in the Spanish character. Besides, it just might work.

It would have to be done quickly. The Spaniards were moving closer, losing their ground. He explained the situation to

Juanita. He thought the whole scheme fantastic, but she accepted it easily, as if it made perfect sense. He pointed in the direction he thought the Spanish leader might be found. She nodded, squeezed his hand, and departed at the run. He wistfully hoped God really was on her side, but quickly rebuked himself for even momentarily subscribing to her childlike faith.

He told the others his scheme, and they agreed. They, too, seemed to have unbounded faith in his judgment. It was entirely unwarranted, but he was glad of it. Manton mentioned the horses and said if they were lost, all of them would be undone. He was right, but he could spare no one to see to their safety. He was betting everything on victory, with no escape if they lost. He could protect Dale and Manton if the day went against them, but Juanita and Morales would surely be put to the sword.

He doubted these particular French chaps knew anything about his mission, but if he were held in captivity even briefly, they would probably find out. He definitely should not be hazarding his own life right now, but his blood was up. It was clouding his judgment, and he didn't care.

The chapel lay four hundred yards away. The tempo of firing increased and the smoke grew so thick it seemed solid, which was both good and bad: it would cloak them from the French, but they might well blunder into them by accident. He heard bugles blaring commands; that gave him a better fix on the French position than his eyes. By the sound, they were at an oblique angle to his position.

He broke into an easy trot; running would have been unwise in the obscuring smoke. The others trailed him closely. He used the cross on top of the shrine steeple as a homing beacon— ironic, given his reservations about conventional religion. Brambles tore at his uniform, and he stumbled several times as his boots collided with unseen obstacles. Dale behind him blasphemed feelingly. The four had to bob and weave to avoid low hanging branches. As they closed, the noise of the fight grew louder. Shouts, screams, cries, and lamentations jumbled into a raucous chorus that defied description.

Without warning, he ran headfirst into a Frenchman who appeared out of the smoke like a spirit summoned by a conjurer. They both recoiled in complete surprise, and the inexperienced Frenchman froze. He would have reacted properly in another few seconds, as he had been trained, but Pennywhistle recovered in a fraction of a second and whipped the dirk out of the top of his right boot. He brought it up in a fast arc and rammed it under the Frenchman's chin so that the tip bored into the brain. He recovered the blade and was moving forward before the Frenchman hit the ground.

Reaching the wall of the shrine, they took cover behind it. Pennywhistle's breath came fast and hard; he had to force himself to breathe slowly until a measure of equanimity returned. His men were with him and intact, their faces tense but expectant. The shouts were very near now, cries of anger, confusion, exhilaration, and fear, and he understood every word of the French, if not the Spanish. He was exactly where he wanted to be. Now, it was all about the timing. The French officers exhorted their troops to rally and straighten their lines. A volley boomed from somewhere, and he heard cries and French curses. The Spanish had not given up the fight. He could not see it, but judging from the musket reports, they actually had some kind of line. They had stopped their retreat.

Musket flashes in the dense smoke reminded him of maddened, blinking fireflies. He saw fast glimpses of midnight blue through the miasma. Slightly above them, he caught sight of barley brown. Skirmishes were tight, local blobs of reality that winked in and out of existence; the grand design hidden. He thought he heard a high, almost keening female voice in the tumult. It couldn't be! But the inflection, tone, and emotion were distinctive. A navy blue boat cloak appeared for a fraction of a second and then vanished into the smoke.

Juanita! God's blood! She had rallied them! She was only supposed to talk to the commander, but evidently he lacked the zeal she so amply possessed. A fiery girl suddenly materializing in the middle of a losing battle would be an extraordinary event, even to jaded soldiers. She really was a Spanish Joan of Arc.

There were more cries from the French. The words were less important than the emotions: terror, puzzlement, uncertainty. His experience shouted to him that the crisis of the battle was at hand.

He spoke in hushed, urgent tones to his men. "We need to pour it into them. When I give the command to fire, shoot for the muzzle flashes, and aim low. Once you get the first shot off, reload as fast as you can and keep firing. I want them to think they have a company of Spaniards to their rear. I want you to shout..." he paused and tried to summon something from his limited Spanish that sounded fierce and angry. People learning a language tended to remember the curses best. What was it? Something about mother. Then it came to him. "Shout, *¡Chinga tu madre!*" It was crude, the ultimate Spanish insult.

Dale spoke little Spanish, but shouted boldly. Manton added his voice a second later. Morales laughed openly and joined both.

They loaded their weapons and balanced them on the wall. They peered into the thunderheads of smoke and their trigger fingers tensed. They could not even discern silhouettes. Pennywhistle waited. His intuition said, not quite yet. Flashes rippled again and again through the brimstone fog. He heard sounds of retching. Natural enough with the low hanging, sulphurous cloud, not to mention the other, inevitable odors of fear, death and dying that accompany every battle.

For a few brief seconds, he saw the frayed end of a line of men, and they were wearing blue. "Fire!" he shouted. Red-orange tongues flicked into the grey-white murk. The noise of their guns was smothered by a Spanish volley, more ragged than the last one, but still substantial.

Pennywhistle and his men reloaded and fired again. And again and again. He fired considerably more often because of the capabilities of his piece. His band turned from human beings to machines dedicated to sending lead into the French. It all blurred into a routine that left them hot, sweaty, and covered with layer of grey grime. Biting open cartridges repeatedly made their lips dry and cracked. The powder tasted gritty and bitter. It was only a few minutes, but it felt like hours. There were blurred shapes in the cloudscape, angry noises, then for a fraction of a second, nothing. Nature held its breath.

The silence exploded into a tumult of noise and things happened very fast. He heard a piercing, authoritative voice yell Charge! in Spanish. "I'll see you damned first!" someone retorted in French. A bugle blasted a command, but was abruptly silenced. The lines were close, shredded, on the point of disintegration. He saw bits of brown move quickly forward, bits of blue flow backwards. The shouts and ululations rose to a crescendo and challenged the crack of gunfire for supremacy.

His ears rang and his tongue felt like sandpaper. The acrid smoke stung his eyes and he blinked rapidly. It was madness, it was chaos; a furious hell of unbridled energy cascaded over his body, a wanton waterfall of brutality and destruction. His face changed to a bright crimson and a wave of heat rose from his feet and engulfed him. He hated it, but loved it at the same time. You were never more alive than when violent death was near. The insane joy of battle raced through his veins and his eyes widened and muscles swelled as he felt the decisive moment approach. The beast within, the predator, knew the prey was ripe for the kill. The flank of the blue line was mere yards away.

The air grew oppressively heavy with the noise of men cursing, cheering, weeping, and the smells of blood, vomit, and excrement. The howling confusion overloaded all the five senses and stunned many into a daze. Some men simply refused to move, while others wandered aimlessly, ships without rudders. It was frenzied, stifling work: gun barrels grew hot enough to singe fingers and muzzle blasts heated the air like coals stoking a furnace. Weapons exploded from every direction, pan flashes scorching off eyebrows of the men next in line. Black bruises blossomed on shoulders as muskets repeatedly slammed back in savage recoil.

"Now!" he yelled to his men. They jumped to their feet; bayonets fixed, wills steeled, and charged headlong into the smoke.

"*¡Chinga tu madre!*" they yelled as they ran. Battle cries damned the French as bastards, whoresons, blackguards, and commanded the lot of them to die. Pennywhistle himself shouted "*¡Cago en tu leche!*"—I shit in your milk—the odd insult surfacing to memory like a shark from black water. He struck fast and hard with his bayonet and became a tower of scarlet strength that stunned the French. He plunged his blade into blue backs and chests as they appeared out of the smoke, withdrew it violently, and sought new targets. He continued to yell like a madman, but his actions were anything but crazy. There was a cold, practiced, efficient skill in his movements. His mind assessed the scene: he had hit them at exactly the right spot. Push them hard and they would break.

The shocked, astonished French recognized an English officer, but where had he come from? They saw a sergeant too and their fevered brains told them English regulars had joined the fight—much more dangerous opponents than Spanish militia. French resolve wavered, on the point of dissolution. Manton viciously gored a man in the stomach, as expertly as the best soldier. He twisted the bayonet and braced his foot against the dying man's thigh to extract it. Dale blocked a bayonet thrust and buried his own blade in the volitgeur's sternum. Morales lacked their skill but used his weapon effectively as a large club; his opponent's skull smashed like a peach hit by a pile driver.

Pennywhistle heard someone shout in Spanish, "Form on the Englishman!" A breeze lifted some of the smoke and he saw tense Spanish faces and peasant cloaks to his left and right. Cold steel flashed. As if in response to some hidden signal, the ragged French line disintegrated. Most men break and flee rather than be gutted. One minute there was a vague semblance of a line, the next, scattered fugitives running headlong down the hill, making the fastest escape possible. The air was filled with shouts and screams of terror and madness. The Spaniards ran in pursuit.

Pennywhistle's eyes blazed with the raw eagerness of the hunt. He wanted to join, hounds chasing foxes, but he was too experienced to succumb. The French were dazed, but experienced troops could rally much faster than peasants. Flushed with success, militia overestimated their fighting prowess and were inclined to run wild in pursuit. They could easily be scattered by any disciplined force, and the French probably possessed considerable reserves. Fresh troops could easily scatter even the most exultant soldiers, reserved energy far more important than that of enervated triumph. The militia had to be recalled quickly. He had to find the Spanish commander, but he had no idea who that was.

Out of the swirling, smoky confusion he heard a voice shout, "¡Santiago!" It was the battle cry of St. James. Juanita again! She would serve just as well. She had inspired the troops, now she could rein them in. He dashed through the smoke toward her voice. His men followed, uncertain of their destination, but trusting their commander. He found her, and she grabbed him in a wild embrace. She was flushed with joy and power. He pushed her back and looked deeply into her eyes, which blazed once more with the fiery dedication of the zealot. She was a female Savonarola.

"We must stop them," he said with urgency. He wished he had a bugle, whistle, or a drum handy to sound the recall, but thinly trained troops probably would have not understood anyway. On the other hand, his uniform was bright and distinctive among the earth colored peasants. His rangy, whipcord frame was easy to spot. "Tell them to halt and regroup on the Englishman."

She nodded once, her expression grim but approving. She squeezed his hand firmly, then ran forward and began shouting commands loudly into the smoke. Her distinctive voice carried far. A minute later, the gunfire ceased. He did not so much see it as feel it: a change in the energy that suffused the air, a sense that Nature herself willed men to take notice, slow down, and let reason return. As the sun rose higher and heated the landscape, the mists that blended with the gunfire began to dissipate, and a cool wind started to blow.

Now Pennywhistle could see more clearly as the smoke wafted away. The ground was covered with a bloody and awful carpet. It was not entirely still, as men in both brown and blue writhed in agony. The smell of excrement pervaded the air, as dying men voided their bowels. Flies covered both the dead and wounded—indescribable, irremediable wounds that made death a release. Some men tried to crawl to a place of imagined safety, and some pleaded in Spanish or French for water. The battle was a minor skirmish in the grand scheme of the War, but the men were just as dead. It was nothing he not seen before, yet it sickened him, and he was glad. It meant at least a part of his humanity was still intact.

Six angry Spaniards prowled the field. They stopped every now and then to bayonet any Frenchmen who showed signs of life. Those most likely to recover, those still able to beg for water, attracted their immediate attention. Their pleas for mercy caused them to die first. The last ones to go were those with the truly horrible wounds, those barely clinging to life. In a few minutes, there would not be a single Frenchman left alive.

Not content with merely inflicting death, one Spaniard lowered the front flap of his breeches and urinated into the unseeing eyes of a French lieutenant. He then sliced off the corpse's left ear, punched a hole in the lobe, and added it to string of similar trophies he wore round his waist. It was a repellant sight to witness, but he could no more stop it then he could stop a tidal wave with a gesture of his hand.

For the first time, he truly grasped the depth of Spanish hatred for the French. They were more intent on killing, degrading, and mutilating French soldiers than attentive to the needs of their own wounded. French weapons littered the ground, which soldiers had dropped in order to run faster. They were far better pieces than the Spanish had; the militia could certainly rearm themselves. Men began to return, singly and in small groups. Their faces looked drawn and grey, but many wore smiles of satisfaction. They had done something remarkable, something extraordinary. They had faced down French regulars! The girl had been a marvel, and the unknown Englishman had fought with a fury that astonished them.

Pennywhistle felt an overwhelming thirst as he walked the battlefield. The constant biting of cartridges had left his mouth as parched as the sandy wastes of Egypt. He picked up a dead voltigeur's canteen and drained its contents greedily. The water tasted old and brackish, but nevertheless refreshed him.

Juanita directed him to the Spanish commander. He was a small, wiry man with beady, brown eyes and a large, dark mustache. He had greasy olive skin and a beaky nose ill-suited to a thin, long face straight from an El Greco painting. He looked less a soldier than hard-nosed merchant selling trinkets at a carnival, but his ferret-like countenance changed when he broke into a wide grin upon seeing Pennywhistle. "*¡Mi amigo! ¡Mi* *compañero!*" he bellowed merrily. He ran up to the marine and threw his arms around him in a gesture of gleeful triumph. Pennywhistle found this distasteful, but reminded himself the Spaniards were demonstrative creatures and it was the custom of the country. He forced himself to return the hug, but only managed to do so half-heartedly.

The man identified himself as Colonel Estéban Aguinaldo, laying heavy stress on the *colonel*. Militia types always placed great emphasis on rank; probably a compensation for their lack of training and professionalism. Aguinaldo burbled on enthusiastically, testing the limits of Pennywhistle's inadequate Spanish. He finally had to beg the man to slow down. As he listened, he realized Aguinaldo was proud of himself and wanted someone of rank to hear his story. A lot of it was obviously poppycock and piffle, but Pennywhistle commanded himself to attend. Aguinaldo related the conventional tale of how his men had been surprised by an overwhelming French "horde." Privately, Pennywhistle wondered how Aguinaldo had had allowed himself to be surprised. Militia types often neglected elementary precautions, like deploying scouts in front of the main force. He interrupted to ask, "How many French?"

"A full battalion!" Aguinaldo replied excitedly. Hardly a horde, but green troops always exaggerated enemy numbers, and the colonel wanted to inflate his own achievement. Pennywhistle estimated they had actually faced half a battalion, around 300 men. It had been a typical skirmish in the Peninsula, but with an atypical result. It would never make the history books, but Aguinaldo was convinced it would someday become the stuff of legend. Twenty minutes later, Pennywhistle had the entire story, a few helpful details, and Aguinaldo's undying friendship. Aguinaldo demanded he join him in a celebratory drink, but Pennywhistle suggested quietly that he should see to his men's needs first. Aguinaldo was so consumed by self-exaltation that he was forgetting the end of a battle leaves a thousand details which demand immediate attention. Reluctantly, he conceded the Englishman was of course right, but must join him for that drink in an hour. The marine agreed, and the colonel bustled off and self-importantly began to shout orders, sounding more a carnival barker than an officer.

******

Pennywhistle and his men trudged back up the hill to their camp. Battle was the most physically demanding activity in the vast catalogue of human actions, and it generated a huge appetite. They didn't bother to cook. The bread, manchego cheese, and chorizo tasted unnaturally good, and the garnicha seemed a prime vintage. Everyone ate in silence, hunger being more compelling than the inclination to chatter. Pennywhistle was glad for the quiet. He needed to assemble the events and information of the last insane hour into some sort of coherent framework. He also needed to freshen up for his meeting with Aguinaldo. It would revive his spirits, and a clean, crisp face bespoke a professional attitude, always significant when dealing with amateurs.

Manton brought him his ditty bag, which contained a small looking glass, toothbrush, his shaving kit, and soap. He also conjured up a heavy cotton towel, and filled a bowl with water from a nearby brook. "Thanks, Manton. You are a most resourceful servant," Pennywhistle remarked, sincerely grateful. Manton helped him off with his coat; he would give it a thorough brushing. The death's head face that stared back bleakly at Pennywhistle from the looking glass shocked him. It looked more like a chimney sweep's than a gentleman's. It was covered in powder grime, lined with care. The lips were dry and cracked; the teeth stained a blackish grey. The eyes looked weary and haunted, and he noted a small gash near the left eye. When had that happened? He was not even thirty, but looked a hundred.

He mixed a few drops of lemon juice into the pouch of baking soda and stirred it with his horsehair toothbrush until he had a heavy paste. He scrubbed his teeth energetically, as much to get the gritty gun powder taste out of his mouth as to clean them. He checked the looking glass and was pleased to see white. He lathered his face with the fine, lemon-scented soap Manton had purchased at Floris in London, and splashed himself vigorously with water. The heavy cotton towel felt luxurious against his skin. The powder stains vanished and his face looked tanned and fresh, but he had plenty of stubble yet to attack. He again doused himself and slapped on heavy shaving lather, another delightful confection from Floris. He applied his straight razor with efficient determination. Five minutes later, he felt greatly refreshed, no longer an apostate from civilization. He glanced in the mirror and decided he only looked about fifty.

He reviewed the situation, as the Colonel had explained it. The Spaniards had been on a rescue mission when ambushed. Twenty of their compatriots, prominent citizens all, were being frog-marched to the town of Guijuelo for a very public execution by firing squad. This tactic was meant to send a wide ranging message that the best people would be killed at the least hint of resistance. It was a much more calculated and studied response than the usual burning of villages.

Someone had thought this through, and yet missed the essential point. Acts of terror, rather than cowing the population, enraged them. Killing their leaders had not stopped the Spaniards, but turned local resistance movements into mass uprisings. The Spanish visited blood-curdling retaliations on the French, including skinning, boiling, and burning alive any soldiers they captured. Undying hatred of the French and a commitment to rid the country of them had become an article of faith. It was no surprise that priests were heavily involved with the guerrillas.

Pennywhistle pondered courses of action. It was not his job to take over someone else's mission, but an officer was expected to use his initiative. He had fumbled his task through misjudgment and trapped himself behind enemy lines, yet he was now in a position to cause considerable discomfiture to the French. He might be at the right place for the wrong reasons, but it was an officer's duty to harass, confound, and unbalance the enemy. He was sure he could get through to Wellington, but it would be much more satisfying to cause damage along the way. Aguinaldo had bungled the rescue. If the citizens were to be rescued, it was up to Pennywhistle. Guijuelo was on a longer route to Wellington's army, but it would still get him there, and who would think to look for a British officer in the wake of a French unit?

He could use the Spanish militia as camouflage, if they could be kept under some order and control. There were perhaps three hundred of them, but they were certainly not the 300 Spartans, however much Aguinaldo believed them so. Pennywhistle knew that as many as half of them, given the opportunity, would quietly slip away and return to their homes and farms.

Of those who remained, only a few had the potential to become real soldiers. Those were usually easy to pick out, by their look, bearing, and attitude. They were usually men from the margins of society, often the unemployed, outcasts, or the poor—not family men. They were people who did not fit in. Family men had something to lose, these people did not. Often the same qualities of fire and restlessness that fitted them for soldiering rendered them ill suited to civilian life. He might be able to pluck twenty men. He would put them under Morales, who had shown commendable loyalty. He was one of their countryman and a regular, if a barely trained one. More importantly, they had seen him fight well and heroically.

The problem was Aguinaldo. He was punctilious about honor and command; he would not suffer someone stealing his men.

Of course... if he knew nothing of it, he could make no objection. He would have to be set aside with finesse, his ego soothed and his pride puffed up. Pennywhistle knew a way. He would indeed join him for a drink, and he would make it memorable.

CHAPTER TEN

He needed to do a bit of hiking first. He was not familiar with the flora of Spain, but guessed there was probably something similar to the plant he knew from the Scottish Borders, something from the *Papaver* genera, of the *Papaveracace* sub family of plants. He finished his breakfast and left Dale in charge. He said nothing about why he needed to poke about the hillside, but Dale knew him well enough to discern he was not doing it for pleasure.

He found what he was looking for after half an hour. It was a slightly lighter shade of red than the one in Scotland, but he was certain it was of the same family, and the juice or seeds would have similar properties. Extract of poppy had long been used as a sedative for babies plagued by the pains of teething. A small quantity would be mixed with milk or honey. Wet nurses swore by it. It was not nearly as powerful as opiate specimens of the Far East, but he was certain a heavy dose would put an adult drinker to sleep. He wondered if the taste would be detectable mixed with wine or spirits.

Aguinaldo was a small man physically, and Pennywhistle suspected the same was true of his character. He would probably be feeling the post battle fatigue about now, and even ordinary alcohol would have a pronounced effect. Blended with a soporific, the concoction should have the desired effect. He needed Aguinaldo down for the rest of the day. He would make excuses for Aguinaldo to his second in command and would undoubtedly be believed. The word of a British officer carried great weight, and excessive celebration after such a great victory was to be expected. The commander's indisposition would give his second-in-command an excuse to let Pennywhistle do some bare-faced poaching of men.

Pennywhistle had to cast about to find plants among the flowering blossoms that had already produced their seed pods; these he gathered and deposited in his haversack, then headed back to camp. There he sat by himself and quietly scored the pods. He kept a small, sterling silver brandy flask with him that was seldom used and currently empty. It had been a humorous gift from a fellow officer who was amused by Pennywhistle's disinterest in quality spirits. He could make the concoction before he met with Aguinaldo, if he could procure some brandy. It would obviate the difficulty of secretly dosing the Spaniard's drink. He would simply offer the flask to Aguinaldo as a toast to celebrate Spanish triumphs.

Dale was an expert scavenger. The language barrier would make no difference. NCO's like Dale had a magical ability beyond the understanding of merely mortal officers to find the most obscure items in the most unpromising of circumstances. His orders were curt. "I need some brandy and I need it in twenty minutes. Quality would be appreciated, but immediate availability is the key. It's important." He took a guinea from his purse and gave it to Dale. "Make whatever bargain you need to." Dale saluted smartly, said, "Aye, aye, sir," and departed smartly, a half-smile on his face as he turned away. He had recognized the flower parts.

Pennywhistle checked his Blancpain and saw it was only 9 am. The morning's fight had not taken long. Plenty of time for movement, once Aguinaldo was out of the way; they could make good progress towards Wellington. Aguinaldo had said to join him in an hour, but Spaniards never expected one to arrive on time, which puzzled and annoyed Englishmen accustomed to punctuality. Here, if someone said nine, arriving at ten was fine.

Dale returned in thirty minutes, wearing a sergeant's poker-face. He handed Pennywhistle a small jug. "Best I could do, sir. Its local stuff; not sure if it's very good, but the man I got it from kept saying, moo-ey boo-eno. He seemed to think it fit for a king."

"Thanks, Sarn't, I am confident it is exactly what I need." He removed the cork and sniffed the contents of the jug critically. You could tell a lot about brandy simply by the aroma. This one seemed a callously blended expediter to oblivion, but if it were poured from an engraved, superbly crafted silver flask proffered by a British officer, the recipient would assume it was a superior spirit, and he would believe his expectations before his palette. He took a quick sip, which confirmed his nose's opinion of the evil stuff. A far cry from French brandy, but it would serve.

He filled his flask halfway and tipped in ooze from the poppies. He closed the top and shook it violently, hoping shaken was better than stirred. He opened it, sniffed again, and took a tiny sip. There was no change in the taste. The rawness overpowered any subtle differences. He filled the flask to the brim with more brandy, fastened the top, and shook it once more.

This ready, he hunted up Morales and alerted the soldier that important work lay ahead. He did not elaborate, and Morales, intrigued, seemed both flattered and eager to help, especially after hearing that Juanita would accompany them. Pennywhistle had the idea that Morales considered the girl a good luck charm. Nonsense, of course, but he would use any superstition that helped. Next he directed Manton to break camp and be ready to depart directly he returned, and told Dale to accompany him to headquarters. Dale had an excellent eye for soldiers, better even than his own.

Pennywhistle and Dale arrived ten minutes later at a dust-colored, ramshackle farmhouse that served as the Spanish headquarters, distinguished by colorful banners and two guards who stood at some form of attention. The troops nearby sat around talking, eating and drinking, and seemed in no hurry to do anything but soak up the sun. It was no worse than he'd expected. Raw troops usually behaved thus. Dale departed to nose out twenty prime recruits. Mentally, Pennywhistle wished him luck. Now he had his own part to play, and that involved beguiling Aguinaldo, but first he had to find the man. He consulted one of the guards and followed his directions to the small parlor that Aguinaldo had grandly designated his "war room."

Aguinaldo greeted Pennywhistle heartily and unexpectedly in English. "Good friend and noble sir, come in, come in!" He looked skyward as he struggled to remember the few English words he had carefully rehearsed; they came to him and he grinned. "You are most welcome here, most welcome." He opened his mouth to say more, but checked himself. He had come to the end of his English.

Pennywhistle came to the rescue in Spanish and said he was honored and pleased to share the gracious hospitality of such a fine warrior. Aguinaldo replied that he wished to discuss the current situation, but first, there must be toasts to their brave victory. He acted blissfully blind to the fact that the hostages he had attempted to rescue still remained in French hands.

Pennywhistle sat down in a beautifully crafted rococo chair next to a very plain, slapdash walnut table. The contrast between the pieces of furniture struck him as similar to the contrast between a regular and a militia officer. A map of the area covered the table top. It looked to be recent, detailed, and of good quality, which struck Pennywhistle as extraordinary. He'd make certain to take that with him. Aguinaldo poured some red wine into an ugly green clay mug and handed it over. He then raised a similar one and proposed an elaborate toast, the essence of which was "Death to the French and success to our armies." Pennywhistle drank slowly and found the wine pleasantly smooth, not the raw red plonk he had dreaded.

From the rosy glow on the Spaniard's face, this was not his first sip of the day. No, Pennywhistle gauged, the man was already well into his cups.

They laughed and joked for half an hour. The Spaniard talked mainly about himself, although Pennywhistle's gentle prodding elicited a few useful military details. Aguinaldo turned dark when he spoke of French depredations and his hatred of everything Gallic, but brightened noticeably when his guest suggested he had some charming brandy he would like to offer to return the colonel's grandly diverting hospitality. This was even easier than with the hussar in Cordona. No guile or persuasion necessary.

He poured some of the doctored brandy into Aguinaldo's empty mug; the man gulped it and smiled broadly. His cheeks flushed more noticeably. Hardly the way to drink a fine brandy, but perfect for the cheap swill he'd offered. It would speed the effect.

"I am delighted it pleases you; permit me the honor of offering you more." Pennywhistle held up the flask.

Aguinaldo agreed happily. Pennywhistle poured. He asked Aguinaldo a few harmless questions about his family and waited patiently for the syrup to take effect.

Aguinaldo sat heavily down in the chair and mopped his brow with one hand while he clutched an official looking valise to his chest. He droned on about his lovely daughters, then his eyelids grew heavy and his speech began to slur. He spoke more deliberately; as if each syllable were of such importance it needed special consideration. He told Pennywhistle he was confident he would soon be promoted to general. He was in mid sentence when the leather case slid to the floor and his head fell gently forward and onto the table. Pennywhistle reached over and nudged him. No response; he was firmly in the grip of Morpheus.

The marine opened the valise and methodically inventoried the contents. Evidently, Aguinaldo was a barrister in private life. Many attorneys thought that the same blustering, soaring rhetoric that made them effective in a courtroom would make them great battlefield leaders; a dangerous conceit. Nevertheless, lawyers were among the most vocal opponents of King Joseph, knew a lot of influential types, and were good at inflaming crowds and galvanizing resistance. Most of the contents were writs and depositions, but at last he came upon the details of Aguinaldo's mission.

He read as quickly as he could, frustrated again by his lack of Spanish. His knowledge of French helped him recognize cognate words. Ah, here it was! The captured dignitaries were listed, along with their positions. They were an impressive cross section of influential society; he had heard two of them named in the officers' mess in Lisbon. Their loss would certainly do great harm to Spanish war efforts. Hence, their rescue was would benefit British interests in the long term, and his in the short.

The town of Guijuelo, the prisoners' destination, was a mere ten miles away. The prisoners were to die by firing squad at ten 'o clock tomorrow in the public square. The French clearly had anticipated some sort of rescue attempt, hence the heavy escort. Only a portion of the escort had been engaged by Aguinaldo's militia, and while the French had lost tactically, they had won the strategic victory, for the prisoners had not been recaptured and would still die on the morrow. The Spaniards had predictably attempted to rescue their own and had just as predictably failed; now the French would relax. Pennywhistle was counting on that. They would not expect a second rescue attempt in a garrison town where they were strongest. It amused him to turn the tables: the hare chasing the fox. He would carry out Aguinaldo's mission—by making certain Aguinaldo was nowhere near. The irony was delicious.

Pennywhistle finished his inspection of the papers, rolled the map into a leather case, and checked Aguinaldo's pulse. The man would sleep for hours and awaken with a bad headache. When he stomped, stormed, and roared about the disappearance of his troops and the Englishman's perfidy, his remaining men would listen, nod, and agree volubly, but they would see him for the silly, strutting, rooster he really was. Partisan leadership depended on respect; his days of command were numbered. Pennywhistle laughed out loud. He had rendered a great service to the Spanish people!

Now, down to business; there was work to do.

CHAPTER ELEVEN

Pennywhistle wanted to dash and set things moving, but knew an ounce of preparation was worth a pound of blood. What he contemplated was efficient from a military point of view, but ambiguous from a moral one. Well, the scales balanced. He had saved a girl, a good deed as society reckoned things; now he intended to make use of her in ways that had little to do with goodness. It troubled him that he was going to use her regard for him to further his own military ends, but a wise commander kept the military goal first and foremost in his mind. All interests were subordinate to those of the British Crown.

He left the farm house and quickly found Major Miguel Fernández, the second in command. Fernández was a staff type, not a field soldier. He appeared as eager to evade responsibility as Aguinaldo had been to exert complete control. He seemed unsurprised by his commander's indisposition; evidently the colonel had a reputation as a tippler. He also had no problem believing Aguinaldo had tasked the Englishman with borrowing a few troops to complete the mission. This suited the major, as long as he himself was not called upon to go. The Englishman would do the work, but the Spaniards would get the credit! And if things went wrong, the English would bear the blame.

Pennywhistle found Dale cleaning his Baker and waiting patiently. Dale had indeed identified twenty sturdy recruits. Dale's lack of Spanish was a problem, but non-commissioned officers always seemed to have a way to communicate with rankers that bordered on the psychic. It was time to bring in Juanita and Morales to complete the little drama.

He set off to find Juanita and found her easily, as she had been looking for him. She was smiling, energized, jubilant. She talked proudly about her people handing the hated French a nasty surprise. He had wondered how much he should tell her; now he decided that withholding information would only provoke her curiosity and would not conjure forth her inspirational efforts. He would tell her everything—everything about the immediate mission, nothing about its place in the greater design.

As he told her his plan, her eyes grew wide and bright, but he could have sworn he saw a flicker of red when he told her there would probably be a skirmish at the end of the trail. She really was a creature of fire. War had the effect of bringing out qualities that might normally have gone unremarked, never resorted to. He told her he needed to work with Dale, and she said she would quickly return with Morales in tow.

He and Dale studied the map he had pilfered, plotting a route to Guijuelo that was parallel to the main road the French were on. They were out of the mountains now, but it was still hilly country and they would have to ask Juanita about the terrain. They debated timetables. The execution protocols would start hours before 10 a.m., and soldiers would be alert. The best time to attack would be just before dawn. Men's responses were typically dullest around 3 am. Even the most attentive sentries instinctively relaxed their vigilance at that time.

Tactics would have to be basic, something part-time soldiers could understand. He would have only a few men, so he would have to strike for the jugular, hit the tipping point of their operation. Trouble was, he had no idea exactly where that was. He needed a map of the town and the dispositions of French troops. That would require informants. He also needed an escape route, and a diversion. He had no intention of dying nobly in an orgy of gunfire that had value only to propagandists of mad heroism.

The men would also have to be provisioned. They probably had plenty of powder and shot and better weapons than before, but he guessed they were short on food. Militias might be keen for glory, but were generally dim about the art of logistics, forgetting that men with full bellies fight longer and more valorously than those with growling stomachs. He had a way to remedy the food problem; things he remembered from his boyhood.

He was getting ahead of himself. Nothing could be done until he had the men firmly under his command. For now, here came Morales and Juanita, both looking sprightly and eager, alive with misplaced confidence in some magical faculty he did not possess. He carefully explained the specifics of his plans to them. He calmly told them both to lie for the greater good. They would tell the Spaniards the same story he'd told Fernández. The militia was already in awe of the rangy Englishman who had fought so fiercely; they were to say that he needed to move fast and so could take only twenty of their number. It would appeal to their vanity and become a contest, but a contest that was rigged, since Dale already knew the men he needed. Juanita's oratory and Morales' rank would sell the story very effectively. He asked Juanita for a description of the country ahead, and it was as he'd guessed. There was one stream in the area, and after all of the recent rains it was probably swollen and fast running. Perfect for what he had in mind.

He wanted to be sure, so he had Juanita and Morales repeat his instructions before he sent them along to join Dale. He would sit and review the maps and let Dale handle the recruits.

That was something best done without the direct presence of an officer who might inhibit spontaneity and rough language.

The men would need sleep, even if it were only a few hours. When the exhilaration of battle wore off, it often left men torpid and listless. He was tired; the morning battle had denied him his rest, but he reached deep inside himself and summoned up a small reserve of nervous energy. A steaming cup of strong coffee helped greatly, at the cost of depleting his limited supply of beans. He looked at the map for a place where they could rest and still be able to defend themselves, and decided he could get at least four hours of marching from the men by appealing to their newly found faith in themselves, their patriotism, and their desire for revenge. He needed to strike a balance between good discipline and what could reasonably be expected from once and future civilians. He didn't need them to be good soldiers for the duration of the war, merely for the next twenty-four hours. He made calculations and scanned the map to find a spot hard by the brook.

When the others returned, Dale and Morales marched proudly. Dale led from the front and Morales brought up the rear, with a file of marching men in between. Their uniforms, if they could be called that, were makeshift, but they all had full cartridge boxes and Charleville muskets in good working order. Dale had seen to that. They looked enthusiastic and chipper, not a trace of resentment at being dragooned into an enterprise that might well get them killed. Juanita walked with an easy stride at the side of the column, and the men looked at her with admiration rather than desire. The cult of the Virgin Mary was popular, and Juanita was a battlefield Madonna. Superstition perhaps, but Pennywhistle knew it would be a great help to what he had planned. Men often fought for the most fantastic reasons.

******

Dale called a halt. He was not sure if the recruits understood the English, but Morales echoed the order a second later in Spanish. The column parted and bulged, as some of the men stopped promptly and others reacted more slowly. Dale and Morales conferred quietly. Morales then barked a word of command. The men shuffled and bumped, but formed something like a horizontal line. Dale wanted them in position for Pennywhistle's inspection.

He made the inspection cursory and only examined two muskets carefully. They were clean and well oiled; Dale's intervention Pennywhistle had no doubt, since militia were not usually so particular. Dale had made sure all of the men were now armed with French muskets, instead of antique fowling pieces and rusty shotguns. The cartridge boxes had also been looted from the dead French soldiers, so that the cartridges fit the bores of their new weapons—a most important detail; each man carried sixty rounds. The men tried to maintain the famous Spanish dignity, but more than a few smiled at Pennywhistle as he passed before them, flushed with recent success and confident more lay ahead. Dale, Juanita, and Morales must have put on quite a show.

Pennywhistle knew they expected some kind of speech. Spanish commanders and troops loved battlefield oratory, while English officers and soldiers generally scoffed at it. He tried to think of phrases the now indisposed Colonel Aguinaldo would have employed, but only a few came to mind. He decided to open with some shameless bombast, then give them the bare details of the mission and impress its importance upon them. He would keep it short.

"Who will help me teach *Monsieur* Johnny Crapaud that Spain belongs to the Spaniards and is a place where no frog-eating Frenchman dare show his face? Who will help me give the French such a hiding that their screams will be heard all the way to Paris? Who will help me smash King Joseph's lackeys so hard that they will forever run from the sight of an angry Spaniard with a musket?"

His opening brought cheers and a loud chorus of "I will, I will!"

They would win a glorious victory, he proclaimed. Not just a minor victory, but one that would save lives, contribute decisively to the safety of their country, and earn them the undying gratitude of many generations yet to come. He was honored to command them and had great faith in their cause and their fighting ability. He laid it on pretty thick, and it surprised the rationalist in him that they ate it up like children gobbling candy at a county fair. He made it sound seductively easy. They merely had to follow orders, since every detail was carefully planned and every eventuality foreseen. Success could not fail to attend them. He fervently wished that were true. His final words repelled him, but he felt they would have a good effect. "God and the Virgin Mary smile upon you this day!"

That did it. They erupted in mighty cheering. He slapped a pleased look on his face, but he knew he had cruelly tricked them into a bizarre eagerness to surrender their lives. Maybe that was the role of a partisan leader, after all, to fool men by means of personal magnetism, flattery, and oratory into believing the impossible was child's play. It was distasteful, but it was also about giving them something valuable and real: confidence in themselves.

Dale and Morales formed them up and they moved out toward Manton and the horses. He promised them rest and refreshment after only eight short miles. He could march with them, show them he was willing to share their privations, but decided that would be a mistake. They wanted a father figure, someone aristocratic and important, and such figures were always mounted. Lightning would have a rider today.

CHAPTER TWELVE

Manton had been his usual reliable self and had everything disassembled, stowed, and ready to move when Pennywhistle returned, leading twenty new recruits. He was surprised by the new entourage, but too well trained to let his face betray it. He was used to unusual actions from his captain and knew each one was always a means to a definite end. He took his place at the rear of the column.

Pennywhistle asked the men to select from among themselves the two who had fought most valiantly for the privilege of riding the two bays. It was a fine way to let them know he cared for their welfare, as well as showing he trusted them to make a good choice. Privately, he guessed the men would see action that night, and it was as well to do what he could to conserve their energy.

Morales marched with the men and already had a possessive attitude toward his new-found charges. He was eager to redeem himself after the surprise at Cordona. The men responded well to him. Something could definitely be made of the man.

Dale rode close by Morales and exchanged quiet words with him from time to time. He was picking up pidgin Spanish quickly. He had expected to have to give Morales advice on discipline, but that was proving unnecessary. He looked at the infantry's step as they marched and observed their facial expressions. No one appeared resentful, surly, or disgruntled, common among men pressed into service; most looked expectant. They talked freely as they marched, something British soldiers would never do, but it sounded full of encouragement and curiosity rather than resentment. Dale decided they were not a bad lot. If he could have them for a few months, he could make them fit to stand alongside British infantry.

Pennywhistle asked Juanita to ride one of the spare horses, but she preferred to ride with him as before. She explained she felt safe with him. He started to remonstrate, preferring not to encourage her growing affection, but her flinty look of determination told him it was a waste of breath. Besides, he needed to talk with her about what lay ahead, and the Spaniards believed he rode tandem to allow one of their men to ride rather than walk, so it actually worked to his advantage.

Juanita knew the town of Guijuelo well. She had been there many times with her father on drives. It was a prosperous market town of 3,500 souls, centered round a large plaza and an ancient church dating to Roman times. The plaza would naturally be the site of execution; it would accommodate plenty of unwilling spectators. "They will surely confine the prisoners in the monastery, next to the Church of San Felipe," she said confidently. "The old monk's cells will be very effective prisons. It will amuse the French to imprison Spaniards in a holy building, since they have such contempt for our faith."

He found it disagreeable that he would be compelled to trust and depend on priests to accomplish his goal, but they formed the stiff spine of Spanish resistance. He normally considered them grasping purveyors of superstition and fear, but in the Peninsula, religion increased the fervor with which the war was fought, as well as pushing people to commit atrocities in the name of their God. It was contradictory, illogical, and outrageous. War was like that, though: mixed motives, odd bedfellows, unexpected consequences. His mission was proof of all three.

The next few hours passed uneventfully, although the marchers showed signs of fatigue and were glad to halt when they reached the bivouac. He told them to rest and smoke their pipes. Their haversacks were nearly empty of food, but he assured them they would not go hungry.

Pennywhistle found a quiet spot near a gnarled old oak. It was secluded and peaceful, yet he still had a clear view of the men. Dale and Manton did not disturb him; they knew his methods far too well. Juanita was not more than twenty feet from him, but the expression on his face made it clear he was a thousand miles away. It startled her when she realized he was meditating, just as St. Teresa of Avila had done. St. Teresa had gotten great insights from God.

Pennywhistle ruminated on what he would need for tomorrow's attack. It came down to three things: intelligence, secrecy, and cooperation. Juanita was the perfect person to acquire the first. She was a Spaniard, she knew the town and some of the horse traders, and could contact the priests easily. If stopped, her tale of being a drover's daughter would hold up. He would give her one of the spare horses to lend the tale verisimilitude. Tonight, French guards would probably take no notice of a peasant girl going about her business. They had plenty of more important matters to tend to before tomorrow's scheduled execution He needed to know how many troops he faced, their locations, and any information about their experience. The Spanish priests surely knew some of this, and his intuition said they would respond with alacrity to an offer of help and rescue.

His men would need disguises and would have to approach the town in disparate, small groups: twos and threes would work best. The walls of the town no longer stood, but three principal streets marked the site of the old gatehouses. Groups would use different entrances, so there would not even be a hint of something organized. Peasant smocks, common for workmen, would be simple but effective camouflage. Glancing at Juanita, he swiftly decided it would be well to disguise her, too; a beautiful girl was hard to overlook, but even a soldier would not look twice at a shapeless bundle under a dun-colored shawl. A hay cart could be appropriated and pulled by one of the horses, and the weapons could be hidden in the hay for later retrieval. He wanted the men to seem dull and unremarkable, townsmen strolling idly on an early Spanish evening. French contempt for the Spanish meant they would not be recognized as strangers, since all Spaniards looked alike to them. He would establish a rendezvous point and timetable later. That took care of secrecy.

Cooperation was unlikely to be a problem, although the French had certainly developed effective networks of informers. Even with the widespread hatred of the French, there were always a few who collaborated out of expediency. But collaborators could also come in handy, if identified; he could use them to feed false information to their French paymasters.

Priests, however, had even more effective intelligence networks. They would know who could be trusted. They took confession constantly, and even though only a fool would tell his priest he was an *afrancescado*, religion was taken seriously enough that some probably had. Priests were active to the point of actually firing weapons in battle. He thought that quite an original interpretation of the medieval ideal of "The Peace of God."

It remained to find an escape route. That was a thorny problem, particularly as they would be accompanied by frightened and bewildered civilians, quite possibly under fire. A diversion was needed; a spectacular explosion and fire would fill that bill nicely. The town supported a garrison, so there had to be a powder magazine somewhere. He surmised its location was no secret.

He came back to himself after twenty minutes. He could pull this off. It would be risky, but not foolhardy. He remembered an observation of Bonaparte's that, "In war, men are nothing, but a man is everything." It was arrogance, he knew, but he believed himself to be the essential man to pull off this rescue.

His troops would need food and sleep before the event. A few could procure the food while the remainder rested. He would show them how. He cast his eye about and found a suitable chunk of wood. He took out his boot knife and began to whittle. Cork was easy to work with. It only took fifteen minutes to fashion the shape he wished. It was no artistic triumph, but it would serve and could easily be duplicated, even by unskilled hands. He remembered there was a supply of string and iron vent picks in the saddlebags. They would be pressed into service.

He smiled pleasantly and walked over to his little band. Manton and Dale returned the smile, knowing what he had in mind, but Juanita and Morales looked at his creation in puzzlement.

"It's such a splendid afternoon that I think a spot of fishing is in order. We are going to have a wonderful fish dinner today. Shad, barbel, and trout, I should think." He looked at Juanita and Morales with a twinkle in his eye. "Don't worry, I will show everyone how." He saw them cock their eyebrows in uncertainty. He laughed. "Be of good cheer, this is how I spent summer afternoons as a boy in Scotland. No one will go hungry today."

He asked the four to assemble the men in a semicircle alongside the brook. Once everyone was gathered, he explained the purpose of the wedge-shaped chunk of wood.

"Cork floats beautifully, and each wedge will be fitted with four hooks made from vent picks. We put them in the stream, but moor them to shore with string. Baited with worms and with the swift current to move them, they will attract plenty of fish.

One man can easily manage four floats. It will be our flotilla of fishing craft. The rest of you can take a nap and wake up with the prospect of a good dinner. You won't be eating any rotten salt pork or weevil-infested biscuit today!" He saw delighted looks on their faces. Good food assumed exaggerated importance among soldiers in wartime.

Pennywhistle enjoyed fishing. His enthusiasm was infectious, and the men responded like children given an unexpected and highly diverting task. It took them thirty minutes to carve their rafts and another fifteen to unearth legions of wiggling worms from the earth. An hour later, a squadron of newly commissioned fishing vessels commanded the center of the stream. The first hits came within minutes. After ten minutes, most rafts were pitching and yawing energetically. Fifteen minutes later, the water was awash with violent underwater motion. Pennywhistle smiled with real joy and ordered all of the boats in after an hour. Either the worms had magical properties, or no one had fished this steam for a long time.

The harvest was prodigious. The helmsmen of the boats shouted their companions awake, and the hungry men gathered round to watch the proud fishermen untangle fish from the hooks and lay them carefully on the beach: exactly the three types of fish he had predicted. Large too, most specimens at least three pounds; one was actually close to ten. It was extraordinary. Pennywhistle had not expected results this good. Maybe it was beginner's luck.

Juanita said nothing but smiled, looked heavenward, and made the sign of the cross. Morales silently mouthed "Amen." Pennywhistle thought it odd to attribute success in fishing to divine intervention—Ghillie Gunn would have a supplied a woodsman's explanation for why the fish were biting, having to do with weather, current, and time of day, as well as the feeding habits of the species involved—but if the Spaniards believed

Jesus had a particular affinity for him, so much the better for the mission.

The haul of fish was a beautiful thing in the midst of war. Hungry men started toward the fish with unrestrained glee, keen to appropriate the best specimens and have at them with a knife, but Pennywhistle stopped them. It seemed a pity to treat such admirable examples of piscine perfection abominably, not to mention a hungry free-for-all would burst the bounds of discipline. He wondered if anyone else here even knew how to properly clean a fish and prepare a fillet.

It seemed ridiculous to give them a demonstration, but Ghillie Gunn shouted in his mind it would be a crime not to. "A beautiful fish deserves a proper presentation," the voice remonstrated. So he gathered them round and gave instruction, almost like showing them the manual of arms. They watched attentively, all the while licking their lips. He told them that trout was best prepared simply, fried with butter and a bit of lemon. He doubted anyone had lemon, but inquired if anyone had olive oil. Several raised their hands. He knew many of them carried iron skillets in their kit—standard fare for soldiers forced to forage and cook for themselves. "Then go to it, and dine well, my friends."

The men laughed and joked as they set to it, teasing anyone who burnt his fingers or dropped a fillet on the ground. An hour later, there were no words, only burps, smiles, and flatulence. Pennywhistle was pleased. Morale was sky high. Now they would sleep with full bellies and wake refreshed. Good, he needed them ready to go in five hours. They would trust him; they would advance against bullets without hesitation and perish gloriously for a sacred cause. They might even succeed. He had purchased them cheaply. It gratified him in a cold, detached way. He truly was a heartless bastard.

He had always had deep suspicions about the sanity of zealots, and Spain was a country full of them. Their fanaticism made them extraordinarily perseverant, no matter how difficult the struggle, and they could endure privations that would break most men; yet it also blinded them to the appeals of reason, and it lead them to cast civilized restraint to the winds. The same spirit that had defeated the Moors had also spawned the Inquisition.

But Juanita might die too. That sickened him, and he felt ashamed that it did. She was a non-entity, a tool, a means to a necessary end. She was a peasant, a foreigner, and a religious zealot.

It made no sense to have feelings. He had walled up real feeling since Carlotta. He was an apostate of the heart, beyond caring. But a part of him, base beyond reason, made him think Juanita's enchanting oval eyes glistened with promise.

She had an almost other-worldly magnetism. It naturally drew men to her—he could see this in the eyes of all the men, even Dale and Manton; but it was eerie in a way. It was sacred, not carnal. If you allowed her to touch your soul, the result would not be casual or temporary; it would truly be transformative unto death.

Carlotta's death had changed him into a cynical creature with a deformed soul; he viewed the world through jaded eyes, dark with distrust. Still, he was not so far gone as to be unable to appreciate Juanita's fierce idealism and genuine love of country. Her light had touched him. She was creature of heart that walked in the sunlight of grace and justice. The hymn "Amazing Grace" coruscated through his brain when he thought of her. Odd; while the melody was pleasing enough, he had never particularly liked the words, since he associated them with itinerant lay preachers spouting canting drivel.

But no evangelical hymn could distract him from a primitive truth proclaimed by his loins; he had had no woman for a long time. A dark part of him said, *take her, revel in her, ravish her.*

Enjoy the madness and everything else be damned! He would have a splendid release and care nothing for reason afterwards.

Yet stern reason was ascendant. The girl was an innocent thrust by naked villainy into a world turned upside down. She was vulnerable, and her need for safety had caused her to foolishly place great faith and trust in him. To exploit her trusting hero-worship for the sake of low desire was simply wrong. Noblesse Oblige outweighed lust and made his duty clear.

He would not let her die. Three women had died because of his actions. He could not permit another. It was a supreme effort of will to channel his powerful, base energies into a constructive plan of battle. But with will, anything was possible. And his will was strong.

From where he sat, Dale wondered if his commanding officer would make an approach to the young miss, who seemed to wish he would. Many officers would, given such a perfect opportunity. But the captain always put others first and constantly neglected his own basic needs. Even a fleeting wisp of happiness would do him a power of good. Dale was curiously disappointed when Pennywhistle flopped down on his blanket and fell asleep.

CHAPTER THIRTEEN

Perhaps it was Juanita's confidence, or her faith, or French arrogance in assuming that the Spaniards were thoroughly cowed, but Juanita simply strolled quietly into town just after twilight gave way to night. The two guards at the town entrance were engaged in a heated argument about some trifle and she walked right past them.

She saw a handful of French soldiers near the cantina, but they didn't even look her way, focused as they were on their drinks and desultory conversation. The air of the town rippled with tension, and not many people were about in the streets. She was a sensitive, and her special way of knowing screamed as she felt a blanket of collective distress press heavily down upon her. Nature knew something bad was about to happen and was broadcasting warnings to those who could understand.

She went first to the *Posada Dos Coronas*, where most of the drovers and horse traders lodged. She had stayed there many times with her father. It was run down, but prices were cheap. She recognized a few men in the public room. After exchanging greetings and answering pleasant inquiries about her father's health, she was able to start them talking about the situation in town. They knew quite a bit. They came and went, were observant, and the French often did business with them. French tongues had been rather loose. Thirty minutes later, she had an excellent idea of French morale, troop strength, and dispositions. She also secured the name of a talkative collaborator, just as Pennywhistle had instructed her.

She said she would have need of horses and mules, ten of each. She needed them quickly, but did not specify for what purpose. Anyone else they would have refused, but they trusted her because of her father, and her own charisma affected them as well. She said she could pay in gold. She flashed them a guinea Pennywhistle had given her and handed it over to one of the drovers. That caused eyes to brighten. She said more would follow upon delivery, but she expected a fair price. Her eyes grew flinty as she told them what she considered a fair price. They tried to haggle, but she said there would be no negotiating this time, as she was acting on behalf of another. They made faces, but accepted it.

Her next port of call was the imposing gothic Church of San Felipe, where Pennywhistle planned to secretly gain access to the prisoners. When he'd told Juanita this, she'd argued with him. She was a woman of faith; the priests would see that, she told him, and talk freely to her. She knew he was reluctant to share his plan with the priests, but she emphatically told him that complete honesty promised more benefit than secrecy. To relinquish control was a leap of faith that did not come easily to him, but in the end he had conceded that she would be a better ambassador for his purpose.

Juanita entered the church, breathing in the lingering traces of the incense. When she explained her cause, the priests were overjoyed. They had been praying for deliverance from an intolerable situation, and this maiden appeared like God's emissary with an answer. Not a simple "Have faith, wait, and trust," but an answer that carried the risk of danger and demanded their active intervention. Yet the answer offered the hope of salvation in this life, not just the hereafter. She talked with the priests for an hour. They agreed to shelter Pennywhistle's men in the undercroft until they were ready to move, then dispatched people to procure peasant smocks for disguise. They even readied a mule to transport the clothes back to the Englishman's camp.

Juanita relayed Pennywhistle's concern that there might be retaliation against the town, even if the rescue attempt failed. Father Dominquez, their leader, spoke for all of them. "We will do what we must, endure what we must, and trust God to give us the strength to bear our burdens honorably." The brave words made Juanita's heart swell with confidence and pride. Of course they would prevail!

******

Pennywhistle wondered if it would compromise his mission to do what he had in mind. He was supposed to preserve secrecy, but sometimes excessive secrecy worked against success. He had been told all sorts of blather about "need to know," but he also believed an officer was expected to exercise judgment as circumstances demanded. If his hunch was right, this would confirm he had made the correct decision about the rescue, and this misbegotten mission might wind up accomplishing something unexpected; perhaps contradicting the letter of his orders, but consonant with their spirit. He was risking his life and that of others—civilian others. He had a right to know. To hell with his orders!

He removed his left boot and took a small screwdriver from his haversack. He inserted it into one of the tiny screws in the heel and began twisting counter-clockwise. After the first one fell free, he repeated the process on the other three. He removed the heel and took out a small metal container similar to a makeup compact.

He twisted the lid off and unfurled two long rectangular strips of paper. There was something strange about their feel; they were impregnated with some sort of chemical. Probably flash paper, fire would cause each to disappear in an instant. They contained no words, merely a long series of numbers arranged in diagonal columns of ten. Each number probably corresponded to a letter and each column to a discrete piece of information: a person, place, or word. His hunch was that it was the first. He thought these might be the names of prominent citizens who were covertly involved in supplying cash and information to guerrilla groups. He wanted to match names with those he had seen in documents in Aguinaldo's valise.

He knew only the bare bones about cryptography, but thought he was looking at a simple transposition cipher; a classic "rail pattern" pioneered in ancient Athens. The numbers were written downward as if on rails of an imaginary fence then moved upward once the bottom was reached. The message was then be read off by rows, or would have been if the encoder had simply used letters as the Greeks had. But the encoder had added a complication; the numbers first had to be converted to letters. A cipher disk was required to fully decode the message. The disk was a four inch wide cardboard circle with two inner rings that could be turned to various alignments. He had none, but had seen one and its settings at headquarters, carelessly left in plain sight.

He needed to recall an exact and meticulously detailed image of the disk. An ordinary mind could not handle the task, but it was well within the capability of a mind moved to an altered, expanded state of consciousness. Such a mind not only enlarged the reach of the senses, it furnished a key to unlock the innermost vaults of memory. A quick flash of Aadi's weathered face popped into his head.

He had learned meditation as a child from an old Hindu servant. The man had saved the life of Pennywhistle's grandfather long ago in Bengal, although no one had ever heard the details. Indeed, no one even seemed to know the man's formal name or his exact age; he was simply called Aadi, and he appeared somewhere between seventy and ninety years old. He was just under six feet in height, but so exceedingly lean he seemed taller. He walked with a spry step, had skin the color and texture of old parchment, and possessed a long, thoughtful face that perfectly mirrored an ascetic cast of mind. He wore the traditional Indian mundu, a sarong-like garment, rather than European attire. He handled English well when he spoke, which was seldom, and appeared a man who was thoroughly content with his lot in life. Due to his strange ways, people on his grandfather's estate reckoned the man half mad but harmless.

Children are naturally curious about odd ducks. They have not yet been taught to judge, fear, or hate. Tom had heard peculiar stories about the odd foreigner who refused to eat meat and had a magical touch with plants. One day, young Tom took it in his head to meet this unusual man and find out if any of the rumors were true. It took an hour of walking uphill through the most heavily wooded part of the estate to reach Aadi's isolated, tiny cottage. The old man welcomed him warmly and shared a humble meal of beans and biscuits. The two talked. And talked. And talked. Hours passed like minutes, as each seemed to sense a need in the other: one to be understood as a person and the other to understand life in general; one to supply mature wisdom, the other to share youthful vigor.

To Pennywhistle's developing mind, the ancient Hindu was far from the crazy man some had made him out to be. He was just a man who viewed life differently—very differently. Possessions, prestige, and power meant nothing to him; they were chimeral, earthly conceits which oppressed the mind and retarded progress of the spirit. The old man averred that living a simple life in perfect harmony with nature brought riches far more lasting than those enjoyed by princes and kings.

A friendship developed and the boy learned a great many things about life, philosophy, and nature from an Eastern perspective; rich and stimulating counterpoints to the

Enlightenment ideas he was acquiring from Ogilvie, his Scots tutor. Aadi's instruction touched the warmly emotional, intuitive inner self; Ogilvie's, the coldly rational one that assessed the world's machinations. Adults might have seen a conflict in the two approaches, but the young Tom blended them seamlessly.

A year after their first talk, Aadi told Pennywhistle he had a gift for him, the legacy of the Sidda. He said the legacy was something wondrous and amazing; it gave a concentration so profound and intense that it enabled a man to see extraordinary possibilities in even the most mundane of events. The general effect of the legacy was akin to the explosion of color that bloomed when ordinary sunlight was filtered through a prism. Doors of knowledge bolted to most men would be opened and the ephemeral veils concealing higher planes of reality would be lifted. Time itself could be slowed. The smallest fragment of even the most complex physical or intellectual design could be examined in exquisite detail in the twinkling of an eye. The gift brought inner understanding, powerful self-knowledge, and a deep serenity. Sidda's bequest made rubies and diamonds seem mere silly baubles. Aadi made it clear the gift would take years of disciplined practice to master fully and effectively.

"Are you ready for this, Master Thomas?" The old man asked with dread seriousness. "Chose wisely, young sir, for the path is not an easy one. I would not think less of you if you declined. Once you start down this route, your life will be transformed. You will see things you never saw before even though they were in front of your eyes the whole time Your eyes have never lacked the capacity to perceive; you brain has simply lacked the awareness to properly instruct them. The gift is not something I offer lightly. I have never offered it to one so tender in years, yet I sense in you a love of knowledge and a worthiness of purpose that tells me you can handle the intensity of the gift far better than most adults." He sighed gently. "So many adults are frozen in their perspectives and frightened of new ways."

Eight-year-old Thomas Pennywhistle looked the old man deeply in the eye. Something inexplicable passed between them. Deep instinct guided Pennywhistle's words. He squared his shoulders and said with a quiet voice mature beyond his years, " Show me."

"I call the gift, *The Ritual*, said Aadi. "Let us begin."

Pennywhistle heard the old Hindu's voice in his head, instructing him as clearly as he first had twenty years before. He sat down and made himself comfortable. He crossed his feet and extended his hands slightly, palms upward. He closed his eyes, breathed deeply in and out, and started *The Ritual*. His breathing slowed, steadied, and deepened. His heart rate plummeted. His mind filtered out his present environment and everything became intensely quiet. He felt time slowing down and his consciousness beginning to shift, broaden, and intensify. A deep tide of calmness flowed through him. His mind's eye visualized a gentle, wave-less blue sea under a sunny, cloudless sky. He concentrated on that for several minutes. He blew a gentle suggestion into the vision that a cipher disk bubble up to the surface from below. Peace flooded his being as he focused on the vision.

And it happened. The outermost ring of the disk floated to the surface of his subconscious. He saw the numbers in each of the thirty compartments clearly. He rotated it slowly in his mind and perused the numbers. Each square compartment contained ten numbers, all beginning with an eight or a one. They looked to exactly correspond to the numbers in the flash paper columns. He had one more ring to go.

That proved harder, but ten minutes later he saw the ring in its entirety. The inner ring contained the letters of the alphabet in boxes, arrayed in seemingly random order. Yet not quite random; the frequency of the letter Q, the least common letter employed in English writing, suggested terminations or pauses. It would be a matter of aligning the two rings to discover the number and letter correspondence, but the trick was to know the baseline settings. His intuition told him it was the setting he had seen at headquarters. It was the first time he had ever been grateful for a lapse in security. He looked at the first group of numbers at the on the flash paper. It was time to test his theory.

He continued to breathe deeply. His mind's eye began to rotate the wheels. He saw them as clearly as if his hand held them directly in front of his real eyes. The first diagonal column of flash paper numbers formed up as background scenery on his mental tableau. He scanned them quickly. Eureka! It was a name. Manuel Sánchez. He had no idea exactly who Sánchez was, but his hunch about the setting had been right. God's blood, he had the key! He mentally unscrolled Aguinaldo's list, but Sánchez's name was not on it.

Over the next hour, he repeated the process and came up with thirty names. Twenty of them were on Aguinaldo's list and were being held prisoner in Guijuelo. They were certainly persons of value to His Majesty's Government. He re-furled the paper, packed it up, and returned it to the false heel. As he screwed the top back on, he decided he would say nothing to anyone about his unauthorized peek into state secrets. Headquarters types would not see it the way he did; they often failed to understand the need for improvisation in the field.

A picture began to form in his mind. Someone must have seen the list, but probably only part of it. Of course! All of the captured men had been on the first strip. The French were after the second strip! No wonder they had been searching for him. The guide he had killed had meant to lead him toward capture. They had no idea who he was personally, but a good idea of what he carried. The allegedly important dispatches in the case were probably mere window dressing, a distraction.

He was no spy and understood little of their clandestine ways and methods, but he was a good and clever soldier who learned fast. There had to be a mole at headquarters. He speculated about the motive of such a person; perhaps gambling debts had driven him to treachery. Many officers ruined themselves through debt. Whatever the reason, the mole had probably done great damage; but a rescue of those on the first list might undo a measure of it.

He realized he had been in a trance for some time as his concentration ebbed and the ordinary world reformed about him. His head throbbed dully. He heard the Spaniards talking quietly among themselves. Dale and Morales were inspecting weapons and ammunition. He looked up and was startled to see Juanita staring down at him, curious about the unreadable look on his face.

"What is the matter, *Capitan Pennywhistle?* You look as if a mule just kicked you." She looked puzzled, but he guessed she accepted the Lord moved by secret paths, and those touched by him might act in strange ways.

He realized how odd he looked and forced a broad smile onto his face. "Juanita, I am glad to see you!" He was not pretending; he truly was relieved she was returned and unhurt. "I see by your face you have news. Please sit and be comfortable. Speak freely and tell me what you have learned."

She smiled back. He did care, although he seemed unaware of it. He could be so grim sometimes, but a smile changed him entirely. She wished he would smile more often, but responsibility was the enemy of joy. And just now, great responsibility lay on his shoulders.

She remembered to talk slowly and deliberately so he could follow the sense of her words. She included observations and details that she hoped made her report even more valuable. The Englishman was always concerned about the little things. Pennywhistle listened, interrupted her a few times to ask questions, and she could tell by his thoughtful expression he was translating her information into tactics.

Morales coughed a few times discreetly, to attract his attention. "I have the cart, *señor capitan.* The men have hidden their weapons inside the hay. Unless one makes a close and extended inspection, they are impossible to discover." He seemed pleased with himself.

"Thank you, Sarn't Morales, you have done well. Please assemble the men and tell them I will be along directly to acquaint them with their tasks for the evening." Morales saluted smartly. He was looking more like a soldier with each passing hour. He turned on his heel and marched away briskly.

"Juanita, you have taken great risks and done all you can. It is up to soldiers now. I should prefer you to stay here and remain safe." He paused and a look of concern settled on his face. "It would relieve my mind."

She started to snap a protest, but his naked sincerity caused her to bite her tongue. Instead, she spoke quietly and gently. "I cannot do that. You need me. I know horses and I know the ostlers. They trust me. God understood you had need of my knowledge and placed me exactly where I needed to be. I believe God wants me to remain at your side, and I would be foolish to argue with God."

Religion again! He thought of God as a detached watchmaker who set His creation running and then allowed mechanistic laws to disinterestedly enforce themselves, but the girl clearly believed in divine intervention influenced by prayers and supplications. She thought God spoke directly and intimately to her. Under normal circumstances he might have considered that madness, but here it seemed to be the prevalent reality. His icy rationality pointed out that she should not be thought of as a woman, but as an asset, and she would indeed prove useful. If she were killed, so be it. It was the nature of war. He met her eyes and said simply, "Very well; but it is against my better judgment."

She regarded him intently, and her sympathetic expression showed she felt the conflict within him. "You are a deep man," she said gravely, "a man who sees clearly what others miss. That is a heavy burden to bear, but that is exactly why God has chosen you."

He sat back and started to think about their escape route, trying to recall everything he knew about explosives and fuses. The charges would have to be placed strategically, and he wanted to make sure that all his people, militia and escapees, would be well clear when the fireworks erupted. He expected they would speed a few Frenchmen to the next life, but he wanted to spare the civilians. Only he had the skills to do what was necessary with the fuses, but he also had to be in command of the rescue, and he could not be in two places at once. And now he was out of time. He hoped the answer to his dilemma would come later.

CHAPTER FOURTEEN

A lot could go wrong with the plan. The best way to reduce hazard was to patiently explain what was expected to the unit en masse, then chat briefly with each individual about his part. Most commanders never bothered to make sure enlisted men understood the big picture, but in Pennywhistle's experience, men who knew what was going on were more willing to follow orders, and made better decisions when they had to improvise.

It took a full hour to put it to the men. It was dark when they assembled, but the full moon came out from behind the clouds as he addressed them, and the men took this as providential sign. It helped that Juanita preceded him with a smart piece of oratory laced with words like, "God, family, rescue, country, honor, and death." The last was for the French, of course. He watched a variety of emotions play across their faces as she spoke, and when she concluded, he knew she had plowed the field expertly. It had only remained for him to plant the seeds.

He split his twenty Spaniards into small teams and, with Morales' help, gave them directions to use all three of the town entrances at different times. One team of two men would enter through the Rosas portal last, and would report any signs of increased alertness on the part of the garrison.

Using a map of the town drawn by Juanita, Pennywhistle outlined with each team the route they would take to the Church of San Felipe. He made them repeat their instructions to ensure each man was clear on his part in the grand scheme. He told them to temporarily forget the military instruction given them by Dale and Morales. "Don't try to be stealthy; the French will construe it as furtive behavior. Be not stern but easy and unmilitary in your stride. Be talkative, loud, and jolly in voice, and welcoming and friendly to anyone you might encounter. Tell anyone who asks what task you are about, that you are happily carrying out the business of St James, helping to prepare for the grand and glorious festival in his name the day after tomorrow. Tell them they surely must not miss it. The French believe you to be boorish slaves to your religion. Let's give them what they expect!"

He made each man affix a white lozenge-shaped patch to his smock. It was not only a well known emblem of St James, it would also make his men easier to spot should there be any night fighting.

Morales and Dale would take charge of the weapons cart and see that it reached the church. He and Manton would accompany Juanita and obtain the horses. They would bring Lightning and the five remaining animals with them. He doubted they would be stopped, but if they were, he would let Juanita do the talking. He and Manton would keep silent, cringe, and nod.

******

The full moon glowed brilliantly as they set out, riding toward the Rosas entrance. Juanita led, Pennywhistle and Manton followed, Manton holding the bridles of the horses that brought up the rear. The dark smock covered all trace of Pennywhistle's scarlet uniform and the floppy round laborer's hat he affected hid most of his face. Manton's smock, of similar brown earth tones, looked as dull and unremarkable as its owner was trying to appear.

This time one of the guards decided to do his duty and stopped Juanita. She betrayed no fear. He asked his questions in a pidgin Spanish nearly impossible to understand, but she answered him directly and even with a little coquettishness. That surprised Pennywhistle, but the smile she flashed the guard seemed to go a long way toward setting him at his ease, and he waved them through. Her magnetism clearly had dimensions to it other than spiritual, and she appeared able to project it at will. She was full of surprises.

They reached the posada ten minutes later. The ostlers and dealers were as good as their word, and the ten horses and ten mules were ready, snorting a bit and nuzzling at Juanita as she looked them over. He was not sure if Juanita was in earnest or merely playing her part, but she demanded an inspection before taking possession. She was convincing because her expertise was not feigned. Pennywhistle did his part and paid the men from his purse. One of his greatest fears had been that the gold English guineas would cause trouble, but these were businessmen; they hated the French, and they loved hard coin. Spanish paper currency had become so debased by the war that it took a fistful merely to buy a loaf of bread.

One man volunteered some useful last minute information about the two roads east of town. Both were only lightly guarded, because large detachments of French troops were at the other end, and both roads had been effectively cleared of resistance. Since no action was expected on these roads, the garrison commander had assigned four of his least reliable people. The guards were frequently drunk or even absent. Pennywhistle nodded; the second road was the one he had selected as an escape route.

He also received alarming news. The current garrison was three hundred men, but the execution was to be a showy thing and more troops were on the march. By ten a.m. tomorrow, the plaza would be swarming with over a thousand French soldiers. He had no idea of their direction of approach, but for all he knew, it might be along the escape route. The odds were acceptable now, just barely, and only because the alternative was to do nothing; but unless they were well gone by first light, escape would be impossible. The timetable would have to be advanced.

They approached the San Felipe Church, making a show of quietly tending to the horses in case the guards at the gate looked their way. Dale and Morales were already in place. Manton tethered the horses and mules in back and stood guard over them. Three of the teams were already assembled in the church undercroft, three more were expected momentarily, and the final one of two within fifteen minutes. The priests gave them welcome food and drink. Now it just remained to wait patiently for the other teams. No one spoke much, but the tension was evident on the faces of the Spaniards. Juanita's violet eyes burned with something he could not quite identify, but it was not tension.

Father Domínguez told Pennywhistle the guard on the prisoners changed at midnight. The priests were supposed to accompany the guards to hear confessions and administer the final sacraments. Pennywhistle's men would stage the rescue just after the guard changed. The rear of the monastery backed onto a small stream. There was an old entrance there, used centuries before the river had silted up, barred by a rusty portcullis in some very decrepit masonry. The priests would come in the front way, drawing and holding the soldiers' attention; he and his men would come in the back.

Half an hour passed slowly. The final team of two failed to turn up. Pennywhistle fretted. The plan was already in motion and the time table could not be changed. They were not bad men, simply men who could not face another battle. It was frustrating, but not unforeseen. These were amateurs, after all; he counted himself lucky that most had not deserted. He would simply have to make do.

Two problems worried Pennywhistle. He could blow the magazine or lead the rescue, not do both. The powder magazine fronted on the main plaza and was far enough distant that it would necessitate him being absent from his new charges a bit too long. He alone had the requisite knowledge of explosives and fuses, but Partisan leadership was highly personal, and the Spaniards might waver in his absence. Partisans were far more likely to fight for A Man rather than A Rank. Also, once the French garrison had recovered from the shock of the explosion, they would immediately seek out the authors of their misery. He needed to give the French a focus for their anger and get them looking in exactly the wrong direction.

He decided he would not be missed for five minutes and unobtrusively turned command over to Dale. Dale merely nodded, his eyes showing he understood perfectly why Pennywhistle needed privacy. It was time to give *The Ritual* a quick outing and see what solutions presented themselves. Pennywhistle was no friend of organized religion, but churches were supposed to be places of mediation and reflection, and the main chapel of San Felipe would provide a spot to do just that.

It usually took him a good ten minutes to reach the state of deepest mediation, but necessity drove him to reach it this night in just under three. Usually the process was similar to gradually descending a winding mental staircase to a place of inner knowledge, but today it was as if he plunged over a high waterfall. He felt himself falling fast and hard into the maelstrom of foam and mist at its base. Such violent concentration would provoke a bad headache later. He saw the problems clearly, and several solutions began to emerge from the deep recesses of his mind. His eyes took in the extravagant garishness of the chapel, an oppressive mass of vulgarly gilded surfaces designed to showcase a heavily bleeding Jesus; his heightened hearing detected the sound of a mouse in the pew behind him. A plan suddenly sprang full blown into his mind. He frowned. He did not like the plan at all, but it just might work. He allowed there was a certain irony in it. He had limited faith in how the Spaniards might act if not under his direct command, yet he now must trust three of them enough to operate independently and carry out a design that required more than a little finesse.

******

Chef-de-bataillon Pierre LeClerc knew he was drinking too much, but he was worried. He quickly gulped one glass of the local red horse piss and angrily demanded another from the Taberna's bartender. As the garrison commander of Guijuelo, he needed to make sure that tomorrow morning's execution of the grandees went off without a hitch. Colonel Lazarette, arriving tomorrow to supervise the spectacle, was a man with absolutely no tolerance for error. LeClerc shuddered to think of his fate should even a small thing go wrong.

So far, things had gone well. The rescue attempt had been thwarted, although it bothered him that it had cost the French a bloody tactical reverse. He wondered about the tall Englishman in the scarlet jacket; just what was his connection with the Spanish militia?

Maybe the problem was things were going just a little too well. The evening was too uneventful. The Spaniards had *not* done anything hasty and foolish, which was out of character. He had really thought they might try something tonight. He had already talked to the three *afrancesados* he paid handsomely for information, but they had nothing for him. Damn those bloody Dagoes! They never came through when you needed them! What he wouldn't give for some reliable intelligence! He shook his head, pushed down his anger, and fretfully drained his glass.

The King's Scarlet

Morales and Juanita took shelter in the Widow Juárez's stout stone house just off the main plaza. The widow was yet another acquaintance Juanita had made as drover's daughter. Like Juanita, the wizened old widow despised all things French.

The small front window gave an excellent view of the powder magazine. The magazine was not purpose built, but housed in a circular two story brick building that Morales thought had started life as a church. Judging by the thickness of the brick work, the rounded arch over the entrance, and the tiny, slightly Byzantine windows, the edifice dated from the final years of Roman occupation. The structure was solid, inflammable, unobtrusive, and built to last; an excellent place to store powder. Morales calculated, based on Captain Pennywhistle's instructions, that many barrels of powder would be necessary to reduce the structure to rubble. He hoped it was crammed with powder. *Rather a shame*, thought Morales, *to wreck such a venerable structure*; but the lives of men counted for far more than a delicate appreciation of ancient architecture. Morales observed for a solid hour—not really enough time to establish the guard routine, but the best he could do. As he did so, Juanita knocked on numerous doors. She had the hardest task of all: convincing perfectly reasonable citizens to risk everything to rescue people they barely knew. He was relying on her magnetism and their hatred of the French.

Juanita approached each family with an instinctive blend of humility and fervour. She told them they mainly needed to create large clouds of smoke, not necessarily a huge blaze. Plug their flues, stoke their fires with green wood, and shout *Fire, fire!* at the top of their lungs with all the hysteria the French expected of Spanish peasants. They would then race into the streets with fire buckets and head to the old Moorish fountain in the plaza. The French would turn out the guard and probably pitch in. Juanita and Morales agreed a solitary peasant figure in a drab workman's cloak could probably slip by in all the confusion.

******

Pedro Valdez strode boldly into the *Taberna de los Tres Amigos*. He was merely a portly sergeant in Pennywhistle's little command, but a man with wide and varied connections in civilian life. The place was crowded tonight. A pall of tobacco smoke floated low over the dimly lit main room, and a buzz of low voices engaged in animated chatter assaulted his ears. The noise sounded like the very distant rumbles of thunder before a storm. An old man strummed a fast guitar and a young girl performed a sweeping flamenco dance on a small stage. She did it with great verve: plenty of clicking heels, flashing skirts, and snapping castanets. One French lieutenant, lust sparkling in his eyes, was paying attention, but nobody else. Everyone seemed preoccupied. All of the Spanish regulars were in attendance; most good men, but he spotted two shameless collaborators. Juanita had recommended one of them as a good conduit for disinformation.

The Spaniards were greatly outnumbered by French officers. The place was awash with blue and gold uniforms. The French appeared jolly, probably thinking that a long and hearty embrace of Bacchus's happy product might allow them to forget for a few fleeting moments that they were enduring an unwelcome posting to a country Bonaparte had called "the urinal of the planets."

Yet the jolliness was forced and brittle. Valdez felt a heavy undercurrent of tension and free-floating anxiety among the French officers, far beyond the normal disquiet of being in a country where they were roundly hated. The Englishman was right, realized Valdez. The French expected the Spanish to make some sort of forlorn, final gesture on behalf of the prisoners; probably inept but certainly bloody-minded and determined.

Well, he would give the French just what they needed to confirm their expectations.

He only needed to convince one man, but it had to be exactly the right man. He could use one of the collaborators, but hoped to cut out the middleman in spreading his disinformation. He scanned the crowd carefully. He was in luck. *Chef-de-bataillon* LeClerc, the garrison commander, red faced and feeling no pain, was among the celebrants tonight. As a coffee merchant, Valdez had done business with LeClerc and understood something of his excitable character. LeClerc had such disdain for the Spanish that it sometimes rendered his boastful tongue careless. Some might have called Valdez's interactions with LeCleric disloyal, but he always sold them the poorest beans and picked up handsome profits and much useful information. "'Tis an ill wind that blows nobody good" summed up Valdez's attitude.

"Don't go back to your inn, *monsieur*. Bad men are watching you. They are prepared and desperate. Go instead to the barracks, rouse your men, but proceed only there only with a heavy escort of your fellow officers," Valdez whispered conspiratorially to LeClerc from behind. LeClerc turned quickly round toward Valdez, a startled look on his crimson, bloated face.

"Since when have you developed such a great concern for my welfare, Valdez?" said LeClerc skeptically. "You sell me second rate coffee; you have always refused to sell me first rate information. Why the sudden change?"

"It is simple, *monsieur le chef*. Bloodshed is bad for business. Your death would provoke grim reprisals, end many innocent lives, and probably reduce my customer list to zero. You and I certainly have had our differences, yet for all that you are an essentially reasonable man with whom I can do business. Your successor would surely be far less understanding."

"There is a certain cynical logic to what you say, Valdez. I had hardly credited your people with such a straightforward appreciation of the realities of life. You race is, shall we say, quixotic."

"That may be true, *monsieur*, but we also have a highly developed instinct for survival, a legacy of our long struggle with the Moors. It is because of that instinct, I feel compelled to provide you with some further information you will find useful. It bothers me to tell you, but I have no wish to see this town bathed in blood because of a foolish and stupid enterprise that cannot possibly succeed. My countrymen have sadly failed to draw the proper lesson from this morning's encounter." Valdez shook his head slowly and sadly.

LeClerc laughed grimly in understanding. His eyes became hard, black dots. "Foolish and stupid seems to be a specialty of your people, Valdez. Pray tell, what do they have in mind for this evening?"

Valdez's face assumed the grave cast that LeClerc expected. He had planned his words carefully, but wanted to make them appear emotional and spontaneous. He spoke reluctantly, as if the words only emerged after a deep inner struggle. "There will be a second attempt to release the prisoners. A battalion of men are to approach from the North, along the Ramierz Road. They believe you will expect any rescue to come from the East, along the Alcázar Pike, and so, they anticipate achieving complete surprise. The attack is scheduled to begin at ten, and an English officer will be leading them."

LeClerc blinked twice in complete surprise and his wide mouth assumed the expression of a giant O. He had never expected this kind of information from Valdez, but his warning tallied perfectly with the kind of foolishness he expected from the Spaniards. He had been wondering if that cursed English officer would turn up again. His leadership would make the militia attack far more dangerous. But could this be a deception?

It was as if Valdez had read his mind. "I assure you, this is no trick," said Valdez with a deep, sad sigh. "I tell you this against my better judgment, but my humanity and allegiance to the Blessed Virgin demand that something drastic be done. Better a few armed men die than an entire village of innocents suffer retribution! Can you afford not to heed my words, *monsieur*?"

LeClerc rubbed his chin gently, thinking as deeply as his alcohol-fuddled brain permitted. If the man was lying, just trying to cause a nuisance, nothing would happen. But if he were telling the truth and LeClerc failed to act, the consequences could be dire. He had no wish to face the wrath of Colonel Lazarette. Besides, why would a merchant making a good living wreck his business by telling his chief customer a bald-faced lie?

"I will call out the guard, Valdez," LeClerc said gravely. "But if you are lying to me, I swear I will hunt you down and have you drawn and quartered."

Valdez's eyes widened involuntarily and he rocked back. He knew LeClerc meant his threat literally. But he was prepared to give his life for Spain, even if it were not on the battlefield. His soul, however, was another matter. He shuddered inwardly as he spoke the ultimate Catholic lie to sell his story. "I swear on the Virgin Mary's honor, I speak only the truth."

No Spaniard would sully the Virgin's honor, thought LeClerc. The cult of the Virgin Mary had an ironclad grip on the hearts of most Spaniards. The man must be telling the truth! LeClerc smiled wolfishly. Perhaps this night would be a productive one after all. He would bag the whole lot of Spanish rebels tonight, and the renegade Englishman as well. It would bring great advancement to his career. Yes, he decided, this would be a very fine night indeed!

******

Long after all hope had been given up for the last team, the two men confounded everyone by showing up at the huge church. There had obviously been some debate between them to judge by their faces, but Pennywhistle merely nodded pleasantly and asked no questions. They had made a difficult choice, one that might very well get one or both of them killed, and he would probably never know what had happened.

Sergeant Valdez returned and gave his report. He felt LeClerc had swallowed the bait completely. Pennywhistle liked the man's solid confidence: Morales had been right to recommend him. As an added benefit, Valdez spoke some English. Until Sergeant Morales returned, he would make Valdez his chief Spanish NCO.

Pennywhistle checked the Blancpain; exactly eleven—time to set things moving. Soon the prisoners would be released from cells to absolved before execution. The French did not like the priests but had enough residual respect for Catholicism to allow them to speak with the prisoners in privacy and confidence. Thanks to Valdez's misinformation, LeClerc was pulling guards away from the church. There was only a squad of guards left, and to have drawn this duty probably meant they were not the front line troops—the best would all be with LeClerc. The ones remaining would not be expecting anything to happen in the stone-walled confines of the old monastery.

Pennywhistle sent Manton ahead with the horses and mules to a seldom-used old stable on the edge of town. Father Dominquez and two old priests accompanied him, and one priest carried a small banner on a long pole with the symbols of St James. Any French about would deduce the animals were to be used in the parade that was a key feature of the festival in his name. The four had the hardest task of all: to simply wait.

The priests spent their time in silent prayer. Manton passed his time thinking about Juanita and wished he knew enough Spanish to draw her into conversation.

Upriver from the monastery, the militia pulled their muskets from the weapons cart and relieved them of lingering bits of straw. Dale had them use picks to make sure the vent holes were not blocked and did a quick inspection to make sure the barrels were clean and the locks free and clear. He told four of men to insert new flints; better now than take a chance in a fight. He had them all fix bayonets: the silence of cold steel was preferable to the report of a firearm. He checked to make sure all cartridge boxes were full; they might well need every single one in the days ahead.

Pennywhistle inspected the men. They nodded in assent as he passed by. They looked scared—normal and healthy enough—but also eager. They would be executed as outlaws if they failed, but if they succeeded, they would be rescuing their leaders and countrymen who were the core of the Spanish resistance. They greatly respected Pennywhistle, even if he was a foreigner. He was a professional, a sort of English El Cid, who had performed miracles in the earlier battle. Jesus had clearly laid his hand upon him. They had no reason to expect anything but complete success.

Valdez asked two men their particular tasks. They responded quickly and knowledgeably. It pleased Pennywhistle that Valdez was learning the right lesson about leaving nothing to chance.

Finally, the Spaniards boarded the punts and sat down. There was no talking or murmuring; everyone understood the importance of silence. Pennywhistle took the punt pole in one craft, Dale in the other. Not normally a task appropriate to either, but being part of the Royal Navy, they were the only two who knew anything about boats. Each punt towed a companion filled with men. The waters were dark, muddy, and surly. The current was barely perceptible, but flowed toward the monastery, to their advantage. The only thing that added cheer to the journey was the stunning radiance of the moon.

He spotted no French lookouts of any kind. Why patrol an unimportant stream that led nowhere? The bulk of the old monastery loomed up before him. The punts gently fetched up against a reed-lined bank. The men splashed ashore. There was still no talking.

Pennywhistle and Dale found the portcullis, which was indeed in an advanced state of disrepair. A few smart kicks from him and Dale would smash it down, but that was hardly their job, and it would deprive the militiamen of a chance to demonstrate some team spirit. The four Dale selected ran at it, turned sideways at the last second, and shoved violently. It separated easily from the decayed old masonry easily and crashed backwards. Pennywhistle moved inside the entrance and wrinkled his nose. The smell was rank and of things long dead. Something furry and not dead scurried past his feet.

He brushed aside some cobwebs and walked forward a few paces and a few centuries. He found the old stone stairway, its steps hollowed by a millennium of use. He walked slowly upwards through the darkness, operating more by touch than sight, until he found the door. The hinges were rusty and it would not take much to make it yield. So far, everything tracked. He had no reason to believe what lay on the other side of the door was anything other than he had been told. No light showed under it, confirming the entrance was not in current use.

He went back down and formed the men up. He and Dale would go through first, swords drawn. Ten men would follow, bayonets fixed, weapons unloaded, so no accidental discharge could give the alarm. Ten more would follow, a little later, with loaded weapons. Pennywhistle enjoined them to fire only upon his signal. It occurred to him that any guards at the end of the corridor would have their backs toward him. He would have his hands full with the freed Spaniards and could not afford any prisoners. He would do it efficiently; a split second jolt of pain, then darkness.

He applied a layer of tallow and beeswax to the door hinges as a lubricant. Without it, opening the door would make a loud, creaking noise straight out of a Gothic horror novel. He pushed hard on the door and it slowly swung open with nary a sound. The corridor was perhaps thirty yards long, narrow, dark, and empty. He listened for a minute, hearing nothing, his eyes gradually adjusting to the darkness. He turned to Dale close behind, tapped him once on the shoulder, then turned round and moved carefully forward, cutlass at the ready. Dale followed ten paces astern. Pennywhistle reached the end of the corridor and peered down a hall lit by uncertain, flickering torches.

He heard voices; Spanish voices. They were solemn, scared, and sad—what you would expect of people making their final confessions. He could make out the monks' cells, and saw only two French guards. He could see nothing of their faces, but their postures were slovenly. Prison guards generally had poor morale; no sane man welcomed the job, and those assigned it were often men who'd committed minor infractions of duty. Those who enjoyed it were generally bullies. The untimely demise of these two would, he suspected, go un-mourned by their superiors.

He sheathed his cutlass, then made hand gestures to Dale. He took off his cloak. No need to conceal his identity any longer. He was no spy, but a British serving officer. He removed his boots, drew his dirk, and held it in front of him. His movement was lithe and quick, a panther that had spotted his prey and closed for the kill.

The first guard heard nothing of his light-footed approach and moved not an inch. He was thinking idly of a woman when a hand clamped itself over his mouth. Another reached behind and jabbed a knife smartly into base of the skull where it joined the neck, severing the spinal cord neatly. He made no noise, and Pennywhistle caught his weight and lowered him to the floor. A duel had caused him to leave medical school in Edinburgh years ago, but his knowledge of anatomy had constantly proven useful in war. It was strange how knowledge of healing could be easily perverted to harm. At least the man had not suffered.

The second guard died in a similar fashion a minute later. Unlike the first, he made a gurgling sound, but he was just as dead. The Spanish voices grew louder and sadder. Pennywhistle detected the musk-like aroma of fear.

Dale went back down the corridor and brought the militiamen along. Dale's face was its usual mask, but the Spaniards looked at the dead bodies with awe. They were very glad the tall Englishman was on their side.

Dale handed Pennywhistle his boots. He put them on and prepared to enter the first cell. Fleetingly, he thought that, in a story, this would be the moment for a dramatic entrance and a speech that would sound suitably heroic to school children reading it a century hence. But this was no Covent Garden grand opera, just dirty, messy reality. His words would not be poetic.

Instead of bursting into the cell, he swung the door open slowly. There were six people inside, two priests and four civilians. The civilians were men in their forties and fifties and exceptionally well dressed, although their fine clothes were somewhat the worse for travel, rough handling, and imprisonment. Torn and dirty, their clothing showed they had been ill-used. He stepped into the wavering yellow light with a heavy tread and spoke in quiet but authoritative tones. "I am a British officer. Follow my instructions exactly and you will all live to see sundown tomorrow. Disobey or hesitate in the slightest, and I will abandon you to your fate." He hoped his Spanish was equal to the task.

Valdez entered the room. Pennywhistle thought he might help with translation and also hoped his confidence would reassure the frightened captives. The priests betrayed no surprise, but the civilians looked as if the Archangel Gabriel had just arrived. Shock and disbelief held court for the space of several breaths, then three smiled broadly, while one started to weep. They would not die tomorrow!

Pennywhistle eyed them carefully and chose the one with the most confident posture, a man named Vences. He gave a précis of his plans while the others listened. He told him only enough to let them know his scheme was clear and detailed.

"We have little time," he said, "and we must free the others." The priests stayed behind and took up the droning murmur of the confession rite. Any French guard who passed by would assume absolutions were still in progress. It was a thin ruse, but it might delay discovery; on the other hand, it could cost the padres their lives. The priests agreed willingly and crossed themselves. Faith again! He wished he understood it.

CHAPTER FIFTEEN

Twenty minutes later, all of the prisoners were moving. Juanita had been right yet again. The priests' foreknowledge and cooperation had proven essential: it was ultimately their confidence in Pennywhistle that had persuaded some of the prisoners that the rescue attempt was what it seemed, and not a cruel hoax intended to cheat them out of their devotions. As soon as they had been released, a low buzz of chatter erupted. His attempts to enjoin silence prevailed only for short intervals. They all wanted to talk to their fellows about they had been through. They had seen edge of the precipice, but had been miraculously delivered. A few reasserted their status as very important people. They had been utterly powerless until a few minutes before, and now they wanted control back.

Unhelpful, impractical suggestions rained upon his head and taxed his patience. He tried to listen and appear interested, as the British were naturally concerned with the grandee's on-going good will, but his diplomacy was unequal to it. These fools were wasting precious time. It was far harder to think with all of their chatter than it was with bullets buzzing about his ears. Their agitation caused them to speak so swiftly he only understood half of what was being said. He could lead or wet nurse them, he could not do both. He finally put Valdez in charge of them and simply said, "Shut them up." The grandees grumbled in resentment at being fobbed off on an underling, but Valdez rose to the task. He moved up and down the file of shambling aristocrats, flashing ready smiles, speaking a few pleasant words, and nodding often. After perhaps ten minutes, the babble had dropped to an occasional murmur.

Getting in had been easy, getting out, with 20 rescuees, would be less so. He and Dale carried out a quick reconnaissance. The monastery, Juanita had found out, housed a squad of soldiers as a garrison. There were too many to be disposed of stealthily, and he simply could not trust to luck and hope that their escape would go undiscovered. Damn, it looked as if gunplay would be necessary after all. He made a careful survey of the ancient walls. They were of stout construction, several feet thick. They would be highly effective sound dampeners. In a confined space, gunfire would be loud, but the noise would not carry far, and if Morales was doing his job, the French garrison outside would be preoccupied. The monastery guard were scattered; that was a problem. He needed to take them down in one fell swoop.

This was a task for the militiamen. It was their country after all, and they were full of fight. They had limited training and experience, but if he set it up right, they only had to fire one volley. He would have to make sure they did not take pent up frustrations on wounded Frenchman. They would either murder them out of hand or prolong their agony with torture. He grasped the savagery of war in the Peninsula, but he could not allow that to happen under his command. Besides, dead Frenchmen would be no distraction to any arriving troops, while wounded, ones pleading for help, certainly would be.

He picked out the ten men he thought would obey the difficult order to leave wounded enemy alive, and asked Valdez if the men knew how to perform a right wheel. Valdez said they did, although it would be ragged. It would have to do. He hoped surprise would outweigh their lack of training.

Swiftly, he got the men in position and had them lie down on the floor. They had been surprisingly quiet in their movements, giving nothing away. They were out of sight, at right angles to the main corridor. Then Dale doffed his cloak, drew his sword, and marched boldly down the hall. He saw a startled French soldier and shouted, "Here, you, yes you, you French windbag!" The Frenchman had no idea what Dale had just said, but its tone of challenge was unmistakable. Where the blazes had the Englishman come from; was he mad? He thought for a second his mind was playing tricks and blinked quickly. The Englishman was still there and steadily advancing. The look in the Englishman's eyes was ice and steel. He shivered at the prospect of facing him alone and began to yell for backup.

The shouts were heard, and ten Frenchmen ran down the hall, muskets poised and bayonets fixed. They stopped alongside the man who had given the alarm. What the hell? A lone Englishman with malice in his eye in a monastery in the middle of the night? Just like the first man, they could scarcely credit their eyes. They debated quickly; kill, or capture? Killing would be easy, but it would leave a great mystery. Their superiors did not like mysteries. Better to let higher ups have the worry. They would take him alive.

No NCO was around, so the group advanced hesitantly, in a ragged line, bayonets leveled. They hoped against hope that the Englishman would miraculously see reason and surrender. The Englishman raised his sword arm above his head. There would be a fight. Perhaps the mad Englishman sought blue suicide.

In one quick, smooth movement, the Englishman sheathed his sword, fell forward onto his hands and dropped to the ground. The rapid movement caused the Frenchmen to halt.

Pennywhistle ordered the Spaniards to their feet. "By the right wheel, march!" The line of shouldered muskets swung like a door hinge out into the hall. "Make ready," They brought their muskets to the vertical position and there was a loud "click" as they full cocked them. Their targets were less than twenty yards away, jumbled together. "Present." The muskets were leveled. "Aim low." He was not sure of the Spanish equivalent of the last command. At least they got the idea. Their muskets were pointed low and their rounds would probably take the Frenchmen in the chest. "Fire!"

It sounded like thunder in the narrow corridors. The hall imprisoned the smoke and everyone coughed from the brimstone smell. He heard moaning at the end of the hall. As the smoke dissipated, they saw the French line was down. Most were dead, but two moved slightly and made low, animal noises. The threat was gone.

******

Morales checked the timepiece Pennywhistle had given him. Just after midnight; time to start things rolling. He had neither the time nor ballistics education for any systematic job of demolition. The best he could manage would have to be quick and dirty. At best, he might have five minutes to set the fuses.

The magazine guards looked bored and stupid. It took them a full minute to respond when they saw thick thunderheads of smoke billowing down the street and heard the frantic shouts of the peasants. They had split a bottle of rum earlier, and it was taking effect.

Peasants from other homes saw and smelled the smoke and flooded the streets. Juanita's instructions were followed with glee. The peasants loved the idea of tricking the hated French. The town had lain under a yoke of tension and fear, and the energy expended running around like panicked chickens was a great release. Even children joined, unsure of what was happening but treating it like some street carnival. From somewhere distant a bugle sounded, and a few French soldiers began appearing. The guards left their posts and ambled slowly down the street to investigate.

Now! Morales dashed across the street and flew through the magazine entrance. He looked at his watch and noted the time. He had to make every second count; the guards could return at any moment. The powder would be on the lowest level. Morales pelted down the stairs and came to a solid oak door that had no lock. He threw it open and entered. The low, groin-vaulted ceiling overlay a room filled with at least three hundred barrels of powder. Excellent! More than enough to do the job. He scanned the room for a place fuses might be stored. It was hard to see; the heavily shielded lantern he carried was a wise precaution, but it gave poor light and cast peculiar shadows.

He left his boots at the door of the cellar; there was always the danger of a boot heel generating an unwanted spark. He found a battered walnut bureau with many compartments that looked like it belonged to the chief armorer and frantically rifled through its many compartments. At last, he found an array of fuses in the bottom drawer, all color coded to signify burn times. He looked at them but had no way to puzzle out the codes. He would simply use as many as possible and only discard the shortest ones. A multitude of fuses reduced the problem of duds. He decided five should do the job; probably too many, but he knew Pennywhistle counted on this diversion and he simply could not fail.

He found a big axe in the corner and took solid swings at ten barrels. The energy of fear, tension, and joy flowed through his arms and multiplied the solid, smashing force of the blows. The barrel staves creaked, cracked, and ruptured and powder cascaded onto the floor. It was all very messy. He laid out the fuses as French and Spanish shouts from the street grew steadily louder and more mixed. He bent down and lit the fuses with his flint and striker. The fuses hissed into life, like slow, malicious snakes.

He spun away from the fuses, grabbed his boots, and bounded up the stairs. He forced on the boots and dashed into the night, panting and stumbling. His heart pounded and his feet raced over the cobblestones. Suddenly, the brightness of midday lit up the night. A giant fist knocked him to the pavement. A great noise followed, roaring, a second later.

CHAPTER SIXTEEN

The faces of LeClerc's two hundred men paled, then grew mottled with fury when the huge explosion rocked the night sky. They had waited stealthily for two hours for the Spanish rescuers to appear and absolutely no one had materialized. Now thunder, flames, and eerily illuminated plumes of smoke blossomed half a mile away. *"Merde, merde, merde,"* snarled LeClerc. That bloody Dago had tricked him! He should have known better! There would be hell to pay when Lazarette arrived. He ordered his men to double quick toward the magazine. It was all he could do. He fervently prayed he could salvage something from this night's debacle, but he was not optimistic.

******

Morales' back and chest ached. His head felt as if it were a bell pealing. His legs hurt and his hands were badly scraped. That he felt anything at all, told him he had not lost consciousness. He moved slightly and inventoried himself. Everything seemed in working order, if slow. He sat up and shook his head a few times. He was dazed and his hearing was muted, but his vision was intact. Juanita looked down at him, her face contorted with worry and concern. The edge of her skirt had burn marks, but she looked healthy. His brain was functional enough to feel relief.

He struggled slowly to his feet. The powder magazine lacked a roof, was one story shorter, but much of the blast had been funneled upward and the ground floor could be salvaged. Still, the damage to the town was substantial. Flames and smoke poured into the night sky. Several peasants lay dead, partly covered with debris. One was a child. A few scarecrows in rags stumbled about, no longer resembling townsmen. French soldiers at the far end of the street performed a survey of the damage. He wished he had gotten things right, but he could not be said to have gotten things wrong. It was time to go, before more French soldiers pounded up, as they would surely do. He heard the melancholy alarm of fire bells.

He decided to make directly for the monastery, trusting that Pennywhistle had completed the rescue. He and Juanita shambled along, picking up speed as coordination returned with each step. Juanita walked behind, a one woman rearguard against further harm. The unnecessary death of innocents saddened him, but stiffened his resolve to make sure their unexpected sacrifice was not in vain. Whatever else happened tonight, the French had lost a great deal of their fire power.

******

Pennywhistle had been peering out the half-open oak door of the monastery for five minutes when he heard the loud explosion and the shouts and fire bells that followed after. He checked his Blancpain. 12:30; right on time. He smiled slightly in relief. He had been right to trust Morales and Juanita! The diversion had worked, but things could unravel quickly. He went back inside, dashed down the hall, and issued orders.

Five minutes later, the procession was on the move. He and Dale marched in front, followed by half the militiamen. Valdez and the grandees came next, and the other half of the militia brought up the rear. The grandees behaved themselves and moved in silence. Pennywhistle reviewed the speech he would give at the stable. He doubted they would like it, but they would have no choice but to accept his verdict or allow themselves to be recaptured by extremely irate French soldiers. At least the weather was good and clear, and the full moon gave excellent illumination.

He could hear French shouts as his little column marched, but they were very faint, at least half a mile away. Morales and Juanita came racing up the street, broad smiles of relief on their faces. Pennywhistle was delighted to see them, but less delighted when they both insisted on giving him hearty hugs of congratulation.

Señor Vences had been particularly outspoken earlier, so Pennywhistle put him in charge of the grandees. He appeared to command respect from the others, and Pennywhistle had neither the time nor inclination to convene some impromptu forum to determine the best leader among them. He had done all he could for them and had endangered his own mission by doing so. It was time for them to be on their own. He might have taken the most important rescuees to Wellington's headquarters, but he had no idea who they were. It was best to return them whence they came and let them do their jobs. He would suggest, however, they head south, toward General Hill's small army. With luck and a little prudence, they should be able to avoid any French patrols.

They reached the stable and things were ready. Now was the time to drop the bombshell. He gathered everyone round. He spoke crisply in a severe command voice that brooked no argument. Internally, he struggled to keep the conflicted emotions he felt safely manacled. "Listen carefully. I will not be going with you. I—" A collective gasp stopped him. Looks of disbelief blossomed and people turned to each other in shock and confusion. How could the indispensable man desert them?

Juanita's eyes fixed his gaze. They blazed with angry disappointment. Morales and Valdez looked like children who had just been told there would be no Christmas.

It shook his composure, but he struggled manfully on. "I have made plans for your safety. Follow them, and you will see your loved ones again. I will give your leader this," he held aloft four golden guineas, "to purchase the food and drink you need. The horses and mules are yours, a gift of my government. I do this because of duty, not from any lack of regard for you. I am badly needed by Lord Wellington, and cannot violate my oath and honor by remaining any longer." Some nodded; Spaniards understood the idea of personal honor.

He looked through the crowd and locked his eyes onto Vences. "Señor Vences will be my replacement. He is one of your own leaders and he has my complete trust and confidence." The last part was a lie, but he could not let the crowd know that. Vences was surprised. His furtive eyes blazed like two black holes burned in a blanket, but he recovered quickly. His chest swelled, and he broke into a mirthless smile. He was finally being accorded his due.

Pennywhistle addressed the grandees. "The militiamen will escort you. The militia will ride the mules; you, the horses. You will all have to ride two to each mount. Celerity is important; everyone must be well clear of Guijuelo long before dawn and French reinforcements arrive. Sarn't Morales will be in charge. Sarn't Valdez will be his second. I will leave it to Señor Vences to decide when to release the militiamen and allow them to return to their homes."

He paused for a second, and favored the militiamen with an approving look. "I wish to congratulate you for your gallant conduct today. You have brought great honor to Spanish arms, and it has been a privilege to command you."

The militiamen smiled with pleasure at the compliment. He was happy they were all still alive to enjoy the accolades. He had brought them pride, success, and glory and knew they would be sorry to left to their own devices. He hoped this show of confidence would fuel their determination to protect the grandees, even if it did nothing to ease his conscience for abandoning them.

"I will speak with Señor Vences, then take my leave of you." He was about to wish them good luck and Godspeed, but the Spanish salutation was better. "*Vaya con Dios*." He saw tears in some Spanish eyes. He wondered how an entire people could wear their hearts on their sleeves. It struck him as odd that their sympathies and alleged devotion to God had done nothing to mitigate the savagery of war here. Perhaps the Moors had left a more lasting legacy here than he thought. The Peninsular War had many elements of Islamic jihad.

The crowd reluctantly accepted his words. They understood the Englishman had to follow orders, and they had no reason to expect that the provision he had made for them was anything less than the best he could manage. He had provided a military escort, as well as horses, mules, and gold to pay their expenses. English gold had a bewitching effect on those used to fluctuating paper currency.

Men vigorously clapped him on his shoulders, smiled brightly, and shook his hand heartily as he moved through the crowd. It added to his feeling of guilt. While he spoke to Vences, Manton matched grandees to horses and militiamen to mules. Vences was more intelligent than Pennywhistle had first thought and appeared to readily grasp details. He told him little enough, and it was all true, except for one consideration. He said he was taking a more circuitous route than the one he had actually chosen. If the man were captured he might be compelled to talk, but he would send the French off on a fruitless quest.

Vences solemnly thanked the Englishman for choosing him and said he knew many who would help on the route ahead. Pennywhistle cut him short with a flourish of his round coachman's hat and made a quick courtly bow, signifying the audience was at an end. He spun on his heel and walked away, leaving Vences smiling uncertainly, not quite sure if he had been complimented or rudely dismissed.

The Englishman felt reassured, but an angry Juanita shattered his equanimity. She stomped up to him in a fury of indignation. "No, no, no, I will not go with them. It is not right, it is not your destiny; it is not God's plan. He has chosen me to help you and I cannot leave your side." Her fire subsided and her voice changed oddly, as if another identity spoke through her. It was calm, but steadfast of purpose. "If I leave you, you will die."

CHAPTER SEVENTEEN

Colonel Lazarette was furious, but his voice was clipped and barely rose above a menacing whisper; his sentences studded with jagged icicles of sarcasm. *"On t'a bercé trop près du mur, LeClerc?"*—As a child, was your cradle rocked too close to the wall?—he asked contemptuously. *"Vous avez le cervau d'un sandwich au fromage!"*—You have the brain of a cheese sandwich—he continued derisively. *"Tu es bêtes comme tes pieds"*—You are as smart as the bottom of your feet—he concluded with disdain.

"You had a simple job to do, LeClerc, and you bungle it. I arrive ready to make a very public point with these Spanish clods, and I find everything in chaos." Colonel Lazarette's voice continued coldly, but his face began to flush a deep red, betraying a passionate Gascon heritage that long years of service had not entirely disciplined. "Your powder is destroyed, the prisoners have escaped, and you have done nothing to recapture them! A callow, first-year subaltern could have done better than you—a field grade officer. I can tell you this: Marshal Marmont will not be pleased. If you have any thought of salvaging your wreck of a career, you will tell me what I need to know immediately."

LeClerc blanched and stammered. "Yes, yes, of course, Colonel." LeClerc had given the Empereur ten years of solid, reliable service and had never received such a dressing down. Then again, he'd never earned one before, and there was no doubt he was being served his desserts.

Marcel Lazarette always got what he wanted and never suffered fools gladly. His splendid uniform was a perfect accompaniment to an outsized personality. The expensively tailored outfit flattered his solidly muscled, powerfully built figure. He was of medium stature—cavalrymen were rarely of great height—but the beautifully tailored uniform created the illusion of someone considerably taller.

He wore the uniform of a colonel of hussars. His circular bearskin busby was anchored to his jaw by a gilt chinstrap and featured a red and green plume, two cords of gold in a u shape across the front, and a red, hanging bag top. His navy blue dolman jacket was closely fitted and heavily gilded, with cherry red collars and cuffs. The jacket had ten, chest wide horizontal rows of gold braid, five silver buttons in each row. A large rectangular splash of gold adorned each side of the jacket. The tunic underneath was crimson. A red and gold sash circled his waist and a sapphire blue pelisse, fringed in fur, clung to his right shoulder. His riding gauntlets were of the finest, softest brown leather.

His skin-tight trousers were also cherry red, and had five overlapping gold cloth lozenges covering each thigh. The inside seams of the trousers were reinforced with brown leather. His boots were black, trimmed with gold tassels, and stretched to just below the knee.

Because of the brightness of the trousers, his regiment of hussars had been nicknamed "The Cherrybums" by the British.

The uniform was gaudy, but it did not in any way make the owner seem a circus figure. People could never quite pin it down, but they sensed a Faustian presence in the bright attire.

Perhaps it was the oversized handle bar mustache, although that was a common enough conceit among hussar officers. It was not so much the mustache itself, as the arrogance with which the owner wore it. Matched with thick, beetling eyebrows, piercing, deep-set eyes, and high cheekbones, the mustache seemed to flare, like a bull walrus'. It was not a handsome face, yet it was a memorable one; alive with unusual planes and angles an artist would have found compelling. A two-inch scar below the right earlobe completed the impression of someone hard and dangerous.

Lazarette could be bluff, expansive, vulgar, refined, angry, and jolly, all in the space of a few minutes. In other words, a typical hussar, albeit one of high rank: volatile emotions and loads of dash. Moreover, he hailed from Gascony, a region of France famed for birthing great soldiers with dramatic personalities. Bonaparte himself had once proclaimed, "Give me an army of real Gascons and I will cross a hundred leagues of hell."

What most failed to note was that this typical hussar exterior masked a very atypical brain. It was brilliant, cold, calculating, and ruthlessly logical. He liked the fact that his public persona and garish uniform caused both soldiers and civilians to underestimate him. They did so at their peril, and he cunningly exploited their misapprehensions.

Lazarette had expected to supervise an execution with plenty of pomp and circumstance meant to overawe the Spanish peons and quell any nascent rebels. He had worn his dress uniform and brought banners and a band. He had with him two companies of hussars and a full battalion of light infantry to provide a suitable official backdrop for the mass execution. His men were to have formed the firing squad.

Now it was all a shambles. He would fix it. That's what he did, solve problems. He did not think himself cruel, just superbly efficient. The Spanish saw things differently; they regarded him less as a problem solver than a problem eliminator. He quite liked the fact that the Spaniards were afraid of him. They nicknamed him "El Castigador," the Punisher, because of his swift and brutal retaliations against Spanish villages. He had a large price on his head, and it amused him. He followed its rise the way a man might follow stocks. You could tell a lot about a man by the hatred he inspired in his enemies.

It took him a while to piece together what had happened, and even then the information was sketchy and the picture confusing. The magazine explosion had been no accident, but part of a plan he had to admit was clever. It would not have fooled him, of course, but with an oaf like *Chef-de-bataillon* Leclerc in charge, it had worked well. You could pull all sorts of tricks on a garrison soldier that would never work on a field officer. The one survivor of the guards at the monastery was sure about the two Englishmen. The exceptionally tall one in a red coat, a captain, had directed everyone, the wounded fusilier said. Lazarette did not doubt him; the Englishman sounded a resourceful leader, one after his own heart.

It had to be the same officer that headquarters wanted. He had something they needed, something valuable. Maybe it was something he carried, or something he knew; in any event, Marshal Marmont had made it clear he wanted the man taken alive. The Englishman had eluded capture repeatedly, despite a massive combined arms sweep. He was believed to have fought in a small engagement early yesterday in which the French received a sharp defeat. French soldiers had remarked on the furious figure in the scarlet coat. Certainly Spanish militia could not have pulled off that smart little victory without outside assistance. It all tracked with the cleverness of last night's escape; squabbling, poorly led Spaniards could never have accomplished it. They were little better than stupid, brainless pigs, and like pigs, good only at rutting.

His primary task was to recover the prisoners and assure their deaths in some public venue, although it might be necessary to kill them on the spot once he overtook them. He would track and extirpate the Spanish cockroaches, and he would apprehend this intriguing British officer. Whatever he had or knew was considerably more important than a few more dead Spanish notables. Lazarette cocked his head in thought. He doubted this resourceful officer was actually English; the *Roastbifs* were thick-headed, hide-bound, phlegmatic or choleric, never truly sanguine. It was only the Norman-English, or the Norse-descended, or the Celtic tribes who ever showed true élan or greatness of soul.

The English officer was a real soldier, not a pretend one like LeClerc or the brutish amateurs who were the Spanish militia. His conspicuous gallantry in yesterday's battle had advertised his presence in a contemptuous way. He had exposed himself in battle while on a mission of secrecy, positively sneering at French efforts to capture him. That sort of arrogance intrigued Lazarette. It would be an exciting challenge to stalk, capture, and interrogate him. He had led the French a merry chase, but he would not escape Marcel Lazarette. It would be another personal triumph in a career full of them. He was up for promotion, and this was the very thing to assure it.

He wondered if the famous British stoic resolve would stand against his methods of extracting information. He wanted see what sort of man this officer was when there was no chance for heroics. He had piqued Lazarette's curiosity. What was the point of having extraordinary abilities if you only were pitted against dull, unworthy opponents? It would be a pleasure to face a truly formidable antagonist and put his own considerable skills to a real test.

It was nearly 9 am. The prisoners had a lead of many hours, and they had horses and mules, which made catching up with them more difficult, even as it made tracking them so easy as to be a task for children. He would deploy cavalry to race on ahead and fix them in place until the infantry arrived. He had two companies of hussars, roughly two hundred and eighty men. He could divide them evenly to cover all three roads, but that would dissipate their strength and seemed a crude approach—the method of a mindless man. No, he would make a logical deduction and deploy most of them on one road. He had to get inside the Englishman's head.

He prided himself on his orderly thinking. It was the concomitant of his experienced professionalism. The Englishman certainly was a thoroughgoing professional and probably thought that way as well, so he asked himself, *What would I do?* He looked at the maps again. The Englishman would want to take the quickest route toward safety: that road toward Los Lobos. Yes, that town was the logical destination.

Lazarette was sure he had things right. He summoned his aide, Captain Chaumette.

"I want both companies mounted and ready to move within the hour. See that the men have ammunition and provisions for three days."

Chaumette saluted crisply. "Of course, Colonel." Chaumette was briskly efficient. Two years with the colonel had taught him good work brought quick reward, just as botched work brought swift punishment.

Lazarette's route selection was partly correct. It was the road the fugitives had taken. But he could not know Pennywhistle was no longer with them. He would find that out soon enough, but for now, the Englishman had gained a little time.

******

Pennywhistle, Dale, Manton, and Juanita stopped at a tiny hamlet just after dawn, 4 leagues away from the Grandees and the militia headed to Los Lobos. They needed rest, and now that they were no longer in the mountains, night travel was safest.

The place bore the welcoming name *El* Corazón, the heart, and was but a dot on the map.

It was the circling hawks that first alerted Pennywhistle. He recognized them as carrion feeders. The stench drew him on.

They rode into an eerily silent necropolis, deserted and in ruins. Stray weeds blew down the arid main street. The few buildings had been blasted apart and most of the inhabitants murdered. No one had done anything to clean up the mess. It reeked of death, and bodies lay rotting on the hardened dirt thoroughfare. All of the bodies bore signs of predation. Crows had plucked out most of the eyes.

Dogs scattered at their approach but did not move too far off. They had clearly been feeding on the corpses. He guessed they were domestic animals turned feral. They were always more dangerous than wild dogs because they knew man and did not fear him. It was time to put some fear into them. He stopped and dismounted, then shot two of the more aggressive. Dogs were pack animals and he wanted to establish himself as a dominant male, a dangerous beast superior to anything in the pack. The dogs ran off howling. He had bought perhaps a day's respite, but he told everyone to keep a sharp eye out for their return.

He carefully examined one corpse and his woodsman's eye detected an unexpected shape to the bite marks. Wolves! They usually avoided humans, but played havoc with corpses and unattended horses. They always came at night, and since the sun was up, they were no danger for now. Still, if they stayed, he would have to keep the horses close.

Juanita said it reminded her of Sodom and Gomorrah after the Lord's wraith. *Typical*, thought Pennywhistle. The Lord had at least wiped things clean with his fire; the authors of this ghastly massacre were very, very human. The animals were merely doing what their natures demanded and cleaning it up.

He wondered what these poor devils had done to merit obliteration. El Corazón was a town with its heart cut out.

He directed Dale and Manton to find a sheltered spot for their camp, one that could be defended against dogs. He told them to take Juanita with them since he wanted to spare her any more grisly sights. Alone, he walked down the street, looking at the human remains. He had seen far worse on the *Bellerophon* at Trafalgar. He spotted two hogs chewing on a child's body. He fired the Ferguson at fifty yards and shot the first sow in the head. Her companion ran squealing off. He reloaded rapidly and killed the second pig at eighty yards. Last night's exertions had left him with a ferocious appetite, and he expected it was the same with the others. It was a repellent thing to do, but the need for survival trumped his sensibilities. He walked over and carefully covered the dead child's body before calling Dale over. Dale came running up and promptly began to dress the meat.

It was a terrible, inhospitable place to stop, repulsive to any human in his right mind, which was precisely why it was so safe. The French had come and gone, the inhabitants were dead or fled; it was a place no one would think to look. Even if they thought to, or were so ordered, the search of such an abattoir would be cursory at best.

He decided to explore what was left of the town. As he walked, he considered. Staying indoors afforded better defensive possibilities against the feral dogs, but staying the night in this terrible place might be a bad idea—both for their morale and because it was unwise to remain in any one spot for too long. A few homes were intact and might have beds in which they could snatch a few hours rest, then move on. He went into three of the most promising, one by one, and made a thorough inventory. Two of the homes had been looted, and only fragments of furniture remained. The way things lay, smashed and broken, seemed to indicate the French had been more concerned with vengeance than plunder. He could almost feel traces of a lingering, violent anger. In the second home, he saw a rag doll in the corner. Its head had been wrenched off. He wondered about the fate of its owner. A lonely crucifix clung to the kitchen wall. Faith had not defended them from the French.

The third home was intact, complete with beds, linen, and even cooking utensils. It looked well tended, save for two weeks of accumulated dust. There was a kitchen table and four chairs, rough peasant furniture, but quite whole. The French must have gotten bored with their depredations. There were no traces of blood, unlike the other homes. Perhaps the family had fled early. There was even a pleasant smell; some decayed lilacs in a crude earthen vase. It was a great relief after the sickly smell of putrefaction that suffused the streets.

He sat down at the table. He closed his eyes to think. He put his head back and stretched out his feet. It felt good not to be sitting on a horse. He jerked his head back upright. He had fallen asleep! That would never do; he needed to be alert and thinking. He was thirsty. The kitchen had a jug full of some rotgut spirits, but he wanted none. Coffee, that's what he needed. Yes, hot and luxurious, a splendid idea. Manton still had a few beans for his hand grinder in the saddlebag. He leapt up, energized with the prospect, and dashed out the door and back to Manton. Manton looked dubiously at the few beans he had left. He said he could either manage one strong cup or two weak ones, but that would be the end of the beans.

"Make it one," sighed Pennywhistle. He handled most hardships stoically, but the prospect of being deprived of the blessed nectar for even a short time seemed a cruelty beyond measure. Yet another sacrifice for King and Country!

While Manton made coffee and Dale cut the gammon steaks, Pennywhistle walked with Juanita. He knew it was a mistake to have taken her along, but he had assumed she would want to go with her own people and had been unprepared for her defiance and almost holy certitude of purpose. He had repeatedly taken the easy, coward's way out because he had not had enough energy to dispute with her at the time. A sterner man would have rid himself of her long ago. He had no idea what to do with her, but an expedient part of him argued she had indeed proven useful in unexpected ways. He was procrastinating, he knew, but promised himself he would figure things out when they made it to the safety of Wellington's headquarters.

He decided to show her something pleasant after the horror of the town. She was bearing up well, but it could not be easy. He took her inside the unscarred home and showed her the kitchen. He got her talking about cooking, and she seemed content to ripple on about it. Cooking gave her something to focus on in the midst of all of this death. She simply could not understand why the English tolerated such bland food when there were so many different types of peppers available. She checked the cupboards and found a number of spices. She said she could use them to make the ham tastier. She was very practical and always thinking how to be useful.

An hour later, everyone sat down around the intact table to a wonderful breakfast of ham steak enhanced by paprika and oregano, and some reasonably fresh bread that had been a gift from the priests in Guijuelo. Juanita picked some fresh peaches, which were a splendid counterpoint to the ham. Manton and Dale consumed a salvaged bottle of inoffensive mistela and Juanita drank cool water brought from the one well the French had neglected to poison. Pennywhistle savoured his hot, bracing coffee. There was little talking, and they ate with quiet relish. When they finished, everyone sighed and sat back, enjoying a moment of fleeting, false domestic bliss.

Perhaps drawn by the scent, an orange tabby cat materialized from one of the rooms and began meowing loudly for food and attention at the foot of Pennywhistle's chair. He fed her a few bites of ham. His hand began to stroke her idly, and she started to purr. It was strangely soothing, reminding him of pleasanter days back home. He meant to close his eyes for only a second, but it felt so good not to open them again.

His companions at the table smiled as he nodded off into sleep, half the cup of coffee still before him. They saw no point in disturbing him. He had earned it.

CHAPTER EIGHTEEN

It was a deep, deep sleep that comforted, restored, and renewed. He remembered no specific dreams, merely fleeting impressions, but they had all been good and left him with a feeling that all things were possible. He awoke gradually, like rising up to the sun after having swum through a sea of fleecy clouds. He felt bathed in white, luxurious softness. It took him a few seconds to realize he was in a feather bed with clean linens that smelled lightly of lemon. His head was on a pillow, not a rock. He opened his eyes slowly and held his hands up to his face, a rote action. What he saw surprised him. There were no flea bites. Fleas were a great problem in beds found in Spanish inns.

It took him a few seconds to realize he was not in a Spanish inn, and even longer to recall where he was. He was still in the home where he had eaten breakfast, but he had no idea how he came to be in a bed. The solution came to him and he smiled. He saw his coat hanging on a nearby chair. Manton must have brushed it. The window was open and a pleasant breeze wafted in. It surprised him that it was not fetid, but carried the scent of mulberry trees. The wind must have shifted. Years spent at sea made him very conscious of wind.

By the light, it must be early afternoon. He had probably been out for four or five hours. They had thought he needed rest and they had been right. He stretched luxuriously, and a part of his mind said a few more minutes of languor would not be out of line. Then another part of his mind shouted at him: Something is wrong! Something is off, attend to it!

He sat up, wide awake, his senses on high alert. He saw nothing out the window that was out of the ordinary, but his senses continued to scream at him. He quietly donned his boots and drew his cutlass, but his trusty Ferguson was nowhere in sight. That alarmed him. It was his most valuable possession and he always kept it close. He hoped Manton had taken it for cleaning. He listened intently. He walked to the bedroom door, ducked his head—the frame was not designed to accommodate his six-foot two-inch physique—and was about to open it when he abruptly froze.

It was the absence of noise he noticed. No birds, no small creatures, no insects; no singing, chattering, or chirping. Even in this town of death, there had been the background chorus of wildlife, now all was silent. Well, not quite. He heard a scratching noise at the foot of the door. The tabby he had petted earlier managed to paw it open. The cat bounded over to him and began energetically meowing and rubbing herself about his ankles. She stopped after thirty seconds, apparently feeling her message was not getting through. She turned, arched her back, and hissed menacingly in the direction she had come. It seemed Nature would not stop sending dire warnings.

Pennywhistle quietly closed the half open bedroom door to the point that only a sliver of light passed between it and the doorframe. He peered through the tiny opening into the kitchen and listened closely. He heard a low rumble of voices with definite hostile undertones. They were speaking in both Spanish and French, which struck him as odd. The voices gradually grew louder and more distinct. He heard loud thumping and boots entered the kitchen. Now he could make out what the men were saying. They were debating what to do with the prisoners. One group wanted to shoot them now, another later, after they had provided information. When he heard one man say, *Kill these pigs immediately, we don't know English*, his blood froze. He stealthily opened the door just a tiny bit wider for a better view, and his worst fears were realized.

Pennywhistle could make out five of them standing in the kitchen. They were, dirty, ragged, and scruffy. All had bad teeth, and all carried carbines. Their faces showed not a trace of kindness or mercy and bore many scars; these were hard men positively eager for trouble. They wore leftovers of what might have been uniforms, some French, some Spanish, but that was in a former existence. French and Spanish working together left but one conclusion.

They were scavengers. Probably deserters who had leagued together and found it profitable to enrich themselves by plunder in the no man's land between armies. Every war spawned these human jackals, but the brutal nature of the guerrilla war in Spain was generating them more rapidly than usual. Pennywhistle could just make out that two of them had their weapons pointed directly at Manton and Dale.

Manton and Dale were unarmed; quiet but with defiance on their faces. The scavengers continued to argue about their fate. Juanita was nowhere around, and he hoped fervently she was safe; he had to act quickly before these scoundrels did something precipitate. It was only a matter of a few feet and he could probably take two with the cutlass, but the other three were problematic. Dale and Manton would react, of course, but they had only their fists.

Juanita decided things. She came out of nowhere and silently opened the outside door. The loud arguing blanked out her approach. She stepped into the kitchen, full cocked and raised the Ferguson to her shoulder. The men turned in shock at the click sound; they knew exactly what it was. The sight of a girl with a weapon confounded them for the critical moment.

Her expression was one of focused hatred. She held the rifle like a professional, seated hard against her shoulder. There was no uncertainty or hesitation. It was point blank range, less than ten feet, but she used the V sights. Speculation changed to certainty in Pennywhistle's astonished mind: she had seen service with the partisans. Certainly, she had observed him loading the unusual weapon. She pulled the trigger and the weapon slammed back against her shoulder. There was a boom that resounded in the closed space and one man's head exploded in spray like a rotten watermelon hit with a cudgel.

The rest of the brigands froze in shock, but Pennywhistle acted. He slammed open the bedroom door, cutlass held close his side, and rushed at the center man.

Dale and Manton spied Pennywhistle and took their cues from him immediately. They jumped at their oppressors, batting their carbines aside and knocking them to the floor. They struck out with their fists before the brigands could even begin recover the weapons. The sergeant and servant rained blow after blow on the two scavengers, Dale much more expertly and brutally than Manton. Not surprising; Dale had had a reputation as a bare knuckle fighter before entering the Service. Dale blocked a flailing left hook and executed a smashing right cross to his opponent's lantern jaw: a hammer crushing an eggshell. The man collapsed on the floor like a limp dishrag. Manton's opponent put up more spirited resistance. He was a giant of a man, four inches taller than Manton's six feet, and he knew how to use his fists.

The momentum of Pennywhistle's running approach forced the cutlass through the scavenger's chest and out his back, spitting him against the wall. The scavenger wheezed oddly, the sound of air leaving a balloon, as life deserted him. The man next to him tried to wield his carbine as a club, but the marine sidestepped neatly and slammed the heavy brass clamshell guard upwards under the man's chin, actually lifting him off the floor. The man fell heavily to the floor. He still breathed but did not move.

Manton staggered from a punch to the chin, but a rifle butt to the back of the head brought down his giant opponent. Juanita again! The expression on her face was fearsome, and she continued to slam the butt into the man's head as he lay on the floor. Pennywhistle was not sure which of the blows killed him, but the back of the man's head was a mushy pulp by the time he was able to grab her and stop her. Brain matter leaked from fissures like oatmeal. She struggled for a second, and then went limp in his arms, exhausted and shaken, but unrepentant.

Manton smiled a smile of gratitude toward her. She had probably just saved his life. He had never seen an avenging angel in action before.

Pennywhistle had never seen an avenging angel, either. He had never underestimated anyone so consistently. He'd had no idea she was capable of the wrath of a Fury. Juanita walked over to the corner, crossed herself, and began moving her lips in silent prayer.

Three men were dead, but two lived: unconscious, damaged, but their wounds were far from lethal. Manton, Dale, and Juanita looked at them and then looked gravely at Pennywhistle. He nodded with resignation. He did not like it, not one bit. But there was nothing else to be done. He was the leader, it was his job. He could not permit anyone to endanger his people or his mission.

He had no idea where these men came from, how they came to be in this situation, or if they had once had a spark of humanity. He would never even discover their names. He might not know who they were, but he knew exactly what they were. They had surely compiled a soul-destroying catalogue of dark deeds and placed themselves beyond both the laws of civilization and of war. The fate of deserters, traitors, and brigands was clear, unequivocal, and one of the few things on which all of the principal combatants of the Peninsular War agreed. If either the French or Spanish had caught them, they would act as summarily as he. Even if his three companions had favored them with an imitation of a jury verdict, their fate was sealed.

He would be quick and efficient about it, showing them more mercy than they had probably shown many others. He took one last look, conscious of the fluctuations of their chests as they silently drew breaths. Absent the dirt and scars, their faces in repose were ordinary and unremarkable. They could have been men you might have passed in any town in Europe without giving them a thought. He searched in vain for any special hallmark of evil. He was a gentleman by birth and training, and gentlemen always offered opponents sporting chances. But war had changed him. He was an officer first. Gentleman's code be damned, he would do his duty. If it was harsh and unforgiving, so be it.

They each had a pistol in their belts. He removed them and checked to make sure they were properly loaded. He turned the bodies on their sides, positioned himself above, and shot each one through the temple. He felt distaste, but not a trace of sympathy or regret. A deep part of him worried that it had been too easy. He was a soldier, not an executioner. Wasn't he? For an instant, he was not sure.

Neither Dale nor Manton said anything. They were grateful not to have had the responsibility.

Juanita walked up to corpses, looked at the spreading pools of blood next to their heads, and spat upon them. "*Bueno*," she said with disgust. The blood filled the room with the smell of old iron.

Manton watched her in horror. How could such a lovely angel do such a thing? He briefly remembered the circumstances of their first encounter, and it all made grisly sense. She had at least left them untouched. He had heard chilling stories of female partisans relieving male corpses of their private parts and stuffing them in their mouths as warnings.

Juanita looked at the conflict in Pennywhistle's face and loved him for it. Only a man with a great and generous soul would feel compassion for brigands. Her soul was hard. She should ask God to forgive the dead men, but the fire in her heart wished them a speedy passage to hell.

The English captain was a remarkable man, steadfast and fearless, save when it came to matters of the heart. He seemed to understand nothing of that. Perhaps it was something in England's climate. Impure thoughts raced through her mind when she looked at the lanky Englishman, ones her priests told her were wrong, unless one was married. Strangely, she felt no sense of sin. She had been warned Desire was like that. It startled her she did not care what the padres would think of her. The tingling in her loins would not be denied.

Why not? All of the girls in the village would want him, even if he were a foreigner. He had a beautiful, angular face, shaped like an inverted triangle, with a well formed nose, sensual lips and deep, thoughtful green eyes. You could lose yourself in those eyes. His soaring frame dwarfed most villagers, and his sandy red hair was exotic. He might speak in a tongue they could not understand, but the deep, resonant tenor of his voice spoke a sensual language that needed no translation. He kept such a formal and strict distance; why could he not yield to simple feelings?

Pennywhistle debated whether to bury the bodies. It was calculation talking, not humanity. He worried they might have friends who would look for their murderers. But such people had no real friends, merely allies of convenience. Those allies would be more interested in looting the bodies of valuables. The sight of their bodies would be both a warning and a mystery.

Burial was a waste of time and energy. This was a city of the dead anyway; what were five more corpses? A cruel part of him remembered a Bible verse from long ago, "They shall pass into the lower portions of the earth and be a portion for foxes." In this case, it would be for dogs and pigs.

Dale interrupted his thoughts. "I am very sorry for my conduct, sir. This should never have happened."

Pennywhistle said in puzzlement, "You fought well just now, Sarn't. There is nothing to feel sorry about."

"I mean getting jumped, sir. I was carving up the rest of the hog to take with us, sir. I was so intent upon my work that I did not hear them come up from astern. I should have had my rifle closer."

"You were acting for our benefit, Sarn't. You were foresighted to think of our food needs. I should have been awake. If the fault lies with anyone, it lies with me. I thought we would be safe from regulars here, but I had quite forgotten about scavengers. They may have friends. We need to pack up and evacuate within the hour. Sorry I cheated you of a good rest."

"Don't worry about it, sir. Got the best cuts packed into a barrel of brine. One of the horses can carry it. At least we will eat well tonight." Dale managed a smile.

"Excellent, Sarn't." It was something to look forward to.

CHAPTER NINETEEN

Miles away, Colonel Lazarette had discovered a name. His source of information was bloody and unconscious. No matter. "Pennywhistle," the colonel said out loud, savoring it; an unusual name, even for an Englishman. He heard a low rattle from the man he had been interrogating. He touched the carotid artery and found no pulse. Señor Vences was dead. No great loss to humanity, but he had been most useful to Lazarette.

The ambush had not gone quite as planned. The militia had put up a much more spirited resistance than he would have expected. It puzzled him. Spaniards were brave enough, he admitted, but they were invariably ill-trained, poorly led, and forever squabbling among themselves. It was normally easy for hussars to stampede militia, sweeping peasant soldiers before them as easily as housewife with a broom swept her parlor. Thundering horses ridden by men arrayed like martial gods and wielding over-sized sabers was enough to unman even the stout of heart, let alone ignorant peasants.

But the hussars had not achieved complete surprise. One of the hussars had discharged his carbine early and alerted the militia. As a result, they had failed to catch the Spaniards in the open where they could be savaged. The militia took cover in the village of Los Lobos, behind stout stone walls and inside sturdy homes. They opened up an intermittent but galling fire on the troopers. Instead of a gallant, overmastering charge, the hussars had to engage in a prolonged, man-killing firefight. It was the sort of warfare at which they did not excel. The officer in charge of the ambush would have to be disciplined. Lazarette rewarded success extravagantly and punished failure in the same way.

In the end, the contest had degenerated into a grueling, house-to-house struggle, much of the fighting hand-to-hand. Each house became a fortress, and in the tightly confined spaces death lurked around every corner and materialized without warning out of clouds of choking smoke. The militia fought with a ferocity that bordered on fanaticism. This was the sort of struggle where training counted far less than sheer tenacity generated by undying hatred. The militia sold their lives dearly and died to a man; but thirty of his own men lay dead or too wounded to go on. Well, the Spaniards died *almost* to a man. Their leader, a sergeant, had escaped at the last minute. Worst of all, most of the notables they protected had escaped during the battle.

Even the man who had just died had possessed a stronger core than he'd expected. By his clothing, he was some kind of a grandee, yet he had fought stoutly with his short sword before being clubbed into unconsciousness. He had not been summarily executed because his troopers had the wits to see he might be of some use to the higher ups. The prisoner had been hard to break. He had not been lured by drink, he had ignored threats to his family, and he had not been snared by cleverly oblique methods of questioning. In the end, it had taken a severe beating to ring the truth out of him. That had worked as it invariably did, but the soldier tasked to carry it out had done so with rather more enthusiasm than skill. If only the man had not died prematurely, he would have surely have surrendered the names of all of his contacts. Nevertheless, Lazarette had pried five names out of him. He would see to the extermination of those men in the days to come.

Lazarette did not relish using torture, unlike some; but it did not really bother him either. It was a means to an end. Death had to be viewed with detachment. To kill for no reason was uncivilized and illogical, but if a particularly harsh death brought information that advanced one's cause, it made perfect sense. He did admit how men bore up under pressure was of some intellectual interest to him. He did not enjoy their pain, but he found it instructive to see what core lay underneath the veneer of civilized behavior. The complexity of the human condition both perplexed and fascinated him. War was a terrible business in most ways, but it was an amazing laboratory to reveal both the utter frailty and robust strength of mankind.

Most hussars were gallant hearts, but not deep thinkers. He was both at home and out of place among them. He loved the thrill of the chase and the clash of swords, but bringing that about so that he always fought with foreknowledge and advantage amused him even more. He knew the gaudy uniform amplified the impression of show over smarts. It was fine for the ego to be thought brilliant and clever, but rather more useful to be easily dismissed as a mere archetype. It made it so much easier to do the unexpected, because everyone only expected the obvious.

One thing Vences had said troubled him. The route the Englishman was supposed to have taken made little sense. He knew Vences believed it; his face, tone, and body language shouted it was the truth as he knew it. But it might still be false. If so, it meant the Englishman had a considerable fund of guile and had deliberately deceived his Spanish ally. It looked like this Englishman believed in maneuver; all the more interesting. Vences had also described the curious round hat worn by the Royal Marines. Lazarette had fought the English on numerous occasions but had never encountered their marines. Perhaps they were different in some way.

Lazarette unfurled a map and began to study it. He stopped, realizing his eagerness to bag the marine was making him get ahead of himself. The essential question had to be answered first. What did the Englishman want? That would tell him a great deal about his quarry's destination. The man traveled with no armed escort, so stealth had been a consideration. Were it not for the mole in Lisbon, they should never have taken note of him. He had something headquarters badly wanted. He traveled in uniform rather than incognito, which indicated he was a soldier tasked to become something else, rather than an experienced intelligence agent.

Marmont's army was closely shadowing Wellington, and Lazarette had just received a bulletin on their current location. The Englishman was heading towards Wellington's headquarters. Two possible routes presented themselves; one that ran toward Ciudad Juárez and one that ran through Los Robles. The first was direct and a good road. The second was rough, twisting, and fringed with small plots of forest at intervals. It provided places to hide or defend. It would be rougher on cavalry. The marine seemed a tough fellow. The harsh road would not bother him. It had to be Los Robles.

He bellowed for his secretary, who appeared quickly and sat down at the small, collapsible writing table. Lazarette began to pace slowly back and forth as he dictated orders. The secretary wrote quickly and in silence. He recognized the pacing: the longer the stride, the more detailed the orders would be. The strides were long today. He was blocking out a plan of campaign, not just a quick raid. Action would follow very soon.

******

Pennywhistle and his companions rode in silence. The sun was high in the sky and it was a hot, lazy afternoon. The only noise was the steady clop, clop, clop of the horses' hooves on the road. Lightning plodded along good-naturedly and radiated a calming presence. Pennywhistle reminded himself it was unwise to anthropomorphize, but the beast always seemed agreeable. He was pleased his seat continued to improve. Equitation was the one gentleman's art he had never mastered, but there was hope for him. He felt rested and alert, but the same could not be said of his companions, for they'd had little sleep. Dale fought to stay awake, Juanita drooped in her saddle, and Manton slumped forward, arms around his horse's neck, drifting in and out of sleep.

Pennywhistle did not mind. Being a soldier, he knew rest was hard to come by. He had developed the habit of taking catnaps, able to summon sleep quickly and in the most unpromising of circumstances. That was the only kind of sleep he had gotten for three days when the huge storm hit *Bellerophon* after Trafalgar. When he catnapped, an innate sixth sense and superior internal clock apprised him of both danger and time.

Los Robles was only an hour away and they were making reasonably good time. Wellington's Army and safety were not more than twenty miles from Los Robles. With luck, they might encounter a patrol of British cavalry. Of course, French cavalry was probably out and about. They had seen little traffic, just one itinerant muleteer and his small caravan, a dealer in blankets and trinkets, but it was when things seemed their most ordinary and benign that disaster struck, like the violent waterspouts he had seen at sea. They came down with no warning, riled the ocean beneath, and retracted quickly into the clouds. He kept a weather eye open for places to quickly take cover.

The small patches of forest he saw from time to time along the road reassured him. He was at home in the woods, even in a foreign land. Customs and people varied from nation to nation, but the forest signs and the canons of predation never did. A forest could be a dark, threatening place to those who had lived too long in towns and cities, but it was a place of marvelous wonder, resources, and refuge to one trained in its ways. A townsman alone, without training and tools, might easily starve, but Pennywhistle's knowledge of edible plants and deadfall traps ensured he would never go hungry.

Right now, the road was devoid of cover. It was arid, stony, and poorly maintained. At least he could see several miles in every direction and would be able to detect any approaching horsemen. He noted patches of woodland in the distance. He wondered if the escapees had made it safely away. Perhaps he should have gone with them; but they had been keen to run their own show and had only accepted his help out of desperation.

The problem with the Spanish was they wanted foreign help but disdained to accept foreign advice and training. Everything had to be on their terms. He had been told upon arrival that they were the worse trained and worst officered army in Europe. They boasted, swaggered, and promised much, but mostly failed to deliver on their pledges. They were incredibly touchy about outside interference and refused to admit their country was too weak to fight on its own. Because of that, they were the authors of much of their own misery.

They had plenty of men, but never seemed to be able to bring them together at a decisive point; egos and poor discipline always got in the way. They had done it right at Bailen, although uncommon French ineptitude had helped, and had bagged Dupont's whole army. But that had been four years ago, and nothing had worked since. Their leaders focused on the pettiest of matters, scrapped with each other more often than with the French, and refused to coordinate their plans. Wellington fought a constant military battle with the French, but also a constant diplomatic one with his unreliable Spanish allies.

The British had done amazing things training the Portuguese army and had turned a rabble into very competent soldiers. An NCO like Dale could work wonders with Spanish troops. It was a shame the Spaniards did not put more effort into building a regular army rather than dissipating their strength in the form of ill-coordinated guerrilla groups led by feckless opportunists. He wondered if at least some of the scavengers at El Corazón had been former guerrillas that had tired of making war for their country and decided to make war upon it instead. Killing always had to be kept under the tightest control and discipline. When men crossed the line into barbarity, profit became a much more important consideration than patriotism or humanity.

A low level electric current issued from his alert subconscious and caused the hairs on his arm to prickle and rise. He turned in his saddle and looked astern. His attention fixed on a distant, slowly rising cloud of dust. From the size of it, it meant horses, and a considerable number. The cloud continued to swell and he started to estimate numbers. Company strength. Trouble.

CHAPTER TWENTY

Lazarette pushed his troopers hard. It was his job to demand the best from his men, but it was also his nature. He was a fighter, but more than that, he was a driver. When he got the bit in his teeth, it was impossible for him to let go until his object had been attained.

The men and horses wearied, panting heavily, but Lazarette did not particularly care. A Company was relatively fresh, since B Company had borne the brunt of the fighting against the militia. He had left B Company behind to see if they could pick up the grandee's trail. The troopers had been in their saddles for more than sixteen hours and had covered nearly forty-five miles. They had searched two towns, none too gently, without finding their target. The people had been cooperative, in a surly fashion. His chastisement of El Corazón was still fresh in the minds of all villagers, and no one wanted it repeated. He had taken no joy in that business, but it had proven a useful object lesson. No one along the way had seen or heard anything of a tall Englishman, and he had no reason to doubt their veracity.

He wondered if the oddly-named Pennywhistle was on the move or had holed up someplace. This was the road he would use; Lazarette felt sure of that in his heart. His quarry had to be somewhere close, but where? There were small patches of forest at irregular intervals, and the man taken refuge in a forest once before. Perhaps that was his element, a place he felt safe.

Three small forests lay directly ahead. If his hunch was right, he would be within one of them. It would be tedious work to track him, not well suited to dashing horsemen, but it could be done. He looked at his map. *Bosque del nubes, Bosque del sol, Bosque del rey*; the first two looked small and easily searchable, the third larger and more daunting. *Bosque del nubes* was only two miles ahead and was a reasonable place to begin.

******

Pennywhistle saw the dust cloud growing thicker and closer. It was time to seek shelter. He had been foolish to travel by day, but he'd wanted to gain some distance from the oppressive malevolence of El Corazón. The Bosque del sol was a few hundred yards ahead; they could get a few hours of sleep and resume moving after dark. With luck, whatever was in the dust cloud would pass them by.

******

Lazarette passed the word to the junior officers in the long column, and they all but cheered. The men needed a rest, and their horses needed water. They could grab something to eat before they began their search. With luck, the colonel's intuition would be proven right, they'd capture their quarry, and they could bivouac for the night.

******

Pennywhistle ranged alongside each of his three companions in turn and explained his plans. The prospect of rest was welcome, and cool shade would be a pleasant relief from the late afternoon heat. Pennywhistle cantered on ahead and found a trail that led into the woods. The ground rose slightly as he entered and the trail wound uphill. It was not much of an elevation, but he should be able to find a spot with a clear view of the road.

He found what he was looking for: a small clearing with a creek that promised potable water. He also noted damson nearby; a purplish fruit that tasted like plums. There were ligonberries as well. They dared not risk a campfire, but Dale had cooked a small amount of ham for the journey and that could be eaten cold. Decision made, he returned to the road and lead his weary party to the shelter. He got everyone bedded down, and exhaustion took them. While they slept, he tended to the horses, who were no less glad of the respite, then walked uphill until he found a lookout point.

He plucked a damson, took a bite, and drank coffee from his canteen. The beverage was cold, leftover from the morning that now seemed long ago, but the caffeine still worked, and it helped to sharpen his already acute senses. He unshipped his spyglass and looked down the road. He could see the tail end of the column and the colors blue and crimson. He had been right: hussars.

The column wheeled right and moved toward the woods a mile distant. Troopers dismounted at the edge and withdrew their carbines. Every fourth man acted as a horse holder, while the rest spread out in a wide arc and moved methodically into the woods. It was a general sweep, a sort of military scavenger hunt to find something they believed hidden in the woods. He knew what they sought. Of course, they would find nothing, and a systematic search would take time.

He debated whether to break camp immediately or stay put on the assumption that hussars would cease work at nightfall and not search his present position until early tomorrow morning. The parched road was devoid of cover and movement would send up a beacon of dust. If he could see them with a spyglass, they could certainly spot him. He observed the hussar's slow progress and decided to remain. His companions needed sleep and any further deprivation would literally make them stupid with fatigue.

As he watched, a few of the horse holders produced long, slim sausages from their haversacks and began to eat, even as their animals buried their heads in feedbags. The horses looked well cared for and were perfectly suited to the terrain: small, sleek, and fast. The hundred or so hussars moving into the woods held their carbines expertly; they were no novices. The interval between troopers was sensible, enough to cover a lot of ground, but never enough to be out of supporting distance. They were clearly men who had been well trained; exactly what you'd expect from a veteran unit.

If they caught him and his people in the open, they had no chance. If that happened, much as he hated to consider it, he would do the necessary thing, the honorable thing, and surrender. Heroic resistance was foolish if no possibility of escape existed. He could fight to the bitter end, take a few of the French troopers with him, but he would surely die, as would his companions. It was far more sensible to survive, trust to bluff and guile, and await an opportunity to escape.

He would see how the next hours unfolded. It seemed pointless to just watch flashes of blue and crimson appear at intervals in the distant woods. He decided he would do something useful to pass the time and headed back to camp. He would clean his rifle.

He was walking down the slight hill when he saw flashes of color moving through the brush, directly beyond the camp. Crimson and blue! Hussars! What were they doing here? Apparently, he was not the only one who did the unexpected. He had been flanked. He did not think they had seen him, but they would reach the camp before him. It looked like no more than an under strength troop, but the heavy woods let him see only blobs of color, and it was impossible to know their numbers for certain. It had never occurred to him there might be a secondary detachment. He had focused all of his attention on the shiny objects ahead and missed the real threat from behind. He truly was an idiot!

He was grateful he never went anywhere without the Ferguson and suitable accoutrements. It was like a third arm to him, a part of his being. He eased down behind a low rock, waited until he saw a quick glimpse of crimson in the heavy brush, and fired. He heard a scream, then a dull thud. A chorus of shouts erupted below.

He rose to a crouch, dashed thirty yards to his right, rolled on his back, and reloaded in ten seconds. He reversed onto his stomach, waited until he saw another splotch of crimson, lined up the V sights and fired.

He did not wait to see the results of his actions. He ran to a position midway between the first two shots, reloaded, and fired again. He saw no more movement, but heard plenty of yelling. They were confused. The three shots had come in too rapid a succession to be the work of just one man, as most soldiers reckoned these things. He had to reinforce the illusion.

He moved back up the hill and to the left. It was a few minutes before he saw any movement. He fired. He was not sure if he hit anything, but the there was no more rustling of the bushes. He sprinted down the hill and moved far to the left. He could only guess their location, but hoped to convince them they faced a line sufficiently long to enfilade their position. This time it was about bluff. He had no target but fired blindly. He moved left again.

It was discharge and dash, discharge and dash, discharge and dash, classic Shorncliffe Doctrine. It appeared to be working. He saw flashes of crimson only at odd intervals. He wanted to warn his friends, but dared not approach the camp. He hoped they had awakened and would make a run to it. Dale would want to reach him, but he was no fool. He would see that Pennywhistle was cut off. He would do the prudent thing: clear off, head for safety, and know his officer would find a way to rejoin him.

A French head popped up for a quick peek. He put a bullet through the forehead. He was only fifty yards away! He heard talking, very low, too indistinct to make out the words. He moved lower down the hill and closed the range. He leaned his back against a tree and reloaded from the standing position. He waited patiently and breathed deeply. His pulse slowed and his hands grew bone dry on the stock. He saw a flash of metal thirty yards ahead. Someone was crawling slowly and methodically forward, preceded by his carbine. Sound tactics! He saw it again a few seconds later and fired a foot above and behind the metal. He heard a squawk like an angry bird, but saw no more metal.

He decided to test a theory. He took up a handful of pebbles and threw them toward what he thought was the main French line. They landed with a rustling patter.

A volley of bullets crashed through the trees. One missed his head by inches. They were not aimed shots; they were shots of rage and exasperation.

Another volley roared. This time it was high and damaged only the upper branches of a tall pine twenty yards away. French carbines were far better at distance than English Pagets and were not to be underestimated in an open field fight, but cavalrymen were not used to firing them uphill in heavy woods. Men usually failed to correct for elevation when firing uphill. Not a mistake he would make. From the sound of the two volleys, he guessed he faced about thirty men.

Another volley, wildly off the mark; but fire enough bullets and you were bound to hit something.

Cavalrymen were used to facing an enemy openly, charging with striking hooves, raging shouts, and flashing blades. Hussars were trained to ride ahead and hold a crossroads until infantry support arrived. They could use their carbines effectively, but it was a secondary weapon. Fighting a concealed enemy of unknown strength in dense woods with bullets alone was not their style. The forest was his element, not theirs. They had no experience of this kind of warfare, where dash and daring counted for little, and marksmanship and patience counted for much.

He moved again, loaded and fired. He did want them to think they would have even a second's respite, wanted them constantly off balance and scrambling. If only he had some way to move behind them and get off even one shot, he might even be able to stampede them.

He was about to reload when he heard a twig crunch behind him. All had been perfectly quiet a second before. His mind knew instantly what had happened; the man must have removed his boots. He jerked his head round to look, and the butt of a carbine crashed into his head. He saw stars, blackness, then nothing. The stubby hussar smiled.

CHAPTER TWENTY-ONE

In the end, it was lack of initiative that saved them. The hussars were satisfied to have captured the English officer. He'd led them a long chase, cost lives, and been a difficult catch, but they had gotten their man. After a man-killing day of riding, they were tired and needed rest. They had no orders about other persons; as far as they knew, the officer was traveling alone.

Dale woke instantly when he heard the shots. He was never a heavy sleeper during campaigns. He recognized the distinctive crack of the Ferguson and the rattle of carbines. He assessed the situation quickly and correctly. His impulse was to race to his officer's aid, but he had spent too much time with Pennywhistle to do something that, while natural, was not coldly logical. The French barred the way and he would be killed or captured before he got close. "Save the people and the supplies, come back when the odds are more even. Attack only from advantage. The cloak of night is a useful ally when numbers are not on your side." The captain's instructions rang through his head. He had often expressed his thoughts about battle to Dale, and they were the ideas of a hardened professional, not a heroic amateur.

Dale had spent years poaching; he knew woodcraft as well as his officer, but now safety lay on the main road. He would evacuate the camp and return later. If the French searched at all, they would find an empty camp, and it was doubtful they would come back a second time. Manton and Juanita were also wide awake and already moving. Manton broke camp and packed their gear onto the horses. Juanita followed his lead.

Manton's expression was grim and purposeful, just like Dale's. Juanita's was harder to read. There was no fear, but there was a strange mixture of hatred, anger, and joy. She did not like what was happening and feared for Pennywhistle, but she felt she was exactly where God intended her to be and doing exactly what He intended for her to do. Things might look dark, but that was exactly how God made tests of faith. He would not find her wanting. His purpose was hidden, but she felt a certainty in her heart that He would save them all. She knew the two Englishmen were heretics, but they were good people, unaware that the Lord had appropriated their services, regardless of what they believed.

The horses were restless, knowing something was wrong. They chuffed and snorted, but the gunfire cloaked the noises from French ears. Lightning wondered where his master was. The little band left the woods and cantered onto the road, fifteen minutes after the first shots were fired. The gunfire faded. They halted a mile away and took shelter in a small ravine that hid them from view. They needed a plan, and quickly.

******

Pennywhistle awoke in agony. His head was on fire and he felt as though he was inside a kettle drum being pounded with the fast battle step. He opened his eyes and the light hurt. His vision alternated between clarity and a blur. Being clubbed on the head was not a minor physical event. Fortunately, his memory and reason appeared intact. As his vision slowly righted itself, he identified the source of the drumming: hoof beats. He was draped over the back of a horse and his wrists were bound. Hussars rode wearily in front and behind. His weapons were gone, but they had not relieved him of his boots, which made him fleetingly grateful to have been captured by hussars. The feet were the first concern of an infantryman, since hard marching wore out footwear quickly. High quality boots were a desirable prize of war, but hussars were always well equipped and had no need to scavenge. They were far more expensive to outfit than any other form of cavalry.

It wasn't hard to guess where they were headed. He was going to meet the author of this bit of misery. There would be some kind of interrogation. It might be cursory and civilized, or detailed and grueling. With all of the effort expended in his capture, he thought the latter more likely. Stubborn refusal to say anything would be counterproductive; it would only stiffen the resolve of the interrogator.

It would be easy to assume the caricature of an English officer: brave, well connected, well meaning, but not over bright, wanting judgment. He would give them what they wanted; well sort of. Provide them a persona, tell them a likely tale: small slices of truth sandwiched between lies to establish credibility and convince interrogators they were making real progress. Start with unadulterated truths and gradually feed in half truths and deceptions. Leads took time to pursue. The more believable they were, the more effort and manpower would be consumed in discovering their usefulness, the more time he would buy. Once his companions realized he was indeed captured, he had no doubt Dale and Manton would come for him; probably Juanita too. They would tell her to stay behind, but she would not listen.

His head throbbed as the miles ground slowly past. At least it seemed like miles through the pain, but likely was a considerably shorter distance. It took a real effort to craft the details of his story. Now they were approaching some sort of headquarters area. There was a large, square tent with two guidons flanking the entrance. They flapped uncertainly in the evening breeze and orderlies moved purposefully past them, intent on talking with their master inside.

******

Dale, Manton, and Juanita dismounted and tethered their horses to a large juniper near the rear of the ravine. Dale suggested everybody sit and eat some ham and bread. Juanita glared at Dale with an expression that shouted, *How can you think of food at a time like this!* Dale answered the look in pidgin Spanish. "Survival; first order of business. Everyone will think better on a full stomach. There may not be time to eat later."

Juanita would have none of it. She snatched up Dale's glass and scornfully said she would stand watch. Confidently, she predicted the Lord would dispatch help. Dale and Manton glanced at each other, their cynical eyes indicating they did not share her faith.

She flounced up to the top of the ravine and swept the horizon methodically for ten minutes. She was about to sit down and yield to Dale's suggestion when she saw them. She could not quite credit her eyes and thought it might be a mirage. She lowered the glass, blinked, then put the glass to her eye again. The horse and rider were still there and coming closer. They looked like storybook figures who had wandered out their illustrated page. God was indeed showing her proof she had passed her test of faith. She shouted to Dale and Manton.

Dale and Manton dashed up and Dale took the glass. He carefully examined the horse and rider and decided either Juanita had special access to the Lord's ear or they had just been granted an amazing piece of luck.

Only the British docked the tails of their horses, and the scarlet of the coat was unmistakable. The rider wore slate grey trousers with a red stripe and sported a japanned leather-and-brass cavalry helmet with a short bill and elaborate crest that ran the length of its top, putting Dale in mind of something a Roman centurion might have worn. The officer sat astride an enormous horse that, even to Dale's unpracticed eye, looked to be a very fast, very expensive thoroughbred.

The officer had a fine seat and cantered along slowly, magisterially, looking as if he were on a pleasant evening survey of his estates. He was short, wiry, and athletic, probably in his later twenties; the perfect cavalryman. Dale knew he was one of Wellington's elite, an exploring officer. Those men roamed widely and alone behind enemy lines, and were the eyes and ears of the army. They were chosen for their intelligence and resourcefulness. They rode the best horses Ireland could produce, ones that could outrun even the fine animals of the hussars.

Dale walked out of the ravine and onto the road. He waved his arms and shouted. The officer blinked in surprise at the apparition. He carefully drew his carbine and rode on, warily.

"Advance and be recognized!" he demanded. Dale snapped to parade ground attention and touched his round hat in crisp salute. "Dale, Sergeant, Royal Marines, at your service, sir." The horseman lowered the carbine and studied Dale, seeing a man in his early forties, slightly above average height, solidly built with a round, weathered face that had seen of plenty of hard service. The patches on the uniform bore out what the face showed.

The officer smiled, relaxed, and asked the obvious question. "What the blazes is a blue water marine doing in the middle of this desert?"

Dale responded in a firm voice. "It's a bit of a story, sir, and takes some explaining. I can only give you the short version. My officer has been captured and I need your help."

The lack of deference in Dale's voice amused him, but it was the sergeant's eyes that commanded attention. The blue in them was the hardened steel of pure determination. This man wanted his officer back badly. The cavalryman appreciated loyalty; he put the carbine back in the saddle holster.

"Well, you certainly are a direct and cheeky fellow, Sergeant, but if I can be of help to an officer in distress, I shall certainly pitch in." His tone was breezy, but the offer was sincere.

"I am very much obliged, Captain ...." Dale left the sentence unfinished.

"Steven Thynne, 1st Life Guards, and this is Mandrake." He patted his horse proudly as if the beast were of equal rank: not a servant, but a companion who had saved his life many times. Mandrake was huge, over a thousand pounds and nearly 18 hands high; Wellington's favorite hunter, Copenhagen, stood a mere 15 hands. He had paid more for Mandrake than the sergeant would earn in a lifetime.

Dale face remained neutral, but he recognized the surname as the same as that of the Marquis of Bath who owned the Longleat Estate. He had always thought that estate would make a fine poaching ground. This was probably one of the younger sons. His piercing grey eyes, strong chin, and slightly aquiline nose certainly suggested an aristocrat. His accoutrements were expensive and the cut of his jacket was superb. It all tracked: well dressed officer on a fine horse from a smart regiment. He had omitted the use of Lord, to which he was entitled as the son of the marquis. That told Dale he relied on professionalism for his reputation, not pedigree; an excellent sign. "If you will come with me, sir, I will introduce you to my companions and explain our plight," Dale said.

Thynne dismounted and led Mandrake by the bridle into the ravine. He noticed the horses first; definitely not up to Life Guards standards.

Dale made the introductions. Thynne thought the girl remarkably pretty, although there was a strange look in the violet eyes. The servant seemed protective of her. Part of him wanted very much to know her better, but this was hardly the time or place, and a subliminal part of his brain warned him there was more danger inherent in the proposition than he really needed to bother himself with.

Thynne spoke excellent Spanish, was handsome in a rakish sort of way, and behaved with a courtliness most women would have reckoned charming, yet Juanita found the package uninteresting after Pennywhistle. However, if his zeal could be used to save her man, so she would treat him with solicitude.

Dale explained the situation in a few crisp minutes. Thynne whistled, shook his head, and placed his hands on his hips.

"You are in a bit of a pickle, aren't you! But Pennywhistle seems the kind of man I should like to know better. If we are going to do this thing, it must be tonight. The best chance of an escape is as soon as possible after capture. Every hour a man passes as a prisoner saps his strength. Now, let me think."

He walked over to his saddlebag and made sure the cavalry trumpet was inside. His batman had not forgotten to put it in, after all. It might come in handy for what he had in mind, particularly at night. He sat down and his face assumed a thoughtful cast. He wondered if these three could even remain upright in the saddle. Dale was probably a good man in a fight, but he had doubts about the other two. Still, both looked determined and seemed to share Dale's passion for retrieving Pennywhistle. Lightning bobbed his head slightly and made a snorting sound that sounded like equine support for the mission.

Seeing the look on Thynne's face and divining the thoughts behind it, Dale spoke up. "Pardon me, sir, don't wish to be impertinent, but I have a few suggestions you might find useful."

Thynne smiled. "I welcome suggestions, Sergeant; we need cleverness and initiative right now."

"Well, sir, I was thinking...." Dale began to speak animatedly and Thynne listened with close interest.

******

The horse stopped and Pennywhistle felt hands untie him from the saddle and rudely bundle him to his feet. He was unsteady and dizzy. Two troopers held him by the shoulders, while another shouted rudely in French, "No tricks, Englishman! You are our prisoner."

He replied in perfect Parisian accent, "I would never think to discommode you. I am too eager to meet your commanding officer." He managed an annoying grin. The hussar looked at him in surprise. Few Englishmen spoke their tongue, and those who did usually eviscerated it.

He decided to take advantage of the Frenchman's surprise. "Who is your commanding officer now? I had heard it was"—he swiftly made up a name—"Colonel Bourette, but that he was shot for cowardice. Does that happen often in your service?" His head hurt, and needling the trooper seemed to relieve the pain. It would also tell him something about the morale of the unit.

"That is a goddamned lie, you English dog! The only deaths we die are glorious ones on the field of battle. We have never been beaten. There has never been any Colonel Bourette. You must have gotten your information from the Spanish desperados you fight with. Colonel Lazarette commands here. He is a great man and you are a poltroon." The hussar's eyes burned with fury, and Pennywhistle wondered if he was about to be struck.

"Trooper, come to attention, now!" A voice barked the command from behind and the trooper snapped to attention like a puppet. Pennywhistle saw fear in the man's eyes. "Our guest is an officer, trooper, and must be treated with the courtesies of war. You have not done so, and I will have your sergeant administer appropriate chastisement. For now, you are dismissed." The trooper saluted and turned smartly on his heel.

The speaker stepped forward. He was of medium height, solidly built with broad shoulders. He looked to be in his late thirties, with ruthless brown eyes, decisive chin, and an overwhelming handlebar mustache. There was a sneering savagery in the face, but it suddenly broke into a broad grin which reflected the genuine joy of the hunter bagging his quarry.

"You must be Captain Pennywhistle. My countrymen have tried making your acquaintance for a long time, but you are an exceedingly difficult gentleman to reach. I am Colonel Lazarette. You are," he paused thoughtfully, "a man I should like to know better. I believe entertaining and informative chats lie ahead." The smile and voice shifted character with the last words, making Pennywhistle inwardly shudder.

CHAPTER TWENTY-TWO

The plan, like the name of its author, was thin. Dale liked the officer, could see why he had been selected for his hazardous duty, but was far from certain his idea would work and did not think the man had Pennywhistle's genius for improvisation. It was, however, the best he could hope for, and they were at least moving to take action.

He agreed with Thynne that the recapture had to take place tonight. His officer could not have been moved far. Dale refused to believe the captain was dead. He was just too damned hard to kill, although plenty of people had tried. But if even a day elapsed, he would be far out of their reach, bound for God knows where.

Thynne often traveled at night, but said the French cavalry rarely did. He explained patiently to Dale that the hussars would be bivouacked now and would probably not move until first light tomorrow. Their camp would be easy enough to find. Hussars were confident and there were no Spanish forces of note in the area, so they simply had to look for the twinkling lights of camp fires arranged in an orderly fashion. He had no idea of their numbers, but a careful observation of the camp fires could correct that. It helped that he had a map, and Thynne assured Dale the map was up-to-date and accurate.

Dale brightened when he saw the map showed a small watercourse two miles away. There were few enough of note in the dry Peninsula. It would be a source of water and a logical place to camp, and it might mean boats. Boats were something Dale understood. Even good officers like Thynne failed to appreciate the ease and speed of waterborne movement. If foot and horse failed, boats always worked.

Thynne possessed plenty of experience in dealing with hussars. He had been chased by them on a score of occasions. He knew their commanding officers frequently favored large marquee tents with banners, all part of the pageantry of being elite troops. The command tent would be easy to spot, and Pennywhistle assuredly would be there.

Thynne remarked that the first target should not be Pennywhistle, but the horses. Dale liked that; it was the sort of thing his commander would think of: Divert attention before launching the main sortie. Thynne said a hussar valued his horse above all else and usually kept his mount close at night, yet security in their camps was often far more lax than one would expect, because of simple arrogance. Their mentality was that of attack; they rarely thought in terms of strategic defence. If their horses could be stampeded there would be chaos, and they would forget everything else in the frenzy to retrieve their mounts. Chaos favored the commander with a coherent plan. Thynne remarked that Mandrake was an uncommonly intelligent animal and could help with the stampede. Dale did not quite understand what that meant, but then he knew very little about horses, and if Thynne believed Mandrake had some marvelous ability, it was probably true.

He did understand Thynne's musing that they could double their numbers if they could find a farm, hay, and a few old clothes. He and Pennywhistle had used hats on sticks behind fortifications before to deceive the enemy about numbers.

Juanita knew of some farms ahead; her knowledge as a drover's daughter once again was proving handy.

It was almost completely dark when Juanita spotted a tall, thin figure on a swaybacked horse trudging slowly down the road. The twilight time just before light vanishes entirely often plays tricks on the eyes. She blinked twice, but both were still there. Horse and rider were dirty and weary. Thynne drew his Paget and Dale his Baker. The man did not look at all dangerous to Thynne, but it was as well to take precautions.

Dale recognized something familiar in the silhouette. He put down the Baker, unfurled his glass, and surveyed the rider's face. Dale smiled in genuine surprise. It could not be, but it was: Morales! Dale quickly told Thynne this was a friend. Juanita and Manton waved. A joyful reunion followed, and Morales told his story.

Morales related the ambush and the death of his men. Tears swam in his eyes, especially when he described Sergeant Valdez's sad end, but he brightened when he said that most of the prisoners had escaped because of their heroism. Dale found it interesting that Morales spoke with proprietary tones; he really had become a soldier. Morales continued, saying he had hoped to find Pennywhistle him again. He thought the last place the French would look for a Spanish soldier was right behind them, so he decided to shadow the hussars. He reasoned they might be on Pennywhistle's trail. He had heard gunfire earlier and had seen a man in scarlet splayed across the back of one horse when a hussar column passed a few hours ago. Dale was momentarily alarmed, but Morales said he saw the figure move. He also knew one man could do nothing. He confessed he'd waited, baffled, hoping for a divine intercession. He smiled and said, "I think it just arrived."

Thynne was highly skeptical of both man and story, but Dale vouched for Morales and avowed he had proven himself a steadfast fellow. Quietly, Dale said, "He will fight, sir, and he feels he owes the captain a huge, unpaid debt. Spaniards are very particular about repayment of debts." Thynne nodded and laughed. "We are either the bravest men on earth or the gravest fools. We have only two real soldiers, a Spaniard, a servant, and a girl, and we are going to attack a hussar camp. It's utter madness!" He shook his head, but a moment later, his face assumed an expression of wily resolve. "But because it is, no one will see it coming."

******

The surgeon finished examining Pennywhistle. "He has suffered a severe blow to the head, but the skull is intact, no bone fragments and no soft spot. Still, concussions sometimes manifest after the initial injury, and I would sternly recommend no violent activity for several days. This," he pointed to a large purple welt with the shape of a goose egg, "is undoubtedly painful, but should subside in time. I counsel rest, a bleed, and a good purge."

"Thank you, Surgeon Larrey," rumbled Lazarette. "You have been most helpful, as always. I would like to follow your recommendations, but whether I am able depends entirely on Captain Pennywhistle. If he is cooperative, answers a few harmless questions, I am certain he will make a complete recovery and enjoy a very pleasant confinement in France. We treat British officers well, with food and lodging commensurate with their status as gentlemen. I am informed some of the more dashing ones acquire lady friends. It is quite an agreeable way to sit out the war."

Pennywhistle had a split second of temptation. The pain had not abated and a place of ease, rest and good food sounded wonderful. But then he saw in his mind the faces of his absent three companions who had placed their complete and undying trust in him. The temptation evaporated like a morning mist and his will steeled.

Larrey looked dubious. "As a medical man, it is my duty to request you make sure he receives the best care, regardless of his attitude; but I realize you will do as you will. I would be happy to supervise his recovery, but for now I have done all I can. Is there anything further, Colonel?"

Lazarette smiled. "Nothing more at present, although one can never tell what the morning might bring." The smile was jolly, but the tone ominous. "For now, you are dismissed." Larrey left the tent, feeling uneasy. He knew his colonel too well.

Pennywhistle, slumped in a canvas camp chair, knew that the exchange had been staged for his benefit, at least as far as the commanding officer was concerned. The Colonel had no doubt been informed that Pennywhistle spoke excellent French. The message was clear: We can do things the easy way or the hard way. Pennywhistle got the feeling that, beneath the civilized veneer, Lazarette really did not care either way. He wanted information, pure and simple, and would get it. He saw Lazarette was about to speak and decided to seize the initiative, to disrupt the colonel's control of the situation.

"Colonel, I thank you for the kind ministrations of your surgeon. He is obviously quite skilled. I am hungry and wonder if you could arrange for some food. Pleasant chats always go better when one has a full stomach, don't you agree?" He was signaling a willingness to cooperate and had made a reasonable request. The bargaining had begun. He waited for Lazarette's counter.

"I quite agree, Captain. We French invented civilization and the excellent cuisine that is its hallmark. I have a marvelous steward who has prepared a wonderful *boeuf bourguignon* for my evening's meal. I promise you as much as you like, but first I would like to trouble you for one small piece of information."

Here it comes, thought Pennywhistle. He understood the procedure. Get a foot in the mental door and each succeeding time push it open a little wider. Get a man to give up a trivial piece of information, get him used to going along with what was asked, and request more and more important information with each succeeding question. It was like gradually increasing the heat beneath a pot so that the animal within did not realize he was being boiled to death.

"I, of course, have my duty. Your surely understand that, Colonel,"—he could not be too agreeable,—"but if it is a trifling matter, I see no reason to be uncivilized. What do you wish to know?"

Lazarette smiled mirthlessly. "You were on a mission of some importance; a blind man could see that. I would like to know who sent you."

Pennywhistle realized they were probably reading the dispatches from the circular leather case right now. They would surely have someone who read English. Only a few of the dispatches were in code, and Admiral Martin's name was probably mentioned in several places. He would not be giving much away, but he decided to make it look as if he thought he was.

He tried to assume a pained expression, as if he were undergoing some deep mental conflict. He waited a full minute before speaking slowly. "Vice Admiral Sir Thomas Byam Martin sent me. I was chosen because he is more used to marine than army officers, and because we are as at home on the land as at sea." He volunteered some extra, unimportant information to show he was cooperative, once he had wrestled down his doubts and qualms. He tried to look hungry, as opposed to dizzy and sick.

"I have certainly heard of him," commented Lazarette. "As a captain, he captured *Tamise*, one of our best frigates, in a single ship fight, did he not?"

Pennywhistle was genuinely surprised. Lazarette was well informed for a cavalry officer! He had suspected the man had considerable depth, and this confirmed it. "That is true, Colonel.

The Admiral is a highly intelligent officer. It is an honor to serve under him." Actually, he had only met the Admiral twice and knew little of him, but it was as well to sound as if he were influential back at headquarters. It might mitigate his treatment, as a valuable prisoner of war could be used as a bargaining chip when negotiating exchanges of prisoners. Of course it might backfire, and lead Lazarette to think he knew much more than he actually did. He shifted slightly in his chair and thanked God he still had his boots.

Lazarette was about to speak, but Pennywhistle forestalled him again, wanted to subtlety guide the conversation. The marine gave a smile as pleasant and false as Lazarette's. "I have answered your question forthrightly, Colonel, and now my stomach would like to humbly ask for some of that superb *boeuf bourguignon* you promised." He laid special emphasis on the word "promise." It was important to promote quid pro quo. He didn't want to play the subordinate in a cat-and-mouse game any more than absolutely necessary.

"Certainly, Captain, I will summon my steward directly. A pleasant meal and a good wine are preparations for a good conversation. I have a bottle of *Château Margot* I have been saving for a special occasion, and I am certain this qualifies. That is one of the few things our two nations agree on; the love of a fine claret. When one is relaxed and cares are banished, it is easy to talk the entire night away, don't you find?"

Pennywhistle ground his teeth to maintain his smile. "Absolutely, Colonel. Pleasant discourse is the life's blood of civilization." *Talk the night away* sounded dangerous. He took it to mean Lazarette intended to be extract a great deal of information, regardless of whether the food and wine did their work. He would have to be careful, and reveal things only in tiny portions. He would not pin a desperate hope on Dale for a rescue; he was on his own. But if he stalled for time, an idea might come to him. Perhaps Lazarette would make a mistake. But his head ached, and he was worried.

Chapter Twenty-Three

The meal passed agreeably. Lazarette and the Englishman chatted like old comrades between mouthfuls; on the surface, nothing of any great moment was discussed. It was talk of home, general problems soldiers encountered on campaign, and the women in their lives. On a deeper level, each probed the character of the other man. The Frenchman thought the Englishman's responses a little too flippant, too nonchalant; too glib. He was agreeable, infectiously so. The man had battled his hussars brilliantly, made them believe they fought many instead of only one, yet now he seemed capable of only trivial thoughts. True, this could be the lingering effect of the blow to the head; but it was more likely a ruse, a mask, a stratagem. That would be in keeping with the way the man fought. Lazarette suspected he was a human Trojan Horse: a very dangerous opponent and one who might well fool a lesser man.

"You are a Gascon are you not, Colonel? Your accent is distinctive." said the Englishman with a pleasant, cheerful voice that belied his dark, hard analytical nature. His mind raced and worked hotly, even as his voice tumbled pleasant words. "I visited your portion of Laungedoc briefly during the Peace of Amiens and found both the cuisine and women delightful." He paused and surveyed Lazarette up and down, like a scientist examining an insect for his specimen board. "From your manner, poise, and the quality of your uniform, I surmise you come from a long line of military men."

Lazarette showed a brief flicker of surprise at the Englishman's knowledge of regional accents, but quickly rallied.

"You are perceptive, Captain. I am indeed a Gascon and come from a proud lineage. It stretches back to Roland and the knights defending the pass at Roncevalles against the Moors. My cadet branch had fallen upon hard times, due to a father who was a fine solider, but regrettably a gambler with an affinity for ill-considered enterprises. I am grateful the Wars have afforded me the chance to recoup both my family's reputation and its finances. I started my service as aide de camp to Marshal Massena. I know your Wellington found him a formidable opponent."

"Marshal Massena was indeed a skilled commander." Pennywhistle laid quiet but special stress on the word *was*; the marshal had failed to live up to his reputation as one of Bonaparte's most talented subordinates. One-eyed Andre Massena was the most skilled and industrious looter in Europe. In contrast, Wellington compelled the British to pay for everything they took and punished looting with death. Wellington had beaten Massena thoroughly, but even during his retreat the wily old former smuggler had added to his art collection. If this colonel was his apprentice, then he was nothing more than a damned stinking plunderer, whatever his pretensions to honor.

"Might I return the favor and hazard a guess about you, *mon capitaine*?" Lazarette asked agreeably. "You bear no title, yet conduct yourself with the easy confidence and relaxed grace of one 'to the manner born'. I gather you are what we call a *milord anglais*. You have an older brother, perhaps, who bears the family title?"

Pennywhistle frowned for an instant. He disliked discussing family with strangers. He pasted his noncommittal smile back on and answered in pleasant tones. "I do have an older brother, but he bears no title greater than squire and merits no form of address other than a simple mister. In medieval times, my ancestors were marcher lords on the English frontier with Scotland and were key retainers for the Percys of Northumberland. A number of Pennywhistle tombs maybe found within Durham Cathedral. We rank as gentlemen at present, and that is reflected in our coat of arms. I am quite content with that honorable distinction and have no need of a title, which would merely result in my being overcharged by innkeepers."

"Ah!" said Lazarette in triumph. "I thought so! You are a modest man with no need to flourish pedigrees. A gentleman with many generations of distinguished service in your heritage, heroic likely to the highest degree, yet you behave as if it were all trifles. You let your character and military achievements speak for you. Excellent!"

"Allow me to congratulate you on an excellent tailor, Captain Pennywhistle. Gieves, or is it Hawkes? I see you keep up-to-date with military fashion and have the new short tails on your coat. You seem a very particular man, not the absent-minded stalwart you would have me believe you are. Don't look so surprised, Captain. I spent three weeks in London ten years ago during the brief peace between our nations you alluded to. It is a fascinating city, but I wonder how you English survive on so much tasteless, distressingly bland food."

"Steak and kidney pie may not be in a class with chicken chasseur, but we get by well enough," said Pennywhistle pleasantly. "I would agree with you, in a general way, that we might benefit from a study of your recipes, but I would also argue that you could certainly benefit from a study of our parliamentary system of government. As for my tailor, it's

Gieves, so delightfully understated, and the same as for my father. Clothing should always be in subtle good taste and avoid ostentation. I find smart attire sends a good message to the men. *Vestis virum reddit*, Seneca said; wouldn't you agree? I can see by your clothing that you do, although I must ask if all of the gold on your uniform weighs you down when you ride."

Lazarette smiled at the thinly veiled jibe; he looked as if he had heard it before from French infantry.

The food was delicious, Pennywhistle had to admit. It proved an excellent palliative for the pain hammering his head. But he had a bad feeling his studied persona was not having its intended effect. The colonel was perceptive; he had depth, sophistication, and an observant, worldly cynicism that provoked more from Pennywhistle than he'd intended to reveal.

Pennywhistle knew an aristocratic sprig of an officer, Slade was his name, that was as friendly and brave as he was incompetent. Slade was the kind of ungifted, clueless amateur who meant well but got men killed. He frequently got assignments as a courier because no one knew quite what else to do with him, and as a courier he could only get himself killed. When Lazarette asked about his service, he appropriated this man's record.

Lazarette was impressed by the conviction in the voice, but the record was entirely too spotty for the man who had savaged a whole troop. It was not a lie, he concluded, merely the truth about someone else. He would have to be wary of the Englishman's responses.

"I trust you enjoyed the meal, Captain? The claret was to your taste?" Lazarette inquired like the gracious host he could be when he met someone he respected. He met very few of those.

"The claret was excellent. The French are truly impressive vintners, and their reputation as great chefs is deserved. Those are two areas where, sadly, you put my countrymen to shame. The battlefield is, of course, another matter." He forced himself to laugh. It did not sound hearty, as he hoped, but tinny and hollow.

Lazarette returned an equally humorless smile. "I am so glad. But agreeable though this repast and our talk have been, this is neither a gentleman's club nor Madame de Stahl's Salon. I have great need of information that I believe you possess. You carried dispatches, important ones. The ones in plain text will be easy to read, but it appears some are encoded. We will of course break the code, but it would be so much easier if you simply relate to me their general contents. Just what were you told?" His tone suddenly turned deadly serious and his brown eyes narrowed to those of a hungry predator.

From pleasant circumlocution to hideously direct, all in the space of a few words; the hussar had a fine sense of timing. But this question would be easy enough to field, since he honestly did not know what was in the dispatches. He had been told they were of importance but had begun to doubt that. They were more likely a cover for what he carried in his boot. He guessed if the dispatches were lost or discovered, they would cause some small inconvenience, but without affecting the conduct of the war. The truth was safest.

"Colonel, I have no idea what is in them. I carry messages, I do not read them. I cannot tell you what I do not know."

Lazarette watched his eyes. They were steady and unblinking. Possibly, he was telling the truth.

"A great fuss has been made over you at headquarters and you have been the object of a widespread manhunt. Why do you think this would be so if you were merely a courier carrying ordinary dispatches? Does it not seem a great waste of manpower?"

Pennywhistle decided agreement was wisest. "Certainly, Colonel, but I can hardly be expected to comprehend the thought processes of staff officers at your headquarters. I am but a simple soldier, a commissioned errand boy. I follow the decisions of my superiors."

Lazarette nodded his head in acknowledgement, but his mocking expression suggested he found the 'simple soldier' stuff less than credible. "I do not think they would have made such a great effort without a good reason. Perhaps it is something on your person, or inside your uniform. We have not even searched your pockets. It may be hidden in the most secret of body cavities. We can rip your uniform to shreds and administer the most unpleasant of searches, but I think the solution much more prosaic. I think it is hidden in your mind, and there are many ways to open that up if gentle persuasion fails. I hope you will see reason. I think you are a highly intelligent man who appreciates reason and courtesy. It would be a shame if necessity forced me to dispense with those."

Pennywhistle knew exactly what Lazarette meant. At least he had not mentioned anything about boots. The Colonel was smart and thorough, but it would probably take a full day before he divined the hollow heel. Even if he found it, the message was in code. It would take time to summon an officer from headquarters, time for him to guess it required a code disk, time for him to make the calculations. Still, if Pennywhistle, an amateur, could figure it out, a professional certainly could.

Of course, Lazarette could just beat it out of him. He would resist, but even the best man could be broken under the right conditions, and now the fact that he had decoded the message made the threat of torture a real danger. Too much brutality would simply render one too insensate to respond electively. The most glaring problem was that people in pain would often say any lie just to make it stop. He suspected Lazarette knew all that, had done this often, and had a good idea how to mix pain and guile in just the right proportions.

"I would hope you value reason as well, Colonel. Search me all you like, you will find nothing else because there is nothing else to discover. You have already opened the dispatch case. And I cannot tell you something I do not know. He sat up slowly and rose to his feet. His head hurt but he was no longer dizzy. He dramatically emptied his pockets. What came out were personal items of no military value. "You see, Colonel, I am a dull old sod, with nothing to hide."

The Colonel laughed in spite of himself, he could not but admire the man's cheek. "A fine performance, captain, but I think you have everything to hide. Any man who carries a weapon," he walked to a corner of the tent and picked up the Ferguson, "of unique design and construction is a battlefield artist of a kind; exacting, particular, mindful of details. Just the sort of fellow to whom details of a clandestine nature would be entrusted. I wonder if you have been given some sort of message to commit to memory. It might be a series of phrases, rhymes, or even a poem."

"Sorry, Colonel, that's an amusing theory, but I was told nothing of the kind, merely to make certain the dispatches got through to headquarters. Really, I have no other information to give you. Take what measures you will, but you will have no more information than you do now. And it seems a shame to sully the pleasant relationship we have established."

"I fear I shall have to, Captain, you clearly know something you are not telling. Your headquarters could have chosen anyone for this job, but they chose you; a highly resourceful man with a special weapon who wishes me to believe he is much less than he is. You British are eccentric but you are not fools. They selected you because you could give whatever you carry unique protection. This is your last chance to avoid unpleasantness. Just tell me the truth."

There was both a determination and odd pleading in his eyes that made Pennywhistle believe him in all respects. The man would do what was necessary. He would do the same and endure what he must. He had little time before he would be physically unable to escape. At least he felt better; the pain in his head had subsided to an occasional minor thump, and his mind had returned to functioning with its usual brisk efficiency. His arms and legs were intact, and the colonel had thoughtfully left him unbound. Furthermore, his weapon and accoutrements were within reach.

"My answer is still the same, Colonel. I have nothing to say and no information to give you. However, it would give me great pleasure to discuss that about which I am knowledgeable. I am quite proud of my weapon and you seem most interested. I should be delighted to give you its history and explain its innovations. It performed particularly well earlier this afternoon. Your men will certainly vouch for that." His affable manner translated to "go to hell."

"Another time, I should be most gratified to hear." Lazarette looked directly at Pennywhistle and gave a sigh of resignation. "For now, you compel me to summon my guards.

******

It had taken the five an hour to assemble the four scarecrows now tied down behind the saddles of their human creators. Up close they were unconvincing, but at night, with plenty of shouting in support, they just might work. The flickering, uncertain light of campfires would reflect off the steel and increase the illusion of armed intruders.

Juanita thought the shadow riders were a symbolic version of the Four Horseman of the Apocalypse. With God, even little things flowed toward a predestined end. She would free Pennywhistle, even if she had to do it alone.

It took half an hour of riding before they spotted a hillside festooned with campfires. They halted their horses, and Thynne produced a new Ramsden spyglass from his saddlebag. He unfurled it and carefully surveyed the hillside. His companions were tense and expectant, and Thynne seemed to take a ridiculously inordinate amount of time; they did not know it was his thoroughness that had kept him alive so far.

Finally he spoke. "There are roughly a hundred and forty disposed in the usual manner. There are four vedettes and two guards outside the commander's tent. They are expecting an uneventful evening; we shall make it anything but. Save for the vedettes, all of their horses are all unsaddled and it looks like all of their equipment has been stowed for the night. Even the quickest trooper will take quite a bit of time to organize his tack, mount up, and pursue. Mandrake and I can take care of the horses, but I will leave the actual rescue to you, Sergeant Dale."

"One thing I am not clear on, sir," remarked Dale, "is exactly how will you get the animals to stampede?"

Thynne smiled. "Horses are herd animals, sergeant. They are highly intuitive and follow a leader. Where he runs, they run. Horses naturally want to race each other, which is why cavalry charges quickly become disorganized. No horse has ever beaten Mandrake in a race and I am certain that will not change tonight. Create enough disruption, disorient their human owners, free them from their tethers, and they will dash after any horse that shows them a way to escape danger. It is a matter of separating them from their training and exciting their basic instincts. Mandrake is a highly intelligent animal, a pack leader. He and I are a team. He will follow my lead, and they will follow his. When you dismount and send in Lightning and the other animals with their scarecrow riders, they too will run with the others. The scarecrows will move by so fast, the French will not realize they are dummies, particularly when I precede them with very loud shouting.

"Once clear of the camp and pursuit, I will cull our horses from the herd and circle back toward you. Just head north from the camp. Mandrake has excellent night vision. With tonight's moonlight, he can see as well as you do in full day. He knows you all are the human part of his herd. Trust me, he will find you. The hussars are very dangerous on horseback, but without mounts they are merely second-class infantry. Remember though, you won't have much time. I can't say how long the hussars will chase the horses before they catch a few and mount up. Once you have him, I can get you away from here. I do have one question for you. The girl wants to help. Do you trust her?"

Juanita was picking up English fast and shot a nasty look at Thynne.

"I do, sir." Dale replied with a certainty that surprised him. Combat was man's work, but he was learning that here in the Peninsula everyone who could fire a musket counted. She had used the Ferguson expertly under great pressure. Her ferocity at El Corazón had stunned him. If she had been a man, he would have called her a fire eater. "She will do fine, sir. If anything, she wants the Captain back even more than we do."

******

The guards grabbed Pennywhistle without warning. He steeled himself for the blows to follow. Damn it, just when he was beginning to feel normal again.

CHAPTER TWENTY-FOUR

Thynne argued vehemently with Juanita. He suggested that she stay out of harm's way. If she came along at all, she should stay to the rear and leave the actual rescue to the men. Thynne was appalled by her idea since he was a thorough going gentleman with decided ideas on a woman's place and deportment, but he admitted she made a solid point. She did not really need his approval since he would be elsewhere when it happened, but it seemed important to her that he understand her motives. She talked with the passion of a Methodist bible-pounder, a creature he could not abide, being a good Church of England man, but she made it clear that she would do anything to retrieve Pennywhistle and he must do the same. If that meant using her body as a weapon, so be it. It was as if she was testing him, seeing if his determination matched hers, and if not, she meant to pass some of her fire along to him that it might better help him succeed. He had been right to be wary of her beauty. She seemed less a woman than martial missionary.

If she did not understand him, it mattered little, it would work anyway. He would do his duty and more. He needed no encouragement. He had tired of being known as merely the son of a marquis and wanted to prove himself a real soldier. The sheer craziness of the rescue appealed to the insanely heroic side of him that had caused him to become an exploring officer in the first place. You had to be a bit mad to operate alone, in full uniform, miles behind enemy lines, sometimes in easy view of your opponents. Of course, you had to have the intelligence to know what was important and what was not, as well as figuring out exactly where to look to find it. Your only ally was your horse, and every day he was grateful for the ridiculous amount of money he had spent on Mandrake.

Besides, this Pennywhistle fellow seemed a remarkable sort of chap, someone after his own heart, someone who deserved a sporting chance of rescue. He had no idea of exactly what his mission was, but it had something to do with getting information to Wellington and in a way was not dissimilar to his own. He found it amusing he would be dashing at the French tonight instead of the usual dashing away from them. He checked the trumpet and thought he could manage something dramatic.

He surveyed the camp with the Ramsden one last time. It was on an open hillside, but bordered on a creek. Dale and his party could use the reeds in the creek beds as cover and approach fairly close to the main tent, but he would have no such advantage. He would have to trust Mandrake's great speed to close the distance quickly before they could do him damage. He furled and sheathed the Ramsden and drew his sword.

He had whet-stoned the blade earlier, but he checked the point and edge of the big saber one last time. The 35-inch blade was viciously sharp. He had made sure the armourer reground the point into a triangle instead of the standard quarter circle so that the weapon was just as effective thrusting as it was slashing. He would need to do both tonight: the first for the men, the second for the horses' tethers. He guessed most of the animals were carelessly moored to the hilts of swords driven into the ground. The horses remained more by habit than anything else.

Dale, Manton, Morales, and Juanita moved stealthily along the creek bed, walking slowly with the horses in tow. Dale knew people would be difficult to spot, but the silhouettes of the horses were much harder to conceal. He hoped the French were complacent. Each horse carried a straw passenger. Dale remembered what Thynne had said about the best way to launch the animals. The signal would be Thynne sounding the charge. It was almost time to put the scarecrows upright and attach the swords.

Dale handed Lightning's bridle to Manton and walked along the creek, searching carefully for what he had told Thynne would surely be there. His search was rewarded when he found a flat-bottomed fishing boat, probably belonging to a local farmer. It looked in good repair, had oars, and although it would be cramped, could accommodate six. The creek looked to fluctuate from shallow to non-existent, but recent rains made its depth sufficient to navigate. According to Thynne's map, it flowed north, away from the camp. He'd informed Thynne they would follow the stream for an hour, beach their boat, and make their way on foot. It would work—if the cavalryman was right about Mandrake's night vision.

******

The three guards were short, squat toads with the bowed legs common to hussars, but they behaved like the thugs their ugly, scarred faces suggested. Two guards grabbed Pennywhistle from behind and yanked him to his feet. They held his arms, while the third aimed a blow at his solar plexus. He blocked two punches with his bent, raised knee before his assailant switched his target to the head. He hit Pennywhistle six times hard and expertly in the cheek and jaw. Pennywhistle coughed out blood and a molar before he collapsed into the camp chair. Thinking him down for the count, his assailant incautiously came close. Pennywhistle lashed out with a sharp kick that caught the man squarely in the groin. The guard rolled on the floor, screeching loudly in searing pain. His companions looked to Lazarette for guidance. Lazarette waved a hand: enough for now.

Pennywhistle's head began to throb anew and he felt blood trickling down his face. His right cheek blazed with pain, but the pain strangely increased rather than diminished his alertness. The damage hurt but it was not incapacitating. That would change soon. The quick beating had merely been a demonstration.

"I am so sorry that was necessary," said Lazarette with weariness, "but I felt you needed some slight proof of my sincerity." He strolled over to the prostrate hussar holding his crotch and moaning. "Shut up, you fool, you shame me," he said curtly and kicked the man in the side. He turned to Pennywhistle and said with exasperation, "One of my less useful people, chosen for this duty because of his poor horsemanship."

Pennywhistle looked up and opened one of his eyes. A bloody crust had begun to form on the other. "I suppose it gets harder and harder to find good people with all of the deaths your Emperor has caused. Even with conscription, you must be scraping the bottom of the manpower barrel. I understand you have a big problem with draft evaders and I met several of your deserters yesterday." He put a sneer in his voice. "They will no longer trouble anyone."

"You wish to provoke me?" said Lazarette. "You cannot, but I would have been disappointed if you had not made the effort. All that you say is true, yet I have every confidence the Emperor will prevail. Now let us return to my original question. What are you carrying that is so important? Please tell me now so that I may resume a role I find much more agreeable than this present one. I am a soldier, not a jailer."

"My answer remains unchanged, Colonel. I have nothing to tell you because I know nothing of consequence. Whatever you may do, my answer will be the same in the morning as it is now."

"You British are such a sadly obdurate people. You have a weakness for lost causes and fail to apprehend when you are beaten. A reasonable man would understand his situation and make an accommodation. You are a reasonable man, captain. Would it not make sense to behave as one? You have no hope of escape, but might well look forward to safe, comfortable confinement. What point is there in playing the martyr?"

A loud, blaring clarion call shook the night. It was full-throated and brassy, a series of short, clipped notes, obliterating all of the usual night sounds and commanding everyone's attention, as it was meant to do. Lazarette was shocked, but Pennywhistle managed a hint of a grin.

Lazarette's first thought was, *How many cavalry troopers are charging?*

Thynne blew until he thought his lungs would burst. He stowed the trumpet, drew his saber, and put the spurs to Mandrake. There was no preliminary fast walk, trot, or canter; this was full stop to flat out gallop in a few seconds.

Mandrake hardly needed spurs or reins. He knew exactly what his master wanted and Thynne let him have his head. The gigantic midnight black stallion shoved his forehead down. His eyes burned, he dug his heels hard into the ground and unleashed all of his breakneck, soaring, wild energy. His nostrils grew wide and blazed fire as the supple muscles of shoulders, loins, and thighs pulsated with rhythm and flared out in bold relief. Thynne had always thought him a magnificent animal, but he was less beast now than pure spirit; a force of nature greatly to be feared.

The night whizzed past Thynne like a comet. Mandrake rocketed forward faster than Thynne could ever remember. Horse and rider merged seamlessly into an approximation of the centaur of legend; a terrible singleness of purpose beyond either man or beast. The scarlet and black pair became a bolt shot from a crossbow at the heart of the French. It was if they had both been bred and trained for this exact moment and purpose. Thynne screamed fierce slogans at the top of his lungs, although he later could not recall exactly what they were.

The noise set the stage, attracted their attention, but the French only saw the figure fully when he was thirty yards away. A gentle flick of the spurs caused Mandrake to kick in every last reserve of energy and surge beyond the fast gallop into a full blown charge. Thynne leaned back slightly, rose in his spurs, and thrust the heavy saber ahead at eye level, blade tip pointed toward what looked like an NCO. He braced for the shock of impact. Horse and rider changed from barely discernible objects to a complete blur of motion.

The French were transfixed by the speeding English madman on the gigantic horse. One awed subaltern silently mouthed, *"C'est magnifique! C'est ne pas le guerre!"* By the time they started to move, Mandrake was through them, had ridden two down, and Thynne's sword had begun slicing tethers. In the space of a few seconds, four horses were free and running into the night.

Dale spotted the dark racing figure and acted. He and his companions slapped the rumps of their beasts hard and yelled, "Haah! Haah!" The beasts ran toward the camp, the scarecrow riders with swords held aloft. They blazed past the startled guards at the tent's entrance. One raced after them, completely confused but certain it was some sort of British raid. He shouted the alarm and was soon far gone.

The other guard remembered his duty, and despite his racing pulse, remained at his post. He was even more surprised when he saw the girl materialize out of the darkness. She walked briskly, unafraid, and was dressed in traditional Spanish attire, her chest covered with a particularly large and colorful shawl. She bore a smile that seemed a bit odd, but her violet eyes were compelling and she certainly looked tall, dark, and lovely. Surely it would cost nothing to see what this beautiful apparition was about. As she got closer, he saw her shoulders were bare. His heart beat a little faster. She was certainly bold, but did not look like any of the Spanish trollops he had been with.

He lowered his gun as she approached. She stopped a few yards away and smiled a smile whose meaning was unmistakable. At the same moment she undid her shawl revealing a pair of very bare, very pert, young breasts. It made no sense, but the guard was not thinking sensibly at this moment. His tight breeches suddenly felt ridiculously tight. He could hardly contain himself as she moved forward, hips swaying, and put her left hand on his shoulder. It was pure bliss until the pain slammed into his brain. With her right she whipped up a dagger, plunged it into his chest, and pressed the point home with angry, explosive force. As the Frenchman dropped to the ground she hissed, *"¡Puerco!"*

Dale, Manton, and Morales rushed forward out of the night, weapons at the ready. They darted past her and into the tent. Lazarette could not have been more surprised if all of the residents of Valhalla had returned from the grave to confront him. He was suddenly not the courtly, cruel interrogator but merely an ordinary man reacting as an ordinary man would. It was a moment frozen in time, a fragment of a second that seemed a lifetime, everything carefully suspended waiting for an actor to push the clock hands forward.

One brutish guard made a motion toward Dale, and it was his last. Dale's hanger barreled through his throat. Manton sized up the second toad, vigorously thrust his bayonet into the guard's stomach and shouted, "Taste this, you lily-livered bastard!" He twisted it with real hatred when he saw the captain's bruised face out of the corner of his eye.

Pennywhistle moved much less swiftly than usual because of his injuries. His left eye was swollen shut and his right cheek bulged with black and blue indignity, but there was nothing wrong with his legs. His heavy hessian boot lashed out, connected solidly with Lazarette's seat, and sent him sprawling forward into Dale's arms. Dale jerked the colonel to his feet and finished the business with a powerful right to the chin. Lazarette hit the floor, down for the count. Juanita came out of nowhere and leaped upon him, intending to treat him to the tender ministrations of her dagger. Morales and Manton restrained her with great difficulty; her eyes flamed with hate and her limbs brimmed with its strength. She calmed herself unwillingly and they let go.

Pennywhistle staggered from his last burst of exertion and Dale caught him before he slumped to the floor. Manton and Morales assisted Dale and helped Pennywhistle to his feet. He recovered slightly and tried to say something gallant and important but all that came out was "Thank you."

Juanita came up and looked into his eyes. Her own filled with tears. "What have they done to you, Tomás? She spoke in English, heavily accented, but still English. Stress and necessity had improved her English rapidly. He mumbled, "It is nothing, nothing." She was making such a fuss over a few bumps and bruises. He'd certainly had worse when the Duke of Argyll's minions had set upon him for killing the Duke's grandson in a duel. The expressions on Dale and Manton's faces gave him pause, however. They looked concerned. He must not be a pleasant sight.

"Tomás, Tomás, Tomás," Juanita murmured in anxiety and concern as she squeezed his hand. Manton and Dale looked at her in momentary horror. Peasant girls did not address officers by their first names. It simply wasn't done!

"My rifle, if you please, Sarn't." It surprised him that he slurred the words slightly.

Morales bound and gagged the colonel. He made sure everything was tight, very, very tight. It would probably hurt a bit when he came to, but he did not care. This man commanded those who had killed his men. A part of him agreed with Juanita, but he admired Pennywhistle and realized real soldiers observed the conventions of war.

Dale grabbed the Ferguson and said, "Don't you worry none, sir, I've got it, and Manton and I have you. And, sir, we've got a boat." *Good*, thought Pennywhistle, *we can make it*. And then he passed out.

Chapter Twenty-Five

The force of the slashing saber split the hussar's sword neatly in half and a fraction of a second later, another blow did the same to his head. One second a man, the next, a falling corpse. A second hussar grabbed for the reins from the opposite side, but Thynne had a premonition of it. He used the kinetic energy of the first strike to help him pivot in his seat and guide the sword upward in an arc. He cut off both of the man's hands with the downward stroke.

Contorted faces flashed out of the darkness, hands grabbed for him, and swords darted upwards. Thynne and Mandrake pirouetted expertly as one; both he and the horse were admirably trained for the equitation of close quarter fight, particularly when their opponents were on foot. They dodged or blocked all of the blows of the small knot of men. Thynne's blade sang with skilled energy and darted back and forth in almost balletic movements. He administered several lethal slashes to his assailants and used every ounce of his considerable training. His sword rose and dipped in deadly rhythm and the joy of battle coursed through his veins, but he had to extricate himself. It would be fatal to be drawn into an extended fight. He wanted to keep the stampeding horses moving, but needed the initial island of resistance smashed to discourage others from forming.

Another mob of men ran vainly after the scarecrow warriors. The Frenchmen were surprised the English had not turned to fight, but continued the chase anyway. Even better, the only mounted troopers, the vedettes, impulsively joined in the pursuit. Thynne only faced men on foot. His heavy saddle absorbed most of the enemy blows he was unable to parry and Mandrake stayed undamaged. One man yanked at his tail and got a hoof to the forehead in response. Fortunately, the attackers were sufficiently befuddled and angry to strike at Thynne instead of the logical target, his horse. It may just have been as fellow horseman they were sentimental enough not to want to harm such a beautifully trained and fierce animal. More likely, it was because he would make a wonderful new mount for his captor.

Thynne gutted the last man, put his spurs to Mandrake, and shot free. He yelled at the top of his lungs, raced along, and cut more tethers. He hit several horse rumps with the flat of his sword and urged them forward. Other horses caught the hysterical energy of their brethren and began to yank violently at their tethers. The energy of a bucking horse was far greater than the anchor power of a long blade. It was curious to see running horses dragging swords behind them.

He spurred Mandrake ahead of the running horses, the appropriate place for a pack leader. The intuitive nature of horses was never on better display. They sensed Mandrake's dominance, his energy, his purpose. They wanted to be like him and with him, racing wild and free, heedless of the shouts of their masters pursuing them on foot. It was a kind of equine hysteria for all but Mandrake. He was the speeding embodiment of his master's will.

Thynne heard the passage of several bullets, but none came anywhere close. Carbines were close range weapons and firing at a fast moving target in the dark was a difficult prospect. He slowed Mandrake slightly, even with such a stout hearted animal it was important to conserve energy. The camp receded rapidly and the shouts grew less and less audible. He had not freed all of the animals, but guessed at least a hundred ran behind him. He would ride north for another few minutes.

He spotted Lightning, but not the rest of his party's beasts. It really made no difference. He had his pick of horses now. He only needed five. He hoped the rescue had been successful. He would circle back toward the creek and trust Mandrake's vision and, well, horse sense. It would take the Frenchmen the whole night to round up their fleeing companions and even then, many others would be lost to them for days. It had been a good night's work, regardless of whether the rescue attempt succeeded. He had signed up for adventure, and by God, this night he had had a jolly fine one!

Pennywhistle slipped in and out of consciousness. The now purple bruises on his face swelled and hurt. He saw only disordered images of men running and shouting and later would have only spotty memories of the rescue. Dale and Manton held him upright and his boots moved him forward seemingly without the instructions of his brain. The tumult and confusion made it easy for the little party of five to slip away unnoticed. They reached the safety of the reeds in a few minutes. Juanita insisted on taking charge of him and boarded the boat first. Dale and Manton laid Pennywhistle in next, his head cradled in her lap. His long frame caused his boots to dangle over the boat's port gunwale.

They placed their weapons and supplies in the center. Manton and Morales took the oars and Dale took the tiller. Dale felt they were in a position similar to that of being at an atheist's funeral; "all dressed up and no place to go." Well, not exactly nowhere. They were about to go somewhere, they were just not certain of exactly where that was. But anywhere away from the camp would be good. The brook flowed north, toward Wellington. Dale had no idea how long it would be until

Lazarette was discovered, but when he was, there would be hell to pay and he would undoubtedly mount a vigorous pursuit. Still, it would be hard without horses and it would probably be sometime before he concluded the fugitives had escaped by boat. Dale smiled and remembered the motto of the Marines: *Per mare, per terram;* On sea, on land. It had certainly been that way tonight.

Dale gave the boat a smart shove from the shore and hopped in. "Oars, give way all," he whispered. He realized he had given the naval command without thinking. Manton understood, but Morales was baffled. Manton pantomimed the meaning and the two oarsmen started a shallow and unified stroke. The boat moved into center stream and began steady progress. After a minute the camp was lost from view and the night sounds of crickets, cicadas, and frogs returned. It was soothing, much more pleasant than gunfire and cries of fear, pain, and distress.

Juanita stroked Pennywhistle's hair and spoke soft, comforting words to him in Spanish, the way a mother would to an infant in pain to soothe him into sleep. Pennywhistle heard fragments of it, but it seemed the greatest effort imaginable to pay enough attention to translate. Was she calling him by his Christian name? He barely felt the hard thwarts of the boat on his backside and the tone of her words caused him to experience a relaxed floating sensation. He was desperately short of sleep. His body was doing what it could to heal him.

Dale moved the tiller very little, just enough to keep the boat in center stream. There was more of a current than he had thought and the water was just a little deeper than expected. He told Manton and Morales to boat oars, husband their strength. Let the stream do the work. The boat, even with the weight of five, had at least a foot of clearance and the brook had very few rocks. There were some trees along the banks, but mainly cleared farmland. He spotted a few shapes he guessed were cows. The night was warm with a pleasant breeze. He briefly caught the scent of carnations and gazanias. It would be easy to drift like this and see where the stream carried them, but they had to find Thynne.

Dale borrowed Pennywhistle's Blancpain, and when sixty minutes were up he looked for a spot to beach the boat. He found what looked like a small landing, or perhaps just a spot for cows to ford the creek. He guessed they had come about three miles. The water was shoaling anyway, so it would have to serve. The boat eased onto the sand and stopped ever so gently. Dale grabbed his rifle and stepped over the gunwale. He motioned for the others to wait.

He needed to scout ahead. He moved cautiously out of the low bank and onto a flat grassy plain. He advanced a few hundred yards, stopped and simply listened. His nose sniffed the air for any untoward scents. He moved his head slowly, panning left then right. His woodsman's senses were fully engaged. Nothing presented itself except the utter ordinariness of the terrain and its inhabitants. It was dull but safe. It would do.

He went back to the boat and everyone gathered their belongings. Manton and Morales helped Pennywhistle out of the boat and up the hill. He came briefly to consciousness and absent-mindedly thanked them again for their efforts. He was vaguely aware of the night breeze and movement up a slight incline. His mind wondered who someone named "Thynne," was. He heard the name mentioned several times. He blinked hard a few times to stay conscious. He painfully pulled the crust off and opened his left eye fully for the first time. His vision was unimpaired and he would have rejoiced if he were not so damned tired. Then someone put a colorful blanket down and it seemed the most natural thing in the world that he should become immediately and intimately acquainted with it. A second after he was fully prone, he was sound asleep.

Juanita sat next to him and again cradled his head in her lap. Now came the hardest part, the waiting. Dale, Manton, and Morales spread themselves out in a wide arc in the hope at least one of them might be seen.

Manton passed the time by looking for the constellations his master had taught him. He found Orion, Ursa Major, and Ursa Minor in short order, but it took him longer to find the others. He had just locked onto Cassiopeia, when he felt a low rumble. A few seconds later, he heard it. He would still see nothing. The rumbling grew louder and tall, dark shapes appeared over the brow of the low hill. Thynne had come through after all. Maybe all of that talk about his horse had not been mere boast.

Thynne and the horses slowly clopped down the hill. They had had plenty of exercise for the evening and might need their strength later, so he kept their pace easy. Dale walked up to Thynne and greeted him warmly. "Glad to see you, sir, we made it out just fine, and we have the captain. He took a little damage aloft, but his hull's in good shape." The naval metaphor puzzled Thynne briefly, but he nodded as he deciphered it. "He is sleeping now and Juanita's taking care of him. She won't leave him. How did things go with you, sir?"

"Mandrake and I had quite a sparkling little outing and ran most of the horses off. Johnny Crapuad will have a damned awful time rounding them up after their affair with freedom. We did not encounter any mounted pursuit, although that situation will undoubtedly change. We culled four of the best specimens and have them with us. They all look to be fast and hearty. We brought Lightning, too. I may have been wrong about that horse. He is not much to look at, but appears to have exceptional heart and intelligence. Mandrake likes him and my horse is exceptionally perceptive."

Dale thought it would please the captain. Pennywhistle had never been much of a rider, but he seemed more sure of himself on Lightning than he had on any other horse. Perhaps Thynne had been right about horses having some mystical ability to bond with their riders.

"Did you find out the name of the commanding officer?" inquired Thynne, his expression no longer pleasantly amused. "Captain wasn't feeling talkative, sir," said Dale, "but he mentioned the name Lazarette. I gather that's the colonel we left bound and gagged." Dale neglected to add his fist had put the colonel to sleep.

Dale could not see Thynne's face terribly well in the darkness, but his voice clearly registered concern. "I know Lazarette, sergeant, he is bad news, very bad news. All of us who do this job know him. The peasants loathe and fear him and his men have chased me on a number of occasions. He will not suffer an attack on his camp to go un-avenged and absolutely will not stop until all of us are captured or dead. The girl would be turned over to the amusement of his men. We really must be gone from this place immediately."

"Sir, my captain needs rest, badly. Is there someplace you know where we could fort up for awhile?" Dale worried that he had no plan beyond the retrieval of his officer.

"You are talking to the right man, sergeant. All of us in this singular trade have our bolt holes. We carefully arrange hides, safe houses, places of refuge to disappear for a bit. We keep extra cash, coin, and supplies in a few. We also know which people are willing to assist, although we guard their identities very zealously. If discovered, their deaths would be long and slow. There is a cave five miles from here. It is impossible to see from the road unless you know where to look. Not the most pleasant place, but plenty of room. I have a few extras laid in. It should do fine. It will be light in a few hours. We need to be off the road by then. Stick with me and I will get you all to Wellington."

That was the best news Dale had heard all night.

CHAPTER TWENTY-SIX

Colonel Lazarette endured a full hour of indignity before he was discovered and unbound. He did not vent his very considerable rage immediately. The two officers who freed him expected a spectacular explosion of temper to judge by the frightened looks on their faces, but he could not permit himself that luxury today. He was a man of grand passions, but cold reason always asserted itself at important moments. He was all business and exercised great self control. He forced equanimity into his voice, and demanded a strict and exact accounting of events that had transpired during his captivity. He could do nothing to recover his prisoner until was in full possession of the necessary information; rage, while satisfying, would retard his efforts to set things right.

He listened carefully and his face darkened. He put the details together carefully, like a detective, and admitted his opponent's rescue plan was clever. He wondered who the English officer on horseback was. He had made a spectacular impression on the French and his officers wanted him badly. Lazarette did not care much about him. His death would be an agreeable bonus, but only the marine officer had information he wanted. Pennywhistle had made things personal for Lazarette.

He was not pleased, and yet, he felt more alive than he had in a long while. He had sought a real test of his abilities and this was certainly it. He admitted to himself this was far more stimulating than a simple execution of Spanish grandees. No prisoner had ever had the skill to escape his clutches and he was not about to let Pennywhistle be the first.

He grilled the officers intently about Pennywhistle. No one had seen him escape or knew in which direction he had gone. He described the rescuers to his officers and no one had seen them either. If they were on foot they could not have gotten far, but that would not be consistent with their ingenuity. They had probably taken horses or, the man was a marine officer after all, might have taken a boat. He knew little of watercraft but a man like Pennywhistle would. There was a creek behind the camp. He would have it searched.

He asked how many men still had mounts and could ride immediately. The officers temporized but he finally pinned them down to twenty. Not good at all, disgraceful they had allowed excitement to override every military concern, but he would have to live with it. He would lead the pursuit himself. He told the officers to send the troopers on to him in groups of ten as they recovered their mounts. A man traveling alone at night was still a target for Spanish partisans. He demanded a map and began to make deductions.

Pennywhistle noted Lightning recognized him, even seem pleased, but it was only a fleeting impression in a night full of them. Dale and Manton hoisted him into the saddle and Juanita mounted behind him. He immediately put his arms around Lightning's neck and clasped it tight. His head slumped forward onto Lightning's mane. He closed his eyes and slid blissfully into sleep. Juanita took the reins and Lightning began to plod slowly forward.

The little procession reached the cave just as the first pink fingers of dawn appeared. They had ridden in silence. They all experienced the lassitude and fatigue common after pulse-pounding excitement, but their spirits were heartened by their trust of Thynne's expert knowledge.

Thynne said their sanctuary could last no longer than eight hours, and even that was risky. He knew they needed rest. Otherwise, he would have made the stop brief. He understood Lazarette's coldly methodical, unrelenting methods all too well.

He believed they were a hard day's ride from Wellington's main body. It was likely cavalry patrols were even closer. Once they picked up a patrol, they would have an escort. It would probably be hussars, even the British had them now; same mentality, same sort of showy uniforms. It was somehow appropriate.

Lazarette's men found footprints down by the creek. His guess had been right. He traced the watercourse on his map. He found a fording place a league distant which seemed a likely place to start. With only twenty men, he could not cover multiple possibilities. His men and horses splashed through the water and an hour later found the boat.

Pennywhistle gradually returned to consciousness and realized he was in some sort of cave. It had a ceiling of about ten feet and was roughly the size of a ballroom. He blinked his eyes a few times and was glad to find his vision unimpaired by Lazarette's thugs. His head had stopped aching, but not the bruises on his face. He slowly panned his head around. The cave had a narrow entrance, barely wide enough to admit a horse. There were a few boxes and bales visible, and he noted the horses were all inside. They placidly chewed the contents of their oat-bags.

Manton was sound asleep on his right and Dale was similarly disposed next to the cave entrance. Juanita still grasped his left hand and sat upright against a box, but her eyes were closed. A British officer whom he had not met, but assumed to be Thynne, was the only one wide awake. He calmly ran his long sword back and forth over a whetstone. He glanced at Pennywhistle when he heard movement.

He smiled, put down his sword gently, and walked over to the marine. "Glad to see you are finally awake. It's almost noon and we will need to leave soon." Pennywhistle fumbled in his pocket to see if he still had his Blancpain. He was gratified to see the French had not stolen it. It was ten minutes to midday. He liked to be sure of things.

"I have heard a lot about you, Captain Pennywhistle. You inspire remarkable devotion in your comrades. I am Steven Thynne. I would have introduced myself last night, but you were in no fit shape for me to do the honors. Those purple insults on your face look painful. I gather Lazarette was his usual charming self. All of us in this peculiar calling know what he did to El Corazón." He handed Pennywhistle a silver flask. "This might help."

Pennywhistle took a healthy gulp. Martell Cognac, the best. Finally, some good spirits after all the bad he had dished out over the last two days! "Thanks, kind of you." The cognac was very smooth and mellow, but he would have gladly traded it for a steaming cup of Brazilian Coffee. He made a motion to stand.

"No, don't get up, rest," said Thynne kindly. He reached down and shook Pennywhistle's hand vigorously. "I work for the Peer, that's what everyone calls Wellington, and I am told that you have information of value to him. I do not need or want to know what it is, but I trust I am not misinformed that it is important?"

"No, Captain Thynne, it is very important. Important enough to have turned a simple journey from Lisbon into a series of leaps from one frying pan into another. Nothing has gone right, and it appears I have been shadowed from the very start. I fear security at our headquarters in Lisbon is inadequate and someone is regularly telling tales to the French."

Thynne looked aghast. "I confess the idea of a turncoat at headquarters both appalls and surprises me. What would cause a man to sell out his country, his honor, and his friends? Money, blackmail, love? It is a revolting notion, but you are clearly a man of sense and if you say it is so, far be it from me to doubt you. The Peer will definitely want to hear this. Oh, and let's not stand on formality. It's Steven."

"Tom," the marine said easily. He liked this man instinctively. He also knew the kind of man who became an exploring officer. They would work well together. "We have a lot to discuss, Steven, and I gather not much time to do it in. Why don't you start by enlightening me on our situation and prospects. Please spare no detail. It is good to finally be wide awake and my mind is eager to do something gainful."

"A good map will help. The Peer was hamstrung by the wretched maps provided by the Spanish when he arrived, so he ordered our Ordinance Survey chaps to prepare detailed, up-to-date specimens." Thynne removed a large, rolled up document from a long leather case and unfurled it on the ground. He and Pennywhistle got down on hands and knees to carefully examine its contents. "This is one of their newest efforts and it's based on the most accurate information available." He pointed to a spot. "We are here." He traced his finger in a series of s-shapes outlining a route. "We need to get there." He pointed to another spot on the map. "There is no direct route and we will have to use secondary tracks to avoid French cavalry. Still, there is no reason it can't be done. At least, that's where I think Wellington will be. The armies are never far apart. Marmont is good, I will give him that. The Peer will fall back to Salamanca, I am sure of it."

The discussion lasted for the better part of an hour. Pennywhistle decided he was right to be impressed by the man. He had the details well in hand and his explanation of his part in the rescue was modest. Pennywhistle was experienced enough to read between the lines, and while he believed most so-called heroes were creations of the press for propaganda purposes, this man came as close to the reality as anyone he had met.

"If you don't mind me asking, Tom, what is the situation with the girl? She looks lovely and demure until you get to the eyes. I cannot tell if she is a mad woman or warrior goddess, but there is something dangerous about her, like a powder keg awaiting a match."

Pennywhistle quickly related his association with her. Thynne's eyebrows arched, his expression tensed, and he let out a low whistle. "I am just glad she is on our side," he remarked. "Or is it God's? Perhaps the one thing we can be sure of is that she is very much on your side. I confess, for all of the time I have spent here, I still don't understand the Spanish temperament. For all of their devotion to their Popish Faith, they are certainly excellent haters and don't seem to subscribe to any of the forgiveness stuff. Maybe it's the legacy of the Inquisition."

"Only they could have come up with Don Quixote," replied Pennywhistle thoughtfully. "He's all of Spain in one man; gallant, honorable, proud, but far past his prime and stubbornly clinging to fanciful, medieval conceits that have little bearing on present day problems. Spain is the land the Enlightenment forgot. Juanita has made me realize they see Bonaparte as some sort of Antichrist. They believe he wants to gut The Church here as he did in his own country, reduce it to a mere subsidiary of the State. That helps us, although they still don't like outsiders. Deep down, they know they need our men and our gold, but they are far too stiff-necked to show us any direct gratitude. I am certain that, in future Spanish histories, our part will be writ small.

"I don't know what to make of Juanita either. I just know she has proven valuable. She seems to have attached herself to me the way a remora does to a shark. I want to be shed of her, but in all of the chaos, I have been unable to figure out how. I cannot just leave her stranded."

"She hardly seems the sort of girl who cannot look after herself, Tom. Are you certain you don't have some regard for her? If you do, you would not be the first man to be caught up in a wartime romance. Battle does strange things to our sensibilities. And she certainly is a head turner."

Pennywhistle bristled. It startled Thynne. "I have no designs on her at all, romantic or carnal," he said coldly.

Thynne thought the demurral rather too forceful. "Sorry there, did not mean to touch a raw nerve," he responded with a diplomatic smile. "I am sure there is no need to decide anything just now. It won't matter anyway, if Lazarette gets to us."

"Accept my apologies. Your question was quite reasonable." Pennywhistle's customary tact made a late return. "I want to assure her safety, but I will not permit my concerns to override my duty. I think it's time to wake these worthies," he pointed to the sleeping trio, "and get moving. Don't you?"

"I do indeed," said Thynne. "I don't like to move in daylight, but with Lazarette on us, we have no choice. I am certain he will find this place before nightfall. We can eat in the saddle."

He walked over to Mandrake and extracted a sword from the saddle. He returned to Pennywhistle, who rose to meet him. "You might need this. I noticed your own was missing. It's the '96 Light Cavalry saber. It's a trooper's model that I keep it as a spare. It's well balanced, and the curved blade makes it ideal for slashing. It's got a good edge and the French generals are afraid of it. A single blow can amputate a man's arm. Probably not up to your high standards, but it's all I can offer."

Pennywhistle smiled. "Thank you, you read my mind. I feel naked without a blade." He accepted it from Thynne and flourished it about a few times, to get a feel. It had a comfortable stirrup grip and a 33-inch blade. "It's longer than my cutlass, and heavier. We don't have much room on deck to swing a long blade. I'm more used to something fast and handy. I'll need to practice a bit, swinging it from the saddle. I just hope it will not be needed." He did indeed wish that, but the way things had gone on this mission, he was probably wrong.

******

Lazarette did what he always did: he pushed. He knew his men called him "Old Iron Ass," but he rather enjoyed the appellation. When men started to slump in their saddles he did not relent, but drove them even harder.

The men did not like it, yet it did not surprise them. They knew him to be harsh on the best of days, and this certainly was not one of those. They admitted he always got results. Their performance the night before had hardly been stellar, and they were almost as eager as he for revenge. They had no idea why the fugitive was so important, but it hardly mattered; the colonel believed he was, and they doubted neither his conviction nor his resolve.

Boom! An explosion echoed down the valley. Lazarette looked through his spyglass at a puff of smoke from the top of the hill ahead. One his men had been scouting in that area. He ordered the rest of the troop forward and they trotted upwards until they reached the summit. He found the sergeant and his horse, or at least bloody fragments of them. He dismounted and examined the area. He discovered some wire next to one of the horse's hooves and noticed a cave just beyond. He knew immediately what had happened. The cave was a hide. The horse had stumbled over a tripwire and triggered a cache of explosives. It was a typical, nasty parting gift from the English *goddams*, as he referred to them in private. He was on the right track. They had been here, and not long before. He would have them soon.

Chapter Twenty-Seven

They moved in line-ahead formation, with Thynne in the lead and Pennywhistle in the rear. The day waxed bright and clear, but the road turned dull and dusty. Everyone had mixed feelings: part relief, part anxiety. The journey was close to an end. They might well reach the most distant vedettes of Wellington's army by nightfall. They might also have that outcome forestalled at any moment by an appearance of Lazarette's hussars.

Manton was glad beyond words that his officer had survived, but wondered what would become of Juanita when they reached headquarters. Her interest in the captain was obvious, but Manton knew him well enough to see his concern for her was only that of an upright gentleman doing his manly duty.

He, on the other hand, had a great deal of interest in her, but she seemed almost as unaware of his presence as the captain was of hers. He was picking up Spanish rapidly enough but only understood fragments of what she said. He didn't care. He simply loved the sound of her voice and everything about her. He hated that he was only a servant and hardly in a position to even consider marriage. His heart whispered they could have a fine life together. Still, the captain had told him on many occasions that nothing was permanent, the essence of life was change, and that a man made his own luck and forged his own destiny. He'd certainly never expected to be where he was now, frightened beyond belief yet having the adventure of a lifetime.

Juanita decided to return to her village when this was finished and join the Partisans. She had done that once before; she had received training, but the band she'd joined had been wiped out the one day she had been unable to be with them. She had been spared death then so she could be in exactly the place she was now.

God's will was truly strange and wondrous. A crisis had thrust this man into her life. It was a test of character for both him and her. God had guided him to her to show her how to fight, to show her what mattered in life, even as He directed her to protect and love him. She would surrender her life for him, just as she would freely surrender her body to his passion, but she realized his regard for her, while kind and benevolent, was on the order of a gentleman's concern for a well-beloved pet. He saw her not so much as a flesh and blood woman to be loved, but as a ward to be protected. She sensed a terrific shield around his heart, a high barrier to wall off some unspoken pain. He acted a stranger to his own emotions. If only she could batter down the portcullis of his heart and reach the deep passion within!

Dale carefully observed the countryside as he rode. He was eager to be done with the mission. He liked Spain well enough, although the landscape was far too barren for good poaching. He missed the sea. He thought briefly about retiring. He had put in twenty years and saved enough prize money to open an inn. He stayed out of loyalty to the captain and a perverse inability to give up the adventure his captain always delivered. His captain looked a lot better this afternoon then he had the previous day, and it pleased him. He wondered idly why Pennywhistle disregarded Juanita's affection. If a woman like that made eyes at him, he certainly would pursue her with vigor and enjoy all of her womanly charms at the first possible moment. But then, he was just an old soldier from a country background, a man of simple tastes and desires, who tended to see things in blacks and whites.

His officer was a much more complicated man who continued to blame himself for a death he had not caused. Carlotta had been a fine and remarkable woman, but it was a shame the captain had become obsessed with her memory. The captain practiced forgiveness and compassion toward everyone but himself. He found himself hoping Pennywhistle would have a moment of weakness and simply take the girl. She clearly wanted him. He wished his officer would forget his iron code and simply be human, but he knew that to be unlikely.

Morales, riding behind, had come to admire Dale. He was the epitome of the good NCO. Morales had found he liked soldiering and had some talent for it. He decided his cause was just, but that the British Army would do more to free Spain than anyone else. His own regiment was gone. He wanted to fight with real soldiers. When they reached Wellington, he just might sign on with the English.

Thynne senses stayed on high alert. The road was clear, as was the horizon in every direction. Nothing had happened this afternoon; all to the good. They were making excellent time and each mile brought them closer to safety. Yet he felt great unease, and he sensed Mandrake felt the same thing. The beast snorted and chuffed every so often uncharacteristically. That worried him. Horses apprehended danger long before their human masters did.

He wondered about Pennywhistle and the girl. The marine treated her with an exaggerated respect. The question he'd posed had elicited a testy response. If he had feelings for her, why did he fight them? He seemed to have turned the girl into an exhibit at a gallery of things brave: a feminine object of warrior art, to be contemplated but never touched. It would be the most natural thing in the world to forge a connection with her, even if only for one night. He certainly would have, but then he was a cavalryman and most of them were utter cads with women. He felt no shame in admitting he loved women, loved them often. He determined to enjoy himself a bit before his family arranged the inevitable "marriage for advantage" to some dull, aristocratic heiress with a plain face and dumpy figure. He cheered himself with the fact it might never come to pass. There was a good chance he would not survive the war.

Pennywhistle and Lightning trotted gently along. He was pleased no headache troubled him. He touched his eye and found the swelling greatly reduced. His bruised cheek was still tender to the touch. All other body parts were in fine fettle. He felt the need of more sleep, but that had been habitual on this mission. He told himself he had every reason to feel good: he had escaped captivity, and despite the varied problems of the past few days, he was hours away from accomplishing his mission. But he did not feel good.

It was the damn girl. Thynne's question was innocent enough, but it had opened a Pandora's Box of thoughts he would have preferred to have kept locked up. It was ridiculous, he told himself; they had no possible future. Her religious views alone should disqualify her. She might even be half mad. Danger and privation, however, often made even the most ill matched people feel attraction. It was temporary, fleeting, of no moment. It would vanish entirely when he resumed his normal duties. Two ships at sea who passed within hailing distance, exchanged greetings, and continued on their way. It was monstrous to even think of boarding her.

Yet the thought would not go away. She was attractive and would probably be as passionate in love as she was in battle. He had not been with anyone for quite a period and he was tired of loneliness. It would be so much easier if she had been just a high born nonentity; a woman of beauty and poise with no depth or substance. They were easy to discard and forget.

It was the force of her spirit he feared. It had no aristocratic pretension or refinement but was pure, earthy fire. If it touched you, you would not be the same after. It would be impossible not to feel anything. It had the force to burn through all of the protections he had established. He both wanted it and recoiled from it. It could be much more than a palliative; it might actually heal. It would also make him face the truth about his past. He was not sure he was equal to that.

He had become used to living with his pain; it was a part of him, and he could no more forget the memory of what caused it than he could stop breathing. It drove him to excel, to take great risks, to hazard his life in defense of others. He sought no glory or emoluments. He only hoped the atonement of brave deeds would bring a surcease of pain and guilt. It had worked, but only to a certain point.

He feared if he healed he might start to forget Carlotta, what she had been, how she had loved, the grace she had brought into his life. She had been a magnificent Italian beauty of heroic stature, an even six feet of stately loveliness, gifted with a brain and heart of equally impressive proportions. Few men were ever vouchsafed the sort of love he had had, and lightning never struck the heart twice. His pain kept her alive in a way, and its absence might turn her into a mere memory. She had been buried at sea; there was not even a grave to visit to make her death seem real. If he moved on, he might find love again. It was both an alluring prospect and a horrible one. He never wanted to forget her, but many brother officers had told him to do just that.

He had allowed his love for her to distract him at a critical moment. He should have seen it coming, but he had been tired after the battle with *Pomone* and HMS *Active* had been badly damaged. The heavy, speeding block on the severed ship's rope would have killed him if she had not shoved him out of the way. He told himself no other woman could ever compete with that. A distant part of his mind said, *Have a caution, Juanita might be willing to do exactly that.* Rather than comforting him, the thought angered him. He felt responsible for three women's deaths, and damn it, he would not be for another. He had enough blood on his hands to last a lifetime.

******

The hussars murmured and the column buzzed with a low anger. Men no longer slumped in the saddles and their backs became ramrod straight. Energy vibrated through the formation and fatigue faded. All of the horses sensed it and quickened their pace unbidden. Lazarette was saddened by the death of the sergeant, but it had proven highly useful: it had made the persuit personal to every man in the column. The sergeant had been well liked. He had not even died in battle, but as the result of some infernal device. They badly wanted its designer.

Lazarette had also received reinforcements. Twenty more men had joined him, doubling his force. He spread the reinforcements out widely over several miles, increasing the width of his net. Once the quarry had been spotted, he would concentrate his forces quickly. He sensed they were getting close. The thrill of the chase was as much about anticipation and suspense as it was the capture or destruction of its object.

He spotted a horseman racing across the plain at breakneck speed, raising huge clouds of dust. His heart missed a beat, for he had an excellent idea of what the hussar was about to report. Fifteen breathless minutes later, the man gave him his confirmation. The English had been spotted, a league ahead. The scout had watched them for ten minutes to be certain. Lazarette told the trumpeter to sound the recall for the other scouts.

Lazarette wanted to make a mad dash after them, but he was too experienced for that. He would pace the horses carefully. He did not want the horses to arrive blown and unable to execute a grand, final charge. The men deserved that, and he wanted to set things up so that no one escaped. He cared nothing of the fate of the others and was perfectly content to let his men relieve their anger. He did want Pennywhistle alive, however, and enjoined the men not to offer him fatal violence.

They had not liked that, but when he said he would deal with Pennywhistle personally, they ceased grumbling immediately. Lazarette was the supreme master of his craft. The Englishman might be a fine marine, but he was as out of place on horseback as Lazarette would have been on the rolling deck of a British frigate.

******

The sun sank lower on the horizon and the miles ground slowly past. Pennywhistle was far from becoming a cavalryman, but he was coming to appreciate horses. To his amazement, he actually started to believe that the instincts of a horse might have real value. So when Lightning started to become agitated and make low, snuffling noises, he paid attention.

He reined Lightning up and withdrew his spyglass. He extended it and pivoted in his saddle. It took a minute, but then he saw it: a cloud of dust, advancing quickly in his direction. His ear caught the very faint sound of a trumpet, which banished all doubt. He estimated the horsemen were two miles distant. He looked for cover, but there was none. They could make a fight of it, but the outcome would not be in doubt. They would all die, except himself, and that angered him. He would not be allowed to go out in a flurry of heroism, but would be brought back in chains for further interrogation.

At sea, he could look at a ship's design and sail plan, assess wind strength and direction, then closely approximate what speed it was capable of and for how long. It frustrated him he could not do so with animals on land. If they ran, as they must, he had no idea how the animals would perform and for how long. He might be out of his depth, but this was Thynne's element and he would surely know.

He put the spurs to Lightning and dashed up to Thynne. He explained things and the cavalryman listened closely. Thynne's face darkened, then brightened. "We don't want to start too soon, we need them closer. I am certain Mandrake can outrun them—isn't a horse in the French army that can touch him. I can't answer for the rest of the mounts, but I chose them for their lines and they are at least as fast as those chasing us. Lightning is slower than the rest, but Tom, that animal has heart and likes you. He will find the speed. What concerns me most is that I am the only experienced rider."

He weighed things for a minute, and then actually laughed. "By God, we might just be able to pull this off! We'll give them a damn good run for their money! You've never run a steeplechase before, have you? I've done plenty, but it's a good bet those French chaps never have. There is some broken country just ahead and it's very bad news for horses. I know it well; just tell everyone to follow Mandrake's lead." He moved Mandrake closer to Lightning and extended his hand to Pennywhistle. "Whatever happens, it's been an honor, Tom."

Pennywhistle smiled at the prospect of action; it was so much easier than thinking about women, dead or alive. "The honor is mine, Steven. If we get out of this, I shall send you a leaguer of brandy!"

Chapter Twenty-Eight

Thynne talked to the three others after he finished with Pennywhistle. "There is a walled farmstead five miles ahead. We will make for that. Might be something there for us. I hope to lose our pursuers before then. The ground is rocky with plenty of holes, and there are quite a number of stone walls. It's tricky, but I know what to avoid. The French won't. Trust your horses. Let them have their heads. Don't interfere with them, don't get in the way. They will follow Mandrake. When they reach a wall, they will imitate him and jump. Don't rein them in. Just lean forward, low as you can, and hold on tight. You'll get the hang of it soon enough."

They looked at Thynne with dubious expressions, but would do as instructed. They had little choice.

Pennywhistle took Manton aside. "Listen to me, Manton. I have great trust in you, and I am about to tell you something in the strictest confidence. I must have your word it will stay between us."

Manton was all eagerness, but assumed a grave look which he thought more appropriate. The captain usually did not sound conspiratorial. "Of course, I shall be discretion itself. You have helped me in so many ways, sir, I shall be most grateful to anything I can do to repay and increase your trust in me. Tell me how I can help."

"They are after me, Manton, not everyone else. I have something they want. It's in my left boot. You are only two inches shorter than I and look to have a similar size foot. I propose an exchange of boots. They may get me, but they won't get the cargo. Even if you are captured, they would not think to search you, but I think there is a chance you may get away simply because they consider a servant unimportant." He paused and gave a hint of a grin. "The more perceptive among us know, of course, the opposite is true."

Manton was used to curious events with his captain, but this was wholly unexpected. He put his surprise aside and assumed the steady manner of the good servant. "Certainly, sir, although you are definitely getting the poor end of the exchange. Your boot-maker did a wonderful job. I've never worn a hessian boot before, sir."

They made the switch quickly. Manton's foot was a bit wider than his, but the fit was not a bad one. Manton walked a few feet in his new boots and smiled. In the midst of great danger, he got to play the gentleman for a moment. He had to remember that the boots were not just boots, but something as valuable as gold.

They mounted up and departed in the same order as before, with Thynne leading and Pennywhistle bringing up the rear. They moved at a steady trot, although not a fast one. He wondered at the significance of the walled farmstead, but he had not pressed Thynne on the point.

Pennywhistle loaded the Ferguson before mounting and placed it in a saddle holster next to the sword. He had never fired a weapon from horseback before, and he knew a long weapon presented challenges, even to the experienced. Moving horses presented legions of problems, and they would want to keep moving today, but if Lightning stopped for even a minute, he might not be a bad approximation of a steady platform. He had one advantage. The Ferguson would be much easier to reload on horseback than a conventional carbine or musket. He felt much more comfortable with his rifle than he did with the new sword.

He held the reins with one hand and flourished the saber about with another. He had to get used to its weight and balance, not to mention adapting to its use from atop a moving horse. It felt very heavy, and he realized he could not use the same swift strokes he favored with his cutlass. He was used to quick wrist movements. He would have to be much more deliberate with this piece. He was very skilled with the cutlass, but felt like a novice schoolboy with the saber. He continued to practice as Lightning trotted forward.

******

Lazarette's column quickened its pace from a brisk trot to a fast canter. He told the men nothing, but the faster pace he ordered revealed everything to the experienced riders. Moods brightened and an air of expectancy coursed through the formation. The scouts folded into the column; they were no longer needed as outriders. Lazarette led from the front, as usual.

He could see the enemy through his spyglass. His men rode determinedly on. They steadily closed the gap from two miles to less than one. The enemy had not made a run for it. Perhaps the hussars had not been spotted? He dismissed that immediately. The two English officers were too observant for that. They were probably husbanding the strength of their horses until the decisive moment. That is what he would have done.

Thynne suddenly altered course, striking away from the main road, and Mandrake broke into a gallop. Lazarette spotted it immediately. This was where the English meant to give him the slip. He yelled to the trumpeter, who blew the appropriate flourish. The horses increased speed to match the Englishman's gallop.

Thynne bounded up and over a small hill. Ahead lay a line of stone walls about four feet high composed of rocks gathered from the field. Mandrake put his head down and dashed toward the first at a full gallop. He cleared it with ease and grace and again slowed to a fast trot.

Dale followed, and closed his eyes when the horse left the ground. The animal landed with a resounding thunk, and Dale bobbled about, but opened his eyes to find he was still in the saddle. Maybe it wouldn't be so bad after all.

Juanita's horse cleared the wall with less ease but equal success. She found the whole thing exhilarating and finally understood why men loved riding.

Manton was almost unhorsed but recovered himself quickly when the beast landed. Morales cleared the barrier without incident. Lightning, while not fast, proved to be a natural jumper and sailed over the barrier with dash. Pennywhistle decided, rather than being cheated in Lisbon, he had actually struck an excellent bargain.

Pennywhistle knew he shouldn't, but he had to give it a try anyway. Two hussars had foolishly dashed far in advance of the rest and were just too tempting to ignore. He halted Lightning and aimed a shot at the hussars. It was a clean miss. He reloaded and the second shot scored a hit on the trooper's shoulder, but he decided it was the result of pure luck, unlikely to happen again. He put Thynne's spare spurs hard to the big horse.

He noticed plenty of holes, divots, and hidden declivities in the field, but Mandrake navigated them expertly. The other horses followed his lead, just as Thynne had promised. Pennywhistle hated to think what would have happened if he had been on his own without a guide.

******

Lazarette had closed the distance to a third of a mile when the British party disappeared over the hill. He would not lose them now. The French covered the ground quickly. They had just departed the road when a horse stumbled, twisted, and fell heavily sideways. The animal let out a cry of surprised pain. The rider went down with the horse, leg held fast in the stirrup, and was pinned beneath the massive weight. The horse had hit a rabbit warren. The ground was honeycombed with them. Hussars reined in to help their fallen comrade, but Lazarette shouted a terse, "leave him." The men obeyed, but were naturally displeased. Strangely, they blamed not their commander, but the Englishmen they pursued. It stiffened their already angry resolve, but it did cause them to slow their pace.

Thynne saw the first hussars come over the hill. The farmstead was three miles distant. This was as good a time as any to see what the other horses were made of. He put the spurs to Mandrake and barreled ahead.

Another wall loomed. Mandrake flew over it and the others followed. The four amateurs and their mounts did better this time. None of them exactly relaxed, but the jump seemed easier because their confidence in their mounts was increasing. They found their beasts possessed an intuitive sense of terrain that their riders lacked. The scenery stormed by like lightning in the night.

Pennywhistle glanced over his shoulders at their pursuers. They had changed from a column to a line. The evolution had slowed their progress and they did not appear to be gaining ground.

Another French horse stumbled as it caught its foot in a warren. Its rider flew over its head and pitched into the ground with a heavy thud. He lay dazed and unmoving. The French line blew past him. The rough nature of the ground played havoc with the French line and split it into disparate groups. Because each horse made its best speed, the line became uneven, resembling the hills and valleys found in a compressed Christmas ribbon.

Lightning cleared the third jump perfectly. The horses in the British line were about two lengths apart from each other. Thynne actually had to slow Mandrake so the others could keep up. If he had had his head, he would have left everyone else far behind.

Lazarette lost two more men to holes but refused to slow up. His anger increased even as he admitted to himself the cleverness of the English cavalryman. He would still have the English bastards!

Pennywhistle saw that the French were gradually, almost imperceptibly dropping behind. The horrible terrain was wreaking mayhem on the French, and despite orders to the contrary, the troopers were slowing. God's blood, they just might make it!

Lightning had just cleared a fourth jump when Pennywhistle saw a ragged line of farmers with guns rise discordantly up from behind the wall twenty yards distant, which would be the next jump. Spanish militia, exactly what he didn't need. He knew they meant to help; they were probably supposed to spring an ambush and shoot the French troopers in the back once they cleared the wall. Perhaps the thundering English horses had frightened someone, and that man miscued the line to rise far too early.

They had clearly never seen action before and held their weapons stupidly. The most elementary rule of fighting was form square in the face of oncoming cavalry, exactly the opposite of their current posture. There looked to be a hundred men. Lightning thundered ahead and was now only ten yards from their ragged line.

The Spaniards saw the on-rushing line of hussars brightly clad in crimson and blue; their resolve and reason departed in a quick second of deadly understanding. Real battle was far different from how they'd imagined it. Their ears recoiled from the sounds of pounding hooves. The French looked huge in their saddles, their expressions fierce and angry. They could not be allowed to come close. Utter, complete, overmastering panic seized one man after another and transmitted itself down the line like a banner rippling in a high wind. They knew they were supposed to have waited for English help. Their bold initiative had exploded in their faces.

Instinct, not design, told them to do something, so they discharged their weapons at the French in a sad imitation of a real volley. They did not bother to wait until the smoke cleared to see the result, but turned tail and ran, a mad, pell-mell scramble to anywhere that promised sanctuary.

Lightning let out a strangled cry, rose up briefly on his hind legs, and rolled heavily to the left. He battled briefly to stay upright, but death won and he slowly toppled toward the ground. Pennywhistle swiftly extricated himself from the stirrups and jumped clear. He crashed into the ground and it knocked the wind out of him. He crawled over and saw the bullet hole just above the left eye. He touched the hole gently, hoping it was some kind of cruel illusion. His eyes misted over and his face flushed a violent crimson. Goddamned amateurs! Idiot ploughmen pretending to be soldiers! The fools had killed Lightning with a shot intended for the French. He had lost a friend. Alas, there was no time for mourning.

It was stupid to run. He could use the horse for cover. Even in death, Lightning was his ally. He lay down behind the corpse, balanced the Ferguson on the torso, and waited. His vibrant anger was unprofessional, but he didn't care. He would take as many of the miserable Crapauds with him as he could. Manton had the boots and would get clean away. His mission would be accomplished even if he did not live to see it. He waited, not patiently.

Manton was a full four hundred yards ahead when he looked back and saw his captain no longer followed. He naturally wanted to halt and turn back, but his captain had given him strict orders for just such an eventuality. "Keep moving, forget me, and save the boots. You are now the most valuable person on this mission." So with every instinct protesting loudly, he turned forward, put his head down, and galloped on. Juanita and Dale had not looked back and continued unaware.

It was a very, very slight change in Mandrake that caused Thynne to look behind. The horse always knew things. He saw no Pennywhistle, but plenty of fleeing Spaniards, and he made a highly accurate guess at what had happened. Damn it! He could not stop now, and even if he did, it would just mean four more lives thrown away. It was one of the hardest decisions of his life and it offended every ounce of chivalry in his body. He spurred Mandrake harshly and hoped to God his guess about the farmstead was right.

The hussars were three hundred yards out now, just about the maximum aimed range of the Ferguson. Pennywhistle methodically spread out all of his accoutrements for rapid reloading. If he kept low, he made a very poor target, while they made excellent ones: gaudy uniforms perched high and naked atop their mounts. He would be hard to reach, even with swords, and horses always tried to step over a prostrate figure. He looked at the sword next to him. He wished he'd had time to practice, but he might get one or two strokes in before he went down; fast, upward strokes to equine bellies. Whether with gun or sword, his policy was always the same; strike at the horses, not the men.

He would make one exception: Lazarette. The other troopers were of no importance. He would wait until he was close to be absolutely certain he would not miss. He wondered if the colonel's demise would have any effect on his men, cause them to pause or slow up. The world would surely be a better place and the French Army noticeably weaker after Lazarette's demise.

He centered the Ferguson's sights on a tan stallion's chest. The horse plunged ahead at full gallop, his rider with his sword outstretched. Pennywhistle breathed deeply and let it out slowly as he gently squeezed the trigger. The horse veered to the left, lost his balance, and rolled on to his side, pinning his rider's leg beneath.

He reloaded with dispatch and quickly leveled his piece. He led a dappled grey a bit, then squeezed the trigger. The horse reared, as if in indignation, and tumbled backwards on to his rider, crushing the man's neck when they both hit the ground.

The horses thundered on, the pounding hooves causing the ground to vibrate as if in an earthquake. A hundred and fifty yards now, not much time left. He reloaded again. He could get off two more shots, and then he would use the sword. The sight was terrifying, as it was meant to be. His rational mind merely noted the fact, but his overmastering anger rejoiced in the array of fat targets.

Thynne and his party galloped on. A quarter mile later, just over the low hill, he could make out the walled farmstead. He brought Mandrake to a halt and withdrew his spyglass. The others stopped as well. Juanita let out a cry of horror when she discovered Pennywhistle was not with them. Thynne saw horses and flashes of blue and yellow ahead. Their bell crown shakos and high collared Spencer jackets were distinctive and unmistakable. They had made the rendezvous. His heart leapt and he smiled in relief. It could still be done. He had never been so glad to see any group of men in his life.

It was A Troop, 12th Prince of Wales Light Dragoons; members of Fred Posonby's crack regiment out on an extended scout. There was hope!

CHAPTER TWENTY-NINE

Pennywhistle shot a black horse in the shoulder and its right foreleg buckled. Horse and rider folded up into a dark bundle and hit the ground hard. He reloaded and glanced at the sword. This would be his final shot before they could ride him down. They were only fifty yards away. These might be his last few seconds on Earth. He would make them count.

Lazarette bellowed, "He's mine!" at the troopers, and they veered off. The fleeing Spanish backsides were just too tempting: red meat to hungry dogs. The hussars hated them and had them in the ideal situation; running men on foot, defenseless against horsemen with swords. They tore off after them, shouting with glee and hate.

Five troopers stayed with Lazarette. Pennywhistle was about to fire when they reined in hard, a mere ten yards in front of him, then came to a full stop. He was expecting a fight to the death, not this. What in hell were they playing at? In his battle fury, he'd forgotten they would want to take him alive.

Lazarette dismounted. The five troopers remained in their saddles but drew their carbines and pointed them menacingly at Pennywhistle. Lazarette paced toward Pennywhistle; but, strangely, he did not draw his sword. It was a perfect opportunity for Pennywhistle to kill Lazarette; well, perhaps not perfect, since Lazarette's men would cut him down an instant later. Pennywhistle's careful calculation coupled with sheer curiosity overcame his anger. The marine put down the Ferguson, picked up the cavalry saber, and rose to his feet. He brought it quickly to a vertical position in front of his face and executed a perfect sword salute. He had the feeling some sort of peculiar parley was coming, and a bit of military courtesy did not seem out of place.

"Captain Pennywhistle," said Lazarette heartily, "you left unexpectedly before we had a chance to finish our conversation. I found it quite stimulating and am giving you another chance to complete it properly. Surrender now and I promise you an honorable captivity. I have no wish to kill you, quite the contrary. You have earned my respect; few men ever obtain that. You have done everything a good officer should and more. You escaped, led us a merry chase, killed some of my men, and guaranteed the safety of your countrymen. The honor of your prince is satisfied, the requirements of duty well propitiated. Why not yield to the logic of the situation? There is no escape for you. Surely there is no point to a death that serves no purpose?"

Pennywhistle kept a bland, unreadable expression on his face, in complete contrast to the violent arguments proceeding in his brain. The man had a point. He had done his duty and the mission would succeed. His four friends were beyond harm. He could now tell Lazarette about the boot and it would help the French not at all. In fact, he could have a good laugh at Lazarette's discomfiture.

Pennywhistle was a brave man, not a stupid one. He had no time for the "death or glory" arguments that civilians at great distance from the battlefield loved to applaud. It made perfect sense to yield to the inevitable. He would survive and could contrive to escape at a later time. And yet, he hated to give up, supinely surrender his freedom. He had no wish to wait out the war in comfortable confinement. No, he did not like that idea one damn bit.

Some distance away, the hussars had a field day. Untrained peasants were no match for hardened cavalrymen; they were as flies to wanton boys. The fleeing Spanish were either ridden down or sabered down. Horsemen dashed about in a mad fandango of blood and death. The majority of the Spaniards died with swords thrust through the backs and never even saw their attackers. Others had their faces slashed in half, as French troopers dashed ahead of them and used a backhanded stroke; a common technique used against regular troops, whose necks were protected by high stiff collars. A few threw themselves down and abjectly begged for mercy, but the Frenchmen laughed and struck with fury. The hussars let fly with all of their frustration over the deaths of their comrades and gloried in the extermination of Spanish vermin. Every drop of French humanity fled as hearts grew cold and blood hot. It was not battle, it was butchery.

A priest hid behind a boulder, quivering. He put down his musket and took up his rosary. He knew it was hopeless but recited the prayers anyway. He summoned up the identities of every saint he could recall and asked for their help and deliverance. He made all sorts of promises to them. He asked for the Virgin Mary's special intercession.

Pennywhistle stalled for time. "Colonel Lazarette, it is indeed unexpected to see you again. I wish I could call it a pleasure, but you would lose your respect for me if I lied to you so obviously. Before I give myself up, I should like to hear a full accounting of the terms you offer. If you are the man of honor you claim to be, you will surely favor my request." His manner was courtly, as if debating whether to accept an invitation to palace ball. He carefully observed the troopers on horseback to see if they had relaxed their guard. They had. This was the colonel's show, not theirs. He judged distances and measured the determination in their faces. One in particular looked weak and stupid. He would serve. The Ferguson was still loaded and was within reach.

"Of course, Captain, I am not a barbarian. It is as I told you before, we treat British officers honorably. You are professionals, completely unlike the Spanish scum you sadly support. You will be lodged in Verdun. You quarters will be in an excellent inn with a fine chef. We have many British officers confined there, so you will have comrades to talk to. I am told they have organized amateur theatricals, music concerts, and even publish a small newspaper. Many have acquired women friends. You will be allowed letters and parcels from home. You will have the freedom of the city as long as you give and keep your parole. You will be able to move anywhere in town as long as you return by sunset. You will wait until you are properly exchanged for an officer of equal rank. You can have quite a pleasant war. All it takes is for you to be a bit more forthcoming about the information you carry."

He had no doubt the man spoke the truth. Lazarette might be uncommonly brutal and cunning, but his sense of honor was very punctilious. A sane man would accept his terms with alacrity. Perhaps he was just perverse and stubborn, but it would gall him to live in comfort while his brothers bore privation and death with fortitude.

******

A quarter mile away, just below the brow of the low hill, Lieutenant Charles Vandeleur acknowledged the salute of his scout. "They are down there in the valley, Lieutenant. I looked for the funny round hat and the scarlet uniform and spotted him right quick through the spyglass. Looks to be talking to a French colonel, but the colonel's men have him covered. The Spaniards we were supposed to meet are being cut to pieces." Sergeant Barksdale said the last without great concern. "Maybe thirty or forty French, having a fine time, don't look to be expecting any company."

Vandeleur nodded. "Thank you, Sergeant Barksdale. Doesn't sound like anything we can't handle. In fact, might be rather amusing. Now let's get the men into formation."

"Very good, sir," said Barksdale. He saluted smartly and smiled brightly. It would indeed be very good, for the British.

******

Pennywhistle continued to stall for time. "It all sounds very pleasant. I require your word there will be no further beatings. My cheek," he touched it for emphasis," has not yet healed from our last encounter."

Lazarette replied, "I was hasty and careless. I see such methods with a man like you only strengthen his resolve to remain silent or take more dramatic action. I had quite forgotten the British penchant for quiet endurance. It will not happen again, I give you my most solemn assurance."

Strangely, Pennywhistle believed him. He realized it was not about honor, but simple logic. If something did not work, it was pointless to reapply it. His opponent was a rationalist.

******

Vandeleur formed the troop into two lines of thirty. The lines were a yard apart and the men in each line were close enough for knee-to-knee contact. Sabers were drawn and held vertical to each trooper. The fading light of the late afternoon sun glinted off their well burnished blades.

It was an intimidating sea of blue. They may have been officially styled the 12th Light Dragoons, but their uniforms were fully as showy and eccentric as their French counterparts; they were in all important respects British hussars. Troopers sported tall blue and white shakos with a single large red and white circular plume and gilt chinstrap; the Prince of Wales' distinctive feathered insignia in a circular white frame adorned the cap front. Their short, tightly fitted, deep blue Spencer jackets featured wide, v-shaped amber facings which tapered to meet a wide, thick sash with three horizontal bands of yellow alternating with two blue ones. The crisp, short tails of the jacket were amber as well, matching the cuffs and color. Their charcoal grey breeches fit every bit as tightly as their jackets and featured a wide stripe down the outer seam; amber, of course. They were not only as colorful as the French; they had just as much dash and vigor.

"Trumpeter, sound the advance," said Vandeleur calmly.

The trumpeter blew a distinctive flourish. A French trooper heard it, but seeing nothing, dismissed it as just overheated imagination.

The two lines moved forward at a brisk, carefully-cadenced walk. They did not have far to travel. Both horses and men advanced with the well disciplined movements of classic battlefield equitation. The lines stayed beautifully intact, magnificently theatrical and intimidating. The troopers had every confidence in themselves, their horses, and their commander. This was far from their first combat and they were used to victory. Battle was never completely predictable, but the British troopers had an excellent idea what lay ahead.

They advanced up and over the brow of the hill and lowered their sabers to a horizontal position, wrists angled slightly downward to increase force, tips thrust toward the enemy. Unlike French hussars, there was no shouting or cheering. The line advanced in quick, deadly silence. They moved to a fast trot. The French did not see them; they were far too beguiled by the swirling cyclone of blood and gore they had created, and the screams and shouts concealed the sound of the quiet advance.

Pennywhistle's peripheral vision detected the distant line of advancing blue death, but realized Lazarette did not. Keep him talking, then act. "Very well, Colonel, but we British tend to be formal chaps, and like things in writing. I wonder if you could whistle up pencil and paper from your saddlebag and prepare a quick note which I might sign."

The British lines increased their pace to a fast canter. The French noticed nothing.

Lazarette sighed in exasperation. He clearly felt the formalities a nuisance. "If that is what you wish, it can be easily arranged and put to paper." He turned and walked back toward his horse. His troopers had relaxed and no longer pointed their weapons at Pennywhistle.

******

"Charge!" yelled Vandeleur. The trumpeter blew loudly. The horses went immediately to gallop, then a second later, to charge. The troopers thrust their sabers fully forward and braced for impact. They covered the last twenty yards to the French in seconds.

Lazarette snapped his head round at the trumpet blast and beheld the blue nightmare with astonishment.

A moment later, the dragoons collided with the hussars. Men erupted in shouts, cheers, and curses and their mounts neighed, snorted, and whinnied. Horses reared and hooves rose and fell. Sabers flashed. There were no sounds of crashing horses because they did not physically collide; one horse usually moved aside. The French were engaged in their pursuit of peasants and had abandoned any pretense of an actual line. The British line was a tide that overflowed the discrete rocks of French resistance. Individual hussars slashed back, but the British encircled them swiftly and cut them down without mercy.

Vandeleur dueled with a strange French officer who nattered on about trifles even as he slashed repeatedly at the Englishman. The man chattered incessantly; pleasantly even, almost as if he sought to initiate a friendship. The one-sided conversation ended when Vandeleur's sword pierced his belly.

Sergeant Barksdale parried a crude slash to his neck from a very angry hussar lieutenant. Barksdale's face remained calm but his saber was full of fury when its point expertly slipped past the officer's guard and buried itself just above his navel. The lieutenant blinked in surprise, touched Barksdale's blade briefly in utter bewilderment, and slumped forward in his saddle without a sound.

The dragoons became one giant slashing machine of blued steel. Any hussars who survived the onslaught of the first line were destroyed by the second. The cowering priest gave thanks to God, astonished his prayers had been answered so quickly.

The slaughter of the hussars by the dragoons was almost as complete as that the hussars had inflicted on the peasants. Vandeleur despised the stupid peasants who hadn't followed orders and royally cocked things up, but he admitted they showed real talent as bait. Bewildered hussars, unused to defeat, galloped headlong down the hill, pursued eagerly by shouting, fierce-eyed dragoons. Vandeleur knew the hussars had no chance. The British had better horses and, he thought without even a hint of self congratulation, better riders.

In a blur of motion, Pennywhistle switched the sword to his left hand, dashed right, and grabbed the Ferguson. He did not have time for a well aimed shot, but fired from the hip at point blank range. The trooper's face disintegrated. He dropped the rifle, ran left, and rammed the sword into the chest of the next trooper's horse. He had already withdrawn it before the horse started to fall. He jabbed quickly at the belly of the next horse in line. A bullet sang past his ear. A trooper slashed at him with his sword. He turned sideways at the last second and riposted with a thrust to the man's leg. A fountain of blood shot forth; he had severed the femoral artery. Another trooper fired at him and missed. Pennywhistle hit the ground and rolled sideways. He came up underneath the belly of a chocolate-brown horse. He sprang upwards and put the full force of his shoulder behind the saber that sped upwards into the unfortunate beast's stomach. The animal cried out in startled pain.

Lazarette advanced on him now, no longer the detached, reasonable officer, but a wronged, angry man out for vengeance. The impulsive, excitable Gascon nature he had struggled so long to control burst forth in full cry. The sensible move would have been for him to mount up and join the hussars fleeing down the hill at breakneck speed. The ones unhorsed by Pennywhistle had already joined the exodus on foot. The dragoons would be on him in a minute, but he was too far gone in the embrace of rage to consider this. He didn't care about information, honor, or duty; he simply wanted this stinking British cur dead. He held his sword aggressively, looking for an opening.

Pennywhistle reposed complete confidence in his old cutlass, but the long, curved saber felt leaden and uncertain in his hand. Nevertheless, he swiftly deflected Lazarette's first two strokes to the head and belly. He responded with two thrusts at Lazarette's belly. They were parried, but with much less skill then his own blocks displayed. Lazarette was used to wielding his heavy saber on horseback, not on foot. It showed. The saber was better for slashing than thrusting.

Lazarette made a powerful slash at his neck, which he deflected with a vertical block. He took several quick steps backward to gain more room for maneuver. Lazarette advanced with more aggression than wisdom—useful to know. The marine retreated even more, wanted Lazarette to think he had the advantage. The Frenchman was already becoming careless. Pennywhistle purposely let Lazarette dominate the fight and merely blocked while Lazarette initiated. He made his blocks sluggish and less exact, and saw the glee in the Frenchman's fierce eyes. They widened with triumph and the veins in his neck pulsated visibly. His body was in full thrall to his hot Gascon ire. His rippling neck and shoulder muscles made clear to the marine's observant eye that he was about to launch the game-ending stroke.

Lazarette slashed mightily at his sword arm, clearly intended to amputate it. It was the perfect opening for Pennywhistle. Amidst an avalanche of blue sparks, he hammered down Lazarette's sword. It descended in a violent arc toward the Frenchman's right thigh, leaving him wide open and defenseless. The marine freed his blade from Lazarette's and slashed sideways at the base of Frenchman's neck. He put the full strength of his calf muscles into the stroke. He connected solidly and the heavy blade passed through skin and muscle in an instant.

Spurts of blood shot wildly into the air as the heart continued its duty, not knowing the carotid artery had been severed. Lazarette dropped his blade and brought his hand up to the wound in disbelief and a vain attempt to stanch the bleeding. The blood pumped in mad jets between his fingers. His suddenly pallid face registered amazement and surprise. He locked eyes with the marine and moved his mouth as if to speak, but no words came out. He tottered for a second, his eyes rolled upward, and he collapsed.

Pennywhistle's breath came in hard, labored gasps. He commanded his hammering heart to slow down.

Vandeleur came charging up and quickly reined his horse to a halt. He held a sword in one hand which dripped with fresh blood. "Captain Pennywhistle, I presume. Your friends said you needed help." He smiled broadly. "Looks like they were mistaken. I'm Charles Vandeleur; friends call me Boomer. May I offer you a lift?"

Pennywhistle smiled in spite of himself at the man's sheer, brash insouciance. Maybe that was part of some unwritten cavalryman's code. His merrily thunderous voice certainly merited his nickname. Pennywhistle felt a stress hangover forming. It was often that way after the adrenaline wore off;

great exertion demanded a great payment. The profound physical enervation left him light-headed and slightly nauseous, with arms and legs that felt leaden and doughy. He could not decide which his body craved more desperately; sleep or food. He could barely manage the energy to compose a response and force his powder-stained lips to move. "How could I not accept such a gracious invitation?" he said with a weary courtliness. He cleaned and sheathed the sword with a heavy arm and slung the Ferguson over his shoulder.

Vandeleur extended his hand and cheerfully said, "Hop aboard!" Pennywhistle did just that and the two cantered back toward the farmstead. The rest of the troop formed into a column and followed proudly. Vandeleur thought it a good day's work.

CHAPTER THIRTY

Pennywhistle's return occasioned much rejoicing. Dale and Manton smiled broadly and pumped his hand vigorously. Thynne clapped him heartily on the shoulders and chortled on about hell not being ready to receive him just yet. Morales forgot discipline entirely and grabbed him in a bear hug; distasteful to Pennywhistle, but he could hardly fault a man for being pleased at his deliverance. Juanita, strangely, did not embrace him as he would have expected.

She squeezed his left bicep gently and softly muttered, "*Gracias a Dios.*" Her expression was eerily indecipherable. The violet in her irises seemed lit from behind with an otherworldly radiance. The eyes appeared to be on loan and directed by some sort of higher power at whose nature he could only guess. She contemplated him for a full minute. Her gaze bored into him and it felt as if she were staring directly at his soul, assessing its grace and valuation. It unsettled him. A gentle smile blossomed slowly on her face, as if she had reached some sort of conclusion. She turned on her heel and walked away, leaving him completely confused.

He had a very hearty and pleasant supper with Thynne and Vandeleur. Vandeleur produced a large and tasty ham, as well as a very tolerable bottle of brandy. He told them to thank Sergeant

Barksdale, who had thoughtfully searched Colonel Lazarette's saddlebags. Vandeleur happily filled him in about the state of Wellington's army. Wellington and Marmont had maneuvered for six days in a cycle of move and countermove. The armies were constantly in full view of each other and sometimes as little as 1,000 yards apart. Marmont repeatedly sought to cut the British supply line, which led back to the Royal Navy in Lisbon. Wellington could not do the same to him, since the French lived off the land. The armies were of equal strength and experience. Vandeleur thought it likely the Peer would be on the outskirts of Salamanca tomorrow morning. The men trusted him completely but were surprised and dismayed at his unwillingness to fight. Vandeleur explained that Wellington was merely biding his time, looking for an opening. Marmont underestimated him and believed Bonaparte's disparaging comments that he was a mere "Sepoy General" whose achievements in India were of no account. A grave mistake, where "Old Nosey" was concerned.

The dragoons would depart at first light and would provide him an escort to Wellington's headquarters. Thynne said he would be delighted to make the introductions. Exploring officers reported to Wellington directly, since he usually acted as his own chief of intelligence.

A large and violent thunderstorm cut the supper short. The rain blasted them in interminable sheets and drenched everything. The flashes of lightning were so frequent and the rolling peals of thunder so loud, they frightened horses used to the storms of battle. Electricity hissed through the air. Pennywhistle felt the hairs on his arm bristle. He bid his friends adieu and retired to his bed. Tonight, it was an empty horse stall filled with new mown hay, but he was so tired that it seemed as inviting as a featherbed at the best inn. Manton had thoughtfully laid out his blanket and had scavenged a pillow from God knows where. Pennywhistle eased himself down and slowly stretched out. Despite the sound and fury of the storm, he was fast asleep in under a minute.

A violent spear of lightning, followed by a preternaturally intense boom, woke him some hours later. He saw her, silhouetted against the flashes of lightning. She was wrapped in a calico blanket that extended to her ankles. He was not quite fully awake and wondered if it was the remnant of a dream. Juanita moved toward him calmly and sat down next to him.

He was about to express his surprise and confusion when she reached out and put two fingers over his lips. "Do not speak, Tomás. Listen. Tomorrow we will part, God has told me of this. Your destiny will take you far from Spain. I cannot come along. This, I know.

"You have saved me, taught me so much, shown me what I must do. You do not believe it, but the finger of God is upon you. You are a beacon of light. It is natural that those serving Satan would want to snuff out your light. That is why God has made you a great warrior. It is also natural that those fleeing darkness would seek you out. My people would call you a heretic, but my heart tells me you are The Lord's trusty servant. You perform His will, even if you do not know it."

Pennywhistle was too boggled to protest, and she continued serenely.

"I see the pain in your eyes. You hide it well from the others, but I have the gift of second sight. I know your heart to be a good one, but it writhes in agony. I do not know who she was and I will not ask. She must have been remarkable. You have an ache that you will not allow to heal. Permit me the grace to quiet your heart at least for one night. I cannot replace her, but I can help. The padres tell me this is wrong, but I think they are mistaken. Such a thing cannot be wrong when the heart says it is right. God wants you to forgive yourself and wishes me to help you heal. I want to remember this night for years to come. I also wish to take with me some small portion of your goodness."

She rose to her full height and her violet eyes changed yet again. They danced and grew hot with a fire that was anything but spiritual. She shrugged off the blanket and stood nude before him.

He told himself that this was absolutely wrong, this was madness. But when she sat down, touched him, lovingly kissed his lips, his will power evaporated. He realized he wanted her badly, and her skin felt so soft, so welcoming. The fight went out of him and changed to passion.

The love-making was tender and slow, kind and gentle. He could swear she possessed some kind of magical, restorative energy. She touched him with expert intuition, even though he was certain this was her first time. They lay in each other's arms afterwards and a great peace washed through him as she gently stroked his hair and whispered endearments.

The second time, an hour later, was much different. The lightning and thunder outside was an appropriate backdrop. Everything was fierce and hot, like two hellcats joining. It was wild, reckless, and pulsated with mad, feverish abandon. They bit and clawed at each other and had to remember not to shout and scream lest they be discovered. The end was violent, sweaty, and deliriously happy. The relaxation and accumulated fatigue from the stress of the day hit him at the same time and he found himself drifting, drifting ever so pleasantly. Against his will, he lapsed into a deep, deep sleep.

The next thing he remembered was Manton gently shaking his shoulders. "You said you wanted me to wake you, sir. It's an hour until dawn. I hope you slept well. I got some coffee beans from one of the troopers and have a pot brewing. Just the way you like, black and thick."

Pennywhistle looked around. There was no trace of the girl. It saddened him, yet did not surprise him. She had certainly done something to him. He had not felt this good for a long time. He thought of Carlotta, and for the first time in a year and a half, only a hint of pain touched her memory.

He breakfasted with Thynne and Vandeleur as the first hint of dawn changed the sky to grey. The thunderstorm had departed and left things looking fresh and new. The day promised fair and hot.

They were on the road twenty minutes later. Juanita trotted behind him, next to Manton. She was determined to watch over him until he reached Wellington. She knew in her heart last night had not been wrong. He had been her first, and she would never forget. Someday she would marry, and she hoped she would love her husband, but the Englishman had shown her what passion could do.

She acted as if nothing had happened, but Manton sensed a change in her he could not quite fathom. There was a glow and a peacefulness about her that had not been there the previous day. He had no idea of its cause.

It took them two hours to reach the outskirts of the army. The troops were in motion, as was Wellington. He was not at his headquarters. He was a habitual early riser, usually around 4 am, and had been in the saddle since five. He was out on his horse Copenhagen observing the enemy first hand, constantly recalculating things. Thynne finally found a staff officer who thought he knew where he was, but it turned out the man had not a clue, since the Peer galloped rapidly from spot to spot. It was frustrating beyond measure to both Pennywhistle and Thynne, and it was not until after midday that they finally found him. He was on top of a low, sugarloaf-shaped hill called the Lesser Arapile, in the middle of an old farmyard. It afforded an excellent view of the marching enemy. He was talking with General Alava, his chief Spanish advisor, and calmly chewing on a leg of cold chicken. He was surrounded by the usual coterie of staff officers and aides-de-camp.

THE KING'S SCARLET

Sir Arthur Wellesley, Knight of the Bath, 1st Earl of Wellington, "The Peer," was 42 years old, five-foot-ten, broad-shouldered, and robustly but not heavily built. He was fit and healthy, with prodigious powers of endurance. He had a low forehead, strong eyebrows, firm chin, and an expressive mouth. His heroically proportioned Roman nose dominated his oval face, and his glacially blue eyes sparkled with intelligence and perception. They were not friendly eyes in the least, but they perfectly communicated his coldly rational judgment. No one called him a genius as they did Napoleon, yet there was genius in his uncommon common sense. Pennywhistle felt an imperious self-confidence radiating from the man and a frigidly logical will to match. This was a general soldiers would never love, but would always respect.

A great surprise caused Pennywhistle to laugh loudly. Here was another marine and a good friend: Peter Spottswood. He had acted as Spottswood's mentor and transformed a surly young wastrel into a fine officer of great promise. Spottswood had comforted him when Carlotta died. But what the blazes was he doing here? It made no sense.

Thynne dismounted and strode straight up to Wellington. The two began an animated conversation. Pennywhistle awaited his cue. Spottswood approached, grinning broadly. "Tom, as I live and breathe, it's a pleasure to see you!" He clapped his former captain on the shoulders and looked carefully at Pennywhistle's uniform. It was superbly tailored, but this morning appeared ragged and battered, in stark contrast to his own. "You look like you've had a spot of adventure, Tom. Can't say I have. Absolutely nothing happened to me getting here."

"Peter, you are a sight for sore eyes, but why in hell are you here?"

Spottswood's expression changed to that of a man who had something unpleasant to say and was reluctant to say it. "You won't like it, not one bit. We have both been used. Used as bait."

"Bait? God's blood, Peter, what do you mean?"

"I arrived three days ago, Tom, and I have been hanging about here, feeling useless, waiting to see if you turned up. I confess I was beginning to despair when you materialized this morning. I was greatly relieved, but my conclusion remained unchanged. Turns out, we were on exactly the same mission, and it was not the one either of us thought. Let me ask you, and I think your uniform tells the tale, did you have a lot of unexpected problems getting here?"

Pennywhistle's face clouded. "Problems? That's putting it mildly. It was one misadventure after another. Nothing went right from the start. I felt like a grouse on a Scottish estate, with beaters constantly trying to flush me so I could be shot at. Rather than this being a secret mission, I got the impression someone had been selling tickets."

Spottswood nodded. "You don't miss much, Tom. You will have reasoned it out. You figured there is a breach of security at headquarters?"

"That's the only explanation that answers. We have a traitor on our hands." Pennywhistle spoke with great distaste.

"Martin knew it too, but could not be sure who was the mole. I only found out because Wellington felt any gentleman who undertook a hazardous mission was owed an explanation when it was safe to do so. Martin set this up with him a month ago. Martin had two candidates, Marsden and Peacham, but was loath to accuse either one because they had a set of connections as long as your arm. Both also had heavy gambling debts. He needed indisputable proof. He gave us both the same instructions and the same coded messages. He told one of them about you, the other about me. Whichever one of us encountered problems would pinpoint the traitor exactly. Clearly, he was mistaken about my man, but correct about yours. I think Sir Richard Peacham will have an appointment with the firing squad within the month.

"I gave Wellington the information you carry three days ago. It was important; at least that was not a deception. Some stuff about resistance leaders who can aid Wellington should he move north against Caffarelli. The Peer eventually wants to go for ports on the Basque Coast, I gather. You mentioned beaters earlier. That was the part we played, to flush the traitor."

Pennywhistle's mouth dropped open in amazement. He felt a complete fool. He had risked everything and congratulated himself on outthinking his opponents, but he had been merely a pawn, just a blunt instrument in a greater scheme. The deck had been stacked against him from the start. If he had not come back alive, it would not have mattered to Martin, since it would only have made the result more clear and certain. Martin had probably not even chosen him for his record, but because his brother knew Wellington's younger sibling. The Peer was nothing if not a snob. Pennywhistle thought himself cold and calculating, but he was an absolute amateur compared to Martin. He knew Vice Admiral Sir Thomas Byam Martin to be an able administrator and a clever man, but had never known him to be a hard one. Maybe an utter loss of humanity was one of the perquisites for high command.

He pushed aside his anger and tried to consider things from Martin's point of view. It made perfect sense to sacrifice one to save the lives of many. It was ruthless, but it was logical. War forced reasonable people to make unthinkable choices. He grudgingly admitted he might have done the same thing if faced with Martin's dilemma. He looked back and realized he already had. He had rescued the grandees, but placed the mission ahead of protecting them. Maybe he and Martin were cut from the same cloth after all.

He had at least done some good when he deviated from his expected part in this peculiar drama. If Martin had deceived him, he had not exactly followed orders. He had saved Juanita, helped the partisans win a small victory, and liberated the grandees. He had helped the Resistance and relieved the Spaniards of the presence of the hated Colonel Lazarette. He had unwittingly served another's frigidly cold logic, but he had also honored his own humanity.

Lost in thought, he failed to notice Thynne's approach. Thynne smiled brightly. "Don't look so downcast my friend. The Peer wants to talk to you. I think he has something special in mind."

CHAPTER THIRTY-ONE

The Peer had his spyglass unfurled and was watching the enemy with intense concentration when Pennywhistle and Thynne walked up to him. Thynne made a motion to Pennywhistle to keep silent and wait; Thynne knew his general and his habits. Pennywhistle drew out his pocket spyglass and decided to make his own observations. He could see the enemy line clearly, moving slowly and sinuously.

The army was like a cobra slithering along in the tropical noonday sun, unaware an alert mongoose lurked just over the rise. The majestic king of its realm would never expect a challenge from a dull commoner.

Moving along a six mile front, the 55,000 French made no effort to hide themselves. It was an extraordinary display of color rather than concealment. The midnight blue uniforms and black leather shakos of the line infantry, crimson jackets of the hussars, and burnished metal breastplates and red-plumed silver helmets of the cuirassiers were boldly framed against the early afternoon sky. One voltigeur company even sported forest green uniforms.

The rear part of the eight-division army marched with a slow, contemptuous, careless gait. It bespoke a certainty that their numbers and a cowed enemy guaranteed there would be no fighting this day. Large gaps had opened up between it and the front. The lead division marched with a swift, brisk, sprightly determination that expressed a breezy arrogance. The marching lines reminded Pennywhistle of taffy gradually being stretched, longer and longer, thinner and thinner.

He decided the French had entirely dispensed with circumspection and careful observation of their opponent. Their maneuvering was evidently supposed to be a strategic flanking march against an opponent who had been out-maneuvered before and who would undoubtedly perform his usual evolution of falling back.

The creaking of cannon wheels, the clanking of metal equipment, the clop, clop, clop of regiments of horse, and the unrelenting tramp, tramp, tramp of thousands of feet made an unharmonious music that proclaimed the passing of an army. It was punctuated at uncertain intervals with the base, unwavering rumble of male choruses of complaint, admonition, and angrily shouted orders. It had a certain rhythm and cadence, almost a melody. He knew the noises he was hearing now were the real martial music. It was far more authentic than the smart marching tunes the military bands played. Cacophonous, off-key, and less than inspiring, it was nonetheless the music of real war. It sang discordantly of danger, destruction, and death.

At that moment the Peer snapped shut his telescope and erupted in his distinctive whinnying laugh. "By God, that will do!" He dashed toward his horse, then stopped briefly when he saw Thynne. "Lord Steven, is that Pennywhistle? It is, fine, bring him along. I have a use for him. We'll talk on the way. Not a minute to waste." He jumped into Copenhagen's saddle and put the spurs to him. He shot out of the farmyard like a bullet, destination unknown. His staff knew something was up and rushed towards their horses to follow. Thynne grabbed a horse for Pennywhistle and told him to jump aboard. He rocketed aboard Mandrake and the two went clattering off.

Spottswood, Dale, and Manton saw the whole thing with great surprise but recovered quickly. Spottswood was tired of cooling his heels and feeling like a supernumerary. He was a soldier, not a secret agent.

Dale wanted to fight with his officer. He had skirmished with the French for years, but had never been in a large, epic battle.

Manton knew his duty was to serve his master, but he also wanted to show how much he had learned about soldiering.

Juanita had no right to join the cavalcade, but that did not deter her. The British who met her in the camp had already got a sample of her strong-headed personality. They simply assumed she was Pennywhistle's Spanish trinket and his business. The four shot into their saddles and galloped madly after Pennywhistle.

Morales did not join them; he taken the King's Shilling and signed on as a recruit. He knew if there was to be any fighting today he would be in the thick of it, and that pleased him. Dale had explained matters to the color sergeant earlier, and the NCO was grateful for a recruit who had proven himself. They had found him an old uniform and a musket. He might not understand English well, but he grasped enough of the drill to follow the movements of his new fellows.

It was three miles before Pennywhistle and Thynne caught up with Wellington. An odd conversation followed, breathlessly shouted as the horses tore along: short snippets of information fired back and forth like a mounted tennis match.

"Pennywhistle, good to meet you; know your family. Thynne says you did a fine job, says you know the Shorncliffe protocols. 88th lost all of its light company officers storming Badajoz; sergeant has the company now. I'd be obliged if you'd take it over. There is going to be a fight, I need a good officer in charge. Are you up to it?"

"I'd be honored, my lord," he said with enthusiasm. He meant it too. It would be satisfying to fight as a proper officer with a clear mission instead of being a pawn in some else's intelligence scheme. A thought struck him. "My lord, I have a fellow marine officer and my sergeant who want to fight too. Might I bring them along?"

"Your company, Captain, do what you think best. Report to Colonel Wallace, the Brigade commander, and tell him what I said." Copenhagen shot ahead of them. Wellington had seen something.

Thynne thundered alongside. "I know where Wallace is, Tom, heard some of the staff people talking. Follow me and I'll take you there." Thynne and Mandrake veered left, and Pennywhistle followed.

Half an hour later, Pennywhistle was in animated conversation with Colonel Alexander Wallace.

"I am glad to have you, Captain Pennywhistle. If the Peer believes you worthy, you have must have done something remarkable. Sergeant O' Dwyer is in charge right now. Good man, brave, but lacks experience. He might do, but I far prefer to have a gentleman in charge. Thynne says he's seen you fight and you are damned good. Says you never give up. I like that in a soldier. Be warned though, the Connaught Rangers are a tough bunch; clannish, hard drinking, and cynical. Excellent soldiers, if hard to discipline. They are Irishmen and do not accept outsiders easily. It is a sure bet most of the have never met a marine officer and have no idea what to expect. Don't hesitate to come down hard on them."

"I quite understand, Colonel," replied Pennywhistle. "They need take nothing on faith. I will furnish them with a quick demonstration to eliminate their doubts. I also have some very worthy assistants. The Peer told me I was welcome to employ them as I chose. Please, allow me to introduce them." By this time, the others had caught up, and he had quickly apprised them of his plans.

"Colonel Wallace, I have the honor to present Lieutenant Peter Spottswood. He has saved my life on several occasions." Spottswood bowed and Wallace acknowledged it with a curt nod of the head. Dale stepped forward. "This is Sergeant Andrew Dale. You will not find a better NCO on the planet." Dale snapped to attention and executed a brisk salute, which Wallace returned.

"And this," he hesitated for an instant while a host of thoughts shot through his brain and Manton stepped forward in response to his gesture. Pennywhistle had gone to great trouble to outfit Manton, with the idea that well tailored clothing instilled a sense of pride. He had never subscribed to the common idea that a servant should wear different, inferior clothing that clearly marked him as a servant. Manton looked a stalwart English gentleman: black beaver hat, quality stock, well fitted russet frock coat, good broadcloth claret-colored trousers, and stoutly constructed black boots. He was handsome, six feet tall, and carried himself well. He held Pennywhistle's old fusil, a shortened version of a musket, which was an officer's weapon. There was no reason to believe he was anything other than what Pennywhistle said he was—whatever he said.

He continued smoothly. "This is Mr. Manton, a gentleman volunteer and a cousin of mine." Gentlemen volunteers typically fought with the men but messed with the officers, hoping to eventually obtain free commissions as replacements for fallen officers.

Manton barely concealed his shock at this promotion, but he bowed gracefully with the elegance befitting a gentleman. Wallace acknowledged it with a quick nod of the head, accepting Pennywhistle's explanation.

Pennywhistle himself was somewhat surprised by what came out of his mouth but knew a portion of his brain had a plan. Perhaps the night with Juanita had freed parts of him normally kept in check. Manton had proven himself resourceful, loyal, and worthy. He was intelligent and deserved better than his present station. Besides, Carlotta had thought of him as almost as a son. What he contemplated was fanciful, but it might play out; he had the prize money to make it happen. It might also explode in his face. It all came down to the battle ahead and how Manton responded.

"You obviously have good and loyal people, Pennywhistle. I believe we will receive orders presently, so I will not detain you from assuming command. Good luck to you today." Wallace snapped a salute to Pennywhistle, which the marine returned. His horse turned and he cantered away.

Pennywhistle knew NCOs spoke a language poorly understood by officers. "Sarn't, talk to O'Dwyer and tell him to assemble the men. I want the company formed up and ready to go in ten minutes. I will have a brief talk with them. They need a small demonstration in marksmanship."

Dale grinned; he understood perfectly. "I gather it is time for the Robin Hood gambit."

Pennywhistle laughed without restraint. "It is indeed, Sarn't. We need them to understand what they have been missing."

Dale turned serious. "Remember sir, delicate language has no place, particularly with Irishmen. Give it to them hard, short, and dirty, sir."

******

Copenhagen clattered to a stop that left him panting. Wellington had ridden five miles at breakneck speed and his staff had not yet caught up to him. He cantered over to Edward Packenham, his brother-in-law and the Major General commanding the Third Division. He greeted him briefly and pointed to the French on top of the *Pico de Miranda*, an elevated plateau two miles distant.

"Ned, move on with your division, take those heights to your front, and drive everything before you. The French left has become detached from the rest of the army. Smash it and roll up their flank up smartly. Directly you have done that, I shall inaugurate a general engagement." Wellington's orders were brisk, clipped, and ruthlessly efficient, much like the man who issued them.

"Very good, My Lord," said Packenham matter-of-factly, "We shall drive them most handsomely." He unfurled his spyglass and surveyed the mesa. General Jean Thomière's Seventh Division had indeed become detached from the rest of Marmont's Army. They did not look to be expecting an attack and were ripe for plucking.

******

"The company is formed, sir," said Dale in his best command voice. He touched his hat in salute, which Pennywhistle returned. Sergeant O'Dwyer had not liked the idea his company would soon be under new management, but Dale was a figure of force and power when he chose to be and brooked no objections. He told the sergeant the men were lucky to get such an experienced commander and the odds of them surviving the next fight had shot up accordingly.

Pennywhistle said nothing but walked slowly and deliberately down the line of a hundred men. He looked at faces from time to time, trying to gain an impression of the men he was to command. Nearly all appeared to be in their mid t late twenties, but their faces looked tough, weather-beaten, and much older. All were clean shaven, although many sported the long sideburns that had become fashionable. They were tanned bronze, and their uniforms had faded from brick red to a dusky, reddish-brown from heavy service in the sun. Their well used jackets were frayed at the edges and bore patches of various colors. Their beaten up trousers were grey and thin in the knees; their tall black shakos resembled battered stovepipes. They were not some palace guard wearing pretty uniforms, but sturdy, veteran troops who never shirked a fight. Most importantly, the muskets gripped by their calloused, leathery hands gleamed with gun oil and showed not even a suggestion of rust.

The soldiers mostly kept their expressions impassive, as was usual during an inspection, but he caught hints of skepticism on a few. It was to be expected. They did not give trust easily, but when they did, it really meant something. He took up a position in front of the company. Curiosity showed on the faces of a few men. Just what kind of fellow was this man? They knew nothing of him, and little about the Royal Marines.

"Good afternoon. I am Captain Pennywhistle of the Royal Marines. Colonel Wallace tells me you are a misbegotten gang of bog-trotting bastards, but that you will fight. I hear all sorts of tales of Irishmen being great warriors, but I wonder if it is mostly moonshine. Some call you the Connaught Robbers after your three day sack of Badjahoz, mere looters. You must show me you deserve the title Rangers. I have seen plenty of fighting. I was on the *Bellerophon* at Trafalgar. I trained with Sir John Moore at Shorncliffe, and I can outshoot and outfight any man here." His sneering expression dared them to object. "But I can see my words fall on unbelieving ears."

The men in formation did not visibly shift, but their umbrage was tangible. Soldiers expected to be lambasted by their own NCOs, but who was this upstart? Private McNulty epitomized the attitude of the men toward this unwanted officer who had been thrust upon them, an arrogant son-of-bitch who challenged their hard won reputations. McNulty hated him. And yet, there was something... odd about this officer. He possessed a handsome face, which McNulty quite properly despised, but the large, purple bruises on it made him look like he had just left a prize fighting ring. He did not look or act like an untested aristocratic sprig direct from Horse Guards.

******

"The target is set up, over there, sir," Dale announced loudly. Dale pointed and every eye in the line followed his finger. It was a black army shako mounted on the end of a cut down five foot spontoon driven into the ground. The pike and shako were one hundred yards from where he was standing; Dale had made certain of that.

Pennywhistle picked up the Ferguson and loaded it with quick, precise motions. That amazed the men; they had never seen it's like. They knew it was a rifle, but it was a breech loader, no ramrod; where the blazes had he gotten that?

He swiftly leveled the piece and fired from the standing position. He reloaded and fired again, this time from the kneeling position. His third shot was fired lying on his back, the classic distance position favored by the 95th. He fired his next shot lying on his belly. The final shot boomed out from a crouch.

The men were impressed. His speed and clockwork reloading made him seem more machine than man. Five shots in a minute, amazing! But had he hit anything?

Dale walked out to the target and retrieved the shako. There were five bullet holes in the metal plate on its front. Any one of the shots would have been fatal.

The men waited with great curiosity as Dale walked back. Was this officer just a shameless boaster or really as good as he said? They were about to find out.

Dale handed the shako to Pennywhistle, who regarded it with assured indifference. He said in his best command voice, "You Paddies wanted proof, here it is. I will pass the shako down the line that all may know the truth." He walked over and handed it to Private McNulty who looked at the five holes. He said nothing, but his lips pursed and his eyebrows shot skyward in surprise.

Five minutes later, the Connaught Rangers grudgingly decided he would do. They were still not quite sure what to make of this marine, but it was dawning on them, he was something special. He would do right by them in battle. Manton and Spottswood smiled.

Juanita hovered on horseback several hundred yards away. She had no business being there, she knew, but she needed to make sure Pennywhistle survived the fight. Despite orders to the contrary, there were several other women in the vicinity, wives of some of the private soldiers. The army permitted six wives per company, and they were tough birds. They had chosen a harsh life, were used to privation, and did not shrink from the blood and gore of battle. The army tried to keep them in the rear before a fight, but the stalwarts always made it to the front somehow. If their men were wounded, they would dash in to help them off the field.

Packenham formed his division into two columns of companies in open order and marched steadily toward the French, their progress concealed by undulating ground. Cavalry protected the flanks. Wallace's brigade of 1800 men, composed of the 45th, 74th, and 88th regiments, led the way. Campbell's Brigade marched on their right. 3700 men emerged from the final declivity onto open ground and stopped half a mile from the French. The columns wheeled left and each brigade carefully deployed into a long line, two ranks deep. Pennywhistle and the Connaught Rangers occupied the center of the line.

The appearance of the British came as a shock to the French. General Tomières thought about deploying into line, to increase the number of muskets he could bring to bear, but British artillery opened up an effective fire, which made that difficult. He decided to trust to the powerful intimidation value of a column of 4,000 men advancing downhill. Skirmishers would precede the column to disrupt and unbalance the enemy; the smoke from their muskets would help cloak the column's approach.

Pennywhistle saw the French skirmishers advancing and knew his time had come. Spottswood had command of the left,

Dale on the right; Manton was with him. The light company line was long and loose. Skirmishers fired individually but fought in pairs, one man covering his mate. Two pair typically worked together, firing in chain order. The first man advanced a few paces, fired and retired to the rear. By the time the fourth man had fired, the first was reloaded and ready to fire again. They took advantage of any cover the ground afforded. A number of skirmishers removed their tall shakos and used their stiff crowns as firing stands for their weapons.

Skirmishers from the 74th and 45th advanced on Pennywhistle's left and right at the same time his company moved forward. In all, three hundred men moved toward the French.

The French kept up a steady fire as they approached. Most of the shots were a clean miss. Pennywhistle knew they had a bad case of buck fever: the range was too great.

He was gratified to see his men truly knew their business. His only worry was that in the heat of battle they would become a little too eager and not heed the command to retire on the main body. Their job was not to defeat the enemy, merely disrupt, disorder, and soften him up for the main force to deal with.

Pennywhistle's men opened fire on the French skirmishers at sixty yards. Each man selected an individual target, unlike the way line troops fired. Pop, pop, pop, filled the air as a muskets discharged in rapid succession. The sound resembled bursting bubbles in a kettle of hot stew. Men reloaded and fired at the French from all manner of positions; standing, crouching, and prone. It was now small pockets of men firing into other small pockets of men. Clouds of smoke began to drift and men began to cough.

Pennywhistle fired the Ferguson rapidly, always aiming for officers and NCOs. He saw at least two go down. Manton, at his side, fired his fusil industriously and accurately. He might not have the title, but he was a real soldier.

The French skirmishers had enough after fifteen minutes. They slowly and grudgingly retired up the hill toward the main column. Pennywhistle and his men pursued unhurriedly, pausing now and then to reload and fire.

He was pleased his men avoided running, a natural enough instinct when a predator saw the backside of his prey. He wanted to keep the advance orderly and disciplined. The thrill of success was upon them, but training and experience overcame instinct.

Pennywhistle halted the company forty yards from the massive column. They poured shots into it for two minutes. Then he instructed the buglers to sound "retire." They were bees stinging a quarry and had done their job well, but bees could be swatted if they remained too long.

They retreated slowly down the hill. When they reached the main line of the 88th, they formed as a regular company on the left of the line. Pennywhistle took his place as commander in front on their right. There was no talking in the ranks.

The British lines were oak trees facing a wind. The two lines of the three regiments stood straight as arrows. The men remained stolid and impassive, an iron bulwark of red. The seventeen-year-old ensigns, the most junior officers in their regiments, held the huge silk regimental and king's colors on nine foot poles in front of the lines. The banners were both sources of pride and rally points. They flapped slowly in the rising afternoon breeze. Wallace surveyed the scene from his horse. He told himself to wait; it was all about timing it right.

The French column tramped steadily down the low hill like a juggernaut; slow, menacing, inexorable. It appeared to be one solid formation from the British point of view, but was actually two; 4,000 battle hardened veterans in two massive mailed fists, the second echeloned to the right and slightly behind the first.

Each had a front of 170 men and was 11 ranks deep. From the air, they resembled two solid marching blue bricks sliding ever so slightly left. The 28-inch step of 76 paces per minute of the *pas ordinaire* was far slower than the *pas de charge* rate of 120 paces, but was completely intentional. The disciplined, stately, careful step was designed to give plenty time to the enemy to contemplate the terrifying prospect approaching.

The pace may have been stately, but the formation was loud and rowdy. Men yelled, yipped, bellowed, and cursed, trying to unman their British opponents. Every man shouted his own threat or halloo. French officers liked to whip their men into a killing frenzy. They danced, pranced, and flourished swords about like carnival barkers leading yokels to a county fair. The eerie silence in the British line stood in stark contrast.

The *French* drummers pounded out the advance, the noise rhythmic and mesmerizing. Rubdub, rubdub, rubdub, dub, dub, echoed down the hill. "*Vive la France! Vive la France! Vive la France!*" poured in a low rumble from thousands of lungs. It reminded Pennywhistle of Gregorian chants. Hardened as he was, it unsettled him and his pulse rate jumped.

Colorfully clad bandsmen in extravagant Turkish style turbans and baggy pantaloons marched with the column, loudly playing the "*Marseillaise*". Their trumpets blared brightly, their cymbals clanged, and the small bells on their Johnny jing-a-lings danced wildly. The role of music was not to be underestimated in keeping soldiers steady and resolute.

A stray shot flew straight upwards from the column. It was a replacement who had just joined his regiment from the training depot in Nantes. He had accidentally brushed the trigger of his Charleville. Frightened men often found their fingers clumsy and disobedient in battle. Nasty glares from his experienced comrades caused him to bow his head in shame and focus on the forward motion of his feet.

The band switched to the popular march, *"La Victoire est à nous"*, and the soldiers began chanting *Vive l'Empereur! Vive l'Empereur! Vive l' Empereur!* The rhythm was different from before but the new chant was coordinated with beats of the advance and the purpose was the same. In moments of crisis, the repeated group recital of a key phrase or leader's name exercised a great steadying influence. It distracted mind and mouth from the fear. The effect was particularly notable on green troops, but it worked well with veterans too. It was almost as the words were a magical incantation which would shield them from enemy bullets.

Boom! Boom! Boom! Bursting shells from Royal Artillery six-pounders showered the column with spherical case shot and prevented Thomières deploying into line. His nerve faltered and he impatiently bellowed "Fire!" at one hundred twenty yards; too far for the volley to have much of an impact. Aimed smoothbore .69 caliber muskets could hit an individual only six times out of ten at a hundred yards, and volleys were not aimed: one solid block of men simply fired in the general direction of another solid block of men.

Because the French did not form into line, just the first three ranks could fire. Only 510 muskets could be brought to bear. As often happened, a few men in the second rank died from clumsily pointed muskets fired by the third.

The French were dismayed and alarmed as the smoke cleared to reveal the British standing steadfast. The French reloaded and fired again. A few British soldiers fell, but others stepped forward quickly to plug the breaches. The French band continued to play loudly, brightly, but could barely be heard above the gunfire.

An expertly directed, blue-coated Royal Artillery battery hammered the column with an angry blast of case shot; five six-pounder cannon and a single five-and-a-half inch howitzer focused on the front of the column. Deadly clouds of shrapnel bloomed in the air, heralding a lethal rainstorm of lead upon the French.

A second Royal Artillery battery opened on the column's rear with solid lead cannonballs that grazed the ground, ricocheted up, and bounced on for a hundred yards. The balls carried far more kinetic energy than one might suppose, and it was easy to underestimate their deadly potential. The balls slammed into the back of the column and mowed down two entire files of men as if they were bowling pins. What had been two solid, unwavering files of men changed in an instant to a sticky gumbo of red gristle, body oddments, and bloody things too small to ever be identifiable as human remnants; a crimson mist hung in the air for a brief second.

Tomières realized his mistake, knew he had to close the range drastically, and ordered the column forward at the *pas accéléré*; 100 paces per minute. Drums pounded the advance, men sweated, and hearts raced faster. The band switched to a sharp, sprightly marching tune. The French general halted the column at eighty yards and fired two more volleys in what passed for quick succession to the French, although the British would have considered it slow. But he had made a fundamental miscalculation. Troops advancing downhill, trained to fire on a level field, often elevated their muskets too high. Many shots flew aimlessly into space.

The gentle breeze ceased and a strong hot wind started to blow. French regimental and national flags snapped smartly. The long poles bearing the golden regimental eagles swayed. Their bearers sought manfully to steady them, to make sure the glory and honor they represented was bold and conspicuous.

The forceful wind dissipated the huge, roiling thunderheads of smoke from the volleys. The French column, normally wreathed in smoke and only visible at close range, could be clearly seen. Visibility diminished the surprise and eliminated the shock value of a horde of men suddenly materializing out of seeming thin air. It also made them a clear target for a well-directed volley from an enemy line. All of the troops on both sides could see each other and it added to sense of being in a grand historical panorama.

Tomières ordered French drummers to hammer the *pas de charge*, equivalent to what the British called *the double quick*. The noise sounded like someone shouting "old trousers" to the British.

Tomières again debated whether to deploy into line but realized he was already too close to the enemy for such a complicated maneuver. No, he would stay with the shock value of the column.

Men fell steadily in the British line. The casualties mounted, but the soldiers said nothing. Some men spun like marionettes when hit, then fell to the ground. Other swayed like pendulums for a few seconds before collapsing. Still others folded up like bellows suddenly emptied of air.

Most died in silent surprise, but a few screamed for a brief second before pitching to the ground. Those who did not die immediately lay in untidy heaps of red and moaned. File closers from a third line stepped smartly forward. They ignored both the dead and wounded, stepped calmly over them, and sealed the gaps. Men fell, but the integrity of the line never faltered.

The small British band of bassoons, horns, and clarinets, mostly recruited from Hanoverian refugees, played skillfully behind the file closers. "Lilibolero", " Briton's Strike Home," and "British Grenadiers" poured out and quickened British hearts. The bandsmen played as loudly as they could, since they could hear clearly their French opposite numbers and simply would not countenance being drowned out by any Frog musical volley.

Major Murphy, the popular brigade major, was shot off his horse. The animal bounded away, dragging the corpse, whose boot was still stuck in the stirrups. This greatly angered the men, but since no command had been given to fire, they stood stiff and upright and waited.

"Avancez, mes enfants, courage, encore une fois, François!" Shouted a *chef-de-bataillon* with oversize gold epaulettes. He energetically brandished an ornately pommeled sword in the direction of the British. A loud collective *hourra* answered his exhortation. No one could deny the French had plenty of *cran*—guts—as well as confidence and élan.

The French advanced ten more yards, halted, and volleyed again. The cumulative sound of flying lead reminded Pennywhistle of a chorus of chirping birds. Gunfire heated the already hot air and Pennywhistle felt as if he were standing at the mouth of an oven. Something tapped his cheek, too gently to be lead. He reached up with disgust and brushed away driblets of brains like old grey oatmeal from a soldier a foot away.

The British line never wavered, but biology simply could not be denied. Pennywhistle glanced down the line and noticed several men had wet themselves. He afforded it no meaning; it was far more common than anyone cared to admit. Courage was not about fearlessness; it was about controlling the fear and allowing it to energize you rather than letting it induce paralysis. The men would still do their duty and do it well.

He saw a private lean forward slightly and retch. A few seconds later, he regained his composure and resumed his erect posture.

He saw some men squinting. It was not just the sun. Tunnel vision was a common side effect of the stress of battle.

Another private commenced to shake violently. The man on his left dropped elbow contact, put his hand on the private's shoulder, and looked into his eyes with quiet assurance. No words were spoken, but the shaking stopped. In a good regiment, a man drew courage from his brothers. Death was less frightening than letting his mates down.

The smell of rotten eggs permeated the humid atmosphere as the continuing French fire filled the air with sulfurous gun smoke. The rippling thunder of volleys finally drowned out the music played by bandsmen of both sides.

Battle was smoke, thunder, blood, gore, stench, fear, and above all, confusion. Pennywhistle knew each man saw only a fragment of the whole picture, usually a mere few yards dimly glimpsed through choking clouds of smoke. Trying to reconstruct the whole was as difficult as trying to recall the individual dances at a grand ball. There was indeed honor to be gained, but talk about "the glory of battle" was mostly moonshine written by men who had never been anywhere near it.

Pennywhistle hated the waiting but knew the French had collectively done them little damage by firing far too much from far too great a distance. Still, redcoats continued to fall, like pieces dropping out of a complex jigsaw puzzle. They were ignored and replaced. Men died; the line endured. Wallace knew it was about timing. He wanted the French close in, wanted his first volley to be decisive.

It was also about the number of muskets able to bear. The line greatly overlapped the column and made possible deadly enfilade fire. The French could use little of their firepower potential; with two long, lean lines, the British could use all of theirs. Pennywhistle found it nerve racking to be a stationary target unable to respond, but he knew exactly what Wallace had in mind. It was what he would have done. A low, melancholy whistle passed close to his ear but he paid it little mind. It was the distinctive sound of a bullet nearly out of velocity.

We will win today, thought Pennywhistle, *because of training and discipline*. No troops could stand fire like the British. To see death advancing boldly and do nothing until properly instructed ran completely counter to every animal instinct. It was one thing to seize the energy of fear and fling it away by lashing out at an enemy, quite another thing to clamp shackles on it and patiently endure the writhing, creeping, desperately oppressive burden it inflicted upon the soul.

The French continued to advance. They were fifty yards distant. His acute eyesight allowed him to see their faces. They were very young, but looked hard beyond their years. Most faces showed fierce resolve, but more than few displayed confusion and terror. Almost time now.

A bullet exploded the head of the ensign holding the King's Colors. He pitched forward and dropped his heavy burden. To Pennywhistle's astonishment, Manton dashed out, picked up the heavy silk banner and waved it defiantly at the oncoming French.

"Come and get us, you bloody Crapaud bastards!" Manton shouted belligerently. He followed it a second later with a taunt about their mothers and dared them to advance. He was making himself a perfect target. And yet, in the odd way that sometimes happens in a battle, he stood unscathed and unyielding while bullets whizzed around him. Pennywhistle had never had doubts about Manton's courage, but this deed was extraordinary and deserved reward. Of course, that was predicated on both of them surviving the battle.

Pennywhistle sensed the decisive moment had finally arrived and he saw Wallace knew it too. Shouted commands roared down the two long lines. Drums rattled them out loudly, far easier to hear than a voice in the infernal din. "Shoulder arms!" There was a collective gasp from the French as the immovable British line suddenly moved. "Make ready, front rank kneel." Seventeen hundred muskets were brought to the straight vertical position; every single one would be concentrated on the column's narrow face. A loud "click" echoed down the lines as they were thumbed to full cock. The front rank went down on bended knees, so the rear could fire safely.

"Present!" Redcoats leveled seventeen hundred Brown Besses at the enemy with magnificent, intimidating precision. The Brown Bess fired a .71 caliber ball that, while slow, tended to flatten, balloon, and fragment when striking the enemy. It created no blast wave as high velocity military projectiles two centuries in the future would, but unlike them, generally stayed lodged inside the victim; usually carrying with it pieces of clothing, which were splendid sources of sepsis. The soft lead splintered bones and dangerously compressed internal organs. The French were only forty yards distant. Not a single British musket lacked a target.

Pennywhistle could see the pimples on some French faces; many were little more than overgrown boys despite the deep furrows in their cheeks. Fierce resolve and arrogant confidence had departed. He saw mainly fear and uncertainty. The French knew what was coming would be ghastly.

"Fire!" A long, whip-like sheet of writhing flame lashed out at the French. It sounded like thousands of rattlesnakes shaking their rattles in unison. It was a horrendous wave of fire that was almost a living thing. It tore into the French with battering ram power and wiped the face of the column from the earth as if by the wrathful hand of the Old Testament God.

Strangely, memory played merciful tricks. Despite the awful noise, many redcoats later could not recall hearing the sound of their own muskets discharge or that of the mass volley, even though they saw the flash of the pans, the eruptions from the muzzles, and the long crimson sheet that blossomed from the dusky red line.

The British reloaded quickly and in stony silence. They fired again, the second volley almost as destructive as the first. Huge gaps appeared in the column as if someone had taken a giant sickle to it. The dead fell in rows like stalks of wheat. The column started to buckle. The French returned a very ragged and uncertain volley, fired entirely too high. They were at the breaking point.

Pennywhistle saw Manton flinch from the corner of his eye. A bullet had struck his shoulder, but he did not fall, and he gripped his banner's nine foot staff tightly for support and rooted it in the ground. Pennywhistle hoped it was merely a spent ball, but had no time to fret over it.

"You'll have to do better than that, you froggie whoresons!" Manton yelled before he sagged against the heavy flagstaff.

"Aim for their shoe-buckles!" shouted Pennywhistle. Even the best trained men, flushed with excitement, had a tendency to aim high. The British fired again, low and deadly as before. The French fell like porcelain ninepins on a bowling lawn.

Pennywhistle raised his sword high and turned quickly toward the men. His faced flushed a feral crimson and his teeth sparkled with a wolfish, triumphant smile. "C'mon boys, give a cheer for King George and the Rangers!"

"Hip hip huzzah, Hip hip huzzah, hip hip huzzah!" The pent up tension of hours was released in a mighty roar. All of the other company commanders swiftly followed Pennywhistle's example. It quickly spread down the thin red lines. 1700 men cheered with utter abandon, a tidal wave of sound that crashed harshly upon the French.

It was the utterly confident cheering after the long silence that pushed the battered French over the edge. Soldiers milled about in confusion and bewilderment. Fear closed their ears to the exhortations of their officers and dormant survival instincts suddenly came awake.

"Charge bayonets! Advance!" Wallace bellowed and waved his sword majestically from atop his charger. Drums thundered his commands. The 45th and 74th trudged forward along with the 88th. Bagpipes skirled "Garryowen". Bandsmen and the fifers joined in. The steady, methodical tramp, tramp, tramp of 1700 pairs of feet caused the ground to vibrate strongly. Hundreds of rabbits, red squirrels, and hedgehogs, driven mad by the tumult, scrambled from their hides and scampered crazily in front of the advancing line. They added their own shrill cries to the general insanity of noise.

Manton was in great pain but gritted his teeth, pulled himself erect, and flourished his banner boldly. "Follow the colors!" He shouted. "We have them, boys! They won't stand!" He began walking quickly in advance of the main line.

The half-mile long British line of three regiments thudded steadfastly forward at a deliberate step: determined, deadly, unstoppable, bayonets leveled from the hip. Campbell's brigade moved up in support of Wallace's. Packenham's entire division was on the move and the cold steel of legions of 17-inch bayonets promised evisceration and painful death to the badly disordered French columns.

The columns began to disintegrate, not from the front but from the rear. Soldiers who could not fire saw no point in remaining and waiting passively for death to reach them. Frenchman turned ghastly pale as the blood fled their faces, the better to enable violent actions of the legs. Some men shook briefly like leaves in a wind and other swayed slowly side to side, intoxicated by fear and uncertainty. Some emptied their stomachs, some their bladders, some their bowels. They needed to do something, to take action. They ran. The columns dissolved like kernels of wheat peeled off a stalk by a rising wind.

"Charge!" Wallace yelled with fury. He grinned, waved his sword, and his charger reared in approval. The British advance changed to a trot, then a loping jog, then a flat out run. Pennywhistle caught the fire. He slung the Ferguson, drew the clumsy saber, and waved it toward the fleeing French. "Follow me!" he shouted madly to his men. The Irishmen had already decided he was one tough hellhound and responded with glee.

His men raced forward, some shouting Gaelic slogans he couldn't begin to fathom. No matter, the emotion was unmistakable. Private McNulty yelled loudest of all.

The French lost all trace of cohesion and fled the field in utter, unreasoning fear, impervious to the strictures of discipline. It was always thus when animal instincts overrode training and men thought only of their personal survival and not of the safety of their mates.

The whole division tore off after the French, crazy screaming demons with hellfire in their veins. The instinct of the predator to chase prey was infectious. The field was littered with muskets hastily tossed away, the sure sign of a truly whipped enemy. Even the bandsmen wanted to get in on the unfolding triumph. They threw down their instruments, picked up discarded French muskets, and joined the chase.

A small of knot of brave French soldiers rallied around a stalwart officer. The group had to be smashed immediately lest it inspire others to discontinue their panic. Pennywhistle's men charged at the ranks while he aimed for the officer.

Pennywhistle's blade and the French captain's banged together amidst a shower of sparks that resembled a mist of blue raindrops. The French captain was a fine swordsman and parried Pennywhistle's well directed thrusts expertly. He was nearly as tall as the marine, with long arms that gave his sword great reach. He was light on his feet and slashed with skill and cleverness. The determined look in his icy blue eyes proclaimed he was not used to defeat. In a better world, Pennywhistle would have found it instructive to meet him in a fencing salon and practice well-choreographed, artful moves so that each might learn from the other's polished technique. Today, he had time only for crude efficiency. He parried the Frenchmen's thrust down and to the side and snapped a sharp, savage kick into his genitals. The Frenchmen collapsed, mewling and puking.

Pennywhistle saw not fear but defiance in the man's pained face. The Frenchman knew what was coming and his angry eyes dared Pennywhistle to do it. The marine admired him, appreciated the example he set for his men in a hopeless position, and wanted to spare his life. Yet he could not afford to set a bad example by indulging the luxury of mercy. His men's bloodlust was aroused; it needed to be exploited, not extinguished. He skewered the captain through the throat. At the same time, a private of the 88th gutted the last of the Frenchmen with a savage bayonet thrust. The whole business was over in thirty seconds.

Pennywhistle and his men dashed on. As he ran, he admitted to himself the bloodlust had enveloped him as well. He hated the loss of reason, yet in a strange way he welcomed the exhilaration it brought. He and his men ruthlessly cut down any who attempted to stand, but as the minutes passed, those brave souls vanished entirely. The French resembled a herd of frightened deer fleeing a pack of hungry wolves. He no longer saw the white facings of their uniforms, only the white turnbacks of their coat tails.

British general LeMarchant's cavalry brigade advanced a brisk walk to turn the retreat into a rout. The French ran in little clumps, in no condition to form square. The 800 horsemen moved in two lines. They increased their pace to a quick trot, lowered their heavy sabers, and finally burst into full gallop. Reason returned briefly to a few French who knew a fleeing infantryman's worst nightmare was a man on fast horse with a sharp sword. A badly depleted company of French stopped, turned, and attempted something vaguely like a volley, but the sun was in their eyes and they fired far too high. LeMarchant's troopers crashed into the French fugitives like a tidal wave. In fifteen minutes, Thomière's Division ceased to exist.

It took Pennywhistle twenty minutes to round up and reorganize his men. He was relieved to find ninety of them intact. Five were dead and five wounded, although not badly. He was exhausted, dirty, and soaked in sweat, but had never felt so charged with life. He smiled broadly. It was entirely unmilitary, but he couldn't help it. Cheating death always made life seem sweet. He knew all glory was fleeting and ultimately hollow, but there was nothing wrong with relishing a few moments of hard-earned triumph.

The men were cheerful, nodded as he passed by; many returned his smile. Small gestures, but they spoke volumes. They knew they had served Johnny Crapaud a damned fine thrashing and were proud of themselves.

Pennywhistle turned the company over to Spottswood. He and Dale went to find Manton.

Juanita was leaning over Manton, daubing a wet cloth on a bare shoulder blade. The skin was black and purple, badly bruised but unbroken. Pennywhistle breathed a sigh of relief. Manton had been hit by a ball almost out of velocity. Manton looked up at Pennywhistle and smiled wanly.

"You damned fool," said Pennywhistle with mock anger. "That was a bloody stupid thing to do!" He could no longer restrain the smile that demanded to be released. "But a damned brave thing, an extraordinary thing. How does it feel to be a hero?"

Manton considered carefully. "I don't feel any different. I don't know what came over me. I got carried away and it just seemed the right thing to do." Pennywhistle nodded his understanding. It was often that way in battle, which had a way of summoning up extraordinary qualities from seemingly ordinary people. The swaggering blusterers were almost always eclipsed in battle by the quiet, modest types.

"Manton, I had a presentiment about you and I lied to Colonel Wallace. You heard me call you a gentleman volunteer. You have the makings of an officer in your heart and in your soul; you merely lack social station and prospects. You have distinguished yourself today not just in my eyes, but in Colonel Wallace's and the men. They would be proud to have you as a new ensign.

Manton looked shocked and stammered, "I... I don't know what to say, sir."

"I will speak to Colonel Wallace and see you are appointed to the new vacancy. You have earned it. All of the gentleman volunteers were killed at Badajoz, so none of the usual people are available. Don't look so surprised. You already seen more real battle than the whippersnapper you will replace. You've been around Dale long enough; you certainly know the drill manual. You have been a gentleman's gentleman for two years and know the details of our ways. I have come to notice you copying my speech and manners. You have but to continue that. When you join the officers' mess, do what you have always done. Stay silent, observe, and listen carefully. You will learn the rudiments soon enough."

Manton stared at him, then resolve seemed to settle his features. Pennywhistle noted this, and continued, well pleased.

"Because of the situation, the commission will not have to be purchased, it will simply be granted. I will provide you a small stipend so you can secure some kit and cover your first few months of mess bills. You know better than anyone what you will need. You will be the most junior officer without prospects and will have to live on your salary. It will be a hard life. It will be up to you to carve out your own path and your own future, but it will be one consistent with the many gifts I believe you to possess. You were not born a gentleman, but you are one in every respect by your conduct. Your commission will merely make it official."

Manton felt resounding joy overflow every part of his being. It was far beyond his wildest dreams, but he would not disappoint his master. It hit him then. Pennywhistle would no longer be his master, but a fellow gentleman in arms. It was a heady prospect and moved him to make a decision about another part of his life. It was rash, it was impetuous, but his heart shouted to be heard. He could only do it because he had prospects now where none had existed before. He rose painfully to his feet.

"Captain, my Spanish is improving, but I don't want to garble this. I'd like you to translate for me with Juanita."

"Very well, Man..." He stopped himself. "Very well, Mr. Manton."

Juanita looked at both of them, sensed something important was coming.

Manton steeled himself. "Tell her I love her. I have since I first laid eyes on her. Now that I am to be an officer, I can do right by her. Tell her," he hesitated a second, then the words came out in one quick burst, "I want to marry her, if she will have me."

Pennywhistle could not hide his shock. He had suspected something, but had thought it merely advanced puppy love and simple admiration. What Manton wanted was absolutely crazy, but crazy things happened in wartime, brought people together who normally would not have come within a thousand miles of each other. War breeched boundaries of manners, conventions, and status, and often freed the heart from societal shackles so it might make its own agenda. The two were about the same age. There was no reason it wouldn't work. Pennywhistle translated, but Juanita's astonished looks told him she grasped the meaning long before he finished.

She thought carefully. She had affection for Manton, had seen the looks he thought she had missed. She did not love him, but love could grow. She had fought and bled and struggled beside him. They had only known each other a few days, yet they each understood far more about the other's essence than did couples long engaged. He was a good and worthy man.

She and Pennywhistle could never be together. Last night had been a treasure, but it would remain their secret. Her world and Manton's were not so different. If she accepted, she could stay with the army as his wife and find a way to fight the hated oppressors of her country. The last few days had changed her. She realized she was a crusader, a female paladin of sorts, tasked with something greater than being a simple peasant wife in an obscure village. Danger had shoved her across a threshold, forced her become something much greater than the sum of her gifts. It had done the same to Manton.

Her brother, Carlos, had become a scholar and a fighter for Christ, had given his vows to the Jesuit Order. If only there was a similar order for women. But she realized she wanted a family someday and celibacy was not for her.

She had violated God's law last night, abandoned chastity with an unseemly eagerness, yet it had felt powerfully right and seemed to come from a will beyond her own. God, unlike man, was sometimes willing to bend the rules for a higher good. What had been unleashed was something primal that wanted exploring with a good man. Manton was brave, handsome, and ambitious. Much could be made of him, and he would make an honest woman of her. What she said next was the product of sentiment, calculation, and hope.

"Yes, I will marry you. Manton," she said quietly. "But I must at least know your Christian name." Pennywhistle and Manton both laughed. Officers commonly addressed servants by last name alone, and Manton's first name had never been used in her presence.

"It is John," he said.

"John," she said the name gently several times, as if getting used to it and matching the name to the owner. "I like that name. It comes easy to the Spanish tongue, although we would say Juan. It is the masculine form of my own name, so perhaps we are intended to be together after all."

She spoke it all in English, albeit with a heavy accent. Manton realized that in a few months she would be fluent.

"I have a question for you too, Juanita. What is your last name?" asked Manton with a pleasingly naive eagerness.

"I am Juanita Rosario Dolores García y López. The first three names are given," she said as Manton blinked at the length of name. "The second are my father's and mother's family. Family is important!"

Spottswood walked up, having turned the company over to O'Dwyer after standing it down. Pennywhistle gleefully related the happy and unexpected news. Dale, the oldest among them, had volunteered to give the bride away. Spottswood asked about the wedding date.

"The sooner the better," said Manton decisively. "Tomorrow, in fact." Wartime made it easy to dispense with preliminaries like banns and waiting periods. It would be simple enough to find a chaplain to perform the honors. This was officially a Protestant Army, but priests could always be found around an Irish regiment like the Rangers if Juanita insisted on a ceremony in the Old Faith. He realized she would probably want him to pledge that any children would be raised to follow Catholic teachings, but he loved her and her heart was certainly worth a mass.

He had no living relatives, but Pennywhistle, Dale, and Spottswood were his real family, and as long as they were present he was content. He also thought he would invite Captain Thynne. Pennywhistle would, of course, be his best man.

Pennywhistle decided to stay long enough to make sure Manton settled in with his new regiment. He would introduce him formally to the regimental officers; the word of one gentleman recommending another would be accepted. A uniform and sword would be easy enough to procure, as items left behind by the dead were always sold at auction directly after a battle. Manton could wear them at the wedding.

Then it would be time for him and his fellow marines to return to the Fleet. He trusted the journey back would be less eventful than the journey in. He had no doubt Wellington would score a huge victory today; he would probably be made a marquis. Act One had been a rousing success, and he was gratified to have played a small part.

He surveyed the field of blood and carnage and looked back at Manton and Juanita kissing warmly. Love in the midst of death. It cheered him. It promised hope for the future. Love was stronger than death. Juanita had healed something last night and he was grateful. He felt no guilt. He was happy she was getting a man who would treat her as she deserved.

He thought of Carlotta, and for the first time her memory brought no pain. He blinked in surprise, smiled, and felt physically lighter. He saw her face in his mind and a poignant joy touched him. He caught the scent of lavender she favored and felt her loving presence for a brief second. A flash of insight suddenly made crystal clear what others had told him repeatedly for a year. She had been willing to trade her life for his and nothing in his power could have prevented that. In that instant, he was finally able to absolve himself of blame and accept her death. He heard a rushing noise in his ears and a great wave of peace washed over him. The iron shroud straight-jacketing his heart disintegrated like a fog banished by a wind. Even the purple bruises on his face ceased aching. The sun suddenly seemed much brighter.

He would never forget her, but it was time to let her go. There was a war to fight, troops to lead, and Bonaparte was far from beaten. He would do his duty. Death might lie just over the horizon, but it would not happen today. He felt it in his bones. It was good to be alive.

THE END

The end of *The King's Scarlet*, but Tom Pennywhistle will return in *Blue Water, Scarlet Tide*.

THE KING'S SCARLET: AUTHOR'S NOTES

The King's Scarlet is a work of fiction but the world it mirrors was a very real and terrible one. The Napoleonic Wars in Spain displayed dimensions of brutality, cruelty, and horror found in no other theatre during that long conflict. While the French started things with a needlessly vicious disregard for civilians, retaliations quickly followed on the part of the Spanish and matters swiftly degenerated to the point where both sides routinely committed atrocities. The war morphed into a monstrous escalating cycle of tit-for-tat that moved far beyond an eye for an eye, a tooth for a tooth. It soon became a heart for an eye, a head for a tooth. What we would today label war crimes became commonplace.

The Spanish Army of the time was something of a joke; the French were the premiere military power in Europe. The French intervened in Spain in 1808 during a dispute between the Bourbon King and his son. Both were as inept as they were stubborn; Goya's group portrait of the Spanish Royal Family done in 1800 brilliantly captured the sheer stupidity of this decayed family.

Napoleon was a tyrant but he was also a conscientious provider for members of his family. He married his sisters off to men of great influence and sought thrones for his brothers. The moribund Spanish monarchy seemed a fine opportunity to secure one for his well-meaning but not over-talented brother, Joseph.

Napoleon expected little opposition, a huge misreading of Spanish pride. Joseph's installation as king immediately spawned a revolt in Madrid. Brutal efforts to suppress it succeeded superficially, but the ire they provoked spread like wildfire and rebellious conflagrations soon enveloped the entire country. The rebellion was spontaneous and not well coordinated by a central government; it was chiefly an accretion of lots of smaller rebellions led by local juntas. Priests played a large part since they saw Napoleon as an Anti-Christ who intended to bring the Spanish Church under tight governmental control as he had done to the French. Hatred of the French quickly became a universal article of faith.

With the exception of the General Dupont's ignominious defeat at Bailen, the French armies made short work of the first Spanish armies fielded against them. What they could not defeat was the guerrilla movement that arose. The very word guerrilla, meaning small war, owes its origin to this conflict. Roving bands of guerrillas cut French supply lines, ambushed couriers and messengers, and severed communication among the French armies. At times, all contact with France was blocked. No courier dared move on a Spanish road without an extremely heavy escort. More than half of the French soldiers in Spain spent their time protecting supply lines and thus could not be employed in field armies.

Captured French soldiers usually met long, slow, painful ends after they had been bled of any important military information. Skinning and boiling soldiers alive happened with appalling frequency. Torture techniques achieved new depths of refinement.

The French retaliated with vigor, sometimes burning whole villages. A favorite device was to herd the entire population of a small hamlet into a church—the French had great contempt for Spanish religiosity—and set it afire.

The French and the Spanish soon came to regard the other as something less than human. Only the British under Wellington's strict discipline commanded the grudging respect of both.

The Spanish were loath to admit they were too weak to fight on their own and it was with great reluctance that they asked Napoleon's most implacable foe, the British, to intervene. A brittle yet effective symbiotic relationship quickly developed between the Spanish and the British. The Spanish tied down French forces with constant, unrelenting guerrilla attacks, leaving the British army to deal with the widely scattered field armies.

The quality of guerrillas varied widely. Some bands showed real skill; some became mere cannon fodder; some were little better than militarized gangs who used the French menace as an excuse to engage in protection rackets directed at their own countrymen. Despite a great French superiority of numbers, Spanish guerrillas kept them so off balance they were never able to concentrate all their forces for a decisive showdown with the British. Guerillas also provided the British with constant, detailed, and accurate intelligence information about their French foes.

The British supplied the Spanish with guns and money, but most importantly they supplied a well trained army to oppose the French in conventional warfare. The British commander, Arthur Wellesley, later the Duke of Wellington, was not only a brilliant strategist but also a gifted diplomat who knew exactly how to soothe the sensitive egos of his mercurial Spanish allies.

Although the Spaniards constantly failed to follow through on their well meant promises, Wellington eventually discovered what strengths they had and learned to employ them effectively.

Wellington was a past master of logistics, learned through long experience in India, and he used British sea power to ensure his troops were always well supplied. He always paid for any supplies he needed and punished looting severely. The French lived off the land and encouraged looting, but Spain was a poor country and their troops often went hungry.

Wellington's foresighted prudence was best on display in 1810. Badly outnumbered by the French, he retreated to the powerfully constructed fortifications of *Torres Vedras*. The thirty mile long lines were a series of interlinked forts and earthworks that walled off the Lisbon Peninsula. He had ordered this masterpiece of military engineering constructed in secret many months before. He left scorched earth behind him; the French could not even find even a single chicken or hog. Marshal Massena's troops could not breech the powerful defenses. They stalled and starved. Wellington's Army spent a comfortable winter in Lisbon with plenty to eat, thanks to the Royal Navy. Massena soon had no choice but to retreat.

Wellington was a careful general. He had no blank check on lives and knew the loss of Britain's one large field army would likely be fatal to the allied cause. He preferred intelligent maneuver to battering ram directness and never hesitated to retreat if he felt the odds too great. He husbanded the lives of his soldiers carefully. He refused to offer battle save when he was certain of victory and in his long career never lost one. He acquired a reputation as a great defensive general yet could quickly go over to the offensive when an opening presented itself, as it did at Salamanca.

Wellington developed tactics that emphasized the primacy of the line over the column and maximized the British emphasis on delivering well directed volleys at close range. He typically posted the bulk of his soldiers on the reverse slope of a ridge out of sight of the enemy, making it difficult for the French to guess either their numbers or their exact positions. He often had them lie down during French artillery bombardments, rendering French softening up efforts nearly useless. He used heavy skirmish lines of riflemen to disrupt the French columns at distance then had his main force rise up abruptly in long lines when French infantry columns came up over the brow of the ridge. Surprised, the French usually had no time to shift from column into line. He beat seven experienced Marshals of France with his tactics and made British infantry a force to be respected and feared.

Colonel John R. Elting summed him up well in *A Military History and Atlas of the Napoleonic Wars.* "Something of a toady, more of a snob, he was nonetheless a Great Captain who did more than his assigned duty."

While *The King's Scarlet* is fictional, many of the situations described did occur. The scenario in the opening chapter happened with some frequency, but in the real world a gallant British officer and his NCO would not have been available to intervene. The battle between French regulars and Spanish guerrillas was a fairly typical small encounter, but lacking an experienced British military presence, the French likely would have prevailed. The description of the opening phase of the Battle of Salamanca is substantially correct, although I have made it longer than it actually was for the purposes of drama.

Pennywhistle is loosely based on a real man of the time; Royal Marine Captain Thomas Inch, a Scotsman. The main characters in the book are creatures of my imagination, but they do represent accurately people and perspectives common to the time.

For those readers interested in factual information about the Peninsular War, I have three recommendations. A well written, very accessible general history is *The Peninsular War 1807-14* by Michael Glover. For those wishing for more depth, a fine scholarly treatment is *The Spanish Ulcer: A History of the Peninsular War* by David Gates. For a detailed treatment of the political dimensions of the war an excellent work is *The Peninsular War: A New History* by Charles Esdailie.

For the generalist, the best book on the Salamanca Campaign is *Wellington's Masterpiece: Battle and Campaign of Salamanca* by J.P. Lawford and Peter Young. For those obsessive armchair generals determined to explore in great tactical detail, I recommend *Salamanca, 1812* by Rory Muir.

For those seeking good biographies of Wellington, the most up-to-date is *Wellington: The Path to Victory 1769-1814* by Rory Muir. It is somewhat dry and scholarly, but rich in detail. A less academic and more popular treatment of the Duke is the brilliantly written and insightful *Wellington: The Iron Duke* by Richard Holmes.

BLUE WATER, SCARLET TIDE

August, 1814: The White House is in flames, The Capitol a gutted shell, and the President of the United States is in hiding. British soldiers prowl the streets of Washington, D.C. and organized resistance to the invaders has collapsed. In the young Republic's darkest hour, two Marines who share a secret hold the survival of the nation in their hands. Royal Marine Captain Thomas Pennywhistle discovers a skeleton from his past that will make him question his duty and his destiny. United States Marine Corps Captain John Tracy finds a hidden chink in the British armor, but may have to betray his honor and that of The Corps to exploit it. Starting out as steadfast battlefield opponents, unusual circumstances propel the two Marines into an uncertain and uneasy alliance. A lethal woman tests both men's patience, patriotism, and passions. If the Marine duo makes the wrong choices, it is not just they who will be undone, but an entire nation.

About the Author

John M. Danielski

John Danielski believes you learn best by doing and actually carried out many of the ordinary tasks Tom Pennywhistle performs in *The King's Scarlet*. He worked his way through university as a living history interpreter at historic Fort Snelling, the birthplace of Minnesota. For four summers, he played a US soldier of 1827; he wore the uniform, performed the drills, demonstrated the volley fire with other interpreters, and even ate the food. A heavy blue wool tailcoat and black shako look smart and snappy but are pure torture to wear on a boiling summer day.

JOHN DANIELSKI

He has a practical, rather than theoretical, perspective on the weapons of the time. He has fired either replicas or originals of all of the weapons mentioned in his works with live rounds, six- and twelve-pound cannon included. The effect of a 12-pound cannonball on an old Chevy four door must be seen to be believed.

He has a number of marginally useful University degrees, including a magna cum laude degree in history from the University of Minnesota. He is a Phi Beta Kappa and holds a black belt in Tae-Kwon-do. He has taught history at both the secondary and university levels and also worked as a newspaper editor.

His literary mentors were C. S. Forester, Bruce Catton, and Shelby Foote.

He lives quietly in the Twin Cities suburbs with his faithful companion: Sparkle, the wonder cat.

IF YOU ENJOYED THIS BOOK

Please write a review.

This is important to the author and helps to get the word out to others

Visit

PENMORE PRESS

www.penmorepress.com

All Penmore Press books are available directly through our website, amazon.com, Barnes and Noble and Nook, Sony Reader, Apple iTunes, Kobo books and via leading bookshops across the United States, Canada, the UK, Australia and Europe.

The Lockwoods

of Clonakilty

by

Mark Bois

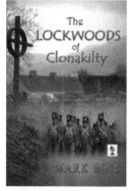

Lieutenant James Lockwood of the Inniskilling Regiment has returned to family, home and hearth after being wounded almost fatally, at the Battle of Waterloo, where his regiment was decisive in securing Wellington's victory and bringing the Napoleonic Wars to an end. But home is not the refuge and haven he hoped to find. Irish uprisings polarize the citizens, and violence against English landholders – including James' father and brother – is bringing down wrath and retribution from England. More than one member of the household sympathizes with the desire for Irish independence, and Cassie, the Lockwood's spirited daughter, plays an active part in the rebellion.

Estranged from his English family for the "crime" of marrying a Irish Catholic woman, James Lockwood must take difficult and desperate steps to preserve his family. If his injuries don't kill him, or his addiction to laudanum, he just might live long enough to confront his nemesis. For Captain Charles Barr, maddened by syphilis and no longer restrained by the bounds of honor, sets out to utterly destroy the Lockwood family, from James' patriarchal father to the youngest child, and nothing but death will stop him – his own, or James Lockwood's.

PENMORE PRESS
www.penmorepress.com

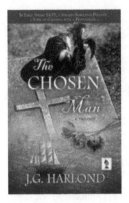

The Chosen Man

by

J. G. Harlond

From the bulb of a rare flower bloom ambition and scandal

Rome, 1635: As Flanders braces for another long year of war, a Spanish count presents the Vatican with a means of disrupting the Dutch rebels' booming economy. His plan is brilliant. They just need the right man to implement it.

They choose Ludovico da Portovenere, a charismatic spice and silk merchant. Intrigued by the Vatican's proposal—and hungry for profit—Ludo sets off for Amsterdam to sow greed and venture capitalism for a disastrous harvest, hampered by a timid English priest sent from Rome, accompanied by a quick-witted young admirer he will use as a spy, and bothered by the memory of the beautiful young lady he refused to take with him.

Set in a world of international politics and domestic intrigue, *The Chosen Man* spins an engrossing tale about the Dutch financial scandal known as tulip mania—and how decisions made in high places can have terrible repercussions on innocent lives.

PENMORE PRESS
www.penmorepress.com

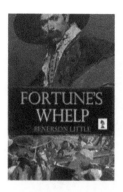

Fortune's Whelp
by
Benerson Little

Privateer, Swordsman, and Rake:

Set in the 17th century during the heyday of privateering and the decline of buccaneering, *Fortune's Whelp* is a brash, swords-out sea-going adventure. Scotsman Edward MacNaughton, a former privateer captain, twice accused and acquitted of piracy and currently seeking a commission, is ensnared in the intrigue associated with the attempt to assassinate King William III in 1696. Who plots to kill the king, who will rise in rebellion—and which of three women in his life, the dangerous smuggler, the wealthy widow with a dark past, or the former lover seeking independence—might kill to further political ends? Variously wooing and defying Fortune, Captain MacNaughton approaches life in the same way he wields a sword or commands a fighting ship: with the heart of a lion and the craft of a fox.

PENMORE PRESS
www.penmorepress.com

Penmore Press
Challenging, Intriguing, Adventurous, Historical and Imaginative

www.penmorepress.com

Lightning Source UK Ltd.
Milton Keynes UK
UKHW021143020721
386521UK00007B/1331